P9-DDR-904

SHELL GAME

SHELL GAME

A V.I. WARSHAWSKI NOVEL

SARA PARETSKY

wm

WILLIAM MORROW

An Imprint of HarperCollins *Publishers*

This is a work of fiction. Names, characters, places, and incidents are products of the author's imagination or are used fictitiously and are not to be construed as real. Any resemblance to actual events, locales, organizations, or persons, living or dead, is entirely coincidental.

SHELL GAME. Copyright © 2018 by Sara Paretsky. All rights reserved. Printed in the United States of America. No part of this book may be used or reproduced in any manner whatsoever without written permission except in the case of brief quotations embodied in critical articles and reviews. For information, address HarperCollins Publishers, 195 Broadway, New York, NY 10007.

HarperCollins books may be purchased for educational, business, or sales promotional use. For information, please e-mail the Special Markets Department at SPsales@harpercollins.com.

FIRST EDITION

Library of Congress Cataloging-in-Publication Data has been applied for.

ISBN 978-0-06-243586-6 (hardcover)
ISBN 978-0-06-286823-7 (international edition)

18 19 20 21 22   LSC   10 9 8 7 6 5 4 3 2 1

For Heather and Rob, Matea and Noah, Niko and Sam—

for many different reasons, all of them good

ACKNOWLEDGMENTS

Gil Stein, Professor of Archaeology at Chicago's Oriental Institute, met with me as I began this novel, when he was the Institute director. His ideas and suggestions were invaluable, but the book has taken so many odd turns that he may not recognize either his Institute or the study of archaeology.

Lorraine Brochu, who worked on digs in Syria, was generous with ideas and advice as I tried to write about various characters' passion for digging. The Dagon was her suggestion. She also advised me on Arabic usage.

Marta Ramirez was kind enough to correct the Spanish in the text. Luana Giorgini offered help with V.I.'s Italian. Marzena Madej helped explore the forest preserves in Cook County.

Eddie Chez, Stuart Rice, and a friend who prefers to be anonymous assisted me in sorting out the business practices of off-shore companies.

I have taken liberties with the Cook County forest preserves, making them denser and more mysterious than they appear in actuality. Weather was a problem in this novel: the winter of 2018 seemed unending, but I've made spring come to Chicago in early April and have arbitrarily set a date for the ice breakup in northern Minnesota. Thanks to my cousin, Barb Wieser, for guiding my treks along the Minnesota-Canada border.

St. Matthieu and the town of Havre-des-Anges are fictitious, as are all the characters in this novel. Hedge fund and real estate billionaires, along with offshore tax havens, exist in real life, but I don't know any; all reference to such people and venues are completely imaginary. However, the Italian artist Antonella Mason, whose work V.I. has in her office, does exist, as do her brilliant paintings.

The Tribal Elders of the Anishinaabe Nation were most generous in giving me permission to set part of this novel in their sovereign land.

Finally, a special thank-you to my editors, Emily Krump and Carolyn Mays, for their thoughtful reading of this book. It is stronger for their advice.

SHELL GAME

BABE IN THE WOODS

THE DEPUTY TURNED without warning into an uncut thicket. Felix and I stumbled after him, following his bobbing flashlight as best we could, the suckers from the bushes and trees snapping back to whip our faces. When I called to him to slow down, he merely picked up his pace.

The meager light from my phone wasn't much use; I skidded on a pile of wet leaves and tumbled into a thorny bush. Mud squelched over the tops of my shoes, down into my socks. Felix tried to free me, but he ended up tangling his own scarf in the brambles.

The deputy was well ahead of us by the time we extricated ourselves, but we could still see slices of his light through the trees and beyond those, finally, the glow of arc lamps. I pushed toward them through the undergrowth.

The deputy was standing behind one of the lamps. He looked around in annoyance when we arrived and said, "About time," then called to someone beyond the light: "Got the kid, boss. He brought someone with him. Claims she's a lawyer."

"That's because I am a lawyer," I said, my voice bright—I'm here to help, not obstruct.

"Bring them over here." The boss had a gravelly voice, hoarse.

After twenty minutes in the dark woods, the high-wattage lights were blinding. I blinked, looked aside, and then tried to make out details of the site. Crime scene tape marked off an area of trees and tangled bushes. A number of officers were searching beyond that perimeter, while techs collected their discoveries—cigarette butts, condoms, beer and cognac bottles—bagging them and marking the locations with yellow evidence flags.

Felix shoved his hands deep into his pockets and stumbled after me into the clearing. He tripped on a branch and nearly fell, but brushed aside my arm when I tried to steady him.

Felix was usually a lively young man, as easy with my generation as with his peers, but he'd barely spoken since I'd picked him up an hour earlier. Nerves: understandable, but when I'd tried probing—why did the sheriff's police think Felix could ID a dead person? was one of his friends missing?—Felix snapped at me to be quiet.

The deputy pushed us toward a man of about fifty, jowly, heavy through the waist but not fat. Lieutenant bars were on the shoulders of his uniform jacket.

"Felix Herschel?" the lieutenant grunted, adding to me, "You're the lawyer?"

"V.I. Warshawski," I said.

The lieutenant ignored my offered hand. "Why'd the kid need to lawyer up? You got something to hide, son? Innocent people don't need lawyers."

"Innocent people need lawyers more than the guilty, Lieutenant"—I squinted at his name badge—"McGivney. They don't understand the criminal justice system and forceful interrogators can intimidate them into bogus confessions. So let's talk about what Mr. Herschel can do for you here."

McGivney studied me, decided not to fight that battle, and jerked his head toward the center of the arc lamps. "Bring your client over, Warshawski. Make sure you both walk in my footsteps: we want to minimize contamination of the crime scene."

I had to stretch my hamstrings to match his stride, but I pulled up next to him, near a log, where the arc lamps were concentrated. Felix stopped behind me but a deputy prodded him forward.

The log was over three feet high at the base, the remnant of some old oak or ash that had crashed in the woods. The bark had rotted to a rusty brown. A black tarp covered its base and a lump beyond it.

McGivney nodded at a crime scene tech. She pulled the tarp back to display the bruised and swollen body of a man. He'd been stuffed headfirst into the hollow bottom of the log. The body's original position was outlined in white—only his feet and part of his legs had been visible, but the deputies had pulled him out.

He was dressed in blue jeans and a dirt-crusted hoodie, unzipped to show a badly bruised torso. He'd been beaten so savagely that his head was a pulpy mess. His hair might once have been brown but was too caked now with mud and blood to be sure.

My muscles clenched. Violent death, nauseating death. Next to me, Felix made a feral gurgling sound. His face was pale, glassy, and he was swaying. I put one hand on the small of his back and pulled his head down roughly with the other, pressing his face as close to his knees as I could.

"You have water, Lieutenant?" I asked.

"No, and I'm not carrying smelling salts, either." McGivney gave a sharklike smile. "Do you recognize the vic—the body, the victim, son?"

"Why do you think Mr. Herschel knows him?" I said before Felix could speak. I had warned him in the car to consult me before he answered questions, but in the shock of death he wouldn't remember.

McGivney's mouth bunched in annoyance. "We have a good reason."

"Perhaps you do, but aside from being pretty sure this is a man, I don't know how anyone could identify him without DNA or dental records. And if you just found him, you couldn't have any of that information already."

"Do you recognize him, Mr. Herschel?" McGivney was keeping control of his temper, but it showed in his clenched jaw muscles.

Felix was looking away from the clearing, away from the body. His color had improved, but his expression was still glassy.

McGivney grabbed his shoulder. "Do you know this man?"

Felix blinked. "Who is it?"

"That's why we asked you out here. We figured you knew."

Felix shook his head slowly. "I don't know him. Where is he from?"

"What difference does that make?" McGivney pounced on the odd question. "Is there a missing person in your life?"

I removed the sheriff's hand from Felix's arm. "He's said he doesn't know the dead man, which means we're done here, Lieutenant."

"We're done when I say we're done," McGivney snapped.

"Oh, please. You've given us zero reason for hauling Mr. Herschel out here at two in the morning. We've looked at a murdered man and felt the horror of his death, which you no doubt intended. Neither of us has seen him before. We can't help you. Good night, Lieutenant."

I took Felix's arm and turned him around, telling him to step in the footprints we'd followed in.

"Why did the guy have Herschel's name and phone number in his jeans?" McGivney demanded.

Felix looked at me, his dark eyes wide with fear.

I muttered to him, "Don't say *anything*," before calling over my shoulder to McGivney, "I'm not a medium, so unfortunately I can't answer any questions about this poor dead man's acts or motives."

"You're at a murder site, not Comedy Central, Warshawski," McGivney snapped. "Your client needs to explain his connection to the dead man."

I turned around. "My client has told you he has no connection. If your search of the body turned up a phone with Mr. Herschel's name in it, then you can learn his identity without any help from us."

"It was on a scrap of paper," McGivney said.

"If we can look at it, we might be able to help you," I said, using the soothing voice of a kindergarten teacher.

McGivney frowned, but he was a reasonable cop, just one I'd pushed on harder than he liked. He beckoned one of the techs, who produced a labeled evidence envelope: REMOVED FROM LEFT FRONT JEANS POCKET, 1:17 A.M. Inside was a scrap of paper with Felix's cell phone number, handwritten with such care that the numbers looked like artwork.

"What do you know about this, Herschel?" McGivney demanded.

Felix looked at me, his face alight with fear. I felt sure he recognized the writing.

"It's been torn from a bigger sheet of paper," I said quickly, before he could give himself away. "Good quality, too. Not just a Post-it or notebook."

"You are Sherlock Holmes," McGivney growled.

"No monographs on paper stock, Lieutenant, just observation and experience."

"And how do your observation and experience explain why your client's number is in the vic's pocket?"

"Still no crystal ball, Lieutenant." I moved from the scene, my hand locked on Felix's forearm.

McGivney followed us. He was phoning orders to underlings, but stopped when we reached the edge of the thicket we'd struggled through on our way in.

"One last question, son," he said to Felix. "Who were you expecting to see back there?"

"I—no one," Felix stammered.

"You asked where he was from," McGivney said. "Where did you think that would be?"

"I don't know," Felix said, shifting unhappily from foot to foot.

Before McGivney could pressure him further, I said, "Who found the body? It was shoved into that log, right? And there's no direct path into that clearing."

McGivney sighed. "High school kids out smoking and drinking. Weed, beer, vodka, cigarettes. Be a while before they do that again."

"You don't think they killed him themselves? Some *Lord of the Flies* fantasy that ran out of control?"

"What, and came back to get stoned at the scene and celebrate the murder? They were scared shitless."

"Whoever killed him didn't want him found," I said.

"You think?" McGivney's upper lip curled in derision. "Let me know if you have any other insights, Sherlock."

2

L STOP

ON OUR WAY back to the city, I stopped at a gas station to buy Felix a bottle of water. "You shouldn't buy bottled water," he muttered.

"I agree, but you need to hydrate yourself. You'll feel better all the way around."

"I'm not a baby," he said, but he drank part of the bottle.

He began to shake, his teeth chattering, his arms wrapped around himself in an effort to stay warm. I turned the heat on high, and gradually, as we got back onto the expressway, he calmed down and drank the rest of the water.

"Thank you for driving with me, Vic," he muttered, staring out the window. "It was . . . quite horrible."

"Yes, that body—the face—were terrible to look at," I agreed. "Do you really not know him?"

"Do you think I'm lying?" he cried, jerking around to look at me.

"I don't think anything. I'm here to help you in any way I can, but I need facts before I can go forward."

"I don't know how anyone could recognize him," Felix said, his voice hovering on the edge of tears. "I never saw him before. Only when they said he had my phone number in his pocket, I couldn't help being afraid. It seemed like that lieutenant wanted to nail me and I probably wasn't very smart."

"Where did you think he was from?" I asked. "Is someone from your EFS group missing?"

"I can't take any more questions right now, Vic, please!"

EFS—Engineers in a Free State—was a group Felix had joined this past winter. Right before Christmas, he and a dozen or so other foreign students had been picked up in an Immigration and Customs Enforcement dragnet. He'd been held in a windowless room in a building whose location he'd never learned. He wasn't allowed water or a bathroom or permission to phone for help.

Felix was Canadian; he'd come to Chicago to do graduate work in mechanical engineering at the Illinois Institute of Technology. His grandfather was Lotty Herschel's brother, Hugo, who'd escaped with her from Vienna to London ten days before the start of World War II. After the war, when Lotty came to Chicago for her obstetrics fellowship, Hugo moved to Montreal, where he married and started a family. Hugo and Lotty remained close, with family visits to Chicago each summer. For Felix, choosing a Chicago university had seemed like a natural decision.

That was before his detention. Afterward, Felix told us that while ICE claimed to be checking the immigration status of all foreign students, only those from Middle Eastern or South American countries were actually detained. As was Felix, whose walnut-colored skin and dark curly hair made him look like Omar Sharif's grandson.

"They held me for five hours. Every now and then someone would come in and ask me the same questions the previous person did, like they were trying to trick me. When I got out, I learned the Europeans and Chinese—and white-looking Canadians—only had to show their passports—no questions asked of them.

"Even when they finally looked me up in their system and saw I was Canadian, they kept demanding my visa. They didn't seem to know that Canadians don't need visas to go to school in the States. Bullies and stupid with it."

Two of his fellow students, a man from Paraguay and a woman born in Sudan, were detained, pending deportation. They'd been DACA kids, the so-called Dreamers, who had come to the States as children but didn't have citizenship or green cards. Like many other Dreamers, they were having trouble raising the five hundred dollars to apply for authorization extensions.

The woman's deportation made Felix even angrier. I wondered if they'd dated, but he said they were just lab partners. "Kitoko's life's in danger in Sudan. Her brother was murdered, her mother was raped. She grew up in the U.S. and everything she knows is here. But that counts for nothing!"

He'd gone to the Canadian consulate and tried to get them to offer Kitoko asylum, but by the time the consul responded, the United States had deported her.

Felix had talked about staying in Montreal after the Christmas break. He'd also talked about some alarmingly radical actions. Over New Year's a group of his fellow IIT students had formed Engineers in a Free State. When Felix learned about the group, he'd returned to Chicago to join them. He'd continued his studies, but he'd also started going to community meetings with students from Latin American and Middle Eastern countries.

He used to come to Lotty's for dinner on Sundays, but he now spent most of his spare time working with his friends. "Peace initiatives. We're following the example of Engineers Without Borders," he said when Lotty asked why he visited infrequently.

Lotty was uneasy. "Yes, it's good that he's standing up for what is right, but I don't want him in his rage to do something irreversible."

When Felix called me at two this morning, panicking because sheriff's deputies were pounding on his apartment door, I was frightened that he had crossed that line.

I'd been heavily asleep after a long day, but when he said "cops at the door" I'd jolted wide awake.

"What do they want?"

I was pulling on jeans, sweater, shoes while telling him to let the police know his lawyer was en route; he'd talk to them as soon as I arrived, but until then he wasn't opening the door.

I am a lawyer, at least on paper: I keep up my membership in the Illinois Bar Association so that I can claim privilege if I'm interrogated about my clients. Or so I can put a thin barrier between them and the law until I find them a heavier legal hitter.

I'd phoned Lotty on my way to Felix's place. I hated to alarm her, but she wouldn't forgive me if Felix were arrested and she found out only after the fact. She'd agreed that it would be best if I handled the situation myself, but to call if he needed the Canadian consul or my own criminal defense lawyer.

It took some doing when I reached Felix's building, but I'd persuaded the sheriff's deputies to reveal their mission: Felix wasn't a suspect in a crime—they wanted to see if he could identify a dead body. They didn't know anything else, or they wouldn't say anything else, except to fight me over driving Felix myself instead of letting them stuff him into the back of a squad car. They lost that argument, too, which probably explained why the deputy left us to flounder through the bracken unassisted.

The body had been dumped in the Cap Sauers Holding, part of a chain of woods, sloughs, and small lakes that make up a large set of forest preserves southwest of the city. Suburbs and gated communities had grown up to encroach on the woods, but Cap Sauers remained as close as you can get to true wilderness in the metro area. It's a minimally manicured remainder of the glaciers that covered the region twenty-five thousand years ago, and the trails are a challenge even in daylight.

As Felix and I drove home, I wondered about the kids who'd found the body. I wouldn't write them off as quickly as the sheriff had. Probably white, possibly from influential families, given the wealth in the immediate area. McGivney would go lightly, but for my money, the youths could have had something more secretive in mind than getting high when they crashed through the woods.

After I left the expressway for the narrow one-way streets near the engineering school campus, Felix began texting. Tension radiated from his shoulders—he was aware of me, but treating me like an outsider.

"I'll let Lotty know what happened," I said. "Do you want to stay with her or with me tonight?"

"No, just take me to my own place."

He didn't speak again, but hunched over his phone, which kept pinging. I wondered if he was checking on members from his Free State group, all up in the middle of the night, none of them knowing anything about a dead man but knowing they had to be on the alert.

I broke the silence when I pulled up in front of his building. "The sheriff's police are likely to get a warrant to inspect your computer. You don't have anything on your server that suggests violence against the government, do you?"

"We're not building bombs! How many times do I have to tell you and Aunt Lotty that EFS is building projects for life, not death." His voice quivered. "Please, no more questions tonight. Okay?"

"Okay." I held up my hands, truce sign. "I don't have friends in the sheriff's department the way I do with the Chicago police and so I don't have any way of getting information about what they're doing. That makes the situation even more worrying as far as I'm concerned and it's why I want to make sure we don't cross any lines."

The sheriff's department handles deaths in the forest preserves. Their police force used to be a byword for corruption of all kinds, including working for the Mob. They've become a professional force these days, but it still made me uneasy, having no one I could talk to on the inside about McGivney, or how his investigation was going.

"I'll talk to my own lawyer," I told Felix. "Freeman Carter has added an immigration specialist to his practice, a woman named Martha Simone. You should see if your mother or grandfather can pay her fees, because they won't be cheap, but you need someone with her skills on your team. Meanwhile, please don't shut me or Lotty out. We may be hidebound reactionaries, but your well-being is important to Lotty, and her well-being is essential to me, okay?"

He nodded mutely, squeezed my hand convulsively, and left the car. It was four o'clock now, a good hour for muggers. I watched him up the sidewalk until he was inside the apartment building before retracing my route to the expressway. The White Sox ballpark loomed on the far side of the Dan Ryan Expressway. In between Felix's apartment and the Ryan were the aged girders to the State Street L. Lotty phoned just as a train was rattling overhead.

I pulled over, waiting for the train to pass so I could hear her. "We just got done with the sheriff's police—I dropped Felix off five minutes ago. It was a strange and tiring outing, but Felix couldn't identify the body."

I told her about the scrap of paper with his phone number, but not my worries about Felix expecting to see a particular body. Lotty is my closest friend, my mentor, my conscience; it felt wrong to keep secrets from her, but I didn't want to worry her when I had only a phantom impression, not evidence.

"You're certain Felix isn't involved in this stranger's death?" She couldn't hide a quaver in her voice.

"I'm sure," I said steadily.

I was sure Felix couldn't have administered those blows. Other things I was less confident of—not just whether one of his team was missing, but also what kind of language his e-mails might contain. I didn't know if I could trust his constant assurance that they weren't building weapons. I didn't know how he and his friends might speak about the United States, forgetting it's prudent to keep your opinions out of the ether these days.

"I have surgery this morning," Lotty said. "I leave in half an hour to scrub. Could you come to dinner this evening?"

I squeezed my eyes shut. My own day was due to start in a few hours, with appointments I couldn't reschedule.

"I'll call you," I said. "I don't think it's going to be possible, but I'll see how things shake out by the afternoon."

As I put the car into gear, I saw a man heading up the stairs to the L platform. Felix's thick curls and the long scarf, which he wore dangling like Tom Baker's Dr. Who, were unmistakable.

During the day, when the streets are so crowded that the L outruns automobiles, I couldn't have followed, but at this hour, it was easy. I waited at each stop, looking for Felix's silhouette among the handful of exiting passengers.

The tricky part came where the tracks ran underground. I had to watch both sides of the street at each L stop until a late traveler or two emerged. I continued north, following what I hoped was his train. And at the Granville stop, eight miles north of the Loop, he climbed down the stairs.

I tracked him to an apartment building near Western Avenue, where a young woman opened the outer door. All I could tell from her profile was that she was slender, with a braid that hung below the scarf wrapped loosely around her face.

She clutched Felix tightly. He clung to her, smoothing her head. The door shut behind them, blocking them from view, but I stared at it for a long moment. Surely this wasn't the person Felix feared he'd see dead in the woods.

3

SISTER ACT

I OVERSLEPT, WHICH meant I spent the day in one of those frenzied routines that Olympic medalists can't handle: a run around the block with the dogs; in and out of the shower; dressing while collecting files and checking messages; eating while driving to my office; combing my hair and putting on makeup as the L jounced me into the Loop.

I was still five minutes late for my first meeting—not so good, since it was with my most important client. Darraugh Graham is the CEO of a firm that had started in transportation and ended up with holdings across so many industries that they were hard to categorize. There are days when I think a truly moral person wouldn't work with CALLIE Enterprises, because it was hard to know what damage its subsidiaries do. There are other days when I look at the outstanding balance on my line of credit and think how lucky I am that Darraugh trusts me to take on some of his private work. Today was one of those grateful days.

During a break from the meeting, I went out to the hall to call the chief deputy medical examiner to see if they'd identified the body in the woods. Nick Vishnikov answers my questions not because of our relationship—which hovers in that gray area between friend and work acquaintance—but because the chronic fraud and mismanagement in Cook County angers him so much that he makes his own rules.

"Caucasian male about thirty, in reasonable health, seemed to have a healthy diet, judging by his arteries and liver and so on, but he was a smoker. The one thing I can tell you is that he didn't die where he was found."

"Was the bludgeoning masking something else?"

"No. Someone with a taste for sadism kicked him in the head until he died of brain trauma. He'd been punched in the gut hard enough to double him over, as I reconstruct it. When he'd gone down, the kicking began. They might not have meant to kill him—impossible to tell."

A brutal, mindless murder. I shivered.

"Did he have any tattoos or moles or anything that would help a close friend ID him?" I asked.

"Nothing unusual. We're prettying up his face—we'll give it to the media when we can make him look like someone a girl- or boyfriend might recognize. Probably on the evening news. You have any thoughts?"

"None. When the kid I took out to view the body saw it, he blurted, *Where's he from?* Is there anything to indicate he isn't American?"

"Did someone issue an edict while I was at breakfast? We can only do autopsies on native-born Americans?" Vishnikov demanded.

"I'm surprised you missed the memo," I said. "That makes it all the more urgent to know where the mystery man was born."

"Can't tell you. If he has signs of cholera or dengue fever, that means he was recently in one of thirty or forty countries, but not that he was born there."

"Does he have signs of cholera or dengue?" I asked.

"I'll check the blood for pathogens. We don't usually, but—just in case. When *you* ask, there's almost always a reason."

He hung up before I could think of a zippy comeback. I looked up dengue fever on my way back to the meeting. It sounded like a good reason to stay out of the tropics.

From Darraugh's, I went to another bread-and-butter client, a small law firm that uses me from time to time. At the end of the afternoon, bloated with meetings, I picked up my car and drove to the building Felix had visited the night before. I'd tried phoning him during my lunch break, to see if he'd had any further visits from the Cook County sheriff, but he let me roll over to voice mail.

The building was in a part of town that typically has a lot of traffic, both foot and car: Pakistani and Indian immigrants have clustered here, and Devon is a South Asian restaurant and shopping hub. This afternoon, the area seemed quiet—too quiet, as immigrants stayed away from any place where ICE agents might be lurking.

It was a neighborhood of bungalows and tidy gardens, with a sprinkling of apartment buildings. These tended to be small, six to ten units, but Felix's friend lived in one of the few larger blocks, with perhaps sixty or seventy units. I sat for a minute, watching adults return from work or shopping, children from school, some in soccer gear, others hoisting younger siblings on backs or hips. I saw men wearing kufis or Sikh turbans, women in hijab, bareheaded women with long braids or short curls, thin women, heavyset women. When people saw me watching the building, they moved fast: only an immigration officer would be staring at them so intently.

I felt a flush of shame, shame that I was inspecting people as if they were specimens, shame that my government could create such fear in people. I drove off. Even if I could bring myself to conduct more subtle surveillance, I would never identify Felix's friend in this throng.

None of your business anyway, I snarled at myself on the road home. It took almost forty minutes to cover the four miles to my apartment on Racine: a just punishment for wasting time on voyeurism. Except for that nagging worry that Felix had been expecting to see a foreigner buried in the tree trunk.

Around half of IIT's student body was international. Ever since Felix had become involved with Engineers in a Free State, he'd gone out of his way to be part of the lives of the African and Middle Eastern contingents. I was sure he was worried about a missing friend, but until he felt like confiding in me, there was little I could do.

I changed into jeans and drove the dogs to the lakefront. A bitter winter had lingered through late March, but today was unexpectedly warm. While the dogs swam, I rolled up my cuffs and waded into the water, but jumped out—the cold froze my bones almost instantly.

The day had been too long: I texted Lotty, saying I couldn't manage dinner; we'd catch up tomorrow.

Mr. Contreras, the first-floor neighbor with whom I share the dogs, came out to collect them. When he started to talk about a visitor, I sketched a wave. "Later, please."

"Ain't no 'later,' doll; she's waiting for you in here." He jerked his head toward his front room. "Says she's your niece. I didn't know you had any, but she don't seem like a con artist."

"I don't have any nieces," I said. If a woman was young and pretty, she could con my neighbor out of his undershorts.

"Auntie Vic?"

A woman, young, with hair the texture and color of corn silk, appeared behind Mr. Contreras. She looked at me doubtfully: Was I going to throw an orphan out into the howling gale? It was a good act—Mitch trotted to her and rubbed his head against her thigh, while Mr. Contreras patted her shoulder. Peppy stayed next to me—the two of us aloof, untrusting.

"Auntie Vic, I—I know it's been forever since I've seen you, but Uncle Dick—"

"Reno?" I stared at her doubtfully.

"I'm Harmony, Auntie Vic. Reno has disappeared."

"I'm sorry to hear that," I said politely.

"Doll, that ain't no way to talk. Miss Harmony needs your help looking for her sis." Mr. Contreras glared at me, arms akimbo. Even Peppy looked at me mournfully.

"Can we talk about this in the morning? I was up all night looking at a murder victim in the western suburbs."

"But, Auntie Vic—" Tears sparkled on the ends of Harmony's lashes. "This is serious. I flew here from Portland because I knew Reno was in trouble, but when I got to her apartment, she was gone."

All I wanted was my bed, three flights above me, as remote as the top of Everest. My brain had all the thinking power of a bowl of stale oatmeal. I collapsed on the bottom stair, leaning against the stairwell wall.

"You live in Portland?"

Harmony nodded.

"And Reno is here in Chicago? Visiting?"

"Doll, you ain't listening," Mr. Contreras said. "She told you Reno has an apartment."

"If she's living here, how come I haven't heard from her? The last I heard, Becky—the girls' mom," I added to Mr. Contreras, "took them out west to a commune. Wyoming, was it?"

"Montana. We only lived there six months, waiting for the guy who supposedly was our father, but he never showed. Then we went on west and stayed out in Oakland. Reno came here by herself over a year ago."

"Why didn't she call me?" I asked.

"She didn't know you and Uncle Dick were divorced until she called out to his house and talked to his second wife. Reno called her 'Auntie Vic' and the lady blew up at her, like we were supposed to know Uncle Dick and you had split up. And then, it wasn't until later she found out what your last name was. We didn't know Grandpa Tony's last name. Anyway, Uncle Dick sort of helped Reno find a job, but he told her that was it, not to come around bothering him again."

Becky Seale was my brief husband's younger sister. When Richard Yarborough and I divorced, the girls were five and six. Linda Yarborough, Dick and Becky's mother, couldn't conceal her delight at the divorce. Both her children had married disastrously: Becky to Fulton Seale, a heroin-using drifter, while her beloved Richard had been seduced (in her mind) by the daughter of a Chicago cop and an Italian refugee.

And then a miracle, at least for my mother-in-law: Dick left me for a petite, femmie woman with a rich father. Teri didn't want a career— she was happy to work in the local hospital's charity store two days a week and to shop or golf with her friends the rest of the time.

I was happy, too: the fights between Becky and her mother had ruined two Thanksgivings and one Christmas for me. My second Christmas with Dick, unable to bear another Yarborough family brawl, I took Reno and Harmony to South Chicago to spend Christmas with my dad. To his mother's delight, Dick stayed at her side in Lake Forest.

The girls and I played hide-and-seek in Bessemer Park, we went to a Blackhawks game—my cousin Boom Boom was still alive, leading the NHL in goals—we roasted marshmallows over the stovetop in my childhood home's minute kitchen. At night I tucked them into the pullout bed in the front room, crooning the Italian lullabies my own mother used to sing to me.

When I returned them to their grandmother's North Shore home, they'd clinched her dislike of me by begging me to take them back to Grandpa Tony. And then I'd forgotten them.

"Anyway, Reno was doing fine," Harmony said. "The finance company where Uncle Dick helped her find work liked her, she got a promotion, and they sent her to the Caribbean for some kind of Mardi Gras party. But when she got back to Chicago, she was upset by the things that went on at the resort they sent her to. All she'd say was she should have known better, but she seemed to get more and more, I don't know, agitated maybe. Depressed.

"I decided to fly out to see her. We were always each other's closest friend, we'd been through so much together that no one else knew about. This was the first time in our lives we'd been apart for more than a day.

"My boss, he agreed: 'Don't let your sis suffer alone,' he said. 'We'll be fine here without you for a few days.' Only when I got here—the janitor, he let me into her apartment, and she wasn't there. I texted her, just said, BIG SURPRISE WAITING FOR YOU WHEN YOU GET HOME! and didn't hear back from her. I couldn't sleep: I kept waiting for her to come in."

"Traveling for her firm," I suggested. "Staying at her boyfriend's place."

"She doesn't have a boyfriend and she'd tell me if she was going out of town. We always tell each other everything."

I don't know how many times I've heard that sentence, usually from someone whose partner is cheating on them. This might have been the first time I'd heard it from a sibling.

"Did you call her office?"

"I did, but they gave me this huge runaround. They have a ton of branches in Chicago and they never did tell me which one she was working at."

I sat up straight. "Who does she work for?"

"Rest EZ, they're part of a—"

"I know Rest EZ," I said.

They're a payday loan company, one of the bigger fish in a scummy pond. A payday loan is supposed to be a bridge, to carry you to that next paycheck, but in Illinois, interest runs as high as 400 percent a year. Even the Mob would blush at that—go to Don Pasquale, one of the few godfathers not in federal custody, and he'd bail you out for 300.

"You're sure," I said to Harmony. "You didn't get the name wrong? There are mattress companies called that."

Harmony flushed. "Are you like everyone else? You think because I'm blond I'm stupid? Reno said she was in financial services. She said she worked for Rest EZ. Does that sound like a mattress to you?"

"No," I agreed meekly. "It sounds like she worked for Rest EZ. Have you filed a missing persons report?" I asked instead.

"With the police? No, I can't go to the police!"

"They have resources way beyond what I can do," I said.

"You think they care about people like me or Reno?" Harmony cried, eyes bright. "They only care about one thing when they see us."

"Grandpa Tony was a cop," I said. "If he were still alive—"

"But he's not, and I won't talk to any cop, not even if he's Grandpa Tony's twin brother!"

I said we could insist we talk to a woman officer, but Harmony was beyond reason.

No police, not now, not ever. "I know you're a detective, I looked you up online. You've solved big cases."

My mouth twisted. "It can be easier to sort out a big fraud than to find a missing person."

"But still, please, can you *try* to find her?"

"In the morning, I can start a serious search, but right now, I'm too tired to think straight."

Mr. Contreras weighed in now on my behalf. "That's right, Harmony. I'm going to cook you a nice steak, you and me are going to watch the races, and then you can sleep in my grandsons' room. We're going to leave your aunt here in peace."

It was a kind offer for us both, but Harmony fought it.

"I have to go back to Reno's place. What if she comes home in the night? I need to be there for her!"

We couldn't budge her. I promised I would drive her back to her sister's apartment. After my bath. After supper.

4

QUEENS DRESSED IN SILK

WHILE I RELAXED in the tub, I checked in with Lotty. She hadn't heard anything from Felix today, and he hadn't answered her phone calls, either. I told her about trailing him up to Edgewater early this morning and my speculations about the young woman, but Lotty had no more idea what he might be doing there than I did.

I started to tell her about Harmony Seale's unexpected arrival, but lacked the energy to convey my own news. Instead, I promised to be in touch and dozed off.

Harmony woke me half an hour later, gently rubbing my shoulder: Mr. Contreras had sent her up to fetch me; dinner was ready. She lingered in my short hallway while I went into the bedroom to dress.

A poster-size photo of my mother hangs there, Gabriella on the brink of a concert comeback before ovarian cancer ravaged her. In the photo, she looks dazzling, her concert gown with its burnt velvet bodice and soft silk skirt making her more glamorous than Callas.

Harmony asked a few polite questions about her. "You're lucky, having a mom you can be proud of," she said. "Although Reno and I got lucky with our foster mom, Clarisse, only now she has Alzheimer's and doesn't know who I am."

"That's very tough," I agreed.

I touched the glass over my mother's face as I passed. It's been thirty years and still Harmony's chance comment could send a spasm of grief through me. There are no balance scales to loss: my mother's too-young death, Clarisse vanishing in the present—there, but not there. All these losses are an opening into an abyss. When we start falling in, it's hard to climb back up.

After dinner, Mr. Contreras tried once again to urge Harmony into spending the night in his spare room. "Vic don't need to be out driving this late."

"I can call a car," Harmony said.

I drove, partly to establish a relationship—I was reliable, I wouldn't leave her on her own in a strange city. I also wanted to see her sister's place: Fairfield and North, the gentrifying northeast corner of Humboldt Park. We brought Mitch with us—the hundred-pound black dog commands respect wherever he goes.

In the ride over I asked Harmony what had brought her sister back to Chicago.

Harmony hunched a shoulder. "Mom went on to Oakland after our so-called father stood her up. She got some kind of job, but everything disintegrated like it always did with her. Mom was begging on the streets, anything she got went for drugs. She tried to get Grandmother Yarborough to take us, or Uncle Dick, but they both said no.

"We slept under viaducts or sometimes in church basements. We ate out of dumpsters. Reno and me—Reno was so pretty, Mom would—she would kind of use her—get men to come around and give her drugs. And me, even though I wasn't as pretty, they—"

She turned her head away. My stomach muscles tightened in outrage, at Becky Seale for putting her daughters through this, at Dick and his mother for turning a cold shoulder, at myself for ignoring them. I didn't say anything—outrage at this point in Harmony's life would be cheap.

"When I was ten and Reno was eleven, we decided to run away, to hitchhike back to Chicago, to see if anyone in the family would take us in. We thought maybe Grandpa Tony . . . but we never made it out of Oakland: a lady picked us up at the freeway entrance.

"We got put in this state home for runaways and discards; we were working on a plan for running away from there when Clarisse and

Henry showed up. Clarisse and Henry Yu. They were a mixed-race couple, see, who couldn't have any kids of their own, so the authorities figured two fucked-up white girls could be dumped on them. We were street kids. We weren't users, but you couldn't tell us anything about drugs. And we knew—a whole lot—about sex."

Harmony's hands went involuntarily to her stomach. I risked a touch on her shoulder. She didn't push me away, but she held herself rigid: she'd been touched too many times without permission.

We'd reached Reno's building. I busied myself parking, both hands on the steering wheel.

"It sounds as though you landed in a good place," I ventured.

"Oh, we did. It took us a long time to trust them, but in the end, it all came together. Clarisse was strict. Not in a mean way, but we weren't used to rules—go to school every day, home after school, do homework and chores before sports or choir or anything, and no excuses." Harmony smiled at some private memory.

"Henry was easier going—if we got a B or a C, he'd tell Clarisse to relax, no one expected us to be Marie Curie. His real name was Heng, Yu Heng in Chinese, but in America he called himself Henry. Clarisse and Henry, when they wanted to be private, they'd speak Chinese, so of course we learned it some, at least to understand. Reno was always better at that than me—I could say 'good morning' or 'how's your arthritis,' but she got so she could really speak in Chinese.

"Clarisse and Henry ran a flower shop in Oakland, but Henry raised fruits and vegetables for the family. That was my favorite thing, digging in the dirt with Henry. Reno didn't like that, but she loved working in the shop, especially when Clarisse let her put together bouquets. Reno's specialty was funerals."

A macabre pleasure, but maybe Reno worked out some complicated emotional puzzle, vicariously taking part in other people's sorrows.

"We went to community college in Oakland, and Clarisse and Henry, when we graduated, you would have thought we were number one at Stanford."

"It sounds as though Reno would have told Clarisse or Henry what was troubling her, if she didn't tell you," I said.

Harmony's lips quivered. "Henry had a heart attack and died five years ago. That was why we moved to Portland. There wasn't any money, or not much, anyway, after his funeral, and we could afford Portland better. Clarisse came with us, but she'd already started with Alzheimer's. We tried to look after her ourselves—we owed her and Henry everything—but she needs so much care, we couldn't do it."

Harmony rubbed her nose with a tissue. "We had to put her into a home. That's what made Reno come out east—it made her feel angry and—and damaged, like every person in our lives leaves us. First Fulton—our dad, assuming he even was our dad, with Mom how could we be sure?—then Mom and all those Yarboroughs, then Henry and now Clarisse—she doesn't even know me when I go to visit. Reno wanted to be in a new place where she could forget all that, but she chose Chicago. I guess she thought Uncle Dick or even our tight-ass grandmother might want to see her now that we're adults. But guess again on that one."

"You said Reno and you didn't know my name. How did you find me?"

"I called Uncle Dick's office. Some snot of a PA wouldn't let me talk to him, but she told me you were a detective who likes stray dogs. I didn't know any of that, but she gave me your address."

"How very kind of her, to both of us," I said.

We'd reached Reno's stretch of North Avenue. Cars honked their way through the park just west of us, and, despite the cold, girls in minis and thick jackets teetered down the street in high-heeled boots, arm in arm with each other or with slim-hipped boys. Skateboarders swerved around us, hooting at "the blond chick" as I followed Harmony to the building entrance. When Mitch curled his lip at one kid who rode too close, the rest of them backed off.

"How did you get keys?" I asked as Harmony undid the outer locks.

"The janitor, he let me in. I was waiting out here"—she gestured to the sidewalk—"when he was leaving for the day. I look a lot like Reno even if I'm not as pretty, so he guessed right away I was her sister and he let me in."

"He gave you keys?"

"No. Reno hadn't taken hers, which makes me even more worried.

How could she leave and not take her keys with her? But hers were where we always put them, in the bowl by the door. When you have a system, you don't waste time hunting for things."

Missing person, possible abduction. Janitor with keys. I opened and shut my mouth. I wasn't up to another battle with Harmony over the police: I'd make my own report in the morning.

Mitch and I followed Harmony up the stairs to the third floor. Just inside the doorway was a small stand with a blue porcelain bowl on it. Harmony put the key ring into it, on top of a few pieces of mail.

I took a quick look around the apartment, checking for signs of disturbance, also whether the security seemed adequate. The apartment would have been easy to search, since Reno had been neat to the point of bareness. The drawers to a desk in the front room held nothing but essentials—the few bills that still come in the mail instead of online, an invitation to a fund-raiser for a youth program, some old letters, including one in Chinese characters. There were also two Chinese prints on the walls of the main room.

In Reno's bedroom, her minimal wardrobe was neatly arranged on hangers and in baskets. She had three handbags, all empty. No computer, no phone.

She had framed family photos on her nightstand and on the wall near her bed. An African-American woman and a Chinese man featured in most of them: Clarisse and Henry. A formal portrait of them with the two sisters stood on the nightstand.

The picture that brought Harmony to life showed her grinning with Henry, both of them wearing dirt-crusted overalls, holding a basket of vegetables so that the camera caught the perfectly shaped eggplant, surrounded by tomatoes and summer squashes.

In another, the woman stood in profile in the flower shop, putting a rose into a wreath. The ghost of a smile was on her lips—she knew she was being photographed and was laughing at the pretense that she didn't. There were several of the girls at their different graduations, the two adults behind them, all four grinning widely with pride.

In one, they were showing off matching gold chains with old-fashioned locket hearts. "Clarisse gave them to us when we graduated from junior college. We never take them off. At least, I never do. I don't know what Reno does these days."

She pulled the chain out from under her sweater. It was of real gold, not plate, an intricate set of links holding a gold locket. Harmony opened it to show me the faces of Clarisse and Henry on one side and her sister on the other.

When I admired the craft in the chain, Harmony said, "It's called Singapore style. Henry had an aunt in Shanghai who used to send him things like jewelry or fancy silks to give to us. One year for Christmas he gave Clarisse and me and Reno silk bathrobes. We used to sit on the back porch in them, pretending we were queens, eating breakfast in our silk clothes."

I looked at all the windows to make sure they had working locks, checked the rear exit, which opened not to the outside, but to the utility stairwell and elevator.

"Keep your doors locked when you're inside," I said.

"I grew up in Oakland," Harmony said scornfully. "I'm not afraid of this neighborhood."

"Something happened to your sister," I said. "She's not answering her phone, she left her keys here. If someone got inside this place once, they can do it again. If you want to come back with me, I'm happy to take you, but if you're staying here, stay smart, okay?"

"Yeah, okay. That's what Clarisse would say, too: stay smart. Do you think you can find Reno?" Her voice broke on the last sentence.

"I don't know, sweetheart. I'll try, but there's a lot of ground to cover. I'll check with Rest EZ tomorrow and let you know what they say. Did she ever mention a co-worker or a boss that she got on with?"

"Her new boss, after her promotion, Reno seemed to like her. She had a name like 'Lute.' Something like that."

"Okay. I'll find Ms. Lute. You have my number, you have Mr. Contreras's; call if you need us."

5

TEAM PLAYER

MITCH AND I rode the utility elevator to the basement. I followed the sound of washing machines to a laundry room. A middle-aged woman who was folding clothes gave a little scream when she saw the dog.

"Who are you? What do you want?"

I held up Mitch's leash so she could see he was under control. "I'm looking for the janitor's room."

"Vern doesn't live here—it's a nine-to-five job."

"That's fine. I still want to find his room. Someone gave something of mine to him; he was supposed to leave it out for me."

She studied me and the dog for a moment, then shrugged—maybe we were robbers, but she wasn't going to get involved. "Down the hall, other side of the furnace room."

I switched on the lights in the hall, low-hanging single bulbs swinging from a wire. The janitor's door was locked, but it wasn't much of a lock. I looked back up the hall; the woman doing laundry wasn't interested in us. I took my PI license, sturdy laminate, and wedged it between the lock-lip and the jamb, jiggled the knob, and we were inside.

Vern had an overstuffed easy chair where he relaxed when his work duties became onerous. The cushion had a deep indentation—the duties must often be overwhelming.

A twenty-four-inch flat-screen TV faced the chair. On the floor next to the chair, a stack of magazines, some about boating and fishing, some a collection of standard porn. A small refrigerator with a salami and seven bottles of Pabst. A sink with a plate crusted with mustard. He should have taken cleaning lessons from Reno.

In the back of the room was his worktable. His tools, at least, he treated with care. Files, screwdrivers, electrical supplies, all in drawers labeled in the round clumsy letters of someone who doesn't often write. Emergency plumbing equipment in racks on a facing wall. Saws.

I didn't touch the tools but looked closely for anything that might suggest blood or hair. I peered behind all the boxes and shelves. I took Mitch next door to the furnace room. We didn't see any signs that a woman had been brought down here and assaulted. I guess that was a comfort.

There was a warren of small rooms and strange bins beyond the boiler room, but searching them would have been an all-night job. It was already past midnight and I hadn't gotten to bed until five yesterday morning.

Mr. Contreras had waited up for me, which was touching, if tiring, since we had to rehash Harmony's story. I assured him that I would help her, although I was beginning to feel as though there were a flashing light on my head that read GIVE ME YOUR TROUBLED RELATIVES, EXHAUSTING LABOR. NO CHARGE.

When I finally made it up to my own apartment, I checked the news to see if any word had come in on the body in the woods. The ME must not have prettied up the face enough yet for the media. Before going to bed, I tried Felix, but had no more luck than Lotty.

I left a text, asking him to check in with his aunt so that she wouldn't worry, turned my phone off, and was, for once, granted the sleep of the righteous. In the morning I had time for my own exercises, a chance to run the dogs, and an actual breakfast at my own table. I made it downtown in good time for my first meeting.

I love having Darraugh Graham paying some of my bills, but it's my small clients who keep me going. The partners in the firm for whom I'd investigated a potential client were so pleased with my work they had invited me to lunch. I declined with regret—they were both witty women, and they enjoyed good food.

Instead of quenelles of pike at the Potawatomi Club, I sat at a counter in a crowded coffee bar, eating a cheese sandwich while I finished responding to a client query. Over my second cortado, I looked up the Seale sisters: trust everyone but cut the cards. I wanted to make sure I was really looking at Harmony Seale. I wanted to make sure she wasn't dragging me into some financial feud with her sister.

It took the better part of two hours to track down Clarisse and Heng "Henry" Yu, to double-check that they had, indeed, fostered Harmony and Reno, that Henry had died five years earlier, and that the modest estate he'd left was invested for the sole benefit of Clarisse Yu's care. Whether the sisters loved or hated each other didn't show up in any tax or probate reports, but they weren't suing each other and neither had much of a bank balance.

Their father wasn't part of their story at all, at least as far as I could see. In fact, Fulton Seale was so far below the radar that he hadn't left any trace of himself. No death certificate had been issued in any of the fifty states, but he could have died as a John Doe or be alive in a cardboard box under the Bay Bridge.

I looked at my to-do list. I hadn't yet called my lawyer, to tell him about Felix's woes. That could go into a text more economically than a phone call—talking to Freeman Carter, however briefly, would automatically add $120 to my outstanding balance, more if we spoke for over ten minutes. "Let me know if your immigration lawyer will talk to him; if not, can you give me some other names?" I finished.

Time to tackle Rest EZ. Their national headquarters were less than a mile from where I was eating—the walk would do me good. The wind cut through my coat as I crossed the bridge over the Chicago River. I pulled the collar up to my ears and huddled down into the coat as deep as I could. I still felt miserable.

Rest EZ's corporate offices were in the junk-filled streets west of Union Station. A bored lobby guard directed me to the seventh floor, where I was greeted by a locked door with a security camera overhead.

A disembodied voice asked me to state my business into the grille to the left of the door.

"Human Resources," I said. "I'm a detective, looking for one of your employees who's gone missing."

We dickered back and forth through the grille. Finally the voice reluctantly told me to take the elevator to nine; someone would meet me there.

On nine, as on seven, no one was in the hallway. I walked the corridor on both sides of the elevator lobby, but saw only locked, unsignposted doors. Whatever the owners of Rest EZ spent that 400 percent interest on, it wasn't their offices—the gray-green drugget on the hallway floor was worn out in front of the doors. I felt as though I were in one of those sci-fi movies where everyone else in the spaceship had died and I was trying to find my way to the control deck without being eaten by an alien.

Back by the elevators, I started work on my vocal exercises. Singing made the empty space seem less suffocating, and the sound might rouse activity in whoever was monitoring me. In fact, after only three scales on "i," a heavyset woman appeared from the corridor on my left. She was wearing a shapeless beige sweater over shiny black trousers. A crucifix on a gold chain was partly hidden by a company ID on a lanyard.

"Who did you say has gone missing?" she said, with the nasal accent of the South Side.

"I didn't, but it's Reno Seale. She's disappeared, her family is worried, and I'd like to talk to her co-workers, to find out when they last saw her."

"You got some ID on you?"

I showed her my Illinois bar membership and my detective license.

"Hmmph. One of those things you can send away for, like a minister's license."

"One of those things you get after a three-year internship with a licensed operative," I said. "Let's find a place to sit down where you can tell me about Ms. Seale."

"You're the one who came to talk about her," the woman said.

"You're absolutely right. Do you have a name? Are you the HR manager?"

She grudgingly admitted to being Audrey Yonkers from Human Resources. She seemed embarrassed to admit she wasn't a manager or a team leader, but she finally revealed she was the HR receptionist.

Audrey led me down the dreary, underlit hall. When she'd opened the door with a swipe from her ID, the space on the other side wasn't much cheerier.

Audrey's desk, a gunmetal affair with a computer monitor, a drooping plant, and a bowl of candies, was just inside the door. She motioned me to a hard chair on the other side and plunked herself down in a metal mesh desk chair.

Three cubicles faced her desk, two containing white women, the third an African-American man around thirty, all working at their computers. They paused to stare at me, a detective on the premises, not an employee with an HR issue they had to circumvent.

Beyond them was an office, door open, where the manager sat. She was a younger woman, with shoulder-length blond hair and careful makeup. She was on the phone. Like the cubiclers, she took note of my arrival, staring at me and nodding a few times to herself, as if something about me confirmed what she'd expected—a middle-aged private eye, nothing to worry about.

"Reno Seale," I repeated. "I'd like the address where she's working. I'd like to know if she's been coming to work the last week."

Audrey double-checked the spelling and typed quickly. "Yeah, here she is. She started a year ago last summer. Did her training, performed well at the For— at her first assignment, so they moved her in September to a tougher location. She was top performer there. They picked her out to go on a trip to St. Matthieu." Audrey's face creased in lines of envy. "She's missing, you say? That explains why they got her marked 'probable grounds for termination'—second day you don't call in is probation, fourth is termination. Maybe she fell in love and flew back to St. Matthieu," she added with a sneer.

"Always a possibility," I agreed politely. "I thought her supervisor thought well of her. Ms. Lute, wasn't it?"

Audrey peered at the screen. "Not Lute, but—"

"Audrey, why are we discussing musicians on the job?" The unit manager had finished her call and came over to join us, smoothing her jacket over her narrow hips.

"I'm V.I. Warshawski." I got up. "And you are?"

"Eliza Trosse. Why are you asking about one of our team members?"

Team members. We're all team members now, not employees, as if being on the team of a multinational will make us overlook our low salaries and miserable benefits.

"She's disappeared," I said. "I need to talk to her supervisor. Ms. Yonkers here has been a most helpful team player; we were just getting to the point where she was going to put me in touch with Reno Seale's most recent boss, whose name isn't 'Lute.' Apparently the company labeled Ms. Seale as ready for termination—is she still part of the team?"

"Discussing internal employment issues is against company policy. Our clientele entrust us with their private financial records; we can't let every stranger off the street talk to our staff."

"Ms. Trosse, Scout's honor I will not ask about a single client, not how they got in debt to you nor if any of them thinks they will ever stop being indentured. I'm trying to find out what was troubling Ms. Seale since her return from St. Matthieu. She might have talked to her co-workers or her supervisor."

Trosse gave me a cool appraising stare. "If you leave me your phone number, I'll contact the people in Reno's office and let you know if she confided in any of them. Audrey, I don't have all the January reports yet. Have you finished entering them?"

"I'm almost done, Eliza." Audrey's cheeks flooded with color; she closed the screen where she'd been looking at Reno's employment history and opened multiple spreadsheets.

"I'll walk you to the elevator," Trosse said to me.

6

CRANK CALL?

MY LEASE MATE at the warehouse where I have my office is a significant sculptor. Tessa Reynolds was in Argentina for the winter, working on a large installation to commemorate the Mothers of the Plaza de Mayo; she'd turned the heat down on her side before she left, which made the whole building feel cold. I turned on all the lights on my side of the floor and flipped on space heaters to create an illusion of a cheery parlor in a room with fourteen-foot-high ceilings and cinder block walls.

My mother's etching of the Uffizi faced an outsize acrylic by the Italian painter Antonella Mason—I'd bought it on my trip to Italy a few years back. With a cup of ginger tea in my cold hands, I sat for a minute, pretending I was in a plaza in Pitigliano under the Umbrian sun.

I'm not good at fantasy. I put the tea down and brought up Rest EZ's Chicagoland locations on my big monitor.

The woman in HR had started to say that Reno worked in the branch on "For—" Rest EZ had seven offices on streets between Fortieth and Forty-Ninth, spread between Wabash and Harlem, along with one at Fourteenth and California.

I began calling them, asking for Reno Seale. I had a backstory ready if anyone asked, but a surprising number of people will answer questions without demanding a reason for them. At the third outlet, on Forty-Third and Aberdeen, the woman who answered the phone said that Reno had left that location months and months ago.

"They moved her to the West Side, I think, but that was a while ago. I heard they sent her to some big gala in the Caribbean. Sure helps to be skinny and blond. Is there a problem? Is she in trouble?" She seemed eager to think that a skinny blonde could be in trouble.

"Did she strike you as someone who might get into difficulties when she worked with you on Aberdeen?" I asked.

"She always seemed like she had some secret she wasn't going to tell, like she thought she was better than us, or smarter or something," my informant grumbled. "And her language—like, she said she moved here from out west someplace, but when she dealt with troublemakers in the office, she sounded like she grew up on West Madison."

Reno and her sister probably picked up a spectacular vocabulary under those Oakland viaducts. They'd seen drug deals, they'd been violated themselves; that leaves a lot behind linguistically, as well as in mind and body.

I probed for examples of lying or stealing. The woman couldn't come up with a specific complaint.

"She looked liked butter wouldn't melt in her mouth, those prim little outfits, that sweet face, but she had a temper on her."

"She ever hit anyone that you saw?"

"No, but she could make big guys back down, way she looked at them. I guess that made the home office excited, so they moved her to one of the high-volume locations where there's sometimes trouble."

"Did she ever have trouble with anyone stalking her?"

"How would I know?" the woman said huffily. "Someone that pretty, you can bet they're beating guys off with a stick. And she had a stick big enough to keep out of trouble, you ask me."

Before hanging up, I asked the woman if she knew anyone in the company with a name like "Lute." I wasn't surprised when she said no—Rest EZ employed more than five hundred people in the six counties.

It was dark outside by the time we finished. My ginger infusion was cold, but I drank it anyway—they say ginger is good for the stomach or the brain or ingrown toenails. The day was catching up with me, but I started calling the West Side branches.

A woman at the second location giggled. "You mean Donna Lutas? She's the manager here. Who should I say is calling?"

She put me on hold; after a wait that went on for close to five minutes, a woman with a deeper voice, one raspy from smoke, announced herself as Donna Lutas.

I introduced myself as Reno Seale's aunt, but before I could say anything else, Lutas interrupted. "Do you know where she is? If she doesn't show tomorrow, I will start termination proceedings."

"I thought she was doing a great job," I said.

"She was, but policy is policy: four unexplained absences. Unless there's a legitimate reason, you are done."

"She's disappeared," I said. "I was hoping someone at work might know where she's gone, like out of town for training or something."

"We haven't heard word one from her. She's a top employee and all, but she can't go wandering off into space like she owns the company."

"When did you last see her?" I asked.

"Monday. End of the workday. Today is day three, Friday will be the fourth day. I can hold off over the weekend, but if she doesn't show on Monday, that's it."

"Could I talk to you, in person I mean? I've heard conflicting reports about Reno. Some people tell me she was such a great asset that she earned a trip to the Caribbean. Others think she traded on her looks. I also heard she's had something on her mind since getting back from her trip. She trusted you; I'm hoping she let something drop that would give me a hint to go on."

Lutas didn't seem to find the questions odd ones, coming from an aunt. "Traded on her looks? Who did you hear that from? If it was Lily Garton, I'll have her stapling forms in the Stickney warehouse for the next decade—she carried on like Reno was a bigger threat than an ISIS bomber. Reno had only been with the company not even a year, but she was one of our top performers out here in Austin. Some people were jealous, and, of course, she's drop-dead gorgeous."

"That's why I'd like to see you in person, Ms. Lutas, to find out more about what had been troubling her this last month."

"Not tonight, you can't. We're closing in forty minutes and I got reports to generate after that. We open at eight tomorrow, though—you come by around eight-thirty, after we get things in shape for the day. I'll tell you what I can, but it isn't much."

After hanging up, I called Harmony.

"What are you doing to find her?" Harmony demanded.

"I'm talking to the people she worked with. You have any other ideas? Did she go to church or sing or anything out of work hours?"

"Not really," Harmony said. "We never went to church. Reno really liked scuba diving, but where would she do it here? . . . I hate to go back to Portland with Reno still missing, but I'm not doing anything and it's getting lonely without her."

"I don't think there's much you can do in Chicago," I said, "but Mr. Contreras and I are still happy to put you up if you're not ready to go home yet."

Harmony brightened. She said she'd think about it and let me know in the morning. I shut down my office and drove home. I took the dogs to a nearby park to chase tennis balls before curling up in front of the television with a bowl of soup.

At nine, I turned on Global Entertainment's *Nightly News Update*. Murray Ryerson, who used to cover crime and corruption for the *Herald-Star*, had been trundled out to present the story of the dead man I'd seen in Cap Sauers Holding.

When Global bought the *Herald-Star*, Murray had been sidelined. He did a Sunday cable show on Chicago personalities but no longer had a regular reporting assignment. For tonight's story, he made the most of the mystery man, describing his beating death in dramatic detail. He included a shot of the crime scene and the toppled tree where the body had been hidden.

"This is where our dead man lay and where his body would have disintegrated if not for the enterprising acts of some Palos Hills teens."

Murray had managed to interview one of the kids who'd found the body, a gap-toothed youth who looked too wholesome to be smoking weed and getting drunk in the woods. The boy's parents were stationed behind him; from the way his mother's hands moved, I thought she was wishing she could throttle her child.

I couldn't resist texting Murray: EXCELLENT WAY TO DESCRIBE UNDER-AGE WEED & ALCOHOL CONSUMPTION. AND GREAT LEAVE IT TO BEAVER KID.

On-screen, Murray finally showed the ME's reconstructions. Their artist had put together a face that didn't look convincingly alive, but at least had both eyes in their sockets. The hair in the portrait was thick, with a slight wave and a part so far to the right that it seemed to be on the side of the skull.

Global flashed their number on the screen along with the ME's number to call if any viewers recognized him. I was getting ready to turn off the set when I was startled to see my own face appear.

"Chicago's crack private investigator V.I. Warshawski was on the scene at Cap Sauers Holding as well. Since her specialty is corporate fraud, we can only guess that the dead man was involved in serious financial crimes. Stay tuned to Global as we follow the story: we cover Chicago and the world."

I texted Murray again, this time not so flippantly. WE NEED TO TALK, RYERSON.

It was half an hour before Murray got back to me, but a dozen other people had called in the meantime, including Lieutenant McGivney, wanting to know why I hadn't talked to him about the dead man and fraud: Murray's remark meant I, and Felix, really knew the man's identity and why he'd been killed. My anger with Murray built as I tried unsuccessfully to persuade McGivney I didn't know the dead man.

"Guess what, Murray—I've heard from reporters at every TV and radio station in town, plus the Cook County sheriff. This should make you happy: everyone in the six counties watches Global. Maybe you'll get a real job one of these days."

"What got you involved with this corpse?" Murray asked.

"Why didn't you ask before you went on the air?" I demanded. "You blindsided me. I know nothing about the guy, but you got the sheriff's police breathing hot and heavy down my neck. And my client's, for which I absolutely don't forgive you."

Murray was unrepentant. "The assignment editor turned this over to me at five. I had that much time to find the kid, talk to the parents, get a crew out to Cap Sauers, and all the rest. The sheriff's office mentioned you were representing one of their people of interest. And you know darned well that where you are, there's almost always a money trail."

"There's no trail anywhere," I snapped.

"Tell me who you're working for," Murray coaxed. "I can help."

"That's bizarre," I said.

"What?" Murray was eager.

"That you didn't pry my client's name out of the sheriff's department. I thought you had an in with every law-enforcement office in the state."

"I used to," Murray grumbled, "but I've been on the sidelines too long. My contacts have retired or been fired."

"It's a terrible secret, Ryerson, so this is completely off the record, but I was protecting Kim Jong-un's love child with Dennis Rodman."

"Damn it, Warshawski—"

"Oh, back at you, Murray."

As soon as I hung up, my phone rang again: another reporter. I turned off the sound and went to bed. A little before two, I was jolted awake by a mosquito dive-bombing my ear. I pulled the covers over my head, but the whine continued. My landline, I finally realized. It rang so seldom these days that I'd forgotten to turn it off.

I growled a greeting.

"This is Fee I Warashawaski?"

Close enough; I agreed it was me.

"Dead man in news. Am knowing. *Thinking* am knowing. Name Elorenze Fausson."

He hung up before I could ask anything, such as who he was and how he spelled Elorenze Fausson. I tried calling the number back, but his phone rang twenty times without an answer.

7

BUDDY, CAN

YOU SPARE A DIME?

DESPITE MY HEAVY head, I couldn't return to sleep, even knowing that another workday was rolling my way. After half an hour, I did what the sleep gurus advise: I got out of bed. And then I did what they tell you not to: went into the dining room and opened my laptop.

The phone that had called me turned out to be one of the last pay phones in North America, at an L stop on Randolph and State. Since that was the busiest corner in Chicago, it wasn't going to be possible to trace the caller.

Elorenze Fausson. I imagined different ways of spelling it. My caller had pronounced it "Foessahn," but I finally found a Lawrence Fausson on Facebook. Elorenze/Lawrence. The words merged when I said them out loud.

His most recent post was almost a year old. I would have to friend him to learn where he was from or went to school or to see his profile picture, but his posts were open to the public. How did Facebook handle friend requests for the dead? I sent one on the off chance before scrolling through his last half dozen posts. One included a photograph of a largish group of men and women standing in a ragged semicircle.

The picture had been taken in one of those characterless rooms that you find in poorly financed public buildings—fluorescent lights, metal folding chairs, a number of round tables covered with books and papers. In the background I could see children's art taped to the wall, alongside posters with Arabic captions.

A community room for a community—where? The photo didn't have a caption, nor a location marker. It could have been anywhere, especially anywhere in the Arab-speaking world.

The photo hadn't been well focused. I fiddled with the contrast, studied the faces of all the men under a magnifying glass. There were seven who looked Middle Eastern, three who appeared Western. I held my breath, wondering if one of them was Lotty's nephew, but when I enlarged the faces, Felix Herschel wasn't in the group.

However, the ME's reconstructed face was a good match for a man in a threadbare khaki shirt. While most of the people, women as well as men, were smiling, Fausson seemed almost melancholy. His hands were in his jeans pockets, and he wasn't looking at the camera.

The group included six women, mostly, again, Middle Eastern. Two of the women were slender, with long braids: either or neither could have been the woman Felix had been embracing that morning. There was also a young Western-looking woman whose freckled face and short reddish hair stood out against her darker friends.

The only text Lawrence Fausson had included was WHO FEELS THE STRANGEST IN A STRANGE LAND? Had he been in a Middle Eastern country, feeling alone and disaffected? Or was this in America, where he felt more out of place than his foreign-born companions?

If all else failed, I could find an Arabic scholar to decipher the texts in the photo's background, to see if they shed light on the room's location. For now, I kept trawling for easier data.

Fausson didn't have a landline or a traceable cell phone. He didn't have a credit card, at least not in his own name.

Just as I was giving up, I pried open a back door into the DMV database. Fausson had a current driver's license, with an address on Higgins, just off Neenah Avenue.

According to the DMV records, Fausson's first name was Leroy, not

Lawrence. The DMV photo was a pretty good match with the reconstruction and with Facebook. Maybe Lawrence had a twin.

My confrontation with Murray had made me forget to text Felix before I went to bed the first time. I wrote him now.

LOTTY IS VERY WORRIED THAT YOU MAY HAVE BEEN ARRESTED OR INJURED. IF WE DON'T HEAR FROM YOU BY THE END OF THE BUSINESS DAY, FRIDAY, I'M GOING TO CHECK WITH THE POLICE, FILE A MISSING PERSONS REPORT, AND START CONTACTING AREA HOSPITALS. IF YOU DO GET THIS MESSAGE TELL ME WHETHER YOU KNOW A MAN NAMED FAUSSON.

I hit SEND and fell into bed for a few hours, but my alarm roused me at six-thirty for another day of mad scrambling, this time so I could make my eight-thirty appointment with Reno's boss at Rest EZ.

I carried my breakfast with me in the car and ate in a precarious and unhealthy way, swallowing fruit and yogurt at traffic lights, choking on toast crumbs, spilling coffee on my coat. When I finally parked across the street from the Rest EZ branch, I looked as though I'd been wrestling in a restaurant dumpster. I also hadn't combed my hair or bothered with makeup. I dealt with my hair, but didn't try painting my face, just removed as much food as I could from my clothes.

At least I fit into my environment. I was on a sad stretch of Central Avenue, where McDonald's wrappers and broken bottles filled the sidewalks in front of the boarded-over buildings. The Rest EZ office was one of the few active storefronts, except, of course, for the liquor stores. The facade was covered with flashing neon advertising all the services inside: city stickers, auto loans, payday loans, Western Union office, ATMs.

The centerpiece was a screen showing a couple racked with misery, tossing and turning while their list of unpaid bills spouted from their sleepless brains. You next saw them walking through a Rest EZ door and finally asleep with beatific smiles: FINANCIAL WORRIES KEEPING YOU AWAKE? REST EZ WITH AN EZ LOAN FROM REST EZ.

In the ad, the loan office was a clean, well-lit place, with a sleek white woman, blond hair piled in a knot on her head, smiling invitingly at the customers. In Austin, the big picture windows were dusty.

When I followed a balding man with a walrus mustache inside, I had to step over the remains of a dinner regurgitated by whoever had spent the previous night in the doorway.

The rich are different from you and me, Fitzgerald supposedly told Hemingway, but the poor are even more so. Their waiting rooms in hospitals or loan offices have plastic chairs bolted to scarred linoleum, harsh overhead lights, and a TV screen high on a wall with the sound up, tuned to Global Entertainment's recycling of the morning news.

A bank of computer monitors was bolted to a counter on my left; you could apply directly for a loan there. If Rest EZ needed more information, you waited your turn for one of the cashiers behind a layer of bullet-resistant glass.

Changing screens flashed on the monitors that weren't in use. I stopped to look. Rest EZ's many services, from insurance to payday loans, were advertised. We got a flash for the Stock of the Day, which Rest EZ's financial consultant division recommended. Glacier Trove (GTR.PK) was today's pick. *"Last week when its shares were at three cents, nobody knew this company; next week the whole world will. Buy today and wipe out that debt overnight. Talk to your Rest EZ financial adviser when you fill out your loan form."*

Next to the monitors were a couple of Illinois lottery machines. It seemed fitting—gambling on penny stocks or on the lottery. When I went to a door that might lead to the manager's office, an armed guard moved in on me, demanding my business. I explained that I had an appointment with Donna Lutas and handed him a business card.

He ordered me to take a seat. "You stay away from that door, do you hear?"

I heard. He scowled at me for a few more seconds, then pressed a code on a pad next to the door. Before he went through, he turned around again, to make sure I wasn't going to jump him and force my way through.

The only good thing about the experience was the entertainment it provided the other people in the room. The guard was black, as was everyone filling out forms or making payments. White woman treated like a wild animal on the loose brought a little pleasure to a dull day. I gave the room a half bow in acknowledgment and picked up a copy of the previous day's *Sun-Times*.

The wait stretched from two minutes to seventeen before the guard returned. "Ms. Lutas says to tell you she is sorry for the inconvenience, but she cannot speak with you."

"I can wait," I said: my next appointment was at ten-thirty in the Loop, which gave me about an hour to waste in Austin.

"Doesn't matter. She won't speak to you. Says you told her you was Reno Seale's aunt, and you're not."

I could feel my eyes glitter. Death Star eyes, an old lover had told me when I'd lost my temper in his presence. "I am Reno Seale's aunt. And Harmony Seale's. And neither you nor she can wipe out that relationship."

The guard glowered at me. "You're a detective, right?"

"Many aunts work for a living," I said. "That doesn't end the relationship to their nieces and nephews."

The audience, which had been enjoying my discomfiture, began agreeing with me. "What's this, she can't be an aunt if she has a job?" one woman said; the bald man with the walrus mustache added, "They try to take everything away from us. Now they want our children?"

The guard sensed the shift in sympathies. "I'll take you back; you can hear it from her yourself."

I followed him as he punched the code in once more: 6-1-1-7-8-5, I noted, writing it in the palm of my hand with my finger. You never know.

In cubicles along a short hallway, clients whose situation required more personal attention than a computer screen were meeting with Rest EZ staff whose nameplates identified them as FINANCIAL COUN-SELORS. Reno Seale's name was still attached to an empty cube on the right.

Donna Lutas had an actual office with a door, but it was hard to see how it could be shut, since a chair upholstered with a high stack of documents was pushed against it. A security monitor on the wall provided shifting images of different parts of the public room out front.

Lutas was typing when we came to the entrance; her thick dark hair fell like a curtain, protecting her from the bigger world.

The guard cleared his throat. "Donna, I decided to have you talk to her in person."

Lutas brushed a wing of hair out of her eyes, still focused on her work. "Jerry, I thought you said you weren't letting her—"

"He relayed your message, Ms. Lutas. I'm V.I. Warshawski and I need to know what documentation you require to prove that I am Reno Seale's aunt." I moved past Jerry into the small space in front of her desk.

She was startled into speaking abruptly. "You have to leave. I can't talk to you."

"Not even about Reno Seale, who worked so hard she earned an early promotion? And who has been missing since Monday?"

"Last night I thought you were Reno's aunt. Now I learn you're really a detective."

"It's true I'm a detective; it's true I'm Reno Seale's aunt. Some physicist wrote about how two objects can occupy the same space at the same time, or maybe that they couldn't, but I can and do. Reno's younger sister is in town. She flew out because her sister has been acting troubled, ever since her return from St. Matthieu. Did Reno say anything to you, anything at all, that would give you a hint about what was disturbing her?"

Lutas shook her head. "It's against company policy for me to talk to outsiders about our employees. Even outsiders who claim to be relatives."

"And you didn't know that policy last night?"

"I only just found out," Lutas muttered.

"Ah!" I clapped my hands, inspiration striking. "Eliza Trosse called you from downtown. Did you tell her we already had an appointment?"

Lutas looked past me at Jerry, who was lingering in the doorway.

I moved the papers from the chair that was holding the door open and sat down. "Reno trusted you, according to her sister; I'm hoping she let fall something that would tell us what was on her mind."

Lutas frowned as I put the papers on the floor, but didn't protest.

"I didn't notice anything special. Reno is an ideal employee, or has been. I hate to think of losing her. But she's not like some of the women here, telling you every time their guy hits them or sleeps with someone else. Maybe she met someone at the resort and she took it more seriously than he did—it happens, especially to girls like Reno."

"Meaning?"

"You ask anyone about her, first thing they say is 'What a knockout,' right, Jerry?"

The guard pressed his lips together—maybe he'd made a pass that Reno had fought off.

"But she's the kind that hides her insecurity under an ice robe. If someone melted the ice, she might drown."

It was a poetically inspired insight. I wondered if it were true. I wondered, too, if that was something Reno might hide from her sister—it was a handicap to see only one side of that relationship. Reno was the elder, even if only by a year, and she might not want Harmony to see how vulnerable she could be.

"There's nothing going on at the company that would have troubled Reno, I take it?"

"That's a ridiculous suggestion, aunt or no aunt, detective or no detective." The words were vehement but the tone lacked conviction.

"Tell me more about the St. Matthieu trip. Was this a corporate retreat?"

Lutas fiddled with her rings. "Rest EZ doesn't hold that kind of event, not at places like St. Matthieu, anyway. Once a year the branch managers get invited downtown for a day to go over problems and strategies, but I can't imagine them flying us to a resort."

"So what was it?"

"We were told it was a big shareholders meeting and they wanted Rest EZ staff who could fit in with senior staff." She was mumbling to her keyboard; I had trouble hearing her.

"Reno had those kinds of skills?" I asked.

"She was beautiful," Lutas blurted out. "I don't think she was very sophisticated, but if all you wanted was arm candy—" She cut herself off.

"Did you know that when you picked her to go?"

Lutas reddened underneath her makeup. "*I* didn't pick her. They specifically asked for her downtown. There was a lot of jealousy, let me tell you."

"From you, too?"

"Caribbean in February?" Lutas jeered. "Of course I'd rather be in Chicago freezing my butt."

"How did Reno feel about going?"

Lutas paused. "I think she was worried. But they told her it was a reward for being, like, rookie of the year in Chicago. Anyway, I think if she'd said no, they might not have been happy downtown."

"Fire her?" I suggested.

A longer pause this time, which stretched into silence.

"No wonder they don't want me asking questions about her," I said.

"They don't want you asking questions because it's against company policy to discuss our team with outsiders." Jerry spoke from behind me, loud and authoritative. "You don't belong back here. You're interrupting our workday. Time for you to go."

He put a meaty hand under my armpit and hoisted me to my feet. I could have ducked and swerved, kicked his kneecaps, all those things, but what would have been the point? I'd still have ended in the same place: on the sidewalk on Central Avenue, not quite missing the pile of vomit that I'd sidestepped on my way in.

8

BEST KIND OF TENANT

RENO'S APARTMENT LAY more or less on the route back into the city. I got off the Ike at Sacramento and drove up to Fairfield. Reno's intersection was like the place in the lake where two currents slam into each other—the older Hispanic residents, on their way to Laundromats, dragging carts of clothes while pushing a stroller, and hip young men out with their French bulldogs.

I rang Reno's doorbell but didn't get an answer. I texted Harmony; she wrote that she'd decided to go look at a garden center on Chicago's North Side. At least she wasn't spending her whole time brooding in her sister's apartment.

I pushed the button for the building super, Vern Wolferman. After a few minutes' wait, I pressed again, longer. A thick hoarse voice came through the grille, telling me I could leave packages in the entryway.

"I'm a detective," I shouted back.

"Hold on, then, hold on."

Another few minutes passed, and then Wolferman arrived in person, wearing faded green coveralls. He was a big guy, tall and running to fat, as I'd guessed from the sunken cushion in the chair I'd seen the other night.

He opened the door, but kept his bulk in the entrance. "You really a detective? Let me see your badge."

"I'm private, not public." I showed him my license, at a distance that pulled him out of the doorway; I slipped around him into the hall.

"I'm investigating Reno Seale's disappearance. When was the last time you saw her?"

"Who wants to know?" He had turned his bulk around to face me in the lobby, but he kept the door open.

"I do. And Ms. Seale's sister. And her employers. When did you last see her?"

"She goes to work in the morning, she says hi if I see her in the hall. Same thing coming back at night, but most of the time I'm not in the hall when she's coming or going. The only reason I know she's missing is because of the sister showing up."

"She's a good tenant?" I asked.

"Best kind. Doesn't bug me all day long with crap a two-year-old could take care of. When her toilet backed up last month, she went and got her own plumbing snake."

"Something two-year-olds do routinely," I agreed.

He glared. "There are a lot of units in this building. And it's old in the bargain. Owners are waiting for it to fall apart so they can flip it. Reno Seale is quiet, she doesn't do anything that gives the other residents a beef."

"No loud parties? You ever see her with anyone?"

He scratched his left buttock. "No. She's pretty much a loner. Beautiful girl, you'd think she'd have a million boyfriends, but far as I know, she's on her own. Except for the sis, who arrived all hot and bothered on Tuesday night."

"I'll be filing a missing persons report with the cops," I said. "They'll come and ask you the same questions I did, only more of them. They'll have warrants to search the building, stuff like that—"

"Why?"

"To see if she fell down an elevator shaft. So try to remember when you last saw her, what she was wearing, those kinds of things."

"I can't tell you what I don't know," he protested. "But I guess it was that Monday, the morning. She left for work. She carried her lunch in a little bag tied with a green ribbon, but what she had on, I couldn't say. She worked in an office and she was dressed for the office, not for running or whatever she did for exercise. And that is it, end of story, morning glory."

He held the door open wider. I sidled past his bulk, back to the fresher air. It was time to override Harmony's objections and go to the police, but there was someone else I wanted to talk to first.

9

JOUSTING

THE THOUSAND DOLLARS an hour Crawford, Mead etc. charged its clients was on display as soon as I walked through the open portal to the offices: the receptionist sat behind a highly polished wood counter, with an arrangement of spring flowers the size of the Goodyear blimp on top. She murmured my name into her phone, told me someone would be out for me shortly, offered me coffee or juice, and waved me to a curved couch facing the windows.

Modern sculptures of hammered metal flanked the couch like bodyguards. I walked past them to the windows to admire the view. A barge was being towed toward the lake, but it was still too cold for the tourist boats and cabin cruisers to be out.

I had texted Richard Yarborough, one of Crawford, Mead's partners, requesting ten minutes on a private matter. Dick had written that he had a five-minute window at noon, adding, WHENEVER YOU'RE WITHIN 50 YARDS OF THE BUILDING, WE GO ON HIGH ALERT: TORNADOES, TERRORISTS, WARSHAWSKI—EMPLOYEE SAFETY INSTRUCTIONS ARE THE SAME FOR ALL THREE.

Very funny. I had arrived a minute before noon. Twelve-fifteen. Dick had decided to be a jerk. I perched on the couch and opened my laptop to start research for the project Darraugh had asked me to take on. Meanwhile, three people had arrived and gone into their meetings.

Twelve-thirty. I reminded the receptionist that I was here for a noon appointment. She gave me a sympathetic smile and phoned into the back again. Twelve-forty. I lay on the fluffy rug in front of the couch and started doing leg stretches.

Glynis Hadden, Dick's secretary, bustled out two minutes later. Glynis had been in the general pool during Dick's and my marriage, but she'd recognized his star potential and hitched herself to him early on. Or possibly she'd recognized someone she could build into a star. Either way, they've been together a long time.

"We're sorry you had to wait, Vic, but Dick is carving out time for you in the middle of a complicated negotiation with our Singapore office."

Glynis was never unpleasant with me, but she had a calibrated sense of how to make me feel unimportant next to the big guy.

When we reached Dick's office, he was still on the phone. He was in shirtsleeves, tie loosened so I could read the manufacturer's label: Robert Talbott. I've paid more for rent, but not a lot more. No jowls or wobbly Adam's apple: he was moving into middle age as fit as a racehorse. It was unworthy of me to have hoped for a paunch.

Dick waved me to a chair—a hard one in front of his desk, no doubt for underlings—mouthed a "thank you" to Glynis, and held up his empty coffee cup. She smiled indulgently and slipped from the room with it.

I wandered to the window, where I could look east toward the lake. The view included the cream gingerbread building where Al Capone used to hold court. Symbolic, perhaps.

Family photos stood on a credenza behind him. Dick and Teri were on a beach somewhere with their children, teenagers now, with teeth so white that the sun bouncing off them was blinding even in a picture. Teri's lean, tanned body didn't look as though it had ever been pregnant.

I turned to a document tray and started riffling through the papers. Deposition in *Ti-Balt v. Trechette,* whose routing slip read, *"FYI, Yarborough. Keeping you in the loop. TM."* Behind me Dick began to stammer at his end of the conversation and finally ended it with a hasty "Catch you tomorrow, buddy."

"Vic! Those are confidential papers."

I grinned at him. "Hey, Dick. Good to see you, too." I sat in an upholstered client chair to one side of his desk.

"I don't bill at your rates, of course," I said, "but the forty-five minutes you kept me waiting are worth a hundred-fifty."

"In that case, Vic, let's get to the point, because ten minutes with me will balance that out. And you are the one who wanted to meet."

"Your nieces. You helped Reno get a job at Rest EZ."

"That's not true, strictly speaking." Dick was smirking, which always made me want to deck him.

"Tell me what's strictly speaking true, then." I tried for a saintly smile.

"She called out at the house and talked to Teri, who was furious that Reno tracked down our unlisted number. I had Glynis call Reno and give her the names of some of our corporate clients who hire at the retail level. Glynis!" he barked into an intercom.

When Glynis shimmered in, he asked her to tell me what she'd done for Reno. "I gave her six or seven names. We told her we couldn't help her any further. She must have been sulking, because she didn't let us know that she'd found a place with Rest EZ."

"Sulking?" I tried not to screech. "After you told her to leave you alone? Sounds like she knew you didn't give a rat's toenail about her."

"Don't get on your high horse, Vic: Becky tried so many scams on Mother and me over the years I was sure that was what Reno was after, too. After all, she lived with a master scam artist."

My eyes turned hot, but I kept smiling in an effort not to jump across the desk and strangle him with his Robert Talbott.

"They lived under viaducts, Richard. They ate from dumpsters. They were sexually assaulted. You knew your sister was an addict; you could have guessed what was happening to her children, but even when she begged you for help with them, you and your mother wanted to pretend it was all a big scam."

I paused, watching him squirm a little. "However, you gave Reno a list of contacts and she parlayed that into a job. Now she's missing and I'm looking for her. She's apparently been worrying about something since she got back from a Caribbean trip for her company a month ago.

I will, of course, tell the police about her connection to you when I file my missing persons report—"

"Don't threaten me with the police." Dick's mouth was an ugly gash in his face. "No cop in Chicago is going to bother a partner at this firm."

"I know one or two who might, but that's not the point. If she talked to you, or Teri, or your mother in the last month or two, Reno might have mentioned what was bothering her."

"I'll ask them, but I'm sure both of them would have told me if they'd heard from her." Dick's voice was still laced with contempt, but he was studying his fingernails, as if wondering whether it was time for another manicure. It was a gesture he used in court to gain time during cross-examination, and he'd done it when we were married and he was trying to see whether he could get away with a lie.

Glynis sensed a change in the airwaves that required her to remove me from the office.

"It's one o'clock, Dick, and your next appointment is here."

Dick looked at his console. "Oh, my God, yes. He's out front? Tell them to put him in Conference E; I'll join him as soon as Vic is gone."

A crude but effective dismissal.

Glynis hit a speed-dial number. While she was relaying the message to the front desk, I kissed Dick on the cheek and left. The receptionist was showing a man into a conference room as I came down the hall. He looked like every other rainmaking partner I'd ever met: white, somewhere in the fifties or early sixties, carefully groomed graying hair, custom navy tailoring, slight frown as he turned down an offer of coffee.

Glynis caught up with me and almost pushed me down the hall to the reception area.

"I've had my rabies shots, Glynis, so no worries if Dick's special visitor bites me."

"Dick gave you twenty valuable minutes when you showed up unannounced," she said.

"I requested time before I arrived. And he took the better part of an hour before meeting me, so don't play the billable-hours record for me."

"Of course he won't bill you, but don't you think you can ease up a bit?"

"This isn't an argument over a bill, Glynis, as you damned well know."

"Maybe Dick is tired of you being the moral arbiter of his universe," Glynis said. "In his place, I would be."

"What, when I'm not around he actually is a moral sentient human being?"

"He has many facets and interests that you know nothing about. Art, for instance." She pointed to the statues flanking the couch. "The partners had Dick choose those."

At the elevator bank, Glynis tapped a piece of shiny metal that looked like hardened lava. "This piece actually belongs to Teri and Dick, but they're lending it to the firm."

"Gee, he must be truly sensitive if he can afford to collect big chunks of steel. And I see Crawford, Mead acquired another law firm, too. Was that also Dick and Teri's choice?"

Glynis stared at me blankly. I pointed at the wall around the elevators, where big brass letters announced we were at the international headquarters of Crawford, Mead, LLC. Off to one side, away from the list of the firm's offices around the globe, was a new sign—we were also in the NORTH AMERICAN OFFICES OF RUNKEL, SORAUDE AND MINABLE.

"Oh—that." Glynis gave a tinny laugh. "They're a Belgian firm who need a U.S. address. Elevator D, Vic. I'll let you know if we hear from Dick's niece."

"Yeah, Glynis, you be sure and do that."

Maybe Glynis was right, that I came across as irritatingly sanctimonious. Maybe he was one of those souls who was generous in secret, but I didn't really think so. What bugged me most was that I'd slept with him, that I'd married him.

We'd met in law school. At the end of our second year, we'd interned at the same downtown firm. They'd assigned us to a pro bono case involving neurological damage to children growing up near a commercial hog operation outside Sernas, Illinois.

Dick and I were sent together to Sernas, where we took depositions from parents, the local school nurse, the town doctor, and the managers of the plant. The stench, combined with the sight of hundreds of animals squashed together at food troughs, led to my permanent aversion to pork. The nights I spent with Dick at a local motel led to our getting married the summer after we graduated.

For some reason, I'd thought Dick shared my passion for social justice. For some reason, Dick thought I'd shared his passion for his career. We'd both been hideously wrong, but we stuck it out for twenty-seven months, while he kept trying to make me act like the wife of an upcoming associate and I'd tried to make him act as though he cared about people at the bottom of the food chain.

Today I needed to answer a bigger question than that: What exactly was Dick lying about when he'd been studying his nails? That Reno had talked to the present Mrs. Yarborough, or perhaps that she'd actually spoken to him? Or something even murkier?

10

GOOD COP, GOOD COP

THANKS TO MY dad, who'd been a cop for forty years, there used to be someone at most stations who knew the Warshawski name. Time passes, people die or quit. I no longer hear "Tony's girl? How'd you get to be all grown-up and a detective in the bargain?" when I talk to a desk sergeant.

That was why I was surprised to walk into the Shakespeare District station and see a cop I knew.

"Lieutenant Finchley?" I said.

"V.I. Warshawski?" Finchley responded. "Please don't tell me you're working this beat—it's my first week here; I'm trying to make a good impression."

Finchley's cordiality was also a surprise: he's a good cop, maybe a great cop, but lately his response to me has been somewhere in the low Kelvin range—not because of detective matters, but personal ones.

"You left Thirty-Fifth Street?" In front of his desk sergeant, I didn't want to ask anything indiscreet, but the Finch had been Captain Bobby Mallory's right- and left-hand man at headquarters for the better part of a decade. I hoped Bobby hadn't demoted him, or even more unsettling, was himself quitting the force.

"Captain thought his staff needed more field experience," Finchley said. "Shakespeare drew the short straw and got me. And you? What brings you here?"

"I'm a worried aunt with a missing niece," I said.

Finchley's eyes narrowed. "On the level, Warshawski?"

"I wish it wasn't, but it is. No one has seen her since this past Monday. I've been to her place of work, I've spoken with her uncle, her sister, and her building super. I should have come in sooner, but her sister kept vetoing police involvement. She's going to show hackle when she finds I was here anyway."

"Cops are used to angry civilians," Finchley said. "They only let you into the academy if you can prove you have ten instead of five layers of skin."

The desk sergeant laughed; I smiled politely. The sergeant called in an officer from the back to take all the details. I explained the mother's death, the father's evaporation, the loving foster parents unable now to help. I gave her Harmony's cell, Donna Lutas's and Eliza Trosse's numbers at Rest EZ, along with Dick and Teri's unlisted home number and Dick's private line downtown. I stressed that Reno had called both Teri and Dick during her year in Chicago.

Finchley had lingered in the background while I filled out the report and answered questions, including the last time I'd seen Reno. The fact that I hadn't known her as an adult raised its own inevitable questions. They still accepted my story, since both cops had seen every variation of family dynamic. Mine was no weirder than others.

"There are an array of questions underlying Reno's disappearance," I said. "Because I don't know the sisters as adults, I don't know if Harmony's reluctance to see you guys dates back to bad childhood experiences, or if she knows something she doesn't want to talk about. I left Dick Yarborough's office this afternoon thinking he was sitting on something, but I could be wrong about that, too.

"All I know is that Reno came home from work on Monday and hasn't been seen since. Her keys were where she always left them, in a bowl by the door, but her phone and computer are gone. The building super has keys to all the apartments; maybe he knows something he's not saying."

"So you think the cops do bring added value to an investigation?" Finchley asked as I got up to leave.

"You know I do, Lieutenant," I said formally. "And I appreciate it, especially at a time like this. Frankly, I'm scared. I think she would have surfaced by now, one way or another, if she—well, if she were able to."

I couldn't bring myself to speak aloud the fear that Reno was dead, but the probability underlay all the other emotions in the room. Finchley even took my hand and said they'd give it their best effort.

After I left, I called Harmony to tell her I'd filed the report. She was as angry as I'd expected, but I was past the point of empathy.

"Harmony, either you know something that you don't want me or the police to know about your sister, or you are being willfully blind to the danger she may be facing. Whichever it is, I've been irresponsible myself in not filing this report two days ago."

"You know what happens when you go to the police?" Harmony was shouting, but her voice was tremulous with tears. "Some guy beat you up having sex with you, the best cop says you had it coming, the worst cop rapes you himself!"

I hung up and drove to Reno's building. When Harmony finally let me in, her face was swollen from sobbing. She let me hold her until she was finally calm enough to talk.

"Was that what happened at St. Matthieu?" I asked. "Did someone rape her?"

"She wouldn't say," Harmony whispered. "All she said was she thought it was going to be fun, scuba diving and shit. The first day, she had a good time, but then she said she knew where the rich old guys on Forty-Second Avenue spent their winter vacations. She did her best to stay out of their way, but she couldn't always. And then when she got back here, she didn't know what to do, so she kept going to work. She told me not to worry; she told me she'd figure out how to solve the problem, but of course I worried. After her first week back in Chicago she stopped talking to me, which is when I really got worried. And finally I came out here, but you know all that."

"Do you think she saw someone at St. Matthieu who'd assaulted you when you were children?"

"We didn't know their names," Harmony said. "We'd call them by their car or their clothes or something. The Merc SUV, or the Nissan. Belt Buckle—this one guy had a huge belt buckle shaped like a cow's head. He liked to hit with it. I asked, did she see the Buckle or Fat Baldy? But she said not them specifically—it was just they had the same look in their eyes. Greedy and dead at the same time."

We talked for almost an hour, but mostly it was about her and Reno's life on the streets of Oakland. "Even after Clarisse and Henry took us in, we'd sometimes go back to Forty-Second, where Mom used to work a corner or put us to work. This one girl who sometimes looked after us was still hanging out there."

My arm was cramping from holding her, but I sat still, letting her talk to my shoulder, which couldn't judge her.

"It wasn't like we really wanted to be there, but we weren't used to. . . . Life with Clarisse and Henry was so weird to us, we couldn't believe they weren't going to put us to work. You know, on the street. So we went back to what we knew, and since we were there, you know, we. . . . Only Henry came and found us every time. We were sure him and Clarisse—he and Clarisse, I mean—would throw us out, but they never did. Took us for ice cream and said we needed more sweetness in our lives.

"But the last time, Reno got beat up bad, and we went to the cops and that's what happened. Clarisse was so furious. She sued the Oakland Police Department and the city and everyone, but it was our word and our black mother against all of them. What do you think happened?"

"I think you're right to be angry and scared," I said, stroking her corn silk hair. "I'll be with you when the police talk to you, but don't you see, what you're telling me makes it even more important that we have help finding your sister."

I tried to persuade Harmony to come home with me, or at least let Mr. Contreras cook her dinner, but she had made her own little nest in her sister's apartment; she felt safe there. I checked the window locks and the back door again, again told Harmony to make sure the dead bolts were in place when she was inside. Checked that she had me on speed dial.

There ought to have been something bigger I could do, like erase her childhood and give her one like mine. I left feeling helpless and close to useless.

LEROY OF ARABIA

WHEN I GOT back to my car, my legs felt as though I'd been in a stair-climbing marathon. They were swollen and heavy and unwilling to move.

It was only five o'clock, but I'd been running all day on short sleep. And I'd absorbed enough painful stories to fill a psychiatrist's notebook for a year. I leaned back in the seat and shut my eyes, just a rest for ten minutes, enough time to recharge.

My phone woke me half an hour later: Felix Herschel.

"Have you gone to the police?" he said abruptly.

Reno and Harmony were weighing so heavily on me that I started to say yes, before remembering that I'd threatened to file a missing persons report on Felix if he didn't show by the end of the day.

"Not yet. Where have you been?"

"I'm fine. I don't need a babysitter."

"Felix, if it weren't for Lotty and the love I bear her, I'd bid you farewell on the spot. And tell you to turn to someone else the next time the cops pick you up. As it is, to keep her from anxiety, will you please check in with her every day until your involvement with the man in Cap Sauers Holding is cleared up?"

"I'm sorry, Vic. I'm involved in a, well, the biggest engineering project of my life so far, and I can't always use my phone." He was trying to sound casual—big man used to important projects—but an underlying nervousness betrayed him.

I didn't try to probe into the nature of the biggest project. I couldn't take listening to him come up with lies. "Does the name Fausson mean anything to you?" I asked. "Lawrence or Leroy?"

"No. Why?"

"How about as Elorenze?"

"I don't know him by any name. What's this about?"

"The dead man in Cap Sauers Holding. I'm going to verify his identity, but I'll have to tell Lieutenant McGivney out in Maywood, and the medical examiner as well. I just want to make extra certain that there isn't a trail leading from him to you."

"There can't be, because I never heard of him."

"He knew you, though. Could it have been through a Muslim community meeting?"

"You Americans and your hang-up about Muslims!" he shouted.

"You're working with Middle Eastern students on your water project," I said. "Fausson hangs out—hung out—in Arab-speaking communities—it's not anti-Islam to ask if that's where you met."

"Repeat after me: Felix Herschel has never heard of Elorenze, Lawrence, or Leroy Fausson." He ended the call.

The biggest engineering project of his young life. It couldn't be a bomb. It mustn't be a bomb. But if he couldn't always use his phone, what was he afraid of? Being tracked, or inadvertently detonating something?

I entered his phone number into the Find My Friends app. He wasn't in Rogers Park, but Eau Claire, Wisconsin. He was in motion, heading southeast.

I stared at the pulsing blue circle on my screen, willing it to give me more information, but it suddenly disappeared. Felix knew I was watching him, or feared someone could watch him, and had shut down his phone.

Six P.M. on a gray afternoon, a time when dark thoughts could drag you down a hole you couldn't climb out of. I drove to my office but jogged around the block before going inside, on the theory that exercise lifts the spirits and makes the brain function better.

I was unlocking my office door when I thought again of Leroy/

Lawrence Fausson and Felix. It was only a matter of time before someone besides my anonymous caller recognized Fausson from the reconstructed face on TV. I wanted to go to his apartment to make sure he hadn't left any obvious connections to Felix.

I picked up my go-bag—a canvas backpack with picklocks, a flashlight, latex gloves, and a few other odds and ends—locked my briefcase with my laptop in the Mustang's trunk, and headed north.

Higgins was a commercial thoroughfare, with apartment buildings and strip malls, but the side streets, filled with Chicago's signature bungalows, were quiet. I found parking on Neenah. As I walked back to Higgins, I dawdled, enjoying the crocuses springing up in the scrupulously tended front yards.

Kids were biking in the lavender twilight, while the adults were returning home from work. A woman heading to Fausson's building was balancing a toddler in one arm while chivvying an older child in front of her. I offered to hold the two sacks of groceries she was also hauling while she dug her keys out of a giant shoulder bag.

She handed them to me gratefully, hoisted a hip to balance her younger child. Another unrecognized Olympic event: carrying a wriggling toddler, an outsize leather handbag, and twenty pounds of groceries. No Bulgarian weight lifter could manage the load.

I followed her inside, where she thankfully put the toddler down as well. The little one ran after its brother on unsteady feet, heading toward a rear unit. I carried the bags as far as her front door and left before she could start imagining me as a molester or, worse, a detective about to commit B and E on Leroy Fausson's apartment.

Fausson lived on the third floor. The uncarpeted stairs were made out of a stone or concrete that sent echoes of footsteps up and down the stairwell. Even my running shoes sounded loud on the treads.

The unit was at the top of the stairs. I knocked sharply on the door, waited a full minute, knocked again. A low-watt bulb showed me the door, but not the lock. I held my pocket flash between my teeth and knelt to work the tumblers. It was an old lock; my picks slipped in it a few times before I found the right combination. I was on my feet and inside just as steps sounded in the stairwell behind me. I held my breath, but it was another homebound family, clattering past me to the back of the building.

I leaned against the door and shone my flashlight around, looking for a light switch. No overheads, but lamps, two on the floor, one on a desk. When I switched them on, I was overwhelmed by the outsize photos that covered the walls and part of the ceiling. Pride of place, the wall facing the door, was an aerial photo of what at first seemed to be a pockmarked moonscape with blobs in it.

After staring at them for a time, the blobs resolved into a set of small huts built near a series of trenches cut into a desert landscape. In the near ground, a dark streak proved to be a muddy stream with a trickle of water in the middle. A couple of trucks stood at the edge of the compound. As I peered more closely, I could see the foreshortened bodies of people and the toppled remains of pillars, even the broken head of a human figure.

When I turned to the wall next to the door, I found a framed poster of a museum exhibit: TREASURES OF ANCIENT SYRIA. The poster centered on the head of a stone figure with a curling beard; arrayed around it were pieces of gold jewelry inlaid with lapis and a couple of small figures.

On the left wall, another blown-up photo showed the gates of Aleppo before the bombing, the Golan Heights viewed from both the Israeli and Syrian sides, close-ups of more Syrian artifacts. The display gave me vertigo.

Before exploring the living area, I went into the bedroom. It was just big enough for a double bed and a chest of drawers. Facing the bed, Leroy/Lawrence had hung a large photo of himself with a dozen other people. I studied it, trying to figure out the background, and realized the group was standing in a section of an archaeological dig. The photo in the front room was an aerial overview; this one showed a section with toppled pillars and the giant head of a figure whose hair and beard looked as though they were made of chain mail.

The man called Lawrence Fausson on Facebook was standing between two solemn-faced Middle Easterners. All three wore dirt-stained tunics over leggings, their heads wrapped in cloth, perhaps more for protection from the dirt than for any religious reason. There were three other Westerners in the group, including the freckled young woman who'd been in the Facebook photo.

From Syria to a Chicago forest preserve. How had Fausson made that journey? Was he an archaeologist? He surely hadn't been an investor in the dig—his chest of drawers was made of pressed wood whose varnish was scratched and chipped. The red rug by his bed was worn, not in the way of heirloom Persian carpets, but in the manner of machine-made polyester from Buy-Smart.

The photos were so big, so overwhelming, I felt as though I were falling into them. I wondered if they'd had that effect on Leroy, or if he was so used to them that they'd lost their impact.

Fausson had left paper scraps on his bedside table. These were the usual detritus of daily life—receipts for six cartons of yogurt; for carry-out from the Damascus Gate, a Middle Eastern restaurant on Austin; for razor blades. No phone numbers, for Felix or anyone else.

A dozen or so books were scattered on the floor by the bed. One was a grammar of advanced Arabic. I picked up a slim volume whose boards were covered in azure cloth, with a design like a Middle Eastern tile pattern engraved into it in silver. The book was written in Arabic, but copyright information was printed in English: Tarik Kataba, published in Beirut. I flipped through it and a yellowed piece of newsprint fell out.

Tarik Kataba, recipient of this year's Nahda prize for Arabic poetry, was unable to accept in person: he has been held in one of Bashar al-Assad's prisons since January 2009. His daughter Rasima, who is attending boarding school in Lebanon, accepted the prize on his behalf.

The article included a photograph of Rasima, a diminutive twelve- or thirteen-year-old, with deep-set eyes that looked too old for her narrow face. She was holding up a certificate for the camera while a group of men towered over her. I returned the clipping to the book and tucked it into my backpack.

One of the books was published by the Oriental Institute. I flipped through *Urban Development in the Chalcolithic: Excavation of the Tell al-Sabbah* by Candra van Vliet. I had no way of knowing if it related to the dig in Fausson's photos. There was also a list of the illustrations used in the text; someone had written notes next to a few of those, but they were mostly numbers that didn't mean anything to me.

The book belonged to the Oriental Institute library. I knew the place, sort of, since it was on the South Side, on the University of Chicago campus. When I was in sixth grade, we had a class outing there, where the biggest attraction was a mummy—for days after, the boys would drape toilet paper around their heads and chase the girls around the playground.

It wasn't until I was a student at the University of Chicago that I realized it was a scholarly institute, creating dictionaries of humans' earliest written languages, conducting excavations, and trying to preserve cultural heritage in the Middle East from looters. I added the book to my backpack. I could return it, which might never happen if the cops seized the contents of Fausson's apartment as evidence.

I made a quick search of the chest of drawers squeezed against the far wall. One drawer held graying briefs and worn socks, all jumbled together; another was stuffed with jeans and T-shirts. Fausson didn't own a suit, but he had a sports jackets and three of the safari-style shirts he'd worn in the Facebook photo. I turned out the pockets and went through his jeans and shorts pockets, but I didn't see anything that suggested a connection to Felix, or to the Illinois Institute of Technology. Hiking boots (also well worn), sandals, a set of the kind of leggings and tunic he'd had on in the dig photo, and a couple of black-check kaffiyehs.

Back in the main room, I plumped myself in Fausson's desk chair and opened his laptop. His wallpaper showed him sitting on a camel, dressed like Peter O'Toole in *Lawrence of Arabia*. The lightbulb went off: Leroy of Arabia would have sounded ludicrous, so he told people his name was Lawrence. Elorenze—the man who'd called me early this morning might have been an Arab speaker. Someone who knew Felix from IIT, or Engineers in a Free State?

Fausson's computer was password protected, but my computer consultant would know how to get past a security screen. I closed the computer and tucked it into my canvas pack.

He didn't have any personal photos on the desk itself—no lovers or parents, not even a selfie. A small stone figurine was half hidden under a week-old copy of the *Herald-Star*. It looked like a lion missing part of its front right paw. The stone was smooth to the touch. I stroked its head with my forefinger.

"What can you tell me about Fausson?" I asked it. The lion stared back at me, solemn, unspeaking. I resisted the temptation to add it to my backpack but returned it to the desk while I searched the drawers.

Fausson had jumbled his documents together, just as he'd stored his clothes. I found his passport at the back of the top drawer, in the name of Leroy Michael Fausson.

The pages were full of immigration stamps from many Arabian cities, including Riyadh and Cairo, along with most European airports, but he hadn't used it since returning to America. I squinted at the date and country stamps. He'd had to leave Syria because of the war, but he'd bummed around the Middle East and North Africa for two years, finally coming to Chicago from Tunis. I photographed several of the pages, but left the passport behind along with the lion.

Although he had utility bills among the papers, I didn't find any financial records, no credit card statements, no bank documents, no pay stubs. If he'd done everything online, I'd have to wait until I got into his computer to see anything.

I'd been in the apartment for over an hour; time to move on. I made a quick survey of the kitchen but tripped as a floorboard popped up. When I tapped it into place with my shoe heel, two adjacent boards came up.

I knelt to look. The reason Fausson didn't have any financial documents was that he was part of the cash economy. When I lifted the boards out, I found a cache of hundreds lying in a shallow metal box.

1 2

FREE FALL

I PICKED UP a stack of bills, counted it. Roughly a hundred-fifty. Eyeballing the size of the hoard, I was guessing a quarter of a million. Take it? Leave it in situ?

I photographed the money, the box, the floorboards. Fausson's tools for getting at his savings were under the kitchen sink—a hammer and a crowbar. I nailed the floor back into place as well as I could, but he'd been in and out of his hiding place so many times the nails were loose—that's why the boards had flipped up to begin with.

I turned off the lamps and had my hand on the doorknob when more footsteps pounded up the stairs. They halted outside Fausson's door. I heard muffled talk—two men. I squatted, back against the wall next to the door, as one man barked a command.

They kicked in the door and swarmed past me into the room. I was out, rolling onto the hall floor, and was on my feet at the stairwell before they reacted.

"You, stop!" they bellowed. "Federal agents! Immigration!"

I belted down the stairs. Got hit from behind, knocked down the second flight. I heard the whine a nanosecond later. Bullet in the back. I lay on the landing, gasping for air. Another shout from above: "Federal agents, halt or be shot." A second bullet whined. I rolled instinctively—not paralyzed, get down the stairs. I yanked myself upright, catapulted over the railing to the first-floor stairwell, ran a jagged pattern the rest of the way down.

Doors were opening around the stairwell, people were crying out in terror. "911!" I screamed. "Gunmen on three!"

I bolted out the front, still screaming, "911! Gunmen!" I raced down Neenah Avenue to my car and floored the accelerator before I'd shut the door. The Mustang skidded, squealed, righted itself. I turned onto Higgins, drove the half mile to the expressway like a lunatic, weaving around traffic, hot-rodding through stoplights as they changed color. It wasn't until I was on the Kennedy, heading southeast, that I turned on my headlights. I got off at Belmont, but took a roundabout route to my apartment, circling back west, and then south, farther west, farther south. After stopping in an alley two miles from my street, I finally decided I was clean.

Even so, I parked a long two blocks from my building and came up the alley behind it so I could go in through the back. I seemed to be in the clear. At the bottom step to my own three flights, my arms and legs began to tremble. I sat down abruptly. It was only then, adrenaline depleted, that I felt warm liquid along my spine.

13

AN APPLE A DAY . . .

THE DOGS ROUSED Mr. Contreras. When my neighbor opened his front door, the dogs almost knocked him over in their rush to me. Peppy shoved her muzzle between my back and the stairs: her maternal instinct told her that she needed to lick up my blood.

Mr. Contreras hobbled along as quickly as his arthritic knees allowed. "Now what did you go and do, Victoria Warshawski?"

"Someone shot at me. I guess they hit me." Fear made me short of breath.

He hoisted me to my feet and hustled me into his apartment. He sat me in a hard-backed chair and got me out of my coat before going to his kitchen for peroxide and a box of cotton. The dogs circled around, whining.

"Lift your shirt or whatever that thing is you got on. Sorry to be a Peeping Tom, doll, but it can't be helped."

He tore off a large piece of cotton and swabbed my back with a rough but thorough hand. He worked his way up from my waist. When he reached my right trap I couldn't suppress a cry.

"You got blood and dirt back here, but I don't see no bullet hole," he pronounced. "If we was on a battlefield, I'd say a piece of shrapnel went through your clothes and caught you, but I don't know what caused this. Good news is the wound ain't deep, but it tore about a square inch of skin off. I'm going to tape it up, but you go see Dr. Lotty in the morning, get yourself a tetanus shot and a proper bandage."

While he bustled off to get gauze and tape, I picked up my coat and inspected the back. There was a jagged tear but no sign of any metal. I looked around for my canvas backpack and found it near the door. I sat cross-legged on the floor, pack in my lap.

Mr. Contreras appeared with his new stash of first aid equipment. When I pushed myself to my feet, the bag's contents clinked and rattled. I stuck in a cautious hand. Shards, wires, glass—hard to tell.

He took the pack from me. "It ain't going anywhere, doll. Just hike up your shirt again and let me get this covered. And now you got dirt in the wound again. You're more trouble than both dogs put together."

He swabbed my shoulder blade a second time, smeared on Neosporin, and laid a piece of gauze over it. When he'd finally wrapped me with enough tape to cover a mummy, we looked at the bag together. On one side, a singed hole in the canvas showed a bullet's entry. On the other, a big exit hole. The bullet had pushed something through with enough force to penetrate my coat.

Mr. Contreras took today's *Sun-Times* from his armchair and spread a few pages on his dining table so we could empty the canvas bag. The Arabic book and papers I'd taken from Fausson's desk, my picklocks and flashlight, the Oriental Institute publication, a bagel I'd forgotten. The remains of Lawrence Fausson's laptop.

The bullet had flattened and cracked the case lid, shattering the screen. The impact had propelled something—a piece of the metal case?—into my back. The computer had taken the bullet's full force. Apple had saved my life.

I sifted through the glass and metal shards. In the midst of the computer's innards was a piece of copper that looked like a misshapen flower—six metal petals opened on top of a stubby stalk. The petals were twisted and misshapen; one had broken off. The bullet. It would have looked just like this if it had gone through my scapula and torn up my heart. A violent shudder shook me.

Mr. Contreras put a steadying arm on me. "Who done this, doll?"

"Some guys who claimed to be with Immigration and Customs." I told him about going to Leroy/Lawrence Fausson's apartment. "They yelled the way they do on the cop shows, but I don't know if they were real agents or perps imitating TV cops. I didn't think ICE agents went out armed, but maybe they fear some Mexican or Somali mother is going to fling a used diaper in their faces."

"Why in God's name did you go there to begin with?" Mr. Contreras demanded. "You don't have enough trouble without roaring around town looking for it?"

"Lotty's nephew." I hadn't told my neighbor about my trek to the sheriff with Felix. When I explained the discovery of Fausson's body with Felix's name in the pocket, Mr. Contreras became instantly sympathetic: if I'd been helping out Dr. Lotty, I'd done exactly what I should have done.

"You go on upstairs, doll, you get yourself a hot bath and clean clothes, and the dogs and me will bring supper up to you."

While I waited for the tub to fill, I texted Lotty in case Felix was so angry with us both that he hadn't let her know he was alive and well.

HE WOULDN'T SAY WHERE HE'S BEEN, BUT HIS PHONE SHOWED HE WAS IN WESTERN WISCONSIN.

I gave her an abbreviated version of my adventure at Fausson's, adding that I'd stop by her clinic in the morning for a tetanus booster. I'M GIVING FAUSSON'S IDENTITY TO THE POLICE. I DIDN'T SEE ANY LINK TO FELIX AT HIS APARTMENT AND I HOPE TO GOD I LOOKED IN ALL THE POSSIBLE PLACES, BECAUSE WHOEVER/WHATEVER FAUSSON WAS, HE HAD A LARGE STASH OF CASH UNDER HIS FLOORBOARDS.

I climbed into the tub, putting a plastic cleaning bag around my shoulder to hold Mr. Contreras's bandage in place. I dozed off, trying to imagine what Felix might be doing, when my neighbor shouted my name from my entryway: he didn't want to risk catching me naked. I climbed out, stiffly, half-asleep, the plastic bag clammy against my breasts.

Mr. Contreras's repertoire is small: spaghetti with tomato sauce, steak, or baked chicken. Tonight was spaghetti, the tomatoes ones he'd canned from his own garden last fall. I added Parmesan. I buy it at an old Italian deli where my mother used to shop; it has somehow survived the encroachment of a hundred big-box companies on Harlem Avenue.

Mr. Contreras and I watched *Kojak* reruns on one of the nostalgia channels—those were the days, when the bald cop ran over criminals and his own captain and right, if not justice, always triumphed.

Lotty called, just as Kojak himself was looking at a briefcase filled with money and commenting, "That's a lot of balloons."

Lotty was worried about me, worried about Felix, but we agreed there wasn't a lot we could do. "Except for you to keep an eye on him," Lotty said, "as much as you can without getting him completely alienated."

"I learned Fausson's identity from an anonymous caller, but the sheriff will certainly question Felix again. Were you able to speak to Freeman's immigration specialist?"

"Martha Simone. Yes, and she's ready to help if we need her. Hugo phoned, he and Penelope." She was Hugo's daughter and Felix's mother. "They say they've tried to get Felix to return home, but he claims his engineers group is doing work that's too important to abandon. I'll talk to them again tonight."

We spoke for half an hour, Mr. Contreras listening avidly but silently. Lotty had grand rounds in the morning, but she said she'd alert her clinic nurse to change my dressing and give me a tetanus booster.

My neighbor began gathering dishes together while I switched channels to the local news. The shooting at Fausson's building hadn't made the cut, which made me wonder enough to look at the Chicago news feed on my laptop. No report there, either.

I didn't like that: no blood had been shed, which made the story only minimally interesting, I guess, but gunshots in a stairwell in one of Chicago's quietest neighborhoods? It should have been a story. I wondered if the people who fired at me really had been ICE agents, using Homeland Security to put a muzzle on the story.

All those balloons I'd stumbled on could indicate something like ICE would be interested in. Drug money, for instance. Technically that was DEA or Treasury responsibility, but Homeland was muscling in on a lot of people's turf. I didn't remember seeing a Kabul stamp in Fausson's passport, but I thought about the poppy routes from Afghanistan.

Mr. Contreras stared at the pictures I'd taken, fascinated, even a bit titillated. "Jeez, doll, where'd this guy come up with all that money?"

"I have no idea, not even an idea of how to figure out an idea. I'm more worried about how it might tie to Felix," I said. "And what if the people who shot at me were the ones who killed Fausson? It's possible his death had something to do with cheating people out of their share of ill-gotten gains. In that case, though, why would ICE come charging in, unless they were crooks pretending to be agents. Or agents gone rogue."

"You ain't going back there, are you? Least, not alone, right?"

"I'm not going back there," I agreed. "Whether they're law or outlaw, they'll be staking the place."

When Mr. Contreras had packed up his pots and taken Mitch downstairs—leaving Peppy with me, for comfort and security—I called Lieutenant McGivney in Maywood, to tell him I'd had an anonymous tip on his dead body. That took ten minutes because, of course, he didn't believe I didn't know my informant, nor that Felix—or I—really didn't know Fausson.

"An anonymous call? We'll be checking your phone records."

"With a subpoena, right, not sitting out there in Maywood with a handy hacker," I said.

"You say he called in the middle of the night last night—"

"Early this morning, Lieutenant."

"It's what, twenty hours later and you're just getting around to letting me know? What were you doing in the meantime?"

"My nails," I said. "When you can't afford a salon pedicure, it takes forever to buff down the calluses and trim ingrown toenails. Then trying to get off all the old polish—"

"You're still not ready for *Saturday Night Live*. And your detective skills could use some polishing, too, Sherlock."

At least he hung up.

It was getting close to eleven and I was close to comatose, but I figured I owed Murray a heads-up on Fausson's identity: if he hadn't put my name out on Global's newscast, my informant wouldn't have known who I was.

Murray, like the sheriff, wanted significantly more details than I was prepared to give. My informant's address, occupation, list of enemies?

"Murray, all I know is the vic's name, which I'm sharing with you because he learned my name from you. And always remember, of course, that this call may be monitored for quality assurance."

"You know something you're not telling," Murray growled.

"I know lots of things I'm not telling, mainly because I don't think they'd interest you. You're lucky I'm still sharing information with you after you set me up with the sheriff's department. Do some footwork for a change. Lubricate those reporter muscles."

1 4

WHO LOVES YA, BABY?

MY ADVENTURES HAD worn me down. I fell asleep instantly, but at two I woke and began that restless, useless churning all the sleep gurus warn us against.

The pain in my shoulder was partly responsible, but most of it had to do with my worries about Felix and all that money under Leroy or Lawrence Fausson's floorboards. I wondered if it was still there.

The pair who shot at me could have been the same men who'd kicked in Fausson's head. Whatever the source of the hundreds under his floorboards, if they thought he'd double-crossed them, they could have killed him and then come looking for the money.

On the other hand, maybe my shooters really were with Immigration and had come looking for Fausson for ICE-related reasons: we're breaking in your door because we want to catch you in the act of reading Arabic poetry. They carried guns in case he threw that heavy volume about the Chalcolithic at them.

Finally, around five o'clock, I fell into an uneasy sleep. I was with Felix in Syria. He'd installed an elaborate water delivery system in one of the bombed-out shells of a city, but when he asked me to turn on the tap, the spigot spat out bits of Leroy Fausson's brain.

Around eight, I struggled awake, stuck my head under the shower's cold water tap, gingerly rotated my right trap. Mr. Contreras had wrapped me so tightly it was hard to tell if I had full mobility in the right arm, but the wound didn't protest very loudly when I moved. Besides my shoulder, the most significant damage was a purpling swath on my right hip, the shape and nearly the size of Lake Michigan. I smeared it with arnica and pulled on my sweats.

Saturday mornings in early spring, I usually give the dogs a long workout. I often go to the Y for pickup basketball after, but today we'd all make do with less exercise. I drove the dogs to the park north of Belmont Harbor and limped in their wake as they chased ducks and each other.

On my way home, Harmony called, distraught: a Sergeant Abreu had asked her to come into the station to discuss her sister. Where was I?

"On my way," I said.

I didn't bother to stop at home but drove straight to Humboldt Park with the dogs. Harmony was pacing the sidewalk when we arrived. At the station, she sat rigid, not opening the car door.

"I can't do this," she said.

"Yes, you can. Reno would do it for you, and Clarisse would tell you it's your job, so out you get. I'll be with you every minute."

Sergeant Abreu turned out to be a woman, and one almost as dark as Clarisse looked in her photos. This helped Harmony relax slightly. Abreu had a patient, quiet manner. It took half an hour, but Harmony finally began to speak in full sentences and to give as much information as she could dredge up.

When we finished, Abreu consulted with Terry Finchley. The Finch had already applied for a warrant to search Reno's apartment building. Since it had gone up in the 1920s, with big coal furnaces in a subbasement and long rows of storage lockers, it held a lot of places where someone could have put a body. No one wanted to come right out and say someone murdered Reno on the premises and hid her in an abandoned boiler, but that was the first thought on our minds.

When Harmony nervously asked what they were looking for, Sergeant Abreu did say, "We don't want to find that she was in the building all the time needing help which we didn't give her."

They'd canvass the other people in the building, they'd circulate Reno's photo throughout the CPD, they'd check with the airlines to see if she'd taken a flight somewhere: if Reno had spotted an old abuser when she was in St. Matthieu, it was possible she'd flown off looking for revenge.

"You want to hang out at my place while the cops search?" I asked Harmony when Abreu had said they had all they needed for the present. "I'll be gone most of the day, but you'd have the dogs and Mr. Contreras for company."

Harmony wanted to stay in her sister's apartment. "In case, like Sergeant Abreu said, Reno's sick or unconscious or something. I should be there if they find her. Maybe—could you let me have Mitch, in case, you know—"

"Sure, but you'll have to take him outside periodically. And don't let him off leash."

"I can take care of him: I'm not a baby, you know."

"Of course not."

When I dropped them off, Harmony said, "Do you think they'll find her?"

"They'll do their best," I said, "but I don't know."

"I mean, in the building? If she's there, she must be—"

"Probably," I said gently, when she stopped.

"I guess if they don't find her by Monday I'll go back to Portland."

"You don't have to decide anything today. Right now I'm getting a tetanus shot and a look at my wound, and then I'm going to do some detecting of my own, but I won't be farther than half an hour from you."

I stopped at home on my way to the clinic to drop Peppy off with Mr. Contreras. Dick called as I was getting back into my car.

"Did you tell the cops to come out here and frighten Teri?"

"Hey, Dick. How are you?"

"Vic, don't push it."

"Just trying to give you time to calm down," I said. "If you put together that kind of predicate negative during cross, I'm surprised you ever made partner. Did the cops frighten Teri? I doubt it. Did I send them out to your home? Beyond my powers."

"Damn it, Vic, they must have gotten my name from you."

"Not necessarily. Harmony could have told them, or twenty seconds in a personal history database," I said. "Reno has been missing for nearly a week. You are her second closest relative, next to her sister. It's natural for the police to talk to you and to your wife. What did you tell them? That your secretary helped your niece get a job and that's where your family duty ended?"

"I didn't tell them anything," Dick said stiffly. "Teri and I agreed that we shouldn't answer any questions without our lawyer present."

"And your lawyer was playing golf, so she couldn't come out to Oak Brook on Saturday?" I asked.

"Our personal lawyer does estate planning. She's getting us someone who's familiar with criminal law."

"Dick, there are a hundred different things I'm tempted to say to you this morning, just to get your goat, but I'm not going to because this is serious. A young woman is missing, and it doesn't look good. If you know anything, *anything*—if she called Teri to ask about bus schedules or called you for legal advice, tell the police. I know you don't want her life on your conscience."

I actually wasn't sure of that. In today's America, we've been brainwashed into thinking we don't owe each other any help or support. The richer we are, the more inclined we are to leave our neighbors and indigent nieces to die on the side of the road.

BODYWORK

I NEEDED TO run one last errand before going to the clinic: delivering the remnants of Fausson's computer to my computer wizard.

Niko Cruickshank is a cheerful, sleepy-eyed guy, but the deconstructed MacBook took away some of his usual bonhomie. "Jeez, V.I., this is a valuable machine. You shouldn't be using it as a shield in a sword fight. Unless you buried nuclear codes in the rubble, just throw it out."

"It was a gunfight, not swords," I said. "No nuclear codes, but I'm praying for a lead to a killer. Anything—an address, a name or two. This guy was murdered, and all I know about him is that he liked archaeology."

"I'm not a miracle worker," Niko warned.

"Just a wizard," I said. "Keep me posted."

It was close to two when I finally made it to Lotty's clinic on Damen.

Jewel Kim, the senior nurse, unwrapped Mr. Contreras's dressing. "Halloween is half a year away, Vic, too early to go around looking like a zombie. Your neighbor did a good job on cleaning the wound, though. It's already started to heal. We'll put a light cover on it, give you your tetanus, and send you on your way."

She looked at my bruised hip before I dressed and had me do various stretches and bends, as well as stand on my right leg. "I don't think you need X-rays. You can put weight on it without screaming. Just baby it for a few days. Your body will tell you if you're overdoing it."

She put her own topical ointment on it, gave me a tube to take with me, and called for her next patient.

I phoned Harmony as I drove to my office. She said that the police were still in the building, searching, but she and Mitch were watching a movie on Harmony's laptop.

"First I was going around with them, but it was too upsetting. Every time they went into an apartment or broke the door on an old store-room I'd start shaking, worrying what would be on the other side. Once they found a whole nest of rats, so I started freaking about them, too."

When I said I'd be by for the dog in an hour or so, Harmony diffidently asked if he could stay the night.

"I promise I'll walk him: we've already been out once and he had a good time in the park. He makes me feel safe."

"Sure, of course, just call me if he starts barking or whining to get out and I'll come over. We don't want Reno to lose her lease because of him."

That also eased a worry at the back of my own mind about Harmony's safety in the building. If Reno had been abducted, whether by some chance-met old abuser or some current-day bastard, the perp could well be keeping an eye on a search for her. It's something predators in particular like to do—they think they are smarter than the law, and so they like to gloat nearby as the law tries uselessly to track them down. Someone would have to be well armed and cocky to take on Mitch.

At my office, I re-anointed my sore hip with Jewel's prescription unguent. The bruise looked more like Lake Michigan than ever, with the shoreline turning yellow and green while the center remained a dark purple.

I resolutely turned away from the cot in the back and settled down with my computer.

I started with the books I'd taken from Fausson's apartment, beginning with the slender book of poetry by Tarik Kataba.

International PEN's website gave me more information about Kataba. In addition to his own poetry, Kataba had translated work from Russian and French into Arabic. It was the Russian that got him into trouble: he had translated a poem by Osip Mandelstam written about Stalin back in the 1930s.

In "Stalin's Epigram," PEN informed me, Mandelstam called Stalin's mustache a "cockroach" and described his followers as "a mob of thin-necked leaders, half men. . . . Some . . . meowing or whistling or whining . . . [while Stalin] pokes some in the groin or in the brow."

The poem got its author sent to his death in the gulags, and the translation didn't do Kataba much good, either: Bashar al-Assad seemed to take it personally, for reasons the article didn't make clear. At any rate, Kataba was imprisoned and tortured for twenty-two months. His wife died while he was in prison.

When he was released, the civil war was heating up. He fled to Beirut, along with millions of other Middle Easterners during the upheavals of the 2010s. After that I couldn't trace him. Dead, drowned, disappeared? If his daughter had stayed in Beirut, she might be sheltering him.

I looked at every page in the book, but didn't see anything except occasional marginal notes in pencil.

I put Kataba's book to one side and turned to *Urban Development in the Chalcolithic* by Candra van Vliet, who was much easier to research than Kataba. Although born and raised in the Netherlands, she lived in Chicago and in fact was on the faculty at the Oriental Institute.

It was four-thirty now, and the Oriental Institute closed at five. I called Van Vliet's office and got her voice mail. I tried her home. A man with a lightly accented baritone answered. He was startled, as everyone is when a detective calls out of the blue asking for them by name. He also was Professor Van Vliet, but when we had sorted out that I wanted Candra and he was Gottfried, he summoned his wife to the phone.

"Lawrence Fausson? Yes, I know him, although it has been several years since I last spoke to him. Why are you calling, detective? Has he committed a crime?"

"He may have done, but I'm calling because he's dead."

"I'm sorry to hear of this, but how does it involve me?"

"I'm having trouble finding out much about him; he had a copy of your book on the Chalcolithic and I was hoping you could give me some information about him. I know only two things about him: he was obsessed with Middle Eastern archaeology, and he was murdered."

FAMILY DINNER

VAN VLIET DIDN'T want to discuss Fausson over the phone. "It's a complex story and I need to see you face-to-face before I decide to tell it to you. I will not be on campus tomorrow, but you may come to my office at ten Monday morning."

In her place, I would have been equally cautious, but it didn't stop my annoyance. I agreed to her terms, though, and turned my attention to finding Donna Lutas's home address.

The search was straightforward and quick. Lutas was forty-one, had an associate's degree in accounting from the College of DuPage, lived with her mother in southwest suburban Oak Lawn. She'd never married. There was one sibling, a brother with three children, who lived farther west.

If I phoned, Lutas would undoubtedly stiff me. On a drizzly Saturday, there was a good chance she'd be home. I should be able to talk my way past the front door.

I rubbed my right hip, wondering whether all the flexing involved in driving twenty-five miles would make it heal faster or more slowly. Faster, of course: it would force blood to the area.

Terry Finchley called as I was getting on the expressway to tell me Sergeant Abreu's team had come up empty at Reno's building. "They found a pound of marijuana and an uncut brick of heroin in one apartment, so it wasn't a total waste of resources, but the only bodies they uncovered belonged to a couple of cats who'd died in the old coal boilers. Abreu had high hopes of the boilers—the seals had been tampered with—but nothing came of it except the cats. We did ask the building department to send a notice to the building manager, ordering their removal, but who knows if that will ever happen."

A semi behind me gave a loud goose honk; I'd committed the sin of letting two car lengths open up in front of me on the on-ramp and scooted up to fill the gap.

"Did you have time to ask the airlines if Reno had booked a ticket?"

"I did that one myself—I still have enough connections at Thirty-Fifth and Mich that they listen to me faster at O'Hare. There's no record of the Seale woman flying, or of renting a car, at least from the big agencies. It's always possible she hitchhiked, or borrowed transport from a friend."

The news, or lack of it, was depressing, but I thanked Finchley, both for the CPD effort and for letting me know.

"I've known you a long time, Warshawski: the more you know, the less damage you're likely to do."

I guessed that was a joke, so I laughed. "That reminds me—I had a call from Dick Yarborough this morning, angry that someone had had the temerity to question him about his niece. Was that you?"

"Ah, yes. The lawyer who can't talk about his family without a lawyer present. No, that was Francine. Sergeant Abreu. She went there before she started the search at the building on Fairfield. Made me curious, though. I may call on the counselor in his office on Monday. Maybe wear my uniform with all the badges and so on to give the rank and file at the firm something to wonder about. It always helps a little, when the underlings are gossiping. Pushes the higher-ups into acting more recklessly than they might have done."

I laughed again, more naturally this time. Mean-spirited, perhaps, but I enjoyed the thought of Dick sweating in his office while Glynis tried to shield him from the Finch.

"Later, Warshawski." Finchley hung up.

By the time I got to the Cicero exit, it was six. Suppertime for a lot of households, maybe for the Lutases as well, but Donna would be annoyed by my arrival no matter what she was doing.

Oak Lawn is a blue-collar suburb with quiet streets, except for the jets screaming their way in and out of Midway Airport. Donna and her mother lived on a cul-de-sac in a ranch house whose wood siding had weathered to a soft gray. Two bare rectangles of ground lined the sidewalk, waiting for warmer weather and a chance to turn into a garden.

The attached garage was closed, so I couldn't tell if a car was at home, but there was a light on in the back. I rang the bell, and after a moment an older woman in khaki slacks and a faded blue pullover came to the door.

I smiled politely and introduced myself. "Did your daughter explain that one of her employees has disappeared? The police are not optimistic about whether she's alive. I'm sorry to intrude on a Saturday evening, but every day counts in looking for a missing person."

Donna appeared behind her mother. "*You?* Why are you here?"

Mrs. Lutas looked at her daughter in surprise. "Dini, if the girl is missing, and you know something, you should help the detective."

"She's not a real detective."

"I'm not with the police," I corrected her. "But I am a real detective, licensed by the State of Illinois, with over twenty years' experience. I need to know what Reno told you happened in St. Matthieu."

"You busted into the office, and now you're doing the same thing here, but I have a right to be private in my own home."

"I got the feeling you didn't feel able to talk freely in your office. I thought we could go over details more comfortably in your own home, where there aren't video cameras recording everything you say."

Donna frowned at her mother. "We're getting ready to eat dinner."

"Dinner can wait," her mother said. "She's asking about that girl you've been talking about. You take her into the front room; I'll see that the lasagna comes out of the oven on time."

Donna took me into the front room on dragging feet, like a teenager whose mother had ordered her to an unwanted household chore. The TV was on, tuned to an animal show—parrots and dogs seemed to be doing tricks together. Donna sat on the edge of a stuffed armchair, hands clenched tight in her lap, oblivious to the television.

"Well?"

I found the remote and turned off the set. "It's not well. There are four main possibilities: Reno Seale is dead, Reno Seale has been in an accident and isn't able to identify herself, Reno Seale has been abducted by people who didn't leave a trace that the police can uncover, or Reno Seale has left town on an errand so private she didn't tell you or her sister, the two people she would be most likely to confide in. Which one do you choose?"

The tendons in Lutas's neck moved, as if she were trying to respond but couldn't.

"What's going on, Ms. Lutas?" I tried to speak in an empathic or at least a neutral tone, but I was tense myself. "On Thursday you seemed pleased, even relieved, to hear from me. Yesterday, you'd been shut down by corporate. I get that: no talking to outsiders about company policy, your job's on the line, and so on. When Jerry took me to your office, I thought he lingered to protect you, but now I'm thinking he was monitoring you to report back to someone, probably Eliza Trosse."

Lutas looked at me wide-eyed, as if I'd performed an amazing conjuring trick.

"Do you know what happened to Reno Seale?" I asked when she still hadn't spoken.

Lutas shook her head slowly, as if the tension in her neck made it hard for her to move.

"I'm pretty sure she isn't injured, or at least that she hasn't been admitted to an area hospital, because I've checked all those. So is she dead or is she off on a secret errand?"

"I don't know where she is or what she's doing," Lutas said roughly. "And it wasn't Eliza Trosse. I don't know who it was."

"Who it was what—oh, who told you to lay off asking about Reno. Someone called you?"

Even though it was Saturday evening, Donna was wearing makeup, and flakes of red skin came off as she bit her lips. She gave the smallest of nods.

"What did they say?"

"They told me I was an employee with a good career and a good track record, but that making a fuss about Reno could hurt my future."

"Man? Woman? Jerry?"

"A man. Not anyone I knew. He sounded like one of those TV announcers, or those preachers with the big TV audiences."

"Did he say anything else, I mean, about why it would hurt your career?"

"He said Reno had left the company under a cloud; that she was lucky they weren't going to prosecute her, and they didn't want me to make the mistake of thinking she'd been ill-treated."

"Did you ask the guy who called where she is?" I demanded.

Lutas shrugged but didn't look at me.

"Didn't you want to know? Didn't you care?"

She still didn't speak, but she held her body even more stiffly.

"There's something else, isn't there?" I said sharply. "A carrot or a stick?"

She turned crimson under her makeup. "Pictures," she whispered. "Pictures I didn't know anyone had taken. I—please—"

The humiliations of the vulnerable are unbearable. "Not my business. I only care about Reno, what inkling she gave about St. Matthieu that would help me start looking for her."

Donna twisted her rings so roughly that one tore skin off the inside of her finger. "I don't know. I could tell something had upset her, but—you keep saying Reno trusted me. That isn't true. She came back quieter than when she'd gone away, even though she was pretty darn quiet to begin with. We asked her what it was like, what they'd done, and she said some of it was nice, the beaches were gorgeous, but she said the event was like *Mad Men* on steroids—rich men, young women in bikinis who were expected to lap dance. She was angry. I told her to let it ride, it was just five days out of her life, and she said it seemed like the entire story of her life.

"Next thing I know, I get a call from Eliza Trosse at corporate HR, telling me Reno filed a complaint and it was my job to stop that where it started. 'Senior staff will take note and it will reflect badly on you if this gets publicized.' Meaning I could be demoted or even fired."

Mrs. Lutas came back with a couple of mugs of hot water and a box of tea bags, which she put on an end table near the couch where I was sitting. "You girls look like you could use a little refreshment."

I smiled gratefully. Drinking tea gives all parties something to do with their hands and eases the throat muscles. I took a packet of ginger-turmeric.

"So I talked to Reno and said, whatever happened in St. Matthieu, the company wasn't going to help, and could she let it lie? She went back to work, but when she wasn't with a customer she seemed to disappear. Into herself, I mean."

Lutas drank some of the hot water. "And then I went to look at Reno's personnel file to see if the complaint to HR had generated a written response and I found someone at corporate had put a note in Reno's file. Online, I mean."

"What did the note say?" I asked.

"'What do we know about this girl?' and no initials. You write in someone's file, you initial it. I was on the phone with my manager right away."

"Eliza Trosse?" I asked.

"No, she's corporate. My manager runs the twenty West Side branches—she reports to Eliza. My manager said there wasn't any note in Reno's file and what was I talking about? And sure enough, I logged back in and the note was gone."

"Someone assaulted Reno when she was a child. She never knew the man's name. Her sister wondered if she might have encountered him at the resort."

"Oh, poor thing!" Lutas's mother had been in the doorway without my noticing. "Dini—did she ever say anything about that?"

Donna shook her head. "Maybe she overreacted to what was going on at the resort because of it. Maybe it wasn't as—as creepy as she made it sound."

"Or it was creepier than it sounded," I said. "Did anything special happen on Monday, the Monday that was Reno's last day?"

Lutas's mouth twisted in annoyance. "I asked her if there was some secret she was sitting on that I needed to know about. As her manager, you know. It was that note in her file that appeared and disappeared. I asked her point-blank if she'd had a run-in with anyone on senior staff at the resort. She said when she could ID the company's senior staff she'd be able to answer that question. And then she left the building.

"When she didn't come in or answer her phone Tuesday and Wednesday, I got worried, so when you called on Thursday, I was relieved. But then—I got the message . . ." Her voice died away and she wiped her hands on her jeans, as if her palms were sweaty.

The message threatening to blackmail her if she spoke to me.

I could smell the beef and tomato sauce from the lasagna and realized I was hungry and twenty-five miles from home.

"Were you in your office when Reno and you spoke on Monday? Could anyone have overheard you?"

Lutas gave a wry smile. "You saw that office. Privacy is not exactly our number one priority."

1 7

VACATION SPOTS

I COULDN'T FIGURE out what use to make of Donna Lutas's story. Her last comment was particularly unsettling. Reno was trying to identify Rest EZ's senior staff. Had one of the company's owners assaulted her, claiming it was all in a day's work? "We brought you to this lovely island, now you won't play along?" And then they'd put a note in her personnel file, but removed it when they realized it would draw more attention to the situation.

The rain had let up, but the temperature had dropped. By the time I got back to my own place on Racine, my hip and trap were aching. I limped from the car to the front door, limped as I walked Peppy around the block.

Saturday nights I sometimes go to a club for dancing or music, but tonight I stretched out in front of the television, watching the Black-hawks while I ate pizza and drank half a bottle of Brunello. Partway through the third period, Harmony called me to say that Sergeant Abreu had stopped by to tell her the lack of results in person.

"I feel like Reno disappeared, it hurts me, her doing that, like she didn't love me the way I thought she did."

"Harmony, I don't know what happened to Reno, but I doubt she abandoned you willingly. By now you must surely know that the news about her is not likely to be good."

"Maybe she liked the idea of vanishing." Harmony sniffed. "She left

Portland, left me and Clarisse on our own, but I could still reach her. Maybe she wanted to get away from me completely."

In some ways, it was a bratty outburst, but it also reflected the sisters' essential aloneness. I didn't have a useful response, so I asked instead if Reno had talked about any of the executives from Rest EZ.

"She was trying to get the names of the company's senior management," I said. "Did she say anything to suggest she'd had a run-in with company execs at the resort?"

"She never said anything except, like I told you, about how these johns all have the same look, vultures but dead. Well, also she said Mama Clarisse would have a fit if she knew how stupid Reno'd been, agreeing to go down there in the first place."

She was quiet for a long moment before saying in a small voice, "I know she's probably dead. I can't bear thinking about it, because my mind starts remembering every bad thing that can happen when some man is making—"

She cut herself off. She knew more than most people about every bad thing that can happen when you are in the power of a powerful man.

"Anyway," she added after another silence, "I can't stay in Chicago any longer; it's making me crazy, since I can't do anything to find her. At least when I'm working in the garden shop I'm making things come to life, so I'm going to fly back to Portland Monday morning."

I assured her that I thought she was making the right decision but promised that I would keep searching. Before we hung up, I insisted that Harmony spend her last day in Chicago as a tourist.

For once this week, I had a full night's sleep and woke up full of pep for taking Harmony around the city. Mr. Contreras joined us for a Chicago Architecture Foundation walking tour of the downtown buildings. I'd stopped limping and the map of Lake Michigan had begun turning yellow in the middle, which meant the deep bruise was healing.

We drove down to South Chicago to look at the house where I'd grown up. Harmony had a fragmented memory of the Christmas she'd spent there when she was five, but we couldn't go inside: the current owner shut the front door halfway through my request to look at my childhood bedroom. I was lucky the house was still standing—so many homes in my old neighborhood have gone into foreclosure, or fallen down, that many streets have more empty lots than houses.

My mother's olive tree was still in the front yard. She'd planted it to try to keep a connection to the Italy she'd fled and never seen again. Harmony tried to inspect it, but the owner appeared again in the doorway, this time with a gun.

We finished with dinner at Orvieto's on North Harlem, where my dad used to take my mother for their wedding anniversary every year. It's an old-fashioned restaurant, serving big portions of creamy pasta—not the kind of food my mother ever liked or cooked—but Gabriella loved Orvieto's for its murals of the Umbrian hills where she grew up.

I tried to persuade Harmony to sleep at my place, to make sure we all got up in time to make her flight, but her things were at Reno's; she needed to go back there.

Before going to bed myself, I checked in with Lotty to see if she'd heard from Felix.

"He actually came to dinner this evening. He said he had been camping in northern Minnesota with some of his engineering friends. They were trying to solve a difficult problem and decided that something like a retreat would help them think more clearly."

"Did he come alone?" I asked.

"Yes. I have yet to meet his free state engineers, but he seemed more like his old self than he's been lately." She gave a short laugh. "Like every other older woman with an attractive young man in her life, I choose to believe him, even though at the back of my mind I have questions."

Such as whether the camping/retreat story was believable. Out of curiosity, I looked up the weather in northern Minnesota. It was almost twenty degrees colder than Chicago, the ski resorts were proclaiming a good foot of snow cover, and the lakes were all frozen. I suppose Felix could be a snow camper, but the story sounded more like something he'd cobbled together after he got home.

He was working on the biggest engineering project of his young career, he'd said when we spoke on Friday, not "my pals and I went up to the north woods to think things through."

"Did he say whether the sheriff's police had been in touch with him to talk about Lawrence Fausson? Murray Ryerson's sound bite got the lieutenant all hot and bothered."

"Yes. I think that is why Felix came to dinner: the lawyer you got him, Martha Simone, went with him and turned the interrogation into a short formality. We're both grateful to you. I hope that he also remembers to thank you."

As if on cue, Felix phoned me himself as soon as Lotty and I said good night. He told me pretty much the same story Lotty had reported.

"Camping in northern Minnesota in late March?" I said. "You and your friends are hearty spirits—the place is still covered with snow and ice."

"I'm Canadian, Vic, from Montreal. We love winter camping."

He added a formal thank-you for Martha Simone's assistance. "I'm not sure she persuaded the sheriff that I truly never met Fausson, but she did make sure he knew he couldn't talk to me without her being in the room. She says there's no evidence to charge me with a crime, and I guess she has a pretty good reputation. Lieutenant McGivney let me go, except he told me not to leave Cook County until everything is cleared up. I guess I'm okay for now, but what if they don't have things cleared up by the end of May? I'm going to go home after the term ends."

I tried to reassure him. It would be surprising if a murder investigation stretched beyond eight weeks, but that only made him more nervous: he was sure McGivney would frame him for Fausson's death. My well of pep talk dried up. I didn't know whether Felix was in fact involved with Fausson in some way, and of course Murray Ryerson had goaded the county into deeper suspicions of Felix. That would never have happened if it weren't for Murray's and my relationship. Felix and I finally hung up with no satisfaction on either side.

I went to bed soon after, since I was getting up early to take Harmony to the airport, but I couldn't sleep. My mind kept ping-ponging between Felix's camping story and Donna Lutas's claim that Reno was trying to track down Rest EZ's senior staff. What company shrouds the names of their senior executives in secrecy?

I finally got up and went to the dining room, where I poured Armagnac into one of my mother's red glasses and tried to read a biography of Niccolò Jommelli, who composed the only opera my mother ever performed in. I couldn't focus.

I went back to bed, hoping the Armagnac or Jommelli would knock me out, but at one I got up again to look at Rest EZ. I didn't know anything about their corporate structure, who owned them, whom they owned.

The company wasn't publicly traded. After an hour of hunting, that was about all I learned. There were no SEC filings, but they were a wholly owned subsidiary of Trechette Investments, incorporated in Delaware. Trechette Investments was a company that invested in financial instruments for the benefit of its shareholders, which totaled one: Trechette International, whose business was unspecified. They had been incorporated in Havre-des-Anges, the capital of St. Matthieu.

I'd heard the Trechette name before, but I couldn't place it. I did a search of all the notes I'd been taking since Harmony first came to me, then tried Felix, and finally my closed cases, but wherever I'd seen it hadn't been connected to my own investigations.

And anyway, it was beside the point: no matter where Trechette International was incorporated, if it was an offshore incorporation the owners wouldn't physically be in the same place as the corporate headquarters. They could be in London or New York or right here in Chicago, with a registered agent handling their business from the Caribbean.

Before shutting everything down, I tried a reverse search: other companies owned by Trechette Investments or Trechette International. I found banks in Latvia and Kiev; an insurance company headquartered in Jersey; a holding company based in Buenos Aires that invested in oil rigs. But nowhere could I find a name of a shareholder other than a parent company. In some cases the parent was Trechette International, in others the Trechette Insurance Group. All of them had been set up in tax havens, and none of them listed any personnel. The registered agent was always a bank or, in some cases, the office of a local law firm.

When I looked up the island, I saw that St. Matthieu was near Martinique in the French West Indies. Like so many of the islands in the Greater and Lesser Antilles, their chief business seemed to be manufacturing offshore companies for needy investors. Personal, corporate, I myself could get a trust, a foundation, or a company with a few clicks of my mouse and a little money debited from my bank account.

Could Reno have flown to Havre-des-Anges in an effort to uncover the owners of Trechette in person? If so, she'd used an assumed name, because she hadn't shown up when Finchley queried the airlines.

At two, I reminded myself that I had to pick Harmony up at six-fifteen to get her to Midway on time, which meant I needed to get up at five. I went to bed with that grinding feeling in my head you get when you're trying to shut your brain down but can't.

I had barely dropped off when my phone woke me again. I swore, was about to send the caller to voice mail, when I saw it was Harmony.

"Vic? Vic—I think someone's trying to break in—I can hear—"

"I'm on my way." I was pulling on jeans. "I'm calling 911 and then I'm calling you back. You stay on the phone with me until I get there."

By the time I picked up Mitch on my way out of the building, I'd reached 911. I mapped the route in my head, pushing my panic out of my gut. I ran stoplights, swerved around slower traffic, cut in front of trucks. At North and Ashland my luck ran out: a squad car flagged me.

I jumped out of the Mustang and ran to the squad. "Officer, my niece—she heard someone breaking into her place and now she's not answering the phone. I've called 911 but I need to get there."

I was practically weeping with fury, fear, frustration, which got the driver to take me seriously. The girlie reaction. I hated it but I couldn't control it. The cop checked with 911, then said he'd follow me, siren whining. We did the last mile and a half in two minutes.

A blue-and-white was already in front of the building when we arrived. They had managed to rouse someone to buzz them in, told me to stay in the lobby while they headed up the stairs. With Mitch at my side, I turned and ran down the corridor to the rear stairwell. The dog raced up the stairs ahead of me, growling, hackles raised.

Mitch had bounded into the apartment by the time I got there: the lock on the back door had been forced. I hurled myself through the opening, crying Harmony's name. Police were pounding on the front door, but Mitch had gone back out into the hall. I followed him to the service elevator, where the garbage bins for the floor stood. He was nosing at one, whining and barking.

My stomach turned cold. I could barely bring myself to open the lid. The corn silk hair, filled with food and paper debris, hung over her doubled-up body. She didn't move. Mitch jumped up, paws over the edge of the bin, nuzzling her head.

Harmony, you are not dead, Harmony, you are not dead. I stuck in a trembling hand to feel her neck. A pulse, a flutter.

An officer appeared next to me, a short woman with a leathery face.

"My niece," I whispered. "She's still alive. I don't know—she could be wounded—"

The officer told me to move Mitch and she'd see about my niece. The dog didn't want to leave Harmony; he growled and snapped at me as I braced my legs against the open stairwell door to hold him.

"Don't tase him," I gasped as the woman put a hand on her tool belt. "He's protecting her, he's doing his job."

"You'd better have a good grip on him then, honey."

She gently tipped the bin onto its side and eased Harmony out. Mitch broke from me then and ran to her side, licking her face. The officer decided to leave him alone. I helped her straighten Harmony's legs and arms. We lifted the sweatshirt she was wearing and lowered the yoga pants but didn't see any wounds.

"Shock is my guess," the officer said, "but I'm not an EMT. You stay with her; I'll call an ambulance."

I took off my coat and wrapped it around my niece. Her face was waxen and her breath came in slow gasps. I held Harmony's hand and crooned those meaningless sounds we give each other to show love. Mitch kept working on her face until EMTs arrived and strapped her to a gurney.

It took every ounce of my strength to hold him then: he was frenzied as they lifted her and carried her to the service elevator. When the elevator doors closed, he began a heartbreaking howl. I tried to calm him, but I was only partially successful. I kept him next to me on a tight leash to look at Reno's apartment.

It had been searched with a rough and wild hand—drawers pulled out, Reno's tidy stacks of clothes on the floor, even the kitchen cupboards swept bare.

18

SAFE SPACE

IT WAS NEARLY dawn when Sergeant Abreu and Terry Finchley finished talking to me. They met me at the hospital, where the ER staff told me Harmony was suffering from shock, not from bullet wounds. They were giving her fluids and wanted her to rest overnight, but they let me go to her room and sit with her. Someone had cleaned the garbage from her hair and face. She looked heartbreakingly young and vulnerable.

When I took her hand, her eyes fluttered open. "Clarisse?"

"It's Vic, Harmony. Your auntie Vic."

Her eyes closed, as if she were retreating from me and the ugly present, but when I gently squeezed her fingers, she said, "I was dreaming about Henry and Clarisse."

"That's good," I said. "Henry and Clarisse are your safe place. I'm sorry to make you leave it, but I want to ask you a few questions. Can you remember what happened? You called me to say someone was breaking in."

"I could hear them at the back door." The monitors on her started beeping more loudly and a nurse came into the room, frowning at me for agitating the patient.

"I called you but then the noise and the shouting, I froze, it was like I was eight again in the shelter and me and Reno would hide to get away from Mom and her boyfriends. I—how could I—a grown-up person would have run out the front door and gotten help, but I hid like a chicken." She was starting to cry.

"Don't," I said. "You saved yourself. You did all the smart things. You called me, you put yourself in a space where your attackers couldn't get you. I think you were quite resourceful. I wouldn't even have looked in the garbage bin if Mitch hadn't sensed you were there."

Harmony's teeth were chattering; her hand in mine was cold again. The nurse told me I needed to go.

"No," Harmony whispered. "She's my auntie, I need her."

Finchley and Abreu came into the room at that moment, followed by another nurse who told them they couldn't disturb the patient.

"But the private eye can?" Finchley said. "I don't think so. If Ms. Seale can answer Warshawski's questions, she can answer mine."

Harmony gripped my fingers. "You're not leaving, are you?"

"Staying right here," I assured her.

"Ms. Seale, we aren't here to harass you," Finchley said, "but the more information you can give us right now, while the event is fresh in your mind, the better chance we have of catching whoever broke in. Did you see their faces?"

"I hid behind the kitchen door when they broke in and then I ran to the hall. I only saw their backs. They were huge, they were the biggest men I ever saw."

Prodded by Abreu, Harmony thought there'd been three men; they all wore black leather jackets and fur hats.

"Did you hear them talking?" Finchley asked.

"I was so scared all I heard was my heart, and then I was in the garbage bin and I guess I fainted."

"What can you remember, Ms. Seale?" Sergeant Abreu asked. "How did you know someone was trying to break in?"

"I was in bed, watching *People of Earth* on my tablet, and first I thought it was the soundtrack, then I realized someone was at the back door. I thought maybe it was Vern Wolferman, the super, you know, because the garbage for our floor, it goes in cans out by the elevator, but then the noise got louder, like something breaking, and I knew they were trying to get in, so I called Auntie Vic and then the rest happened."

"The rest?" Finchley said sharply.

"They broke out the lock or the door, I don't know which, and I ran into the hall and hid." Harmony's grip on my fingers tightened. For the rest of their questions, she kept her eyes on me and her hand tightly wrapped around mine.

Finchley wondered what the wreckers could have been looking for—drugs? That made Harmony angry: she and Reno never used, she'd told the police that already, and it was hard to keep talking to cops if cops kept accusing you of lying.

"We don't think you're lying, Ms. Seale," Sergeant Abreu said. "But you haven't seen your sister for a year. You don't know what the stress of being alone in this big city could have done to her."

"We were alone in Oakland and that was more stress than you've ever known, but we never used that stuff. Ever." Harmony's mouth set in a stubborn line. "We saw how fast girls fell apart when they used. We saw what happened to our mom."

They kept at it for a few more minutes, but the floor nurse made them leave as Harmony's blood pressure and pulse rose.

"Are you mad at me, Vic?" Harmony whispered when the police had left.

"Mad at you? Why on earth?"

"For—for saying Clarisse's name when it was you standing there."

"My mother has been dead for over thirty years, and she's still the person I want to wake up to when I'm in pain or grief," I said, bending to kiss her forehead. "You called for the person you need most."

"I was going to fly back in the morning and now I can't and I think—if I stay on—I can't stay in Reno's apartment."

"Of course you can't fly out today, and of course you'll stay with Mr. Contreras and me."

Abreu and Finchley were waiting for me outside Harmony's room, wanting to know what she'd confided in me.

"She misses her mother. Foster mother, the one who loved her. Not the birth mother."

"You think she knew the scum or knew why they were in the apartment?" Finchley asked.

"If she does, she's a better con artist than Bernie Madoff, and be-lieve me, nothing in her personal finances suggests she knows much more than how to sell a rosebush."

My offhand comment made me think of Leroy/Lawrence Fausson and the hoard under his floorboards. I couldn't imagine anything that would connect Reno to Fausson, nothing except me, but it made me wonder whether the sisters had a cash stash. Were the perps looking for hundred-dollar bills?

I'd lost track of what Finchley was saying, but he seemed to be read-ing my mind, or part of it: What did I really know about the sisters, and could Harmony have come out here to check on some scheme of Reno's that wasn't panning out?

"You still going to talk to Richard Yarborough tomorrow—today, I mean?" I said. "You'll find that's a theory that resonates well with him. Good night, or morning, whatever it is."

19

SPECIAL DELIVERY

MITCH WAS IN the Mustang. When we got home, I had to take him for a walk—he'd had a stressful night, first taking care of Harmony, then dealing with agitated cops, and finally being cooped up in a hospital garage.

It was five when I crawled into bed; it seemed a scant second later that my phone alarm woke me with the chipper message: *Your first meeting today, Monday, is at ten A.M. with Candra van Vliet at the Oriental Institute.*

I cursed in Italian, then English, and wished my Polish granny had taught me to swear in that language as well. I had completely forgotten the appointment. I reset the alarm for nine-forty-five—I would call then and say a family emergency required me to reschedule.

When I lay down, though, I couldn't relax. My right hip was throbbing after last night's frenzied action, reminding me that I'd been shot at as I left Lawrence Fausson's apartment.

There seemed to be a bizarre symmetry between Reno and Fausson. Both were connected to people who wanted to break into apartments and ransack them. Come to think of it, I didn't know whether the pair who'd attacked me last week actually searched Fausson's apartment. Maybe they'd gone there to shoot him and been disappointed not to find him, so they'd shot at me as their second choice.

I got reluctantly to my feet and turned on my espresso machine. When I went into the bathroom I saw that some of Harmony's trash bin had gotten stuck in my own hair. I jumped under the shower and scrubbed my hair until my scalp tingled. Maybe that would persuade my brain that I was alert enough to think.

Professor Van Vliet's voice on the phone Saturday had been cool, even arrogant, which made me dress as if I, too, were cool and potentially arrogant. I put on trousers and a sweater in navy cashmere, with a rose blazer whose severe cut balanced the soft color. The Lario boots I'd bought in Milan several years ago. A light dusting of makeup. When I looked in the hall mirror on my way out, my eyes still looked tired.

I stopped at Mr. Contreras's apartment long enough to give him a précis of last night's excitement and to let him know I wouldn't have time to walk the dogs this morning. Conversations with him are never short, but the idea that Harmony had been in danger, and needed a safe place to stay, roused his protective instincts. He started working out a bus route for getting to the hospital to collect her.

"I'll put her in a cab to bring her back here, won't make her stand on a street corner waiting for a bus, so you go talk to whoever you're chomping at the bit to get at and I'll take care of your niece."

I kissed him on the cheek and slipped out while he was deciding what tonight's dinner menu would be. I stopped at my office to print out copies of the pictures I'd taken at Fausson's apartment, as well as the group photo on his Facebook page.

I hadn't taken time for breakfast, but I didn't want to eat at the wheel and risk spilling food over my good clothes. I gobbled a banana and headed south to the University of Chicago.

I hadn't been in the neighborhood for several years. The university had gone on a building frenzy—new dorms, new apartments on the perimeter. It was just on ten when I found the sole parking garage for the campus. I jogged the half mile across the quads to the Oriental Institute. So much for cool and professional.

The Institute, its weathered stone draped in ivy, looks like a Hollywood idea of an academic building. Its narrow facade makes it seem smaller than it is, especially since its two neighbors are the massive university chapel and an outsize shrine to Chicago economics—God and Mammon facing off across the quad, with the Institute caught in their cross fire. Students and work crews sat on the benches between Mammon and the Oriental Institute, most hunkered in front of their devices, drinking coffee.

The Institute entryway was made of stone or concrete, and the lighting was about as bright as the interior of a pyramid. A student at the information desk didn't look up from his computer as I approached, even though the high ceilings amplified my footsteps.

"I have an appointment with Professor Van Vliet. You don't need to look at me, just tell me how to get to her office."

He pointed at the stairwell behind me. "Second floor, down the long hall, turn right, first door on your left. There's an elevator if you need it. And it's pronounced 'Flee-it,' not 'Vleet.'"

I thanked him meekly as I turned away. The stairs were worn and slippery. I held on to the railing after skidding on the landing.

When I reached Professor Van Vliet's office, she was talking to a balding sunburned man who was bent over her desk, looking at her computer screen.

"Where is Jamil these days?" the balding man asked.

"No one's heard from him in months. I am very much afraid—" She broke off when she caught sight of me. "Who are you?"

I could have gone back to sleep after all, but I walked into the office and handed her a card. "We have a meeting for ten o'clock."

Van Vliet glanced at the card. "Oh, yes. The detective."

She looked to be in her forties, her muddy blond hair pulled back into a chignon. Her skin wasn't as tanned as I would have expected for someone who spent her life under the desert sun, but she had squint lines around her eyes. As I'd guessed, she was dressed with a casual elegance: jeans, western boots and beaten silver belt buckle, with an expensive camel hair jacket over a skintight sweater.

"A detective?" the balding man said. "That's premature, Candra, and something I wish you'd spoken to me about first."

"I haven't called the police, Peter: this person says she has questions about Leroy Fausson."

"Fausson?" Peter's face twisted in puzzlement. "He hasn't been part of the Institute for years."

"Yes, which is why before I told her anything, I wanted to know more about who she is and why she is asking such questions. Ms."—Van Vliet looked at my card—"yes, Warshawski—this is Peter Sansen, the director of the Institute. So please tell us why you are asking questions about a man we have neither of us seen for some time."

"He's dead. Murdered."

Both archaeologists became quiet. I could hear phones ringing in other offices and the clanking of a radiator as the heat came on.

"On Saturday you said he was dead," Van Vliet said finally. "Why could you not say he was murdered? Where did this happen?"

That seemed like a strange question: not when, or how, but where. Like Felix, asking where he was from. "We don't know. His body was found in a forest preserve west of town, but he was killed elsewhere. Do you think you know where?"

Her eyes widened in hauteur. "Certainly not. As I said, I have seen nothing of Fausson, really since we evacuated our dig at Tell al-Sabbah. And that was when the civil war in Syria began to spread, so easily seven years ago."

"What made you come to us?" Sansen asked.

I pulled out Van Vliet's book on *Urban Development in the Chalcolithic* from my briefcase. "He had her book by his bed. We can't find out anything about him, where he worked, what his background is. He'd hung outsize photos of archaeology digs on the walls of his apartment, so when I found this book, I was hoping you'd know something about him."

"He stole this!" Van Vliet's eyes narrowed with contempt. "The Institute's collection doesn't circulate."

"Then you can reshelve it," I said. "What else can you tell me?"

Van Vliet spread her hands and I saw her rings, plain wedding band and a wide silver ring with turquoise insets. "He had been a graduate student here in archaeology, but at the time we evacuated, we had already told him we would not be able to renew his graduate fellowship. He didn't return to Chicago with the rest of us."

"You left Syria in 2011?" I asked.

"It was not until early 2012, in point of fact. Probably we should have left sooner—I sent most of our people home, but there were steps I needed to take to preserve—not the dig, that would not have been possible—but the artifacts. Perhaps it was foolhardy; my husband certainly thought so."

"He's an archaeologist as well?"

Van Vliet laughed derisively. "He would not thank you for that suggestion. No, he is a neurologist, and he sent me text after text telling me to leave Syria at once."

"We need to finish our own discussion, Candra," Sansen said, "so as soon as you've told this detective what she needs to know. . . ."

He didn't leave the room but leaned against a filing cabinet, which, like the rest of the surfaces in the office, was covered both with books and small artifacts. I'd seen only his right profile when he was at Van Vliet's desk, but now, his whole face revealed, I saw an ugly puckering along the right jawline and down along the neck. A burn wound, not recent but very visible.

I realized I was staring and looked quickly away—at a stone figurine with eight breasts holding down a stack of papers on Van Vliet's desk. She had horns sprouting from her head, which made up for a nearby cow, whose horns had broken off, leaving only two worn stubs.

I took out a notebook and tried to focus my attention. "Right. You canceled Fausson's fellowship. Why was that?"

Van Vliet steepled her fingers. "He didn't have a strong commitment to archaeology, that is, to the level of detail you need in the field. His interest lay in the romance of the Middle East. He wore a kaffiyeh, rode around the desert on a motorbike. He even learned to ride a camel. I suggested if he wanted a graduate degree, Middle Eastern politics would be more suitable, but I do not believe he has—had—the discipline necessary for scholarship."

Definitely Lawrence of Arabia. "How did he react to the news?"

"He was quite angry—yes, I think anger is not too strong a word, even though we had spoken about this matter many times during the two years he was at the Tell."

"Did he threaten violence against you or the dig?"

"He couldn't have threatened more violence than was already happening," the professor spoke bitterly. "You must remember that your country had by then invaded Iraq; we dealt constantly with refugees and with looters. Fausson did not threaten retaliation, if that is what you are asking."

"He spent two more years in the Middle East after you left. What would he have been doing?" I showed Van Vliet the pictures I'd taken of Fausson's passport stamps. Sansen stepped over to look.

"His Arabic was very good, if I recall correctly," Sansen said. "He might have been teaching English in these countries—there's always a demand for native speakers. He could even have become a tour guide for Americans, or enjoyed being a nomad on his motorcycle."

"He's dead, poor boy." Candra gave a tight smile. *Nil nisi bonum.* Let's just say he had great potential that he squandered."

"Is there anything else?" Sansen looked at his watch.

"Fausson had a collection of poetry by a Syrian named Kataba." I produced the book. "Could he have been working on a translation?"

She took the book from me. "Oh! Tarik Kataba."

When she pronounced the name, it sounded like a series of clicks. "Kataba was someone we met in Saraqib, but he ran afoul of the regime. I was afraid he had died, but someone told me they had seen him here in Chicago."

"Recently?"

She gave a tiny headshake, which made the gold spirals in her ears seem to spin. "Not in the last few weeks, but perhaps at Christmas? I don't remember."

"Fausson had a picture on his Facebook page taken at some kind of meeting. Is Kataba in the group?" I didn't try to pronounce the name as Van Vliet had.

Sansen and Van Vliet looked at the group shot I'd captured from Fausson's page.

"That is in fact Leroy Fausson." The professor tapped the man in the safari jacket.

She looked more closely at the faces, then pointed at a dark man in a plain white shirt standing in the back row. "This could be Kataba, but I met him only a few times. He had a bicycle repair shop in Saraqib and I took my own bike in there once to get a new tire. He also led tours of the region; perhaps that is how Leroy Fausson got to know him. When he should have been digging, Leroy was often out touring other villages."

She wasn't going to tell me directly why she had taken away Fausson's fellowship, but she kept giving side jabs that gave me a picture.

I put the Facebook picture on top of Kataba's poems. "The group was meeting somewhere; there's writing in Arabic on the walls. Can you read it?"

The professor rummaged on her desk for a magnifying glass and studied the posters. "They seem to be slogans: A CHILD CHASES A BUTTERFLY AND RELEASES A DREAM TO FOLLOW ALL ITS LIFE. SYRIA LIVES IN MY HEART, BUT MY HEART IS BIG AND CAN ALSO HOLD AMERICA. They could be lines from poems, especially if Kataba is in the group, but my modern Arabic is far from fluent, and I don't know contemporary poetry." She gave a wintry smile. "The wedding poem of Inanna and Dumuzi is as modern as I get. Not that it was written in Arabic, of course."

"I'll take your word for it. This woman was also in a photograph from the dig in Fausson's apartment." I tapped the freckled face. "Was she one of your students?"

Sansen bent over the picture, palms on Van Vliet's desk. "That's Mary-Carol, Mary-Carol Kooi. I didn't notice her at first. She did a very nice piece of work for her dissertation, even though her time at Tell al-Sabbah was cut short. She's working here as a postdoc. I didn't know she had stayed in touch with Fausson."

"Nor did I," the professor said. "Perhaps she thought we would judge her unkindly. I'm sorry not to be more helpful, Ms. Warshawski, but Director Sansen and I need to continue a conversation of our own."

Sansen straightened and held out a hand, but in the cramped space he managed to knock over the eight-breasted figurine. In his fluster to pick her up and make sure she wasn't damaged, he swept a box off the front of the desk. I lunged at it, but I only managed to grab one of the flaps. A grubby checked cloth fell out.

When I squatted to collect it, a metal figurine rolled out. It was about five inches high. When I looked at it closely, I saw it was a man with a giant fish draped so that the head lay across the man's head and the skin covered his shoulders and torso like a cloak.

20

THE FISH-MAN

I PICKED UP the checked cloth and handed cloth and fish-man to Van Vliet. She snatched the figure and studied it under her glass.

"I don't think it is damaged in any way," she finally said. "Really, Peter, for a man who can take a piece of pottery out of hard earth without leaving a scratch, how can you be so clumsy inside an office?"

"I need the desert air for scope," Sansen said, unrepentant.

"What is it?" I asked Van Vliet.

"We're not sure," she said. "That is, we know it is a figure that the Sumerians used in their dwellings. We know that their sages and deities included these half-fish, half-men in a group called the Seven Sages. We have sometimes seen them in castings of collections of deities and demons, with the fish-men standing at a sickbed. But beyond that we know very little of their function."

"Lawrence Fausson had a cloth like this in his closet," I ventured, holding out the checked fabric.

"Lawrence?" Van Vliet echoed. "You never met him, but you accept his Lawrence of Arabia persona? At any rate, this cloth is typical Syrian weaving. Leroy liked to wear them; it was part of his saying, 'I'm not like the rest of the colonial predators: I understand this land and these people.'"

"You don't think Fausson sent this statue to us, do you?" Sansen said to me.

"I don't know." I was taken aback. "When did you receive it?"

"It was here this morning, addressed to me, although my name was misspelled," Van Vliet said.

I'd dropped the box when I knelt to collect the figurine. PROFESSOR VAN FLEEAT was written across the top in block capitals, but there wasn't any address. I asked if there'd been packing paper around the box when she got it, but Van Vliet shook her head.

"Someone delivered it in person, but it must have been in the middle of the night," she said. "I asked the people in the mail room—the guard found it outside the front door when he arrived to unlock it."

"It can't have come from Fausson," I said. "He's been dead for a week now."

Whoever dropped it off took an enormous chance that it wouldn't be stolen. I suppose they could have lurked nearby to make sure only someone going into the Institute picked it up.

"I want to take this to the police to see if they can get prints from it, but you and Mr. Sansen would have to be printed. Did anyone else handle it?"

"The guard who unlocked the door and the clerk who delivered our mail this morning. Probably other people in the mail room."

"I don't think we're ready for police or fingerprints," Sansen said, "but you raise a good point, Ms. Warshawski. We'll put it in a box to keep anyone else from handling it."

I was going to argue the point: if it matched the calligraphy on the paper in Fausson's pocket, then the prints could tie back to Fausson's killer. But Felix's phone number was on a scrap in the sheriff's evidence lockup in the county headquarters in Maywood. Chicago cops would come to the Oriental Institute. By the time the two jurisdictions shared information, Felix might be a grandfather himself. Or more likely in prison for Fausson's murder.

Van Vliet made a call on her cell phone, asking the person at the other end for a nineteen-inch E-flute drop front, and then looked sternly at me. "If we need more professional advice on detection, we'll be in touch. Thank you for coming in."

I didn't take the hint. "If you need advice more professional than mine, you'd better call the cops. The cloth wrapping says it's someone who wants to make sure you know there's a Syrian connection."

"That doesn't narrow the field," Sansen said. "There are many people at the OI, at this institute, me included, who've spent decades in Syria. We all know a lot of Syrians, Lebanese, and Egyptians, along with Western scholars."

"Do you think this piece came from your dig at Tell al-Sabbah?"

"That is what the director and I were discussing when you arrived," Van Vliet said, reluctantly. "Neither of us has seen such a figurine before. We've encountered this image only in bas-reliefs and castings, sometimes in clay."

A woman in jeans and a sweatshirt with a mummy on it came in, holding a large gray box—the nineteen-inch E-flute drop front, I supposed. Van Vliet asked her to make a label, identifying the contents as the shipping container for the fish-man figurine.

"Date, context, as if we were in the field." She picked the box up by the edges and gently eased it into the E-flute.

The woman nodded and took the box away.

"Is this figurine valuable?" I asked.

Van Vliet made an impatient gesture. "Valuable to whom? To me, if it is authentic, it is a remarkable piece, but not valuable, because it has no provenance. The museum here at the Institute can't possibly display it. We don't know if it's stolen, we don't know if it's even Sumerian. It might be a copy made by a later artisan who was enamored of the fish-man idea. It could be from Turkey or some other place where the Sumerians established colonies. If it was stolen, was it last month, or last century? So for me, personally, it is a fascinating object but not valuable."

Van Vliet was doing a good job of making me realize how inadequate I would be at tracking ancient statues.

"We maintain databases of artifacts with other museums around the world," Sansen added in a kinder tone. "We can't query Syrian museums these days, for obvious reasons, but we can find out if anyone has a piece like this, or if a piece like this is on an international stolen objects watch list."

That did sound like my exit line. I stopped at the doorway to ask about Fausson's next of kin. "Who can I ask about Fausson's personnel file?"

"He wasn't on staff," Van Vliet said sharply.

"He was a student, right? He had to fill out forms. Someone on this campus has a record of his date of birth and mother and so on."

Sansen nodded grudgingly. "Mary-Carol Kooi can help you. She does some administrative work to augment her fellowship. Up the hall, fourth door on your right."

As I walked away I heard Van Vliet say, "Why did you give her permission to poke her nose into our affairs, Peter? You were the one who didn't want any calls to the police, after all."

I paused long enough to hear Sansen say, "Since when does a museum turn down free professional help, Candra?"

That didn't sound as though they were trying to hide, from the cops or from me.

When I went into Mary-Carol Kooi's office and introduced myself, she said yes, Peter Sansen had just sent her a text, she'd pull up Fausson's record for me. "Peter said he's the man who was murdered out in the forest preserve last week?"

"All the local news outlets put the reconstructed face out on their websites. You didn't recognize him?"

"I can't stand to watch the news, it's all so horrible," Kooi said. "Every time they show another site in Syria that's been bombed to oblivion, my heart breaks into new pieces. And every time they babble on about immigrants and ISIS I get too angry to watch. Do you know our stupid invasion of Iraq forced millions of Iraqis to flee? Over a million ended up in Syria. No wonder the country started falling apart. We want to put up walls or expel Muslims, and we created the biggest immigrant crisis in recent history all by ourselves."

She stopped and gave a self-conscious laugh. "Sorry. I get carried away. What was Lawrence doing out in a forest preserve? I thought he only liked desert hiking."

"He was murdered elsewhere; his body was moved there after he died. But we have zero information on him; that's why I badly need to talk to someone he might have been close to."

I gave her my phone number to text the file to me. "Professor Van Vliet said he'd lost his graduate fellowship, but did he come to the Institute when he got back to the States?"

"I think he came to see Candra van Vliet a few times, but that wasn't recently. He might have been arguing about his fellowship." She reddened. "I wasn't eavesdropping, but . . . I was passing her office and heard shouting, and . . ."

"Everyone stops to listen to a quarrel," I said. "It's not eavesdropping, just our biology."

Kooi made a face. "Maybe. Lawrence seemed to think he'd given her enough help on one of her papers that she should restore his fellowship."

I made a note of that, but I couldn't tell if it was important or not. "He got everyone to call him 'Lawrence,' not 'Leroy'?"

"Not just that, but it had to be 'Lawrence,' never 'Larry.' Candra called it an annoying affectation, but he was so young—immature in a particular way. As if he still wanted to live in a make-believe world, where he got to dress up in Arab clothes and play being T. E. Lawrence."

I nodded: the checkered headcloth and the way he'd worn his hair, parted far down on the right side—it was as if he had decided to dress up as Lawrence of Arabia for Halloween.

I asked Kooi if she'd been to Fausson's apartment on Higgins Road.

When she bristled defensively, I said, "He had a picture up on the wall, I guess of your dig at Tell al-Sabbah, and you were one of the people in it, so I was hoping you knew him well enough to talk about him."

I pulled out another print of the photo in Fausson's bedroom and handed it to her. Mary-Carol got up to look at it.

"Oh, my." Kooi's face lit up. "That's Khaddam." She pointed at one of the Middle Easterners next to Fausson.

"He was like an old-fashioned sage—he knew the weather by the taste of the wind, and he was wrong only once that I can remember. When we had a sandstorm, he knew it was coming days before it hit and showed us how to tie up our clothes and protect our water supply."

Her bright expression turned to worry. "I hope he's surviving. It's impossible to get news about any of our people."

"Fausson has a picture on his Facebook page that includes you with a group of mostly Middle Easterners. Were they people you worked with in Syria?" I handed her the print I'd downloaded from Fausson's site.

Kooi frowned over it. "Oh, that—no. For a while I was going to this one Syrian community center to speak Arabic. They have classes in language and culture so that their kids can grow up speaking it, or at least hearing it, and I was trying to keep up with my Arabic, but it's out in Palos, and the commute was more than I could handle. Lawrence's Arabic was so good the Syrian parents actually had him coaching some of the teens in poetry."

She pointed at the same figure Candra van Vliet had noticed. "That's Tarik Kataba. Lawrence used to brag about knowing him."

"The center is in Palos?" I said. "Fausson's body was found in a forest preserve near there. Would he have run afoul of someone at the center?"

Kooi drew herself up to her full height, about five foot two. "If you're trying to suggest that ISIS is active in the Syrian refugee and immigrant community, then you're as bad as ICE. Do they farm out their investigations to private contractors, like they did with Blackwater in Iraq?"

I tried not to grind my teeth, at least not audibly. "People run afoul of each other all the time, and even, sad to report, murder each other, without being part of ISIS, the Nazis, the KKK, or any other extremist group. Maybe Fausson stole someone's girlfriend or first edition of Kataba's poems. Lesser insults than that have inflamed passions to the point of murder. Did Fausson tend to make the people around him angry?"

When Kooi flushed and hesitated, I added, "The way Professor Van Vliet spoke about him, I got the feeling he'd annoyed her."

"You're not saying Candra killed him, I hope!" Mary-Carol exclaimed.

My sleepless night and worry about Harmony were making me clumsy. "I'm doing a great job of annoying you, and I'm not part of a terrorist group. Nor part of ICE. Let me try again. You knew Mr. Fausson, I didn't. What was he like? He obviously loved archaeology, or at least he loved the place in Syria where you were digging. But did he annoy his fellow diggers? Did he upset people like Mr. Khaddam?"

Kooi gave a reluctant smile. "No, no: Khaddam and the other men in the village, they liked Lawrence to hang out with them. It was like a coup for them, you know—an American who listened to them and wanted to learn the local customs."

"Surely that isn't why the Institute ended his fellowship," I said.

Kooi scowled at the pictures I'd handed her, not angry, just debating with herself. "Peter seems to think you're okay. I guess it's okay if I tell you what I know."

LAWRENCE OF CHICAGO

MARY-CAROL AGREED IT would be easier to talk over lunch, away from the Institute. We went to an indie place across the street, where the lunchtime crush meant a long wait for coffee and food.

It was hard to stay focused on questions and answers on my lone-banana breakfast. I heard that fasting is the new fad in Silicon Valley: apparently the competitive engineers out there think the no-food diet enhances creativity. They compete to see who can go the longest without food. I guess that's why I'm a detective, not an engineer. Only an iron discipline kept me from stealing food from the adjacent table while I waited for my own order.

"Lawrence got a job as a janitor when he came back," Mary-Carol said. "He was such a weird guy, I almost thought he took menial labor to shame Candra and Peter Sansen. You know—the Oriental Institute only prepares you to clean toilets."

Although she didn't know where he'd worked, Kooi said she thought it was for a big industrial firm. "A lot of the Syrians out at the Palos Center do that work, since you don't need English and a lot of places like that don't ask about your papers. Lawrence probably liked pretending to be a Syrian refugee himself."

"It doesn't sound as though you liked him," I said.

She flushed. "I'm sorry—I know he's dead—I did like him, when we were in the field, but when I saw him in Chicago he seemed to have a chip on his shoulder."

I asked for a contact at the Syrian community center, at which she bristled: I couldn't put the refugees and immigrants who met there at risk.

"I don't know you," Kooi protested. "I could be betraying—"

"Palos isn't a big place," I said wearily. "I can find the center easily. A contact would be a help, but it's not essential."

Kooi sighed, as if she'd admitted defeat in a larger battle, but she gave me the names of the woman who ran the center and the man who organized the language classes.

My omelet arrived and I began to feel more human. We ground through my questions: Fausson didn't have a family, according to the records in Mary-Carol's office. He'd listed Candra van Vliet as his next of kin. He'd grown up in New Mexico; his parents had been linguists who worked with the Hopi, studying their language. He'd been in college when his parents' small plane had crashed in the Santa Fe National Forest, killing them both.

"He felt closer to Van Vliet than she to him, apparently," I said. "What went wrong in Syria?"

Mary-Carol Kooi stirred her soup so violently that tomato splotches flew onto the table. "Candra said he wasn't cut out for fieldwork. It made me angry at the time. Lawrence loved artifacts and knew more about them than anyone on the dig, except Candra, of course. It wasn't until later that I realized she was right, that he didn't have the discipline to stick with the hard work."

"What? Cooking and cleaning, those kinds of things?"

"No, no. We all pitched in, some more than others, of course, but even if Lawrence had wanted to be a lion king, so to speak, Candra wouldn't have tolerated it. But he loved showing newbies the ropes.

"When I first got out to the field, I turned to him because he had such great morale when we contracted shigellosis or pined for a real bath. One of the older women told me she could tell the newcomers a mile off by how they reacted to Lawrence."

Mary-Carol blushed painfully. "And you might as well know before you ask, we were lovers for a while. Not long, nothing lasted long there, except the land itself, of course, and the pottery shards. . . ."

Her voice trailed off; she was remembering her time in the desert, the affair with Fausson, when life had been physically hard but emotionally pleasing.

"Where did Fausson lack discipline?" I prodded her.

"The finicky work—pick a shard out of the ground, brush it off, see if you can fit it with another shard someone else found nearby—he, well, he shirked his share, to be honest. I was defending him for the longest time, I didn't want to feel like I'd been a fool for sleeping with him, of course, but I finally had to agree with Candra and the others.

"What Lawrence wanted was a big find, a tomb with intact pottery and statuary, something that would get him an international name fast. He used to leave Tell al-Sabbah, go off in the desert with a local guide, like Khaddam, or even once or twice with Kataba, and be gone for days. You have to be a team player if you're part of a dig."

I thought of the money hoard in Fausson's apartment. "He stayed on in the Middle East for two years after the rest of you came home, traveling to most of the Arab countries. Do you think he'd found his tomb and was selling the contents around the region?"

Mary-Carol seemed shocked at the suggestion. "But the provenance! He would never dismantle a tell. He placed too high a value on the history. You never knew him, but you feel free to accuse him of a serious crime!"

"Lawrence lived very frugally, but he had a lot of cash. I wondered if he sold artifacts that he'd brought back with him."

"He wouldn't!" Kooi was vehement. "It would be sacrilege."

"He'd lost his fellowship; he had to change his expectations," I suggested.

"He could have been finding a rich sponsor," Kooi said. "All that time he stayed on in the Middle East after Candra left, he could have found someone. Those oil and mineral sheikhs have money to burn but no glory. Their name on a big find would excite them."

In my mind's eye I saw Omar Sharif, heat shimmering around his flashing black eyes, riding his camel in *Lawrence of Arabia*.

"Word of something like that would get around," I objected.

"Not with all the wars going on over there," Mary-Carol said. "He'd keep a new dig a secret as long as possible to protect it from looters. Why are you trying to connect his death to archaeology, anyway? How do you know he wasn't attacked by gangbangers?"

"He died from a deliberate beating," I said. "Not a random jumping by strangers. His body was found in a forest preserve not far from Palos."

When that sank in, Mary-Carol was angry. "That's an outrageous accusation, that the Syrians killed him."

"I'm not saying it, especially since I only learned about the Syrian center from you five minutes ago. But it suggests a connection to his work in Syria. Someone he met, something he saw—could he have been blackmailing someone?"

"Even if I could imagine Lawrence doing such a thing, no one in the Syrian immigrant community could afford to pay off a blackmailer." Kooi was scornful. "No one in the Oriental Institute, either, for that matter. And Candra, she has money, but she would never give in to blackmail."

"Professor Sansen wondered if Mr. Fausson had sent the artifact that showed up at the Institute this morning," I said. "That bronze fish-man. The timing isn't right—it was delivered by hand, and Fausson's been dead for a week—but could it have been something he found?"

"That's the whole point about Lawrence," Mary-Carol said. "He wouldn't have dug up something like that and sent it off without documenting its provenance, especially if it could get him the recognition he wanted. You didn't find photos or documents like that with the money, or in his computer?"

His computer. I'd forgotten it in the middle of the drama around Harmony and Reno.

"His computer took a bullet for me. My tech master is trying to reconstruct the hard drive."

Kooi didn't seem curious about the bullet—or about Lawrence's cash, for that matter. His personality occupied too much of her mind.

Mary-Carol wrapped half her sandwich in a napkin: she had to get back to work. "You think he's guilty of some crime, don't you?" she said as we left the café.

"I don't think anything because I don't have enough data. A cash hoard is often associated with drug deals, and your friend did spend time in one of the world's heroin capitals, but I didn't see any signs of using in his apartment. He could have been holding the money for someone else, though. Maybe his Syrian friends got him to smuggle cash out of the country so they'd have a nest egg when they got here."

Kooi brightened. "That sounds much more like him. Especially if Kataba was involved. Lawrence idolizes—idolized poets."

My mouth twisted in a wry smile. "We've come up with half a dozen theories but no facts. It's like, I don't know, imagining a dig but not having a single piece of pottery in your hands. Detecting is like archaeology, I guess—we need facts and we need a context for them before they have any value."

We'd reached the museum entrance. I handed her one of my cards. "Call if something else occurs to you. Or if you need my help."

2 2

OUTREACH

AS I TRUDGED across campus to the parking garage, I wondered when the Silicon Valley tycoons would decide that sleep deprivation enhanced creativity, especially when combined with starvation.

I had a long to-do list: I needed to call Mr. Contreras to make sure he and Harmony had made it home safely. I needed to call Sergeant Abreu to see if the cops had turned up any leads on who had broken into Reno's apartment. I needed to go to my office and do work for my paying clients.

I also needed to stay awake behind the wheel. When I climbed into my car, I figured if I shut my eyes for five minutes, I'd be able to tackle everything.

My phone roused me from such a deep sleep that I thrashed around wildly in the car, trying to figure out where I was. I banged my knees into the steering wheel; the pain focused my mind. Car, U of Chicago parking garage, one in the afternoon.

By the time I'd found my phone and woken up enough to remember where I was, my caller had hung up. It was Glynis Hadden, my ex's secretary. She hadn't left a voice message, and I didn't want to talk to her, anyway—I was sure she only wanted to complain about Finchley arriving at Crawford, Mead's offices this morning. Still, it was just as well she'd called—I'd been asleep for almost an hour. My mouth felt as though it had been stuffed with cotton, and my knees were like the Tin Man's without his oil can.

I extracted myself from the Mustang, stretched until my legs and shoulders agreed that I could drive, and returned to my office. Brushed my teeth. Picked up a couple of cortados from the coffee bar across the street and buckled down.

Before starting work on Darraugh Graham's queries, I checked in with Mr. Contreras. He and Harmony had made it home without incident. She was in bed, worn out from last night's stresses and the fact that no one can sleep in a hospital.

I talked to Sergeant Abreu. She said they figured someone had buzzed the invaders into the building. "No one will admit doing it, of course, but none of the outside doors had been forced open. We picked up some possible images from a security camera at the bank on the other side of the street. We wanted to show them to Ms. Seale, to see if they strike any kind of chord with her, but she'd left the hospital and we don't know where to find her."

I gave Abreu Mr. Contreras's phone number.

I looked at my notes for Darraugh. This was a project that would require close concentration; I'd get up early tomorrow to tackle it with all my wits about me. This afternoon, before rush hour traffic became impenetrable, I was going out to the community center in Palos Park, where Lawrence Fausson had taught Arabic poetry to Syrian teens.

The Syrian-Lebanese Community Outreach Center, on 124th Street, rented space in the town's old Carnegie Library. Like other Carnegies, the building looked like a small temple. Carnegie had believed in the power of reading to change lives, so I suppose his libraries were designed to look like temples of learning.

I climbed a flight of worn stone stairs, passed between the concrete pillars and into the entryway. Flyers in a rack near the door advertised everything from AA meetings to Zumba dance sessions. Signs to the Syrian-Lebanese Community Outreach Center pointed me to the basement, where the community rented a small room for meditation and prayer, and two larger ones for classes and community events.

A schedule was taped to the events room door. Tonight there would be adult literacy classes with ESL tutors. Tomorrow night was a program on how to find help in the Chicagoland area. Thursday a chance for training on how to apply for jobs and conduct interviews. Arabic movies on Sunday afternoon. Arabic classes for different age levels on Wednesday evenings and Sunday mornings, Qur'an studies on Wednesday evenings.

Anyone with questions should text or phone Sanjiiya Yaziki, the administrative director of the center; she could help set up a program for groups wishing to use the center. That was the name of the woman Mary-Carol had given me.

The door was unlocked. No one was at the desk near the entrance, but I could hear banging from the back of the room. I threaded my way through a set of bookstacks and came on the space I'd seen on Lawrence Fausson's Facebook page. It looked as though they hadn't changed the posters or the children's artwork in the intervening year.

A woman of about forty, wearing an embroidered lavender head scarf over Western clothes, was taking folding chairs from a dolly and setting them up around two deal tables. She was slamming them open with a force that showed she wasn't happy with the job.

"Are you Sanjiiya Yaziki?" I asked, taking a chair, and hoping I'd pronounced the name in a recognizable manner. "Can I help you?"

"Oh!" She straightened up, her cheeks rosy. "You startled me! The teens are supposed to be taking care of setting up, but of course they'd rather be in the mall or kicking a football."

I took a chair and opened it. "How many do you need?"

While I opened another seven chairs and pushed the dolly to rest against a far wall, the woman went to a cupboard for paper and pencils. Another door led from the side of the room to a tiny kitchen, where she filled pitchers with water. I carried those to the tables for her. When we'd finished with the setup, she finally asked who I was and what I wanted.

I gave her a card. "I'm a private investigator. I've come here because of Lawrence Fausson. You know he was murdered, don't you?"

"Lawrence," Yaziki said softly. She pronounced it as my anonymous caller had, as "Elorenze."

"I saw the news. It was so strange, so unbelievable that a man that gentle could be murdered. And yet, in Syria every day small children are killed, so I suppose nothing violent in this world is unbelievable."

"He taught here, didn't he?" I asked, sitting in one of the chairs.

Yaziki nodded. "He loved Arabic deeply, it was as if he tried to make it his first language, not his second. He read so much Arabic literature—" She swept an arm toward the bookshelves. "He even used to buy books for us when he found we didn't have this poet or that historian. He was impatient with the teenagers for not caring more about their native poetry. They prefer modern music and verse. It's understandable.

"The old people loved his classes. They loved hearing him recite in classical Arabic, especially the women, who feel lonely as their children become fluent in English and don't speak Arabic at home."

"Did any of your people have theories about who might have murdered him?" I asked.

"Some of our members think it was revenge from your immigration authorities because of the work Elorenze did with the Syrian community in Chicago." Yaziki cast a sidelong glance to see how I'd react to that rumor.

"It's possible he enraged ICE agents," I said, "but they would have shot him, not beaten him so savagely."

"And you? Why are you here talking to me?"

"I'm trying to find someone who can put him into a context for me," I said. "A job, a girlfriend, anything where I could start talking to people, so I can learn who was angry enough with him to kick him to death."

I pulled out another print of the picture in the community events room and tapped Mary-Carol Kooi's face. "She told me about his coming here to teach Arabic."

Yaziki took the print from me, her expression softening. "I took this picture. We were having a small party for two men who had passed their GED exams."

"Mary-Carol Kooi told me she thought he was working as a janitor at the same place as some of the men from your center. If you know where they work, could you tell me? Please? Or let me talk to them directly."

Yaziki's face hardened again. "Mary-Carol Kooi has not been here for many months; why is she suddenly sending you here? And why are you caring about Elorenze's death? Perhaps you yourself are working for the American government, wanting to catch undocumented people?"

I started to bristle, then I thought of ICE agents descending on 7-Elevens and arresting hundreds of employees. Of the mothers detained in front of their children, of chemistry professors arrested as they buckled their daughters into their car seats. We had become a nation of bullies.

"A young man, the nephew of a beloved friend, was brought in for questioning by the police. His phone number was found in Mr. Fausson's pocket and so the police think he was involved in Fausson's death. They're not looking any further for a killer."

I brought Felix's picture up on my phone and showed it to Yaziki. "Has he ever come around here?"

She frowned over it. "Is he Syrian?"

"He's Canadian, but his family is from Middle Europe, not the Middle East."

She smiled briefly. "He's a Jew? He could pass for an Arab. Of course, I could pass for a European. We all worry too much about these identities."

The inch or so of hair that appeared underneath her head scarf was light brown, and her face had that cream-and-rose-petal coloring beloved of romance novelists.

"What was your Jewish friend doing here?" Yaziki asked.

"I don't know that he was; I'm just trying to find out how his and Fausson's lives connected."

Yaziki shook her head slightly. "He looks vaguely familiar, but if he came it wouldn't have been for any regular meeting. Maybe a special program?"

"He's an engineering student interested in desert water systems," I said. "Do you hold workshops on topics that would be helpful for people's families back home?"

"This is my home, our home," Yaziki said sharply. "Our workshops help our community adjust and adapt to their new country."

"So no engineering workshops," I said, putting my phone away.

Yaziki eyed me narrowly, as if trying to fathom my hidden motives in asking the question. "Some of our members are engineers or engineering students themselves; perhaps one of them brought him. My ESL students are arriving soon, so I must ask you to leave; they will be afraid that you are from the government."

I got up. "I still want to talk to someone who might know where Lawrence was working."

"I will ask," Yaziki said. "I think it is safer, easier if you don't speak to anyone directly."

"What about Tarik Kataba, the poet?" I said. "Fausson had his collected poems at his bedside and Mary-Carol Kooi said they knew each other from Fausson's time in Syria."

Yaziki's smile became wooden. "It has been many months since I last saw Sayyid Kataba. I could not tell you how to find him."

I tried to think of something to persuade her that I was on the side of truth and justice, not rounding up immigrants for ICE. Before anything occurred to me, the first of the ESL students arrived, two women in black abayas, their heads draped in black, along with a younger woman in skintight blue jeans and an ORLAND PARK HIGH SCHOOL sweatshirt. All three were chatting and laughing in Arabic but stopped when they saw me.

Yaziki greeted them in Arabic; they nodded and sat down, pulling out workbooks and exercise sheets. It was clearly time for me to leave.

23

PAY STUB

I WAS ONLY a few miles from where Lawrence Fausson's body had been found, which made me think there had to be a connection between the community center and his murder. Sajiiya Yaziki didn't trust me—why should she, since she'd never met me or heard of me? But the center was close to Cap Sauers Holding, where Fausson's body had been discarded. Despite Yaziki's protests, I couldn't believe there was no connection between these two places.

I'd grown up in the world of immigrants, mostly the Poles on the Southeast Side, but also with the Italians who were my mother's friends. I know how immigrant communities close ranks against authority from the big Angloworld—you protect your own, even when your own are sleazebags.

That's why I didn't have a high expectation that Yaziki would get back to me about where Lawrence Fausson had worked. She was protecting the people in her community who could be deported at any second. I didn't exactly blame her, but it was maddening that I couldn't persuade her to help me.

Because I was nearby and didn't know what to do next, I drove to Cap Sauers Holding. I wasn't sure I could find the place where we'd parked, let alone the path through the woods themselves, but it turned out to be easy: the shoulder where the cop cars, ambulances, tech teams, and so on had parked was a mess of mud churned with yellow crime scene tape, cigarette butts, and crumpled chip bags.

I pulled onto a patch of gravel near the road to keep my own wheels from sinking into the muck. It was close to five, meaning I had about an hour more of daylight, but on a gray afternoon in a forest, that didn't count for much. My work flash gave better light than my phone, so I took that from the go-bag in my trunk. I'd left my windbreaker in the car when I visited Professor Van Vliet this morning; I put that on.

The narrow trail that Felix and I had followed with so much difficulty had been widened by the number of people tramping through with equipment. The wider path ended near the giant tree, which was still marked, at least sort of, with crime scene tape—they'd tacked it to stakes in a circle around the tree, but the wind had blown enough of it free that the tape was now one more piece of plastic littering the woods.

I shone my flash around as I walked the perimeter. All the coming and going had left bare patches in the heavy leaf cover, but a week of drizzle had melted most of the footprints. My fantasy that I might find a clue the crime scene techs had overlooked was just that, a fantasy.

I crossed the tape to study the tree itself. The trunk had sunk a few inches into leaf mold, making it easy for the killers to shove a body into the hollowed-out core. Roots stuck out at wild angles, like the fingers of an arthritic giant. The trunk base rose higher than my waist, with the core perhaps a yard across. Insects were busy in the rusty outer bark. A detective is never squeamish, so I tried not to mind the mud, the bugs, the squishiness of the whole scene, as I squatted to look inside.

Tendrils brushed my face as I stuck a tentative arm inside. The light, my arm, stirred an angry outcry. A brown creature hurled itself at me.

I jumped back. Brushed my face and arms wildly, trying to make sure nothing was clinging to me. A few yards away, a squirrel snapped its tail, chattering loudly.

"Your home, huh?" I said, trying to calm myself. "You have a right to defend it from giants, I guess."

The squirrel darted away, started up a tree, saw I wasn't following, and raced back to threaten me again. He must have a family inside.

"I know," I said to him. "You have a Fourth Amendment right to be secure in your own home. What did you do when the killers brought Lawrence Fausson here? Did you bite any of them? Take selfies?"

I shone my flash around the rotting leaves at the base of the tree, not wanting to kneel on top of another squirrel or a snake in my good trousers. Even in jeans I wouldn't have enjoyed it. I wondered if snakes and squirrels cohabited. There were so many things I didn't know about the world around me. What kind of detective was I, really?

I spread my windbreaker across the leaves, shone my flash directly in the squirrel's eyes so that he backed farther away, and lay flat, looking into the heart of the trunk.

I scooted forward until I could shine the flash around the interior. The hollowed innards extended a good ten feet from the base. The sides were black, pockmarked with insect holes. The squirrel nest was at the far end of the hollow core, about a yard from my outstretched arm. The mother was screeching, darting toward me and away.

I backed out and found a long stick to use as a prod. When I returned to the log, my Achilles tendons tingled where they were exposed to the male's sharp teeth.

"Sorry," I muttered, pushing the female from her nest.

It was a disheveled mess of twigs and leaves, unlike the tidy weaving done by birds. Pieces of fabric were twined around some of the twigs. I inched forward, terrified of what else I might find, but no human bodies lay inside the log. No naked squirming squirrel babies, either, thank goodness: the female hadn't yet given birth.

Using the stick, I pulled the mess toward me and inched back out of the log. I sifted through the dirty leaves and twigs but didn't find anything of interest. There were several scraps of fabric, one longish silky strand in a bright blue. The others were khaki canvas, the kind used in backpacks. The light was fading; I shone my flashlight on the biggest scrap, which looked like a corner piece. When I turned it over in my hands, shreds of paper came loose and fluttered to the ground.

One was torn from a check showing a bit of the payer's name, "Force 5 Ind." The other was a receipt fragment headed "mascus

Gat" in faded print with a partial date, February 27, the year missing. Someone had ordered $18.37 in carryout food.

I stared for a moment. "mascus Gat"—I knew that name. Yes, the Damascus Gate on Austin. Lawrence Fausson had had a receipt from the restaurant next to his bed.

I moved slowly away from the log, away from the male squirrel (who was holding his ground a few yards distant), shining my flash up and down the underbrush, hoping for more fragments. By now it was dark enough that I could barely make out the yellow crime scene tape; I'd have to come back in daylight if I hoped to find anything else.

I pocketed the paper and the canvas, bundled the leaves and twigs and the long strand of royal-blue silk back together and poked them into the log with my stick. "Sorry for wrecking your home, ma'am," I said to the squirrel. "I hope you can rebuild with these." I felt as though I should give them something to make up for the canvas I'd filched, so I took some tissues from my pocket and stuffed them into the log as well.

As I walked away, the male flicked his tail repeatedly and read me the riot act in the sternest possible language. He took my departure as a sign of surrender and ran back into his hideout.

The brambles that tangled me on my trip out here last week with Felix caught in my trousers. I cried out when a thorn pierced me—the woods taking their revenge on me for disturbing the squirrels' nest.

It was five-thirty now. No matter what route I took to the city, the traffic would be glue. I drove into Orland Park, a nearby suburb, and found the modern library that had replaced the old Carnegie building. I curled up in an armchair and looked up Force 5 Ind.

Force 5 Industrial Cleaners, their slogan: "We Chase Dirt with Tornado-like Force." Their offices were on the northwest side, about two miles from Lawrence Fausson's apartment. When I called, I got one of those annoying messages: *Our menu has changed so that we may drive you to the brink of insanity.* If I was looking for a cleaning crew; complaining about breakage or theft; worried about nuclear war . . .

It was after business hours, but if they were industrial cleaners, they worked at night. I tried different menu options and finally was connected to a live human.

"This is Detective Warshawski," I said. "We're trying to track down some of Lawrence Fausson's co-workers."

The live human couldn't or wouldn't help me; she was only there to take messages and call team supervisors if a team member was calling in sick.

"This particular team member called in dead," I said. "Put me through to the supervisor for his group, please."

In a few minutes I was speaking to Melanie Duarte. She was annoyingly cautious. Yes, she knew who Lawrence Fausson was; she knew he had died. No, she couldn't tell me where he'd worked. If I had a subpoena and presented it to her boss, her boss would tell her if it was all right to cooperate with me. It was the kind of precaution everyone ought to take to avoid scams, but it made my job harder.

I got her boss's name, Pablo Molita, but before she hung up, I asked if she accompanied her crew to the job site.

"If it's a big job, yes. If it's a small job, I come by to inspect it when they're done."

"Was Lawrence Fausson's assignment at a big or small site?"

"You talk to Mr. Molita. If you have the right documents, he'll tell you what you're trying to find out."

She cut the connection. I leaned back in the chair. How much energy did I want to put into this problem? My catnap on the U of C campus had been five hours ago and exhaustion was overwhelming me. The library chair was padded, and I started drifting off to sleep.

As if she'd timed it, Lotty called me. "Victoria—I just heard from Martha Simone. The police came to the IIT campus this afternoon and took Felix in for more questioning."

"The city or the county?" I asked.

"I don't know. Does it matter?" Her voice had an edge.

"Only in the bigger scheme of things. Sorry, Lotty. Is Martha with him?"

"She's with him, but she says they are close to charging him with this man Fausson's murder. I thought you were going to be helping him, but you haven't done anything." She was fighting panic, which made her angry.

"I'll talk to Martha," I promised. "I'm struggling to get a toehold on Fausson's life, but I'll put more energy into it."

I texted Martha Simone, who called me almost instantly. "Vic, things are worrying, but not desperate. We're in Maywood. Lieutenant McGivney and some of his crew are questioning Felix about his trip last week to northern Minnesota. ICE reported that he had multiple border crossings, so the sheriff wants to claim that he was disposing of evidence somewhere in the north woods. Felix is refusing to tell me what he was actually doing there. He says he was camping with friends, but he refuses to name his friends."

"Does he have to? Why can't a person go off to the north woods without the Cook County sheriff and the U.S. Immigration and Customs service getting their noses in a knot?"

"I agree," Simone said. "But in the circumstances, it would be helpful if he could say or do something that would keep him out of prison. Even in late March, it's cold and snowy in the Boundary Waters; everyone, I'm afraid, including me, is having a hard time believing he took a vacation up there. Especially in the middle of term time."

"Right now I'm on the trail of some of Fausson's co-workers," I said. "It's been a slow slog, trying to find anyone who knew him well. Can you spin that into something about his last known associates starting to emerge?"

"Better than nothing," Simone agreed. "Call as soon as you have a name. Any name."

She cut the connection. I felt panicky, not good for an investigator.

I drove back to the Syrian-Lebanese Community Outreach Center. If the ESL classes were still going on, I'd see if anyone would admit to working for Force 5. It wasn't a great idea, but it was the only one I had.

2 4

HITCHHIKING

LIGHT STREAMED FROM the basement windows at the center when I pulled up across the street. A few people were leaving the building, little knots of women laughing and gesturing to each other, but four men stood at the curb. I was getting out of my car to approach them when a grimy van arrived. Under the dirt and the dents was a drawing of a tornado funnel and the announcement that this was Force 5, with their web address and phone number. An overweight man in a Bears jacket climbed down from the driver's side and lumbered over to the back of the van to open the doors. The men climbed inside.

I shut the Mustang door and drove to the end of the street before making a U and following them into traffic. The van made another stop, at a street corner in Oak Lawn, and then turned onto the Stevenson Expressway. Rush hour, poor visibility, I had to stay closer than I liked.

I kept the radio tuned to the news, in case a report came in about Felix. More shootings on the South and West Sides—hurray for a government that lets every citizen arm themselves with enough weapons to kill us all five or six times over. Nothing about Felix.

At the bottom of the hour, there was a brief human interest story about the fish-man I'd seen this morning at the Oriental Institute.

"We can't add it to our collection," Institute director Peter Sansen explained. "We don't know anything about its history, including whether it's stolen or looted. We've sent photographs to Interpol's art crime division and we're comparing them to international databases as well, but it's an intriguing piece. We're glad to have the opportunity to study it."

And then back to somber news—the firing of all scientists from the EPA, nuclear threats, droughts, floods, avalanches. Shooting in progress on East Eighty-Ninth Street, a hop away from my childhood home.

The van exited at Damen Avenue and went north, into Pilsen, the heart of Chicago's Mexican community. This was an area I could get to easily by bus. When the van stopped at Eighteenth and Ashland, I was ready; I took my wallet from my handbag, pulled into a parking space, and flung briefcase and handbag into the trunk. I scrambled into the back of the van with the two other people who were joining it.

The back was crowded; before the doors slammed shut, I could see perhaps a dozen people on the benches that lined the sides. Another eight or ten of us were jammed into the middle, standing.

It was dark inside, but everyone noticed the stranger. Voices called to me in Spanish and, I presumed, Arabic.

"*Mi dispiace*," I apologized in Italian. "I don't speak Spanish or Arabic. My name is Victoria."

Two women's voices answered from the depths of the van, announcing their own names, and then the men chimed in. I could hear a fan whirring in the roof, but with so many of us crammed together it wasn't easy to breathe. Unwashed clothes and bodies created a challenge all their own. I felt lucky to be standing at the rear. With the three people closest to me, I kept my nose near the seam in the back doors.

There isn't a street in Chicago without potholes, and our driver seemed determined to hit all of them. He slammed his brakes at each stop sign. A final halt: the regulars knew by sixth sense we were at our destination; I could feel them gathering jackets and handbags, pushing toward the exit. When the doors opened, I moved aside, not wanting to be the first out, showing a stranger's face to the man in the Bears jacket. I could see lights and the facade of a high-rise, glass glistening in the rain.

People tried to move toward the building entrance to get away from the rain, but the Bears jacket pushed them back toward the street. "Youse know the drill, line up while Melanie calls your name."

Melanie? It had to be Melanie Duarte, whom I'd spoken to earlier. I waited until most of the people had exited before climbing down. I pulled my windbreaker over my head and huddled near the end of the line. I couldn't really hide—I was about the tallest person there.

A woman appeared with a clipboard and an umbrella. The Bears jacket shone a flash on the inside, found someone's sack lunch, handed it to Melanie, and slammed the doors shut. "See youse at one-thirty," he growled. A true local. Only on Chicago's South Side do people call each other "youse."

Melanie began reading off names, ticking them on the board. Each person shouted "here" before moving forward to the high-rise. At the end, only I was left.

"And you are?"

"Victoria. Victoria Fausson."

"You're not on the—" She did a double take. "What last name?"

"Fausson," I repeated, spelling it out. "You recognize the name, I take it?"

"How did you get on this van?" she demanded.

"I was told I could pick it up at Eighteenth and Ashland. So that's what I did."

"You can't work here," she announced. "You're not in the system."

I didn't respond. I couldn't respond. We were in front of the Grommet Building. During the day, the curved glass facade reflected the changing light over the river and the traffic roaring over the Wells Street Bridge. At night, the reflected headlights swooped in and out, the cars and trucks invisible in the night-blackened glass.

My brain seemed similarly untethered. The Grommet Building is where my ex-husband's law firm leases seven floors. Richard Yarborough and Lawrence Fausson—they couldn't be connected. A fluke. Someone had to clean the Grommet Building, but when Mary-Carol Kooi at the Oriental Institute told me Fausson was a janitor, I was picturing a couple of men with mops in the hallway of a rickety building.

Force 5 still didn't seem like the kind of operation a high-end office would use, sending a van around town to pick people up at odd locations. This was what construction or landscape companies looking for cheap day labor did. They picked up undocumented—of course. I felt like slapping myself on the head. It was a cheap undocumented crew. The Grommet Building's management had looked for the lowest bidder.

"Did you hear me?" the clipboard woman demanded.

She was almost in my face. Murmurs in Spanish and Arabic rose from the crew, like the humming of a hundred bees.

"I didn't hear you," I apologized. "I didn't realize Lawrence worked on this site."

"He could interpret for the Arabians on the crew. You're related to him? Do you speak Arabic?"

"Arabians? That sounds like he was a horse whisperer. Sadly, Italian is my only other language. I understand some Spanish but wouldn't try to speak it."

She realized she was forgetting her position as commandant. "I'll finish with you in a minute."

She clapped her hands and ushered her crew inside. It was seven-thirty and the lobby was essentially deserted, but in a building that housed hedge funds and an international law firm, young lawyers were putting in their mandatory hundred-hour weeks while traders were responding to Far Eastern markets; it was morning in Tokyo and Singapore. A young woman hurried past us, exchanged a bantering comment with the guard and then on to the outside.

"Hey, Melanie," the guard called to our leader. "Got an Arab interpreter yet?"

"Not yet. You find anyone, let me know." She reached in her handbag for a credential, but the guard waved her through.

We all streamed toward the elevators in the bay labeled "38–54." Everyone was wearing jeans and T-shirts, even the women, although two had covered their hair. I still had on my good trousers, but they were stained with rust from the rotted tree trunk, so I fit in, sort of.

Melanie gathered us in the bay for our assignments, saying them in English, then in Spanish: we were divided into teams of four, each given four floors to cover. Most of the people were apparently regulars—as Melanie started listing what we had to do—toilets, dusting, trash cans, vacuuming, how to handle food spills—people shuffled, looked at their phones, said, "*Sí, sí, sí,*" impatiently. One woman typed 42 on the elevator keypad. A car arrived almost instantly and her team of four got on board. Another went to 38.

I was starting to follow, but Melanie grabbed my arm. "You and I are going to have a talk and then you're going to leave."

The other workers stared until their elevators arrived. Two teams had gone to the seven floors that Dick's law firm occupied. I thought again of the quarter million under Fausson's floor and the expensive art collection Glynis had bragged that Dick and Teri owned. Had Fausson been stealing from Crawford, Mead to fund the dig he yearned for? Those piles of shiny lava would be hard to smuggle out, but there were plenty of small items—sketches, paintings that could be cut from their frames, figurines—that would be easy to remove.

As soon as we were alone in the elevator bay, Melanie demanded to know my relationship to Fausson and why I had boarded with her crew.

"We're concerned that the sheriff's police haven't made any progress in finding Lawrence's killers, Ms. Duarte. I've been asked to learn who his co-workers were and if any of them know anything about why he died."

"What? Do you think someone he worked with killed him?"

"Do you think that's possible?" I countered. "I thought a co-worker could tell me if anyone had ever threatened him. Perhaps he broke a valuable object and the owner blew up at him. Or—"

"The customers would report that to me," Melanie said. "If they have any complaints, they're supposed to come to the team leader. How else can we know if we're not doing a good job?"

"And had anyone ever complained to you about Lawrence?" I asked.

"His work was always satisfactory." Her lips were compressed.

"He was enthusiastic but didn't like detail," I suggested.

"No one is enthusiastic about cleaning offices," Melanie said, "but you're right about the detail. He spent too much time talking to the Arabians. If he were up there right now, I wouldn't be talking to you—I'd be going up to thirty-seven to make sure he was scrubbing toilets instead of taking all the Arabians' minds off their work."

The guard was standing nearby. "This the guy who was found dead out in the woods last week? I thought he'd been involved in some episode at one of the lawyers' offices."

My heart beat faster. "What episode?"

"It wasn't anything." Melanie was annoyed with the guard. "One of the lawyers went back to his office around eleven o'clock and found Lawrence reading a letter from his trash. I reprimanded him, told him if it happened again he'd be out a job."

The guard was laughing. "That was Mr. Pruette. We all knew why he was back in the office at eleven at night."

"Could be." Melanie's mouth twitched, almost a smile. "But if you clean an office, you can't be digging through the garbage. It's none of your business. Of course, most of the people who clean for us can't read English, so it isn't a problem."

"How did Lawrence end up working for you in the first place?" I asked.

"He knew the men at an Arabian—" She broke off. "I need your ID. If you're with ICE, you'd better tell me now."

The guard went back to his desk—he wasn't going to get involved if Force 5 had an immigration problem. Someone might accuse him of collusion in hiding undocumenteds.

"No, I'm not with ICE," I said. "Lawrence had been a graduate student in archaeology in Syria when the civil war broke out there. He loved the Middle East, he loved the language and the culture, so he went to the Syrian-Lebanese Community Center to speak Arabic—not Arabian. He even taught an Arabic poetry class there. When he needed work, one of the guys who's already on your payroll probably brought him along."

"You could be right, but I want your ID." Melanie's mouth set in an uncompromising line. "Or you can walk back out in the rain."

"You demand an ID from everyone you hire?"

"I'm not hiring you," she said.

I'm not sure where our standoff would have taken us, but the elevator doors opened again. A woman got off, followed by a knot of laughing men. Glynis Hadden had been working late, as had her boss, Richard Yarborough, and three other men.

25

A STRONG HAND

ON THE BRIDLE

"DICK!" I CRIED enthusiastically. "And Glynis. You two must be the hardest-working couple in Chicago, getting off duty after seven-thirty."

"Vic, what are you doing here?" Glynis was elegant in a khaki wool dress and red heels. She'd touched up her makeup recently. I was very aware of my wet shoes and soiled trousers. "You look as though you've taken up mud-wrestling."

"You know how it is, Glynis: no alimony. I have to find the work I can. I'm trying to persuade Force 5 to hire me."

The guard drifted back to our bay to watch the drama.

Glynis tightened her lips. She knew better than to scowl—it deepens the lines around the eyes and mouth.

Behind her, Dick looked like a stuffed owl. I remembered that expression—it was the same way he'd looked when I found out he was sleeping with Teri Felitti, before she became Teri Yarborough.

He surely didn't mind my catching him working late with Glynis, although he might have a guilty conscience there. I studied their faces, but Dick and Glynis were so tightly bound together it didn't really matter if they were having a physical affair.

One of the trio was the man who'd arrived to see Dick last week as

I was leaving, but the power center in the group was a man of about sixty, who combed his graying hair back from his forehead in the manner of Leonardo DiCaprio in *The Great Gatsby*. It must have been deliberate: his pin-striped suit, cut from one of those wools that make you want to stroke it, had the exaggerated lapels and double-breasting of a 1920s garment.

The fourth man might as well have had BODYGUARD on his forehead in flashing neon—high-end bodyguard, to be sure, since it was good-quality suiting that strained over his shoulder holster. His gaze flicked around the hall, looking for menace—he didn't seem to think that included me.

"This your ex?" DiCaprio asked Dick, looking at me with amused contempt.

"Vic and I were married in another lifetime." Dick gave a rueful shrug. "Another planet. I often wonder how I got there."

Dick's visitor from last week laughed obligingly, but the bodyguard remained impassive. The visitor asked what Force 5was.

"This is perhaps a military client?" He had an accent, French, perhaps. Dick held up a palm, signal of ignorance.

DiCaprio shrugged impatiently. "We've wasted enough time. No one is interested in Yarborough's ex's job."

"We're the service your building management hired to clean the offices here, Mr. Kettie." Melanie ignored the Frenchman. She stepped up to DiCaprio, offering a giant grin, the rictus of subservience. "I'm Melanie Duarte, the shift super, but this woman—"

Kettie, not DiCaprio. Gervase Kettie was a big name in Chicago real estate and construction. He popped up in the news at least once a week—deals in Chicago, New York, Abu Dhabi, along with questions about his income tax—but I'd never actually seen him. And he apparently owned the building where Dick's firm leased their offices. No wonder Dick was letting him be the power center of the party.

Kettie deliberately turned his back to Melanie. Giving a great bellow of laughter, he slapped Dick's shoulder. "That's the ultimate revenge, Yarborough. Got to hand it to you. Let her clean your office. Do you both good."

I knelt to kiss Kettie's hand. "Thank you, Massa, thank you. And all our chilrens thank you, too, doesn't they, Massa Dick?"

"Cut it out, Vic." Dick grabbed my arms. "Sorry, Kettie: she's yanking my chain, which means she feels free to pull on yours, too. Unfortunately, with Vic you never know if her bite is worse than her bark or the other way around."

My hair got tangled in a ring Kettie was wearing. When Dick jerked me to my feet, the ring's inlay came out and clattered across the floor.

I picked up the inlay and turned it over in my hand. It was a heavy piece of lapis, not really a he-man's stone, except that it looked very old. Inlaid into the lapis was a gold serpent—that's what I'd caught my hair on.

"You careless, clumsy bitch!" Kettie snatched the lapis and serpent from me and made to slap my face. I ducked. He swatted air and almost overbalanced. The bodyguard leaped to attention, steadied Kettie and grabbed my own forearm, all in a single smooth movement.

"Let's take it down a degree," Dick said. His face had paled, fear over what Kettie might do and how I might react. "Vic, you owe Kettie an apology."

"As soon as Bowser lets go of me," I said.

Kettie scowled but finally said, "Let her go, Mitty: she's not worth wasting time over."

Bowser/Mitty released me but continued to hover.

"I'm sorry, Kettie," I said. "I'm sorry I became as immature as you."

Dick turned whiter, this time with fury, but he knew it was smarter to get out of the building before punches or lawsuits were exchanged. He put an arm across Kettie's shoulders. "Come on, Gervase—martinis at the Potawatomi will turn this into a bad dream."

Over his shoulder, he added, "Vic, you skate so close to the edge that there are times like now where you go completely off the cliff. . . . Glynis, you have the car lined up?"

She nodded and looked at the guard. "Curtis, can you get us an umbrella?"

Curtis retrieved an outsize umbrella from his station and went outside so he could protect Dick's and Kettie's expensive suiting on their way to their limo.

Kettie shook off Dick's arm and glared at me. "You dare cross me again and you will wish you'd never been born."

I was too startled by the level of rage in his face to reply. He seemed to think silence meant I was cowed—he rejoined Dick, slapping him again on the back and telling him he was lucky to get out of his marriage to me "before she sliced off your balls. These feminazis, they need a strong hand on the bridle."

As the group reached the revolving door, I couldn't resist calling, "Reno is still missing, Dick! But enjoy your dinner."

Dick came to a halt. He turned, as if to shout back at me, then straightened his shoulders and kept walking. Kettie seemed to be asking Dick a question, but I couldn't hear their murmured comments from this distance. Perhaps it was about Reno, or his golf handicap.

"I will definitely be crossing you again, Gervase Kettie," I said.

"Oh, no you won't," Melanie Duarte said. I hadn't realized I'd spoken my thought out loud. "You can't come in with my crew and piss off Mr. Kettie. He'll have me fired if he thinks I brought you. One of the girls at the guard desk teased him one night and she was out of work next day and couldn't find another job."

"Kettie didn't notice you," I said wearily. "He's a miniature Stalin who can't stand it if the serfs don't quiver in his presence. It's my details he'll get Dick—Richard Yarborough—to give him, not yours."

"Is that what this was about?" Melanie's voice went up half a register. "Getting revenge on your ex? I have a good mind to call the cops."

My fatigue suddenly seemed ready to swallow me. My lies and subterfuge, which I'd thought would be clever, seemed merely dreary. I leaned against the wall between two sets of doors.

"And tell them what? That I was looking for work?"

"Why did you come here, anyway?" Melanie demanded. "You're not looking for a job, that's for sure."

"I joined your crew because I need to learn about Lawrence Fausson. He doesn't have a next of kin; he'd cut his ties to the archaeologists with whom he'd gone to Syria, so they don't know anything about his current life. He spent his spare time at the cultural center where you picked up three of your team. I'm hoping one of the men can tell me what Fausson was doing lately. Besides working for Force 5. And getting murdered."

Melanie bit her lip. "You said your name was Victoria Fausson, but then you said Lawrence had no next of kin."

The keypad for calling elevators was next to me. Keeping my eye on Melanie, I pressed 38. *Car E,* the keypad replied.

"Yeah, that wasn't skillful. My name is V.I. Warshawski."

"Is Mr. Yarborough really your ex?"

"Really. A very ex ex. He married again, has two kids in their teens. Our decree did not include alimony—what I said just now was a joke." Sort of. I hadn't wanted alimony—I hadn't wanted my fate linked to Dick's decisions to pay or withhold payment. Dick had been taken aback at the time—I think he'd looked forward to tying me in knots for weeks or months with court battles over payment schedules.

"It doesn't sound funny." Melanie's face puckered in confusion. "Who is Reno? One of your kids?"

I'd hopped on the Force 5 van hoping to ask questions, but I was the one being interrogated. Reno would be a good name for a pet, better than as a name for a child. Poor Reno, carrying an unmanageable burden from the day she was born. And here I was, looking for answers about Lawrence Fausson, while Dick's and my niece was still missing.

Car E, my car, arrived across from me. I let it sit until the doors started to close, then rushed past Melanie and climbed on board.

She would have no trouble finding me—Curtis, the guard, would be able to track Car E on his computer. This meant I had only a few minutes to find any of the men who'd gotten on the van in front of the outreach center.

When I got off on 38, I was momentarily paralyzed, staring at the elevator doors. As a pair opened next to me, I braced myself to duck and roll into the car, but a strange man emerged and headed for a corner office.

Somehow that pushed me back into motion. I typed in five different floors on the keypad, then darted down the hall, looking for anything like a hiding place. One of the Force 5 crew had parked a supply cart outside a women's bathroom, leaving the door propped open.

The woman cleaning inside apologized to me in Spanish, apparently assuming I worked in the building, even though the long mirror showed a sleep-deprived figure who'd spent too much time crawling on muddy ground.

I washed my face and hung the windbreaker on a hook inside one of the stalls. When the woman saw me trying to brush the dirt away from my trouser legs with my fingers, she went into the hall to her cart and came back with a sponge; she wet it slightly and worked the worst of the rust and leaf mold away.

"Better," she said.

I mimed lipstick and brushing my hair. She shook her head, but took my arm and led me to a locker room a few doors away from the cart.

I heard Curtis and Melanie barking questions at someone in an office down the hall. My savior shook her head again, but opened her locker and motioned me inside. She had shut the door and was on her way out when Melanie spoke close by, questioning the woman in rapid Spanish. *"¿Has visto una mujer sospechosa con ropa sucia?"*—Had she seen a suspicious-looking woman in dirty clothes? As far as I could tell, my acquaintance responded that she was too busy with her work to examine people's wardrobes.

Their voices faded. I was hunched over in the locker. My calves were cramping, my neck hurt, and the three slits in the door didn't let in much air. Just when I was sure I couldn't last another second, the woman returned and opened the door.

She motioned me out into the hall and returned to her work without stopping for my thanks.

"¿Los hombres della Siria?" I asked, hoping the Spanish was close to Italian.

"¿De Siria?" she corrected me, scrubbing one of the sinks more vigorously. *"No lo sé. ¿Eres un agente de inmigración?"*

Of course she was worried that I might be from immigration. "I am an aunt," I said slowly, first in English, then Italian. "The police are arresting my nephew for the murder of Lawrence Fausson. The Syrian men were friends of Fausson. I want to talk to them to see if they know anything that could help my nephew."

She shook her head, not understanding. Italian and Spanish are somewhat alike, but their vocabularies are different. I took out my phone and showed the woman Felix's photo. "Grandson of my sister," I said. It was close enough to the truth; Lotty has been a mother, a sister, a nurturer, and a critic in my life for many years.

"¡Ah! Entiendo. ¡Su sobrino!"

She started on the mirrors but simultaneously phoned someone. The Spanish conversation was too rapid for me to follow, but at the end she said, *"Piso sesenta y uno."* In case I didn't understand, she traced "61" in the mirror with a finger and then quickly wiped it clean.

As I turned to go, she grabbed my shoulder. *"No phones. Hay guardias. Tomaron una huella dactilar."* I shook my head, not understanding. Finally, exasperated, she pulled my cell phone from my hip pocket, made to throw it away, then took my hand, dipped it in her cleaning solution, and pressed my fingertips onto a paper towel. No cell phones, but they took fingerprints. You needed a fingerprint to get into the sixty-first floor, the top of the building.

2 6

HOUSEWORK

I WAS PRINTED years ago, when I joined the public defender's office out of law school. I didn't want Kettie's security team to get at my identity, not tonight when I wanted a sneak conversation with the Syrian cleaners. I couldn't take a chance on catching up with them after work—they wouldn't necessarily ride the van back to Palos, and even if they did, I'd be stuck out there, miles from my car.

I needed a different strategy. I went down the hall to the locker room where my acquaintance had hidden me from Melanie and Curtis. I hung my windbreaker in an unused locker, with my cell phone zipped into one pocket, my wallet in the other. I hated to leave them in an open locker, but if there was any kind of pat-down for phones on 61, the guards would find not only the phone but also my wallet, with all my IDs inside.

I took a piece of paper from an open office and carefully printed, *"I am the aunt of Felix Herschel. Felix has been arrested for Lawrence Fausson's murder. Please talk to me about Lawrence."* Added my name, phone number, and e-mail and tucked it into my jeans pocket.

A spare cart loaded with cleaning supplies was parked against the far wall. Clean smocks in pale green, with the Force 5 logo—a tornado sucking dirt from a computer screen—on the back, were piled on a shelf. I put one on, added a stack of green cleaning cloths to the cart, and rolled it down the hall to the elevators, where I pressed "61" into the keypad. The pad told me to ride to 48 and change cars.

On 48, while I was waiting for my second elevator, I took one of the green cloths and tied it around my head, babushka style, then sprayed something labeled STAIN REMOVER onto the others. My car had arrived; the stain remover had a musty, acrid smell that made me queasy in the small space; I was glad that the ride to 61 was short and swift.

When I got off, I saw that the elevator bay was sealed at both ends by doors made of heavy red wood. Enormous brass letters spelled out KETTIE ENTERPRISES on the doors at the east end. So all Kettie had to do to meet with Dick was take the elevator down eleven stories.

Security cameras were placed above both sets of doors and all six elevator cars. A guard stepped from behind a console made out of the same deep-red wood as the doors.

"What are you doing here?"

"I have supplies for the workers," I said in Italian. "*Guarda!*—look!" I pushed the cart up against him and held up a bucket labeled HIGH-ACID CLEANER.

"No one said anything to me," the man said.

I kept my face blank—I didn't understand English.

"*Adesso,*" I insisted, adding that I was working on 42, that I would be docked if I didn't get back to my own duties fast. I tapped my watch, pantomimed agitation.

The guard phoned someone on the other side of the doors, explaining the situation. He was apparently told to admit me—he held out an iPad with a square for putting a fingerprint. I made a show of wiping my fingers on the cleaning cloths, rubbing the stain remover into my fingertips. When I pressed on the iPad, a message appeared announcing the print was unreadable, try again. I tried three times without getting a clear read. The guard was annoyed but couldn't decide whether to send me away or let me in.

The smell of the stain remover in the windowless hallway did me in. I pulled a bucket from the cart just in time to catch the trickle of bile I vomited up.

"Goddamn it to hell—get your supplies in there and get the fuck out of the way."

He pushed a button to release the lock on one of the doors. They opened into something like an airlock—on the far side was a set of glass doors. After a moment, another guard arrived and opened the glass doors. He asked his outside buddy if he'd taken my cell phone. The first guard swore—I'd thrown up, he hadn't wanted to touch me in a pat-down. They compromised by having me open my smock and turn around. No bulges in pockets or waistband; I was good to go.

Hand on his gun belt, the inside guard led me past the antechamber to a conference room, where one of the Syrians was polishing a table big enough for fifty or so made out of the same red wood as the outer doors. Speakerphones were hooked up at intervals down the middle of the table, and there were outsize video monitors at either end. Art objects were placed behind glass niches along the walls. I glimpsed a gold bowl with embossed figures and a stone figure of a ram with red stones around the mouth and hooves. The guard moved between me and the display cases, ostentatiously fingering the handle of his SIG.

I turned to the man who was polishing the table, who squinted at me, puzzled. "Not needing," he said, pointing at the cart.

The guard was watching me, but I had to take a chance—under cover of knocking one of the spray bottles from the cart, I pulled the note I'd written out of my smock pocket and slipped it into the Syrian's pocket. I gestured wildly, reciting the lyrics to "Vissi d'arte."

As Tosca mourned her unhappy choices, the guard grabbed my forearm and dragged me to the exit. I kept reminding myself that I was an immigrant who needed a job, not a street fighter who didn't like being manhandled.

The hall guard asked his colleague what I'd been up to in there.

"Who knows what these camel jockeys say. I don't know why we can't have people who speak the language working here."

I willed my face into its impassive lines. I willed myself not to ask who of their language-speaking friends would scrub the toilets in this building for whatever scut wage Force 5 paid.

When the car came, it took me down to the crossover floor at 48. I wasn't finished for the evening: I rode back up to the main entrance to Crawford, Mead's offices. I hadn't reckoned on the big glass doors leading to the reception area being locked, and locked electronically— you needed a pass card to get in.

I took the cleaning cloth off my head and began polishing the elevator doors. As I was finishing the second set, the light above them pinged; a young woman got out, balancing a carryout bag from a Mexican restaurant with a cardboard drinks tray and her briefcase. She put down the carryout bag while she used her pass card on the door. I scurried over to pick up her food bag and hold the door for her.

She saw my smock, not my face. She mumbled a thanks but didn't think it was strange that I followed her inside—cleaners clean. For verisimilitude, I wiped my fingerprints from the doors, waited for her to disappear, and headed down the hall past the reception area to Richard Yarborough's suite.

Glynis had the outer office. The only thing on her desk was her computer monitor. Paper, stapler, pens, any of the paraphernalia of the work life, had been stashed out of sight. A shelf behind her desk held reference books and a photograph of a smiling man in fishing gear with two teenage girls. I had forgotten Glynis was married—she had such a vestal attachment to Dick I never pictured her with her own family.

I clicked on her mouse and the monitor came to life. I needed a password to get in and doubted it was *I'll Do Anything for Richard Yarborough,* although I was tempted to try it.

Dick didn't have his own conference room—the partners were supposed to use the communal ones—but he did have a small round table in a corner of his office where he could hold impromptu meetings. The real cleaners hadn't been in yet: coffee cups and crumpled paper were still on the table. I unfolded the pages, looking for—I wasn't sure what.

There was nothing in the papers that told me anything except that the meeting had to do with the FATCA, the Foreign Account and Tax Compliance Act. I always imagined it stood for Fatcats, because who else was affected by the act? And Dick's practice was nothing if not full of Fatcats.

I remembered my idea that Lawrence Fausson might have stolen something from Dick's office. I couldn't see anything worth the kind of cash Fausson had under his kitchen floor, at least not anything small enough to smuggle out, but what if he'd been part of the Syrian team on Kettie's floors? There were plenty of valuables there.

On the other hand, Dick's clients represented a lot of money. It was possible that Fausson got access to their accounts through Dick's computer. Dick seemed careless enough to leave log-on information around, and the cleaners were alone in the offices for a long stretch.

In my role as cleaning woman, I recrumpled the pages and looked around for Dick's trash can. It was next to his desk, in a spot where visitors could see it, since it was apparently an object more decorative than utilitarian, being made out of a silvery beaten metal with feet that looked like alligator toes. Before dumping the Fatcat documents, I pulled out the detritus already in the alligator.

Dick had eaten a Snickers bar and two peanut butter cups today. The empty wrappers made me realize how hungry I was. Peanut butter—that was what I needed to get me through my weariness.

I shook my head. Remember the Silicon Valley diet: surely you're as tough as any Facebook exec, I admonished myself. Although their judgment wasn't always stellar.

I put the wrappers on top of the Fatcat sheets and removed a fundraising solicitation from Princeton, where Dick had done his B.A., and a letter from a resort in Portugal where he and the present Mrs. Yarborough had recently vacationed.

Buried in the junk was a typed list of Dick's appointments for the day. Phone meetings, lunches, coffee, and, at the end of the day, a meeting with Arnaud Minable concerning *Ti-Balt v. Trechette.*

I knew both of those names, but I couldn't place them. I heard a cart rattling along the hallway and two women speaking Spanish. These would be actual cleaners. I stuffed the paper into my smock pocket and hurried away. The women with the cart stared and called at me.

I paused, smiling apologetically, and hurried to the elevators.

While I was waiting for Car D to take me down, I looked at the map of the world on the wall highlighting all the Crawford, Mead offices. And saw the sign for the new firm attached to Crawford: Runkel, Soraude and Minable.

PART OF THE FURNITURE

ARNAUD MINABLE, ONE of Dick's new partners. Meeting with Dick to discuss a lawsuit involving Trechette. Their plaque on Crawford, Mead's wall jarred my memory loose: Trechette owned Rest EZ. Trechette owned banks and whatnot around the world but had no listed officers or shareholders. I stood, jaw agape, as my elevator car opened and closed without me.

Dick's niece worked for Rest EZ. Dick handled affairs for Rest EZ's nominal owners. Reno had told her sister that Dick "sort of helped her" get a job—in this case, Glynis had given her a handful of companies to try where she could use the law firm's name. Even so, it seemed a strange coincidence for the lawyer for Rest EZ's parent company to show up soon after Reno disappeared.

The door in front of me dinged. I quickly turned away and started polishing a neighboring elevator—in the nick of time: Dick, Glynis, and the stranger—presumably Arnaud Minable—emerged. I dropped my cloth, bent over, head hidden. It didn't matter—I was a maid; none of the trio even noticed me.

They were jovial—whatever flies the Ti-Balt lawsuit, or I myself, had put in their soup had apparently been strained away by the good food and drink at the Potawatomi Club. Gervase Kettie had gone his own way, which also lightened the atmosphere.

I needed more information than Dick's discarded appointment schedule provided. I wanted to shake him until he told me how his niece and Trechette were connected—but for once in my life I curbed the fiercer impulses Dick stirred up in me. I needed more information before I staged a confrontation.

Glynis was informing Minable that the room he'd used today was available through Thursday; Minable said he was heading back to Havre-des-Anges on Wednesday. Glynis swiped her pass card over the door lock and the group disappeared into Crawford, Mead's offices.

I summoned another elevator car and returned to the women's changing room. I'd planned on dropping off the smock, but it made the perfect disguise. Anyone who's cleaning up after you is part of your furniture, not a person. I might want to be invisible here some other night. I collected my windbreaker, which mercifully still held my wallet and phone, and rolled the smock into a tight ball that fit into the hood.

Vending machines stood in an alcove between the women's and men's changing rooms. I'm not much for sweets, but Dick's peanut butter cups sounded irresistible about now. I ate two packets and sat cross-legged on the floor by the machines. I downloaded an Arabic translator to my phone, then dozed until the shift ended and the regular cleaners began returning to change into their street clothes.

When the man I'd approached in Kettie's boardroom appeared, I pushed myself standing and went over to him. He looked around nervously. Two of his co-workers said something bantering in Arabic that made him flush, but one of them said, "Elorenze, yes?"

I nodded.

"Guards for Ket-tie being much angry to Elorenze."

I pulled up the Arabic app and asked it to translate whether Fausson had stolen from Kettie.

The three men looked at the phone. They conversed among themselves and then took my phone and spoke into it.

The translation app was partial to the present progressive. It told me that the men "are not knowing, was Elorenze a thief. Guard is thinking Elorenze is cheating. He is very angry, shouting, and after that we are not seeing Elorenze again, so we are thinking he is losing his job."

"Cheating him of money or of time or of statues?" I asked.

The men all smiled, held up their palms—they were regretting to make me unhappy, but they were telling me everything they knew.

"What about Tarik Kataba, the poet?" I asked. "Did he work here with you and Elorenze?"

They smiled, but their eyes turned hard and they moved quickly into the men's changing room: they weren't going to say anything else.

When I rode to the ground floor, I saw the battered van waiting at the curb. I flagged a taxi to Pilsen for the Mustang. It was still there. It had a seventy-five-dollar parking ticket in the window, but I hoped my accountant would agree it was a business expense.

As I drove home, slowly, keeping to side streets, I texted Martha Simone. Late though it was, she was still working. She called to say that she'd managed to stop the county from charging Felix; they'd let him go home, with stern adjurations not to leave the jurisdiction.

"Did you have any luck with background on Fausson?" she asked. "I told the state's attorney that my investigator was on the trail of some associates with a close connection to him and that they'd look stupid if they charged Felix, who'd never met him."

"I went down a long and difficult trail and I'm not sure if it led any place helpful. The men who cleaned the Kettie Enterprises offices with Fausson say one of the guards chewed him out for cheating. They didn't know, or perhaps wouldn't say, how he'd been cheating."

When I described the encounter, Simone said, "If there's a chance they're undocumented, I can't call them as witnesses. I can use this information as leverage with the sheriff, but not in court."

"There's another thing you should know," I said. "I can't decide if revealing it would help or hurt Felix, but I was inside Fausson's apartment last week."

"Who let you in?" she demanded.

"The door happened to be open," I said, not adding that it was open because I'd undone the lock. "That part's irrelevant."

I told Simone about the cache of money.

"How you got in is not irrelevant if you entered unlawfully," Simone said. "I can't possibly give this information to the state's attorney."

"Confidential informant," I suggested. "The bigger question is whether it would help or hurt Felix to tell them about the money."

We batted it around but agreed that revealing news about the hoard would implicate Felix further—how could we have known if he hadn't told us? And since I'd gone in illegally, it would be assumed it was at Felix's behest.

Simone was interested in the fact that men identifying themselves with ICE had shot at me.

"They could have been muggers parading as feds," I said.

"They could have been ICE—the agency is getting increasingly ruthless," she said. "I'll talk to someone I know in the state's attorney's office, see if they've searched Fausson's apartment and what they've found."

I told her about my discoveries tonight as well.

"My God, Vic, I'm glad Freeman's your attorney, not me! First your B and E at Fausson's, and now this. Nothing you learned tonight could ever be admissible."

"I'm not interested in admissible. I'm interested in usable information," I snapped, "and that is very thin on the ground. I'm juggling two relatives here: Lotty's nephew and my ex-husband's and my niece. You know what's going on with Felix, but our niece has disappeared, and I haven't been able to find one hint of a clue about what happened to her."

I stopped talking while I thought it over. Dick must know something about his niece. If Reno had been harmed when she was in St. Matthieu, Rest EZ's senior staff would tell their attorney, even if they wouldn't confide in Reno's supervisor at the Austin branch.

But nothing in that scenario connected Dick to Lawrence Fausson, unless Fausson had also been cleaning the Crawford, Mead offices. Everyone was in the same building, but as I'd seen tonight, the cleaning crew looked invisible to Dick. If Fausson had been stealing from him or blackmailing him, surely Dick or at least Glynis would have been inspecting every Force 5 employee on their floor.

"Are you still there, Vic?" Martha Simone's sharp voice made me realize I was looking blindly at a gas station.

"Sorry, Martha. Too long a day. I'm glad you got Felix home."

Before hanging up, I asked if she'd kept Lotty up-to-date. Drily, she said that Lotty had phoned every fifteen minutes or so. She'd also talked to Hugo, Lotty's brother.

"They're worried, as they have every right to be, but I told both the doctor and her brother that unless they can persuade Felix to tell me the truth, we run a serious risk of being blindsided."

I reached home thoroughly demoralized. Mr. Contreras had been waiting up. He cracked open his front door, saw me, and came out, resplendent in his maroon bathrobe and matching pajamas. The dogs bounced out behind him, sure we were going for a swim or at least a run.

"Harmony is asleep. It's been a tough day for her, but she's holding up good. What about you? Where you been? I was beginning to think you got yourself arrested or shot or something."

I put an arm around him. "Long day, but I saw Dick this evening, and I'm thinking he knows something about Reno. We'll talk it over in the morning."

He started to protest—if it was something that affected Harmony— if there was a chance we could find Reno, then we needed to go over right now.

"Unless you want to wrap me in bedsheets and roll me out to the car, I am not moving from this building. The only thing I want right now is an elevator, which we don't have." I kissed him on the cheek and started for the stairs.

Mitch went back into the apartment with my neighbor, but Peppy followed me up. She watched expectantly as I surveyed my larder.

"If you'd gone shopping we could have a real dinner," I said. "As it is, the choice is between a cheese sandwich or eggs, and the sandwich doesn't have to be cooked."

I'd forgotten to put my good bread in the freezer; it had turned a kind of steely green. Cheese on rye crisps. Yum. Washed down with Johnnie Walker Black. Better.

I took off my clothes, rubbed arnica into my arms and legs, and went off to bed. Peppy jumped in next to me, but I didn't turn out the light. I opened my laptop and asked LexisNexis to reveal what it knew about *Ti-Balt v. Trechette*.

Ti-Balt was North American Titanium-Cobalt, Inc., a twenty-billion-dollar mining and machining company headquartered in Duluth, Minnesota. They were suing Trechette for recovery of completion bonds bought through Trechette Insurance Holdings of Saint Helier, Jersey. Some construction project Ti-Balt undertook had not been finished, or perhaps not finished on time. Trechette's insurance subsidiary was claiming Ti-Balt hadn't met the terms of the agreement.

This was a typical corporate squabble over a few hundred million. It would take years to work through the courts. Trechette was represented by Runkel, Soraude and Minable; Dick was apparently pitching in—this was his bread-and-butter kind of case.

My eyes were burning. I saved the results, but before shutting down for good I looked up Gervase Kettie. Why had he taken part in Dick's meeting with Arnaud Minable? His name hadn't been on the schedule Glynis had prepared for Dick. Did he have a financial stake in Trechette? As I started reading about him, Kettie seemed to have a financial stake in everything, from real estate to reality TV, but his was a closely held company, so I couldn't see what his holdings were in detail.

Kettie Enterprises was headquartered in Chicago, behind those heavy wood doors I'd just visited. The company was involved in myriad legal actions, about patent infringements, environmental problems, real estate completion bonds, and any number of other issues. Crawford, Mead was only one of the law firms they worked with. I recognized most of the firms, some based in New York or Chicago, others in Australia, Shanghai, and Mumbai. Arnaud Minable's name wasn't among their counsel in the lawsuits I looked at, and the Trechette name didn't appear, either.

I lay down. I'd shut my eyes for ten minutes and then try to dig up personal information on Gervase Kettie. The next thing I knew, Peppy was licking my face. It was seven-thirty and she needed to get outside.

2 8

BRINGING A DOG

TO A KNIFE FIGHT

YESTERDAY'S RAIN HAD passed, but a cold front had come in behind it. The sky was a sullen gray, the temperature not quite forty, but I badly needed to stretch my legs and lungs; I'd been in cars and vans for too much of the last few days. I put on warm running gear and took Peppy with me to collect Mitch from Mr. Contreras.

Harmony was in the kitchen, stirring a bowl of oatmeal while my neighbor clucked at her, urging her to eat. When I leashed up Mitch and Peppy, she insisted on coming with us.

"That's the ticket," my neighbor agreed. "Fresh air with the dogs and Vic, you'll have an appetite when you get back."

I gritted my teeth—I'd wanted to be alone, to have a chance to clear my head before trying to figure out what last night's discoveries meant.

Once we got going I wished I'd left her behind: I wanted to set a fast pace: I needed to work the muscles that had stiffened while I was healing. Harmony didn't want exercise, though: she wanted to worry over the break-in at Reno's, Reno's probable fate, what she herself should do next—legitimate concerns, all, but by the fourth time Harmony said "But if it wasn't drug addicts looking for stuff to sell, who else did it?" I began to feel like an overtightened guitar string, close to breaking the next time Harmony tried plucking it.

"Did Reno ever talk to you about a man named Kettie?" I interrupted. "Gervase Kettie?"

"I don't think so. Who is he?"

"A real estate tycoon that your uncle Dick works with. What about a lawyer named Minable?"

"How did Reno know him?"

"I don't know that she did," I said. "Just trying to find some way to pry information out of your uncle. How about anyone named 'Trechette'? He's listed as the owner of Rest EZ."

"What would Reno be doing with them, anyway? You think she was like a high-priced hooker, seducing men with lots of money? Are you like every other person on—"

"I know you and Reno had a very hard time of it, with men in power abusing your bodies. But that isn't what lies behind my questions. I'm trying to find out what Reno knew, what she was afraid of, in the weeks before she disappeared. Did she name any of these men? Did she say any of them assaulted her when she was in St. Matthieu?"

Harmony bit her chapped lips and turned her head, fingering the gold chain around her throat, as she seemed to in moments of stress. "She didn't tell me anything. I told you that already. Now you're making it sound like the break-in was men looking for Reno to have sex with."

"No, Harmony. That's what you're making it sound like."

I wished I knew more about how to talk to someone with my niece's history. Was she making these statements because her sister had told her one of these men had tried to assault her on her Caribbean vacation? Or was this the place her mind always went to under duress?

"Anyway, why wasn't it drug addicts looking for money who broke in? Why do you have to blame Reno for it, like the victim is responsible."

"It could have been drug addicts," I agreed. "Sergeant Abreu said she had some bank video footage to show you. Did she stop over yesterday?"

Harmony hunched a listless shoulder. "I guess, but I was in bed and Uncle Sal didn't want her to wake me."

"Then that's what you should do next," I said bracingly. "When we get home, you call Abreu and make an appointment. They want to see if you recognize any of the intruders."

She didn't want to go to the police, didn't I remember that?

"Harmony, you can't reject everything I suggest if you want my help. If you're more afraid of the cops than you are of the intruders, then we'll put that episode down to bad luck and I'll tell Sergeant Abreu that you don't want to waste any more police time on the break-in."

She lapsed into a resentful silence and moved even more slowly. When we finally reached the park I felt as though I'd been released from purgatory.

I unhooked the dogs' leashes as soon as we were away from the roads. The paths along the lake are usually as crowded as the start of the Tour de France. There's not much sense of shared space, and the dogs and I have had dozens of near misses and thousands of curses on our way to the water. Today, though, the cold had kept all but the hardiest cyclists and runners away, so I figured the dogs and I could run free.

"Why don't you catch up with us?" I said to Harmony. "I'm going after them to make sure they don't eat garbage or roll in rotting alewives."

I didn't wait for her answer but sprinted across the muddy ground. A small hill blocked a view of the lake, but it offered the shortest route to the water, and the dogs had taken it. I paused at the crest of the hill, saw the dogs on the beach, and turned to make sure Harmony was behind me.

As I looked, a man in a ski mask sprang from the underbrush and grabbed her.

Shock froze me briefly, then I bellowed, "No!" Shouted over my shoulder for the dogs, tore down the hill and launched myself at the man. I landed on his back and jerked his head back.

He let go of Harmony. She collapsed on the walk.

"Run! Call 911!" I screamed to her.

I couldn't see her, couldn't watch her; all my energy went to her assailant. He was enormous; it was like riding a bull to try to stay on his back. He grabbed at my fingers, but I dug them deeper into his neck.

He lowered his head, bit my left hand. I cried out, lost my grip for a fatal second. He bent low to throw me over his head; I dropped to the ground just in time and yanked his left leg, sending him to the grass.

He howled in rage. A second man in black gear and a ski mask raced toward us. I screamed for help, but a cyclist whizzed past without stopping. I gasped at Harmony to run. She didn't move. The second man reached her and put a gloved hand on her neck.

"Lock up," he snarled. "Lock up now!"

The first gorilla was trying to hit my head, to knock me out, so the pair could leave with Harmony. *You don't, you won't. You don't, you won't,* I kept reciting, ducking from his heavy fists, dancing behind him, kicking him, dancing again. I couldn't keep this up. I felt water on my legs. Rain or pee, and then a roar of pain from my man. A wet dog had his calf in her teeth. Peppy.

He whipped out a knife, was pulling his arm back to slice her throat. A murderous rage lifted me and I kicked him in the solar plexus. He toppled, bringing me down with him. I managed to wrest the knife from him, rolled away, hurled the knife out toward the road.

Peppy jumped around, barking, darting in and out of his face. She wasn't an attack dog; she couldn't bring herself to bite him again.

Harmony was huddled on the ground nearby; Mitch was chasing the second man up the path. Peppy went to Harmony, licking her face over and over.

Two more cyclists passed us, buds in their ears, eyes studiously on the path ahead, not the nearby chaos. I staggered to my feet, found my phone, called 911. My attacker pushed himself upright. His eyes glittered red through the holes in his mask.

"I kill you."

"Not today," I panted. "Cops coming."

A moment later blue strobes lit the path and the hulk lurched toward the underbrush. Two cops jumped out of their squad, but by the time they understood my breathless explanation and went into the shrubbery, the man had vanished.

The senior cop, a man close to retirement, whose eyes were watering in the cold air, started to question us about the attack. I tried to stay focused but found it hard. I was worried about Mitch. He'd been gone too long.

I was also fighting guilt, for leaving Harmony alone. Abandoning her. Yet another unreliable relative. Harmony had again retreated into shock. She was cold, her eyes glassy. I wrapped her in my windbreaker. When the cops saw this, they took her into the squad car to keep her warm.

Peppy wouldn't leave her. There's not much room in a cop car's backseat, behind the guard screen, but Peppy squirmed in and lay across Harmony's lap. I stood by the door, scanning the landscape for Mitch and calling to him.

"You're sure he was a white man?" the junior man repeated.

"Yes. I'm worried about my other dog. He went after the second scumbag, chasing him up the path toward the tunnel under the drive. I need to find him."

"In a minute, miss. You're sure about his race?"

"He's a black Lab. Oh, the man, yes, yes, I'm sure he's white; enough skin showed around his eyes to tell."

I went partway up the path the second attacker had taken, calling to Mitch.

"Tell you what, miss," the senior guy offered. "We'll drive along, see what we can see, and you tell us what you can tell us."

I squashed myself in beside Peppy, scanning the landscape; the squad car crept along. The younger cop put out Mitch's description—a hundred-pound black Lab with gold ears and gold fur on his throat.

"Guy's eyes may be gray or blue," I said. "They turned red with fury when he looked at me. He didn't say much, but he threatened to lock us up, and right before you came he threatened to kill us. He had an accent, perhaps Eastern European or Russian."

A report came in—a cyclist had been beaten and his bike stolen about half a mile to the south. Probably by my man, since the assailant had been enormous and was wearing a black ski mask. Our cops decided an injured cyclist took precedence over a dog. As they made a U in the path I pleaded with them to unlock the doors, told them I'd meet them later at the station, but I needed to find Mitch.

They apologized but wouldn't stop. I felt torn in a thousand pieces. Harmony needed a doctor, she needed protection, but I couldn't bear the thought of Mitch injured or—thought denied. Injured. He'd saved our lives; he deserved my help. As soon as the cops found the cyclist and unlocked the doors, I jumped out.

"I'm running back north, following the path out on Addison. If you don't find me, take my niece to my home address."

They hollered at me, but let me go so they could talk to the mugged cyclist. I staggered up the path. I couldn't run; I was beat. Beat and beaten. My right knee squawked every time I put pressure on it; the bite on my hand was swelling. I needed a year in a sanitarium or at least an afternoon in bed, but most of all I needed my dog.

He was lying by the road near the underpass west of Addison. I cradled him, gently touching the bloody mass on his left haunch. He opened his dark brown eyes and gave my hand a halfhearted lick.

"You're going to be okay, boy, you are not going to die, no sir, not today you're not."

I stopped a cyclist, demanded he find me a cab. "I need to get my boy to a vet."

The cyclist dismounted and knelt next to us. "Looks like you both need doctors. You sure he's hurt worse than you?"

"I can walk, he can't." I wasn't going to cry, not in front of a stranger, not when I had to save my dog and reconnect with Harmony, look after Felix, find Reno, all in the same moment. "I think it's a knife or razor cut. It goes all the way down to the bone. He's losing a lot of blood, so please, find me a cab."

The cyclist pulled out his phone, exchanged texts with someone, and said a car would be here in a minute. In short order, a gray hybrid pulled up at the intersection.

"My husband," the cyclist said, helping me lift Mitch into the back. "Kev, the closest clinic is Wessex, Ashland and Montrose."

The squad car appeared on the lake path as I was getting into Kev's passenger seat. The driver leaned his head out the window and shouted at me, demanding where I thought I was going.

"Vet clinic on Ashland." I slammed the door shut. "Let's go," I begged.

Kev didn't move. "Are you in trouble with the law? I don't want to be arrested."

I choked on a hysterical laugh. "If you'll take my dog to the clinic, I'll stay here and deal with the cops. Please, before he dies. I'll get to the clinic as fast as I can. I won't leave you hanging with the bills. I'd text you my name and number but there isn't time."

To Kev's eternal credit, he agreed to deal with Mitch and left me to face the cops. The cyclist spouse had stayed behind, and I gave him my details before getting back into the squad car. Harmony sat immobile, Peppy's head in her lap, silent behind her wall of shock.

2 9

SAFETY MEASURES

AS THE SQUAD car drove us across Irving Park to Lotty's clinic, I told them to get in touch with Finchley or Abreu in the Shakespeare District. "My niece's place was broken into two nights ago. Lieutenant Finchley or Sergeant Abreu at the Shakespeare District can tell you more about it."

"You think this was connected?" The younger officer twisted around in his seat to face me; he was typing notes on his tablet.

"It felt targeted," I said slowly. "They wanted to lock us up, or her—the one bastard kept saying 'lock up now, lock up now.' This makes me think they have her sister constrained somewhere and that they wanted to take Harmony."

I couldn't make it make sense. Harmony and Reno knew a secret they weren't supposed to and so someone had sent our attackers to lock her up? Were my nieces counters in a sex- or drug-trafficking deal gone bad?

"If they were targeting her," I added to the cops, "that means they tracked down where Harmony went when she was checked out of the hospital yesterday morning. And that is terrifying. It would mean they called all the area hospitals to locate her and then traced the elderly machinist who escorted her to our building. They would have followed us this morning. I wasn't looking for a tail." Which added to my sense of culpability, but I didn't share that futile feeling.

"They waited until the dogs and I left her alone on the bike path before they jumped her." I shivered and put an arm around Harmony's unresponsive shoulders.

"*Please* ask a squad to check on my neighbor," I begged the cops. "He's in his nineties, and he's on his own right now."

"This is a mess," the senior cop grunted. "Call the sarge, see what she says."

The younger man was still trying to explain the situation to his sergeant when we reached the clinic. He had to abandon the call to help his partner escort Harmony inside—she was barely able to stay on her feet.

I tied an apprehensive Peppy to a pipe on the outside wall, squared my shoulders, went in to help Harmony with her paperwork. The clinic had its usual complement of wailing infants and squabbling toddlers, of anxious women worried about their families, anxious people of all sexes worried about ICE raids.

Mrs. Coltrain, the clinic manager, took in Harmony's and my battered bodies and summoned Jewel Kim, the senior nurse. To a rumble of discontent from the waiting mothers, Harmony was jumped to the head of the queue. Jewel wanted to take me into the back along with Harmony, but I said I needed to look after Mitch.

"He was knifed, he's lost a lot of blood, I need to make sure—" And then home to see to Mr. Contreras. Or home first, that made sense. I was so rattled by my mushrooming responsibilities that I couldn't think clearly enough to make a plan.

The cops needed me to fill out some paperwork, which I wasn't much interested in at this point. I promised to stop in at the station to finish the forms (when? As soon as possible, I promised, meaning sometime after next Christmas).

Would I testify if they picked up our assailants.

"Yeah, if I can ID them. They both wore ski masks, you know."

"You might ID the voice," the older cop said. "We can also try to get DNA from the bite on your hand, if you haven't sterilized it."

Mrs. Coltrain looked at my swollen hand in horror. "Ms. Warshawski, before you leave, before you take care of your dog, we're taking care of that bite. You men, if you want a DNA sample, you have two minutes, and then I'm cleaning this hand. A tetanus shot—no, you just had one, didn't you?"

No one argues with Mrs. Coltrain—she's managed a clinic full of fractious patients for twenty-three years, and no policeman can intimidate her. She bustled into the back and returned with a swab, a sterile bottle, and a jar of surgical soap. I let the officers swab my hand, then rushed to the waiting room toilet where I scrubbed my hand. When I came out, one of the nurse's aides was waiting with antibiotic ointment and a roll of gauze. As soon as my hand was wrapped up, I headed for the door.

"Tell Dr. Herschel I'll be back as soon as possible," I told Mrs. Coltrain. "I need to talk to her."

"The doctor wants you on a course of antibiotics." Mrs. Coltrain produced a bottle of Cipro.

The cops were helplessly trying to interject themselves into the situation. "Miss, we know you're worried about your dog, but we don't even have your phone number."

"Mrs. Coltrain will give you my details." I squeezed between a woman who was close to her time and a man whose badly swollen feet stuck out into the room and fled.

I'd forgotten to retrieve my windbreaker from Harmony, but I wasn't going to chew up more time returning for it. As I headed east with Peppy, the wind cut through my sweatshirt, freezing my damp undershirt. Neither Peppy nor I had the energy to run.

Measure twice, cut once. My dad told me that every time I came home from school with a demerit, a trip to the principal's office, a fight with Boom Boom. *It's advice for life, Pepperpot. You're always jumping from the high dive, never checking whether there's water or snakes in the pool. You get bit and you're full of regrets, but if you'd looked first . . . !*

It turned out that my route home took us past the animal hospital where Kev had gone with Mitch, so we stopped there first. The first good news of the day: Mitch had arrived, and even though the clinic hadn't received a deposit for his care, they'd taken him in to surgery. I didn't have Kev's last name or a phone number to write him and his cycling spouse a thank-you letter.

One of the techs came out to assure me that Mitch would be fine. "He's strong, his heart's good, and there's no broken bones. Someone cut him hard; we're repairing a nerve and a tendon, so it's going to be a long surgery, but it's going well. How did it happen?"

I shook my head. "I didn't see it. He ran after a man who was attacking someone in the park and chased him off. The creep must have slashed Mitch to get away from him. He's a hero, but this girl"—I petted Peppy—"is a hero, too, and I have to get her home."

I gave them my phone number and Apple Pay; the tech gave Peppy water and dog biscuits.

I called Mr. Contreras as soon as we left the clinic. He was okay, a second point of relief in the morning—no one had tried to break in to kill him or lock him up, but he was distraught at the news about Harmony and Mitch.

"How could you let it happen, doll, how could you?" he cried at intervals.

"Because I'm not Wonder Woman," I said. "I wish I were, but I'm not. Two enormous men attacked us. I maimed one, only slightly, and Mitch went after the other. Mitch is in surgery."

When we reached our home on Racine, Mr. Contreras was on the sidewalk waiting. He started to expostulate with me while I was fifty feet away, but as soon as he saw my face, dirty from battle and with a bruise forming above my left eye, he stopped midsentence.

"Oh, doll, you shoulda let me know you was hurt. And your hand. You gotta get inside, take a bath, get cleaned up. And you, princess"—he bent over Peppy—"you saved Harmony, you get a whole steak all to yourself tonight."

I managed a wobbly smile. "Too much to do today for me to rest. I'm going to get my car keys and wallet and drive you to be with Mitch. I have to go back to the clinic to see Lotty and figure out what to do with Harmony."

I left Mr. Contreras to pamper Peppy while I got myself up to the third floor. I took the time to strip and soap off my dirt—I couldn't stand to carry around any more of the jackal's DNA on my body—but

I turned off the shower after five minutes, turned my back on my bed, dressed in clean jeans and a soft sweater, and got myself back down to my neighbor.

I dropped him at the animal hospital and went on to Lotty's clinic. The crowd inside was as heavy as before, but there was an unease in the air: Mrs. Coltrain looked troubled, which never happened.

"It's Lotty—I don't like how she's acting," Jewel Kim said when I went into the back. "You can see how backed up we are, but she keeps telling me I can do a better job than her. Go talk to her, Vic."

Lotty was in her office, sitting completely still, hands folded across her abdomen, her face a mask set in lines of pain.

I embraced her, stroked her hair, blinked back tears. Her hair was almost gray now, but it wasn't the hair, it was the quietude. Lotty is small but fierce, constantly in motion, projecting six feet. Today she looked as though she'd abandoned hope.

She finally took my hand. "There are days when it feels too enormous to me. Felix—he's my hostage to the future. It's why I've leaned on you so hard to help him. I look at him—he's the image of my father—Hugo's and my father—and he's been like our little penguin baby nestled in our hands. If we lose him. . . . But my worries about him made me forget how hard it is for you with these nieces of Richard Yarborough. I don't want you to kill yourself, working for me, for Felix, for your nieces, but you're my only hope."

"I will work it out," I said, trying to infuse a confidence I didn't feel into my voice. "It will be easier to do if you go back to work. You can look after Harmony in her current condition: I can't."

"Yes, Harmony." She pressed her fingertips against her cheeks, as if she could physically push energy into herself. "She's had too many blows lately. I'd like to recommend hospitalization, but I worry that cutting her off from anyone she knows might destabilize her further. And then, there's always the wretched problem of insurance. You don't know if she has any, do you?"

"I guess I could call her employer in Portland."

"Get the phone number to Mrs. Coltrain; she'll find out all that,"

Lotty said. "In the meantime, I gave Harmony some Ativan. She's sleeping in one of the exam rooms. If I send her home with you, will she be safe?"

"I can't look after her," I said. "And Mr. Contreras isn't strong enough to protect her if someone breaks in. Especially with Mitch recovering from a knife wound."

"There was a wound in her neck," Lotty said. "Do you know if she was cut there?"

"For much of the attack, I couldn't see her." I thought back to the morning, tried to reimagine it. "She wears a gold chain around her neck. If the assailant pulled hard on it?"

Lotty nodded. "That makes sense, given the size and shape of the wound."

She pressed a button on her desk phone and asked Mrs. Coltrain if Harmony had had any jewelry on her when Jewel started treating her.

"The necklace was gone," Lotty said. "Could it have been a random mugging, someone wanting her jewelry?"

"It's possible, but it seemed that they were trying to carry her off. Losing the chain was a side effect. I'm drowning, Lotty. Flailing and drowning," I burst out. "I can't figure out one thing, one reason, for all that's going on, with my nieces or your nephew. I've never felt so useless. I've been looking for Reno for a week now and haven't turned up a single meaningful clue. Innuendos, suggestions, but nothing definite. Same with Felix. And as for my actual clients—" I broke off, too overwhelmed by it all to speak clearly.

Lotty twisted her fingers together. "Victoria, about Felix—"

"Has he been arrested?" I sat up straighter.

"No, but he texted me this morning to say that the dean had called him into his office. The sheriff and then ICE were asking questions about him, and the school wants to know what he's up to. He won't tell his dean or his professors, which means they're not eager with their support. He says the dean implied he could be asked to leave the Institute. I don't know if that's true, or if Felix is so angry and edgy that he imagines everyone is against him, but still. . . ." She didn't finish the sentence.

"Still, it's a worry," I agreed, trying to put some warmth in my voice. "He's on my to-do list, Lotty. I won't let you down."

"It's an impossible situation. I know I'm asking too much of you, but I can't stop myself." Her black eyes glittered with tears.

She went to a table in the corner for a thermos of the Viennese coffee she subsists on and poured out two cups.

"If you don't think it was a random mugging, how did it happen?" Lotty tried for calm.

I told her my speculation that the creeps had called hospitals until they found Harmony at Beth Israel. "It explains how they knew where she was—they followed her and Mr. Contreras from the hospital, and tracked us to the park this morning."

"That means she's still at risk," Lotty said. "If I hospitalize her, I can't guarantee her safety. Hospitals are porous, too many entrances and exits, too many people with reasons for being there. No one stops to question them."

"I'll see if I can hire a bodyguard. Meanwhile, as long as she's asleep here, let me leave her here for now. She should be safe until the end of the day." I got to my feet. "Once more unto the breach and so on."

30

ALL THIS COULD

HAVE BEEN YOURS

A CERTAIN TYPE of architecture seems to appeal to super-wealthy people in modern subdivisions: thousands of square feet of burnished rare woods encased in pale brick or stone, festooned with turrets and pillars and a few dozen gables. Dick and Teri's Oak Brook mansion had all these features along with an indoor-outdoor pool. They didn't need a tennis court or golf course because those were provided by the gated estate that protected their home.

It had taken me over an hour to reach their estate in Templeton Acres. Only part of that was due to traffic on the Eisenhower—most of the time I was hunting for access to the property. I hadn't felt like dealing with the guard station at Templeton's entrance, so I wound around the back of the development, where the golf course lay.

I lurked around a bend in the road near a side entrance, waited for a pair of golf carts to undo the electric gate, and drove in behind them. No one seemed to care.

I followed a road that ringed the course on the inside. Thick shrubs lined the route, blocking the view of the mansions; I had to guess where to turn off for the Yarborough spread. When I came on a parking strip for TEMPLETON ACRES GUESTS, I left the car and finished the final quarter mile on foot.

A curved driveway led from the inner road to the mansion. I could see the house, with its gables and porticos and so on, through the bare trees, although in summer, it wouldn't have been visible.

The Templeton Acres website offered buyers a choice from one and a half to four acres for their dream palace. Dick and Teri had opted for two, my pretrip research had informed me.

Even two acres is a lot of land; their landscaping included randomly spaced trees and shrubs, with ornamental beds nearer the house. I couldn't imagine Dick and Teri doing their own yard work, not with that kind of acreage to plant and weed and prune. They probably didn't clean their six-thousand-square-foot home, either. I wondered what a wealthy woman who didn't work did with her time. Shopping, charitable committees, school aide, lobbyist, strenuous workouts with the club trainers, or maybe she'd taken up riding and foxhunting.

When I rang the bell, it was answered by a slender woman in jeans and a T-shirt, who asked my business in heavily accented English.

"Is Teri Yarborough home? I have urgent business with her."

The woman looked at me dubiously. "Business? No one is bringing business in house. We not letting in salesmen."

I tried to look genial and trustworthy, not beaten up and exhausted. "Not that kind of business. Urgent family matters. Let me write a note for her."

I was pulling a pen and a business card from my bag when Teri appeared. "Who is it, Claudia—oh! You!"

I produced a wide smile. "Yes, it's me, Teri. It's been way too long—we have a lot of catching up to do."

Teri was wearing a fuchsia tank over black leggings. Her breastbone and ribs were visible above the tank, showing that she indulged in the Silicon Valley starvation diet. Her red leather sandals had jewel-studded balls over the toe strap; the heels were inlaid with pearls. Even at home, in the middle of the day, she had put on makeup. Diamond drops glinted in her ears. I couldn't imagine how many hours of spa treatments and workouts went into maintaining her taut body. Fighting muggers on the lakefront felt wholesome in comparison.

"What do you want?" Teri was scowling heavily. I needed to get

Glynis to call her, remind her that a frown like that would leave deep wrinkles between her eyes, requiring regular Botox injections.

"We need to talk about Reno."

"Reno?" She pronounced it as though she'd never heard the word before.

"Your niece," I said, my voice very gentle. "My niece. Dick's niece. She's been missing more than a week—didn't Dick tell you? It's a terrifying situation. But now I've learned that Dick is doing legal work for the owner of the company Reno was working for. I'm sure, with your—"

Teri suddenly realized that Claudia was listening, wide-eyed, to the conversation. She told me to come in, that we'd talk in the back.

We walked in silence down a parquet hallway. Chinese rugs floated on it, like lily pads on a brown pond. Niches here and there along the wall displayed small pieces of the art that Dick and Teri collected. Bigger pieces loomed in the rooms we passed on our journey.

Teri took me into a room whose function was hard to fathom. Leather armchairs seemed to belong to a gentleman's club, a desk with an outsize computer suggested an office, but there was also a treadmill in the corner.

"I thought you'd have a fully equipped gym somewhere in the house." I pointed at the treadmill. "Or do you keep machinery in all the rooms in case you accidentally eat a piece of bread?"

"It's my treadmill desk," Teri snapped. "What do you mean, coming out here with insinuations—"

"I mean to find Reno. And to find who assaulted her sister this morning on Chicago's lakefront. I know that Reno went to Dick when she first arrived in Chicago, hoping for help in finding a job. And I know that Glynis directed her to the Rest EZ company. And I've learned that Rest EZ is owned by a client of Dick's firm, an entity or person named Trechette. It seems that Rest EZ's management picks their most attractive women workers to help the rich owners undergo R and R in the Caribbean."

Teri was watching me as keenly as if we were in a tennis match and she needed to see the ball placement. I paused a beat, but she didn't want to speak.

"Unfortunately, when Reno was at the resort, she learned something that troubled her deeply," I went on. "She went to Dick for his advice. And then she disappeared."

"I'm going to record this conversation." Teri pulled her phone from the hip of her leggings. "Dick needs to hear it so that he can start legal action against you for libel."

"Slander," I said.

"What?"

"Libel is written, slander is spoken." I took out my own phone. "I'm going to record as well. This way we'll each know if the other has edited the audio when we get to trial."

"You accused Dick of getting rid of his niece. You can't make that kind of accusation, not without paying a price for it."

My left hand was throbbing where I'd been bitten. I squeezed the gauze. The flesh underneath felt squishy. I wondered if I needed rabies shots along with the Cipro Lotty had given me. Which reminded me that I needed to start the pills.

"I didn't accuse him of that, Teri: that's your interpretation. But it makes me wonder why you think there might be a causal relationship. You do agree that she went to Dick for advice?"

Claudia came in with a silver tray.

"I don't want refreshments in here, Claudia," Teri said.

"Your niece has trouble, you wanting tea," Claudia said.

She poured something that looked like pale straw into Wedgwood cups and handed one to me. It tasted like pale straw, too. Teri put her cup down without tasting it and went to make sure the door was firmly closed.

"She's always listening in on private conversations."

"Appalling. You should have her deported."

"She has a green card," Teri said. "And—anyway, it's none of your business."

"Right. My business is with our nieces. Reno was worried by something at work, something disturbing enough that she wouldn't confide in her sister. She went to her uncle, the man who'd helped her find the job in the first place, or at least the indispensable Glynis—"

"You don't know anything about Dick or his family. You think of those girls as the adorable kindergartners you met twenty-five years ago; you don't know them as adults, but trust me, they're manipulative and cunning."

"What manipulative, cunning acts have they committed?" I asked.

"Talk to Glynis. I've said all I'm going to." Teri's lips twisted in a tight smile. "You're not as smart as you think you are, Vic: if you were, you'd be living in this house, not me. And you wouldn't be chasing ambulances to pay your mortgage."

I looked at my feet in their Brooks running shoes. The uppers had come away from the sole on the left heel. "I don't run as fast as I used to; I've had to give up chasing ambulances in favor of their coming to me. And one came to me this morning: Harmony was attacked in the park by a couple of outsize musclemen. She was badly injured: it's not clear how long it will take her to recover."

I held up my gauze-wrapped hand. "This is where one of them bit me when I fought them off."

"That doesn't surprise me," Teri said crudely. "Dick always says you have the personality of a pit bull."

"Pit bull marries weasel, I guess that doomed us from the start," I mused, unwisely, since I'd been thinking of putting the bite on her for Harmony's care.

"Why did you come out here, Vic? To call Dick names? To try to make me feel sorry for a couple of con artists?"

"Those are good questions, Teri. I don't have a quick or easy answer. Nothing in my relationship with you or with Dick is harmonious, but I don't wish him ill; I'd hate to think he deliberately signed up a client who could harm his own nieces. I hoped if I talked to you about it, you might persuade him to dig deeper into Trechette's business. Trechette operates very secretively; he should find out what they're hiding in all those offshore operations."

I was watching her face as I spoke; it was like looking at a cue ball: shiny, hard, not letting anything into the interior.

"It's possible if you came to Chicago with me and actually met Harmony, you'd feel—"

"I'd feel exactly what I feel now, that you're butting in where you don't belong. If you're not out of here in thirty seconds, I'm calling the estate security force to come for you." She went to the door, brandishing her phone at me.

I stepped past her into the hall but said, "Your agitation does make me think I'm right about Reno going to Dick with whatever it was she uncovered in St. Matthieu."

"She wasn't in trouble." Teri bared her teeth at me. "She was blackmailing Dick. She was exactly like her mother."

"Blackmailing him? Is he involved in something illegal that Reno found out about?"

Teri gasped. "How dare you? You say you don't wish Dick ill, but that's all you ever do when you're around him, try to create illness for him when everything was going just fine."

"Meaning no one but me ever questions what he's doing."

"You leave now! Or I'm calling the estate security force." She tapped her phone.

"Going, going," I said, but I stopped in the hall to look at some of the art pieces in their glass boxes. Mirrors were set behind the pieces so that you could see their backs without touching them.

About halfway down was a stone cow with massive horns and eight bulging udders. It reminded me of the little figurine of a woman with eight breasts I'd seen yesterday on Professor Van Vliet's desk.

"This is Sumerian, isn't it?" I said.

"Don't touch it; it's ancient and valuable."

"Yes, I know. I didn't realize these Sumerian objects came onto the regular art market."

"Now you know."

I remained in front of the stone figure. "Did Lawrence Fausson get this for you?"

"No one 'gets' our art for us; we go to galleries and auctions. If you think you can afford them, call Glynis—she keeps track of who is carrying pieces we might be interested in."

"And is Lawrence Fausson one of those people with pieces you're interested in?"

I kept looking at the cow, but I could see Teri in the mirror behind it. Fausson's name didn't make her jump with obvious guilt. She was angry, but that was her normal reaction to me.

"You can't afford statues like this, so I don't know why you're interested, but I'll have Glynis send you a list of the galleries and dealers we work with. Now it's past time for you to go."

Claudia appeared to hold open the door for me. I turned on the threshold to add, "One thing that puzzles me about our nieces: Harmony said Reno didn't get in touch with me because they didn't know my name—that is, they didn't know I was 'Warshawski,' not 'Yarborough.' They didn't know I was a detective who might help them out. Why did you tell Harmony and not Reno? It's almost as though you are worried about the mess Dick got Reno into and were obliquely trying to get her help."

Teri stared at me without speaking. She even bit her lips, leaving a smear of red on her teeth.

SAFE HOUSE

A JEEP WRANGLER pulled up, spilling out teens—two girls, three boys—shouting and punching each other. Teri's children and their friends home from school. They pushed past me into the house, as if I were a part of the door. I guess it's a sign of aging when you cluck your tongue over the poor manners of the modern youth. And when you're invisible to them.

I was heading along the road toward my car when Claudia appeared through some shrubbery.

"You are aunt? You are Mr. Yarborough sister?"

"I was Dick Yarborough's first wife. We've been divorced for many years now. Dick had a sister named Becky who died about twenty years ago. Her two daughters are Reno and Harmony; Reno has disappeared. Harmony asked me to help find her."

"You name?"

"V.I. Warshawski. Victoria Warshawski."

"Ah! Now am understand. Teri, she tell your name when niece calling. Teri say, call to Aunt Vic, she detective. Teri say, girl must not bother to Mr. Yarborough and family. Then Teri tell to Mr. Yarborough and he very much angry. Why you give Vic name to niece, he asking. Why you—can't think word—ask, maybe. Why you tell girl talk to Vic, now Vic sticking nose to my business."

Claudia gave me an appraising look. "And you, you are this Vic, this detective? But you not finding girl?"

"Yes. I'm this Vic and I'm not finding anyone," I said. "Did you talk to my niece—Dick and Teri and my niece? When was it?"

Claudia nodded. "She talking me with phone, telling she is niece to Mr. Yarborough, telling name is Harmony. Like music? I asking, and she saying yes, like music."

Claudia stopped to count under her breath in Polish. "Is one week back. She want talk Teri, I get Teri to telephone. I speak Teri, Harmony very worry, no one know where is sister to her. Mr. Yarborough saying, not worry, no problems. Now I go, sons needing snack."

She flitted behind the shrubbery toward the back of the house.

I trudged on toward my car. Had Teri and Dick told their housekeeper to mind her own business because they didn't care about Reno, or because they knew what had happened to her?

My hand was throbbing more painfully and I thought I might be starting a fever. I still hadn't taken my first dose of Cipro; I needed to get on that. Self-care, the gurus are always advising private investigators. Don't neglect your own well-being for that of your clients.

Near the expressway entrance I found a 7-Eleven where I bought a container of hummus and a bottle of water. I sat cross-legged on the passenger seat, took my pills with the hummus, swigged water, and checked my messages. Mr. Contreras said that Mitch had made it fine through surgery; the clinic would keep him overnight. He, Mr. Contreras, had gone home and was cooking a steak for Peppy.

Lotty's message reported that Harmony was awake and responsive; she could remember part of the attack. Lotty hoped I could take her home at least for tonight, since the clinic wasn't equipped for an overnight stay.

I felt the muscles on my head tighten. I did not want to be responsible for Harmony, even for tonight. I had a wistful fantasy of packing her in a rosebush crate and shipping her to Portland.

It was close to five now. The clinic would be open until eight—Lotty was one of the few doctors in America who understood that working people couldn't leave their daytime jobs to see a doctor without being penalized.

I called Lotty and spoke first, of course, to the clinic manager.

Mrs. Coltrain told me she'd talked to Harmony's boss in Portland. "He sounds like a decent man," she assured me, "and even though it's a very small firm, they do have health insurance."

Your first worry when you're sick in America: Can you afford to get treated?

Mrs. Coltrain put me through to Lotty, who felt reassured by Harmony's current condition. "She doesn't need hospitalization, although she would benefit from a full psych work-up. She's had two violent shocks in three days, on top of her fears for her sister's safety."

"Is there any way she could be faking this?" I asked.

"Absolutely not. Why would you suggest that, Victoria?"

I tried to explain the doubts Teri had sown in my mind.

"No, my dear. Even if she were pretending these retreats from self, it's because that's her historic safe space. It's a tribute to her strength of character, and the love she got from the foster parents, that she isn't disappearing permanently. But one more event like this morning's and she may not come back to us. Can you watch over her tonight?"

"I'm sure her assailants knew she was staying in my building last night. They may be camped out there right now, waiting for her. If I bring her back, they'll attack her, or break into the building."

"What do you suggest?" Lotty's voice was ragged from strain.

"Arcadia House," I finally suggested.

"But that's for women fleeing domestic violence," Lotty objected.

"I'd make a strong case for Harmony," I said. "She was abused as a child, the stable family she came to as a ten-year-old has disintegrated, her sister has disappeared, she suffers from PTSD, which puts her mental health at greater-than-average risk after all these assaults."

Lotty and I both serve on Arcadia's board; they would respond to an SOS from one of us, particularly from Lotty.

"And if I know Harmony is in a safe house, I can put some energy tomorrow into working on Felix's problems," I added.

That clinched the argument: Lotty agreed to talk to Harmony and persuade her to go into the shelter, at least for the next few days. She'd also make the necessary call to Arcadia's resident manager. As soon as I got back to the city, I'd drive Harmony to the pickup point. It would have to work. I was out of other ideas, and I was out of stamina for another physical attack.

I picked up Mr. Contreras and Peppy on my way to Lotty's clinic; I wanted Harmony to feel she had a team on her side, not that Lotty and I were bullying her to go into a shelter. I'd alerted the Streeter brothers, whom I often use for surveillance or bodyguarding: they would escort Harmony and help make sure we didn't have a tail.

To my surprise—and relief—it didn't take much urging to get Harmony to go to Arcadia House. We met in the exam room where the nurses had created a makeshift bed from one of the tables. Harmony was squatting on the floor, her arms around Peppy. Lotty doesn't like dogs, especially not in her exam rooms. She was making a brief exception for Harmony's therapeutic needs, but her mouth was set in a tight line.

Mr. Contreras was the hard sell; he couldn't admit that he and Peppy and his pipe wrench weren't enough to vanquish any number of thugs.

"I love you, Uncle Sal," Harmony whispered from the floor. "You make me remember Henry. I've been in shelters before. Some are crummy, but the safe ones are really safe. I need safe right now."

My neighbor looked mulish, but before he could keep up the argument, I said, "I'm giving you a burn phone with Mr. Contreras's number on speed dial. If Arcadia House doesn't feel right to you for any reason, you press hashtag, then one, and he'll know that we need to find you and move you."

I knelt to talk to Harmony. "I drove out to see Teri—your uncle Dick's wife—this afternoon.

"Let me ask you again if Reno told you anything that would help find her. I put my body on the line this morning to protect you. I think you can trust me to stick with you, but I need to know you're telling me the truth."

A long silence, and then, eyes still shut, fingers digging so deeply into Peppy's neck that the dog winced, Harmony whispered, "When you don't know someone, you don't know if they'll get mad at you."

I rubbed my head with my swollen hand; the jolt of pain jerked me into enough awareness to parse what she was saying. "If you lie, and someone gets mad, they're not mad at you—they're mad at the lie?"

Another minuscule nod. "Clarisse used to say, face up to the truth sooner, not later. And me and Reno, we used to try to, because Clarisse—she protected us—but now—now, who—" She broke off in a choking sob.

"Now see what you done!" Mr. Contreras exclaimed. He couldn't bend his arthritic joints to join her on the ground, but he stroked her head. "You got me, Harmony. And even if Vic don't know enough not to bother you when you're low, you got her, so don't you worry none. You ain't alone as long as you're in Chicago."

"It's okay, Uncle Sal." Harmony was still whispering. "Reno said, the richest men only think about sex and money, just like the low-rent jerks on the Bay Bridge. She said this time she would get a name, but until she had that, there was nothing she could do."

I helped Harmony to her feet. Maybe this was what had struck Teri as cunning and manipulative: the sisters' self-protective silences and oblique hints of what they knew. My mother had been like Clarisse, only more pungent: vomit out the lie and you'll feel better at once.

Lotty reminded me, sharply, that she had patients waiting and someone would have to disinfect this room before it could be used again. I made a face: it was good to have Lotty back to her usual acerbic self, but her acerbic self could be annoying.

We bundled Harmony through the clinic's alley exit, where she and Mr. Contreras—along with Peppy—got into a van that the Streeter brothers use in the piano-moving part of their business.

Lotty's lab tech, who was about the same age as Harmony, came out front with me and jumped quickly into the Mustang's passenger seat. If someone was watching, we hoped they'd think it was Harmony.

I drove north while the van headed south. Tim Streeter was driving the van, his brother Tom riding shotgun. The third brother, Jim, had a souped-up Kia that shuttled between me and the van. About three blocks from the clinic, Jim spotted a tail on me. I started evasive action but did it slowly, hesitantly, leading the tail farther from the van. When we were about a mile apart, I let the trailing car, a black Mercedes SUV, close the gap.

In the crawling traffic on Lawrence Avenue, I made a quick U in front of a shop whose sign flashed PLAY GO, SHOGI, JANGGI, OPEN 24 HOURS. I nearly hit a cyclist and had to leap out of the way of a furiously honking vegetable truck. We were crossing Kedzie and turning south before the Merc could react. I made another U, turned into an alley, and cut the lights. Backed up until a dumpster shielded me from the street.

"Your guy is prowling," Jim warned.

I gave Jim my location. "Can I come out on Pulaski?" That was a mile farther west.

"Don't move. He's turned off his lights, he's going down Kedzie heading for your alley. One of them is out of the car. On foot with a high-power flash. Hold tight."

Through the open phone, we heard the squeal of brakes, the shivering of metal on metal, and then Jim screaming, "You flaming asshole, why the fuck you stop in the middle of the road with your lights off?"

Shouting from the Mercedes, then Jim yelling, "I'm on the phone to 911 this minute, dirtbag."

I backed up until the alley forked. Turned south, toward the tech's Pilsen home. We were about half a mile from the alley when Jim came back on the phone. He was laughing and swearing.

"Guy thought he wanted to beat me up for ramming him. He was coming for me with a tire iron. He whacked my windshield, but it held, and I put the pedal to the metal, acted like I was going to run him down. Don't know which made him crazier—getting his Merc dented or having a beat-up Kia do it. Love, love, love the armor plating we put in. But God above, why would you think you could be an invisible tail in a GLS 450?"

This was more than I'd heard Jim say in ten years of working with him. His adrenaline high made him keep repeating the story. I kept making sounds of admiration while I saw the tech into her apartment.

When I was sure she was safe, I finally interrupted Jim to ask for an update on the van carrying Harmony.

Tim and Tom had made it to the drop-off point without interference. They'd waited to make sure a legitimate member of the shelter collected her and now were taking Mr. Contreras and Peppy to their shop. The brothers would transfer from the van to another beater for the drive home.

"Can you get the boys to do a recon before they let Mr. Contreras out? I'm worried that the goons are staking out my place."

I was ten miles from home at that point. Tom Streeter called with an all clear while I was still passing the downtown exits. Just in case the gorillas were looking for my car, I detoured to my office and summoned Lyft from there. The driver had to shake me awake when we got to my building.

I offended Mr. Contreras by heading for the stairs while he was giving me the blow-by-blow on his ride with Harmony to the drop-off point. I just remembered to take more antibiotics; my last conscious thought was gratitude that the Streeter brothers had armor plating on their cars. Although did you really need it for moving pianos? I drifted into a dream of a grand piano with armor plating dropping from the sky and flattening my assailants.

32

METALWORKS

I SLEPT THE clock around and might have stayed in bed indefinitely if Mr. Contreras hadn't leaned on my doorbell: I needed to get up and drive him to the animal hospital to collect Mitch. He'd phoned first thing, and the dog was in good shape, ready to be released.

"I know you, Vic," he said when I objected to his ruthless awakening. "If I don't make you go, you'd be off doing a million things for banks or lawyers or whoever, and you'd forget all about your dog."

Usually I'm "doll" or "Cookie": he calls me by name only when he's miffed. He was still annoyed that I hadn't paid attention to him when I got home last night, or maybe it was because I'd doubted his ability to protect Harmony—he hates any suggestion that he's not as strong as he was when he fought at Anzio.

I reminded him that I'd left my car at my office. He wanted to go with me in a Lyft car to make sure I stayed on mission, but I ran the four miles, to clear my head and stretch my muscles, but mostly to have some time to myself. My hip bruise had eased up and my whole body felt freer for being in motion, not to mention the luxury of a full night's sleep.

While I was at my office, I stopped for a cortado at the coffee bar across the street, took a shower in the bathroom at the back of my lease mate's workshop, put a new dressing on my hand. The swelling was down but the puncture wounds turned my stomach. The thought of the creep digging his teeth into me—I scrubbed the area with a nail brush until the skin all around the wounds was rough and red. Yes, Lady Macbeth, I get it.

When I looked at my message log, I had a new assignment from Darraugh Graham and a note from Lotty: *"Despite my exigent demands, please rest if you can."*

I wished I could follow her valuable advice. I wished I could decamp to someplace warm, free of monsters, where there was no phone or Internet service. Instead, I phoned IIT and made an appointment with the engineering dean, Richard Pazdur, to discuss Felix. The dean's assistant slotted me in for one-fifteen but warned me that Pazdur wasn't going to violate student privacy with a detective. I looked at the clock: if I hustled, there'd be time to drop in on Felix before seeing his dean. Maybe by now he'd be scared enough to talk.

I drove back home to collect Mr. Contreras—he would never forgive me if I picked up Mitch by myself. As I'd anticipated, though, my neighbor turned dog retrieval into a slow process: he questioned the vet over every detail of the surgery, had the tech repeat after-care instructions three times, double-checked that I had the follow-up appointment in my calendar.

By the time we'd established Mitch in a comfortable bed in Mr. Contreras's bedroom, and I'd placated my neighbor by bemoaning Mitch's shaved left flank, worrying whether the wound would leave Mitch with a limp, and listening to the blow-by-blow of his ride with Harmony to the pickup point for Arcadia House, even talking to unresponsive nephews began feeling like an attractive option.

Before setting out again, I spoke with Marilyn Lieberman, the executive director at Arcadia House, about Harmony. Harmony had spent a disturbed night, after the horrors of the last two days.

"She's almost feverish with distress," Marilyn said. "She keeps going over episodes in her sister's and her lives, talking a lot about her foster parents, and worrying about a necklace. We're getting her a psych evaluation; it may be good for her to be medicated to help her through the roughest part of this time. Our advanced practice nurse did finally give her some Ativan to help her sleep, and if you were hoping to talk to her, she's still sleeping."

I asked if Harmony was delusional.

"No. She's anchored in time and place, but distraught. I'll keep you posted."

I hung up more thankful than before that Mr. Contreras and I weren't trying to care for Harmony at home. The necklace she was worrying about, that was the chain I'd watched her fingering over the last week. It had been important to her; I'd try to fit in a stop at the park on the extremely remote chance that our muggers had dropped it as they fled and—even more remote chance—no one else had picked it up.

We were having a rare day of sunshine, but it was still chilly. I put on serge trousers—hoping they'd end the day in better shape than my beautiful cashmere slacks—and draped a silk scarf over a knit top. Professional enough.

The campus flanks State Street and the L tracks, with offices and classrooms mostly on the west side and dorms on the right. I parked in the rutted ground underneath the L tracks, only a few blocks from Prairie Avenue, where I'd dropped Felix last week. I hugged my coat around me, but the wind whipping down the long tunnel under the tracks made me feel as though I'd gone out bare-skinned.

When I reached Thirty-First and Prairie, I looked around for any signs of the sheriff's police. City cops circled the streets around the school. The occasional IIT security car trundled past. When I reached Felix's building, though, I saw an SUV with the county decal up the street, motor idling.

Felix answered my ring after a silence long enough to make me think he wasn't home. When I identified myself, he didn't buzz me in but came down the stairs to open the street door.

"So you're alone, not with the sheriff." His narrow face was gray and puffy.

"Yep, but there's a deputy across the street, so please let me in before they catch sight of you and photograph us together."

"You afraid of being seen with me?" he jeered, but he backed up.

"No. I'm afraid if they connect us it will limit my effectiveness when I'm trying to talk to your friends or your enemies."

"Do you know who they are, either my friends or my enemies?" he asked as he led me up two flights of stairs.

"That's why I'm here, hoping you'll tell me."

I followed him into his apartment. It was a studio, dominated by a worktable that filled most of the room. A bed in the corner was unmade; papers and books littered the floor and much of the tabletop, but he was messy, not squalid—no food or unwashed dishes were sitting around.

Besides the papers, the tabletop held several scale models, dollhouse-size machinery with miniature gears and belts and fans. I bent to study them.

"Looking for bombs?" he said.

"Admiring the craft. Did you build these?" I reached out to touch the tiny gear shaft.

"Don't—they're delicate!" He pulled my hand away. "What do you think they are?"

I pointed to the copper top at the end of one model. "It looks like part of a Scottish whisky distillery."

"Then we're on the right track—this is supposed to be a portable water distiller. It converts human waste into power and steam and water."

I thought he was joking, but his face had come alive. He explained the workings in detail. I was impressed by what he knew and how good a job he'd done building his prototype.

"This is what your Engineers in a Free State are creating?"

The sullen glaze settled over his face again. "That's why you came, of course, to help the police interrogate me."

"I don't want you arrested, Felix, unless you murdered Lawrence Fausson, of course, but I don't believe you did, so why won't you tell anyone what you're doing, or who and what you know?"

He bent over one of his miniatures, making a minute adjustment to a gear. When he spoke, it was barely a whisper, addressed to the gear.

"I just can't. If I could, I would tell you, but I can't."

I looked for a place to sit and finally pulled a chair away from the table. A book was open to something like an architect's drawing, a figure of a ram with a long curling horn overlain with circles and grids.

Numbers and letters in small print were explained in italics on the left. A photograph fluttered out. I bent to pick it up, but Felix was ahead of me, so fast our heads bumped.

I backed away, rubbing my temple. The glimpse I had of the photo was of a bright gold shape, but Felix grabbed the book from me and put the photograph into it before I could see either the book or the picture clearly, although I made out the title along the spine: *Art in Copper: A Technical History.* Beneath that was the Library of Congress call code, along with the IIT Library stamp.

I stared at him, astonished that he felt so secretive about a technical book.

"It isn't mine," he muttered, and stuffed the book into his backpack. "I don't want anyone getting it dirty."

"Yes, of course . . . I'm committed to helping Lotty and your lawyer save you from an arrest. One thing that would help is some reasons why Fausson might have had your number, since you say you didn't know him."

"I never met him; I never spoke to him." The muscles in his throat worked as he swallowed convulsively. "I have no idea why or how Fausson had my number."

"He spent a lot of time at a Syrian-Lebanese center in the southwest suburbs. Did you ever go there, maybe do a presentation for them with some of the Engineers in a Free State?"

"That sounds like a cop question," he protested.

I gave a sad smile. "I am a kind of cop, I guess, but it wasn't meant as a cop question. I was thinking maybe someone at the center knew both of you and wrote your number down for him. He might have wanted—I don't know what he might have wanted. But he could have had a reason for trying to reach you."

He shook his head, but the worry lines in his face deepened.

"What about Force 5, the cleaning company?"

Felix became completely still. "How did you find out about them?"

"Lawrence Fausson worked for them. Do you?"

He shook his head, in slow, jerky movements, almost like a machine he himself might have created.

I tried several other gambits, but I couldn't get him to say anything else. Force 5 had shut him up thoroughly. I couldn't even figure out if the tense headshake meant he didn't work there or was a guilty reaction to my uncovering the cleaning company's name.

I finally gave up. "I have an appointment with Dean Pazdur. Lotty says he threatened you with expulsion?"

"Not that crude," Felix muttered. "Just—I haven't done well in my classes this winter. He said I should take a leave of absence, go home to Canada, see whether it all blows over."

"I presume he knows the U.S. has an extradition treaty with Canada. But maybe if you left it would slow down the sheriff's juggernaut. Do you want to leave?"

His dark eyes flickered to a chest of drawers by the door. "Yes. No. I don't know."

That was all I could get out of him. I urged him to call me at any hour, day or night, as soon as he wanted to talk, and turned to leave.

On my way out, I stopped at the bureau. On top was a book I recognized, a slim volume, azure, with a design inlaid in silver.

"Tarik Kataba's poems?" I was amazed. "Fausson had this same book next to his bed. And you *still* tell me you never knew him?"

Felix grabbed the book and clutched it to his heart. "Damn you, Vic, damn you, I never met Fausson, I never talked to him. Why can't I have a book of poetry of my own. Do you know every person who reads—I don't know—whatever poet you like yourself?"

Angry tears spurted from the corners of his eyes.

A kaleidoscope turned in my head: the woman with the long braid on Devon Avenue. The daughter who'd accepted a special award for Arabic poetry while Tarik Kataba was in prison.

"Kataba—his daughter is a student here, isn't she?" I said softly.

He looked at me, yearning, loss, impotent fury chasing across his face. "Oh, go away, just go away."

He collapsed onto the edge of the bed, clutching the book, silently weeping. I went to him and kissed the top of his head, but he refused to look up.

3 3

BLINDSIDED

I HAD TO sprint to get to the engineering building in time for my appointment with Dean Pazdur. I ran past something that looked like a giant warehouse, darted between the cars on State Street, and was presenting my card to Pazdur's executive assistant as the clock hanging from the ceiling read 1:24. Nine minutes late, close enough—especially since Pazdur himself kept me waiting for another ten.

Pazdur's office was in the corner of the second floor, where I could see across State Street to the L platform. The station looked like a large corrugated tube; maybe it was supposed to make me think of daring architecture, but it looked rickety, like a place where muggers could lurk to attack students getting off the train.

Pazdur rose to greet me as I came in but repeated his warning. "I'm not sure how useful it is for you to meet with me, because I am not going to discuss student academic performance or private lives with anyone unconnected with the Institute, or who isn't a family member."

He was a man perhaps in his forties, with thinning blond hair and a square face, the kind that people think betokens authority. His desk held the normal paper clutter of an administrative office, along with the requisite computer, pictures of his family—three grinning blond kids, a smiling wife, an eager terrier—and models of different buildings and machines, none as intricate as the ones Felix had created.

I sat down. "I have to start someplace, Dr. Pazdur. I was with Felix

Herschel when the cops took him out to Cap Sauers Holding to identify a dead body, so I have significant skin in the game, so to speak."

"Even so—"

"Even so, Felix couldn't identify the dead man. He's been questioned
numerous times by the sheriff's police, who aren't happy to give him the
same privacy you value. It's my understanding that you spoke to someone from the police about their reaction to their interviews with Felix?"

Pazdur frowned. "Who told you that?"

"Is that an outraged denial? You didn't speak to the police about
Felix?"

"He's a student here. If he's committed a crime, the school has a
responsibility to the whole institution to act. And since he won't tell
anyone anything, it makes it hard for us to spring to his defense."

"Felix told us that you were concerned because he wouldn't tell the
cops what he did on his vacation in the Boundary Waters. He says you
suggested he drop out and go back to Canada. Did you?"

Pazdur studied the street below us, where students were crossing
State Street, heading into the warehouse-like building, or coming back
toward us with cups of coffee and sandwiches.

"Felix is a talented young man," he said at last. "All of our students
are talented in one way or another, of course, but Felix has a particular
gift with metal, almost a sculptor's understanding of what and how it
can be shaped. He also has the mathematical interest in stresses and
alloys and so on that we expect here. He has the potential to be an
outstanding metals engineer."

"Have you told him that?"

"Oh, yes." Pazdur smiled briefly. "It doesn't do anyone any good to
be praised behind their backs, any more than it does to be criticized
there. But he's been neglecting his work. Ever since that disastrous day
in November when ICE agents came on campus, Felix has become a
sloppy student. If he'd performed like this his first term, he would be
on academic probation. He was so gifted, so above average, in his fall
performance that I've been cutting him a fair amount of slack. But the
police inquiry, adding to his own anger over ICE actions—it's making
it hard for him to be the student he not only can be but needs to be."

"You don't think he's doing, let's say, radical work, do you?"

Pazdur curled his lip. "Making bombs, you mean? If he is, he's not doing it on campus. No, the students he's working with are designing a prototype to turn human waste into drinking water and power. It's been done, but on a large scale. They're trying to build something that's genuinely portable. Portable and potable." He smirked—it was obviously a joke he liked to repeat.

"Felix showed me a prototype," I said. "The crafting was beautiful, but of course I have no idea whether it would work or not. Was Lawrence Fausson ever connected to the school?"

"Fausson?" Pazdur was puzzled. "Oh, that was the dead man in the woods, wasn't it. If he was connected to IIT, I haven't heard anything in the rumor mill, and that's the kind of thing the mill thrives on. Why? Do you have evidence he was a student here?"

"Nope. But I assume you know why the cops are focusing on Felix—they found a scrap of paper in Fausson's pocket with Felix's phone number on it. Felix claims they never met, but why did Fausson have his number? I thought if Fausson had been on this campus in some capacity, their paths would have crossed. Can you check?"

Pazdur muttered something that I chose not to hear, but he called his assistant and asked her to look up Fausson.

While we waited, I said, "I don't know why you think Felix would be better off at home. We have an extradition treaty with Canada. Besides, if he leaves Chicago, the cops will take it as an admission of guilt."

"If he stays here and doesn't cooperate, there will be a mess—arrest, spotlight on the campus, student protests, everything I'm trying to avoid."

"That's disappointing—I was hoping you had some plan that would help Felix, but you want to jettison him to save the school."

"I'm responsible for the whole engineering school, not just one student—and one who's difficult to deal with—oh, thank you, Kim." He hung up. "We've never had a Fausson here, as a student or janitor or even a lacrosse coach. Anything else?"

"Why did you say 'janitor'?" I asked sharply.

He glared at me. "The first word that came to mind. If there's nothing else, I have a student waiting with actual engineering questions."

"You're right. One last question. Do you have anyone here named Kataba?"

"Is this a trick?" Pazdur was suddenly furious, his fair skin turning a blotchy red. "You already know the answer to that."

I shook my head, bewildered.

"If you've been talking to young Herschel, I'm sure he told you. I resent you trying to trick me."

"Honestly, Dr. Pazdur, I have no idea what you're talking about. And Felix said nothing to me about anyone by that name. Is it a man or a woman?"

Pazdur's face was still rigid with anger, but he got up to shut his office door. "We have a student here named Rasima Kataba; she was taken into custody by ICE on Thursday afternoon. Tell me that you didn't know about this."

I gaped at him. "Was it on the news?" I managed to ask.

He narrowed his eyes at me, trying to decide if my ignorance was real. "We've tried to keep it quiet: our international students are already under too much pressure. You really don't know about this? Felix didn't tell you?"

"Is she undocumented?"

"She has a student visa, but ICE agents came on Thursday to question her about her father. They say he's here illegally and that she's using her visa status to hide him and block his deportation. When she refused to answer their questions, they took her into custody. They've been interrogating me and my staff, as if we were somehow fomenting terrorism by admitting her as a student."

Felix and his tears, hugging his copy of Kataba's poems. He was in love with a Syrian woman with a long braid who'd run afoul of U.S. immigration laws. If she was still in Chicago it would explain why Felix himself was unwilling to leave.

"You said you were keeping this quiet, but you also thought Felix would have told me. Does he know?"

Pazdur bit his lower lip, reluctant to let out more information, but finally said, "The Engineers in a Free State were meeting in one of our common rooms down the hall when the ICE agents arrived. Herschel and seven or eight others were there."

"You know this means everyone on campus will have heard by now," I said. "I'm surprised you don't have protestors lining the sidewalks."

Pazdur's shoulders slumped. "You're probably right. But you're sidestepping my question. How did you know about her?"

"I don't, not really, but I'm pretty sure her father is a Syrian poet named Tarik Kataba. Lawrence Fausson had a copy of Tarik's poems in his apartment; there was a newspaper clipping inside about a special poetry prize Rasima Kataba accepted on her father's behalf when he was in prison. Some people in the Syrian community think they saw Tarik in Chicago recently. Fausson's connection to Kataba is one of the few facts I've uncovered. If Tarik's daughter is a student here, that might show me how Fausson learned Felix's name, even if the two never actually met."

"You're sure this poet is her father?" Pazdur asked.

"It's a pretty good guess," I said. "I've never met either of them. But Rasima Kataba is the daughter who's named in this clipping about the prize."

"I've had to go through all her documents, of course, since the government has been interrogating me," Pazdur said bitterly. "In the personal statement Rasima submitted with her application, she said her father was a bicycle mechanic in Saraqib—the Syrian town where she grew up. She didn't mention poetry."

"I don't imagine poets make any better a living in Syria than they do here—he had to work at something," I said. "If he was a bicycle mechanic, maybe she grew up taking engines and gear shafts apart." I thought of the beautifully wrought chain belts in Felix's model; had Rasima created those?

"Her fundamentals and her abilities were strong. We had every reason to admit her."

He sounded defensive enough that I asked if he thought Rasima was guilty of some crime that the school should have known about.

Pazdur fidgeted in his chair. "No. I don't. But I never looked at her record until these immigration agents questioned me about why we didn't do a background check on her family. There doesn't seem to be any record of how she arrived in the States, or who she came with. It didn't matter so much three years ago. Now, of course—" He flung up his hands.

Now, of course.

"I heard her mother is dead," I said.

"A fact I only learned during the interrogation ICE put me through. The agent seemed to think we were damned near colluding with ISIS by not have a dossier on every one of Rasima's relatives."

He slapped the desktop hard enough to make his scale models jump. "Felix Herschel is a complication I don't need right now."

I ignored that outburst. "Does ICE think Rasima's father is dangerous, or are they just trying to get every person not born here out of the country?"

"I don't know. This is a hideous time on a campus like mine, and Felix—if he's involved in something illegal—I need to know sooner, not later. I can't afford federal scrutiny of every aspect of my school."

Pazdur's PA opened the door just wide enough to stick her head through. "I'm sorry, Richard, but Keith Lamont has been waiting twenty minutes now for his appointment."

I went to the door. "I'll call you if I learn anything helpful. Why don't you do the same?"

Pazdur nodded wearily. He was looking again at the L, as if he wanted to jump through the window and ride it to the end of the line.

3 4

THE ACCUSED

BEFORE I GOT into my car, I craned my neck to stare at the corrugated tube overhead. It wasn't made of cardboard but layered metal beams whose rusted bolts made it look unstable.

ICE had detained Rasima Kataba, threatening her with deportation because she wouldn't tell them where her father was. My own mother came to America in 1944 at nineteen, illegally, after her Italian-Jewish mother was taken into custody by the Fascists. Gabriella's life here hadn't been easy, but no one had tried to throw her out, throw her back to certain death. How had we become the country that imprisoned children for the crime of not having a birth certificate?

I called Felix.

"Now what?"

I put a finger in my ear as a train roared overhead, rattling the rusty joints. "If you haven't told Martha Simone about your friend, you should. Martha can find out where she's being held and get her the legal support she needs."

"How—who—" He choked.

"Dean Pazdur told me what happened. I'd rather you not say anything else on the phone: your calls are almost certainly being monitored. I'm still on campus—do you want me to stop by before I leave?"

"No. I have class in twenty minutes. Vic—thank you, Vic." His voice cracked—perhaps relief that he wasn't carrying his grief alone. "Could you call Martha for me?"

I used a burn phone to call the lawyer. Communications with Simone were privileged, so even if someone listened in on my calls, they couldn't use them, at least not legally.

Simone promised to get on the case as soon as possible. "Is Dr. Herschel going to cover these charges?" she asked.

Of course Simone couldn't work pro bono. "Add your fee for Ms. Kataba to my bill with Freeman," I said.

My six-figure bill for legal fees was a guarantee that I'd be working until I was older than Mr. Contreras.

"Before you hang up, I need to be able to prove I'm on the side of the angels," I said. "I'm on my way to Rasima Kataba's apartment and it would help if you sent me a document stating you represent her and that I'm assisting you, so that her neighbors believe me when I tell them I'm not with ICE."

"It would have to be right this minute? Okay." I could hear her typing as she talked. "How did you get her address?"

"Felix made a beeline for her building after we left the woods last Wednesday," I said. "But I don't know what surname she uses on her door."

"So Felix went straight to her but didn't think to mention it to his counsel? What else is that young man hiding?"

I didn't try to answer. As I started my car, I couldn't believe it had been only last week that all this had started. Felix and the dead Fausson in the woods, followed instantly by Harmony's appearance at my front door. I felt seven years older, not seven days. I looked at my face in the rearview mirror. Gray hollows under my eyes, almost like misapplied eye shadow, deepened my hazel eyes to a matching gray. Very sexy.

I bounced across the rutted gravel to the street, heading east to the lake. ICE agents had undoubtedly been at Rasima's apartment ahead of me, but they'd been looking for evidence about her father.

The Syrians I'd spoken to in the Grommet Building had acknowledged working with Fausson. They'd clammed up and backed away when I brought up Tarik Kataba's name. They knew him, obviously, and were protecting him. Kataba knew Fausson in Syria, so the two were connected and connected to the Grommet Building through the cleaning service. If Kataba had left any evidence connecting him to Fausson, ICE would have seized it. I wasn't sure what I hoped to find, but I felt a need to look.

I'd debated asking Felix for Rasima's apartment number, but I couldn't do that on the phone, and I had a feeling Felix would object, hotly, to my exploring her home—especially if he realized I'd followed him there the night we'd looked at Fausson's body.

I was waiting at the light on Cottage when my phone rang: the University of Chicago exchange. It was Candra van Vliet at the Oriental Institute, demanding Ms. Warshawski.

"Who did you talk to about our Dagon?" she asked without preamble.

"Your what?" Cars behind me were honking; I pulled to the side.

"The Dagon—the fish-man that you saw here on Monday. Who did you talk to about it?"

"I'll be glad to tell you if you explain why you're asking," I said.

"It was on the news Monday night."

"So it was," I agreed. "I heard it myself."

"And that is why you need to come down to the Institute at once to discuss who you talked to about it."

"I didn't get the memo," I said.

"What are you talking about?" she snapped. "What memo?"

"The memo that said today was the day to call me with irrational demands. Do you want to start this conversation again from the beginning, or shall we hang up so I can get to my own meeting with my own clients?"

A pause, while she thought it over. "Very well. Please tell me if you described the Dagon to anyone."

"No, ma'am. I talked about it with Mary-Carol Kooi. Period, end of story."

A longer pause. "Someone broke into the Institute last night and stole it."

"Wasn't me," I said.

"I wasn't accusing you," Van Vliet said stiffly.

"Your call began with an idiotic accusation."

"I apologize." Her voice was even frostier. "I am so disconcerted that I am not thinking clearly."

"I hope you reported the theft to the police."

"Of course we did, but once an artifact that rare has been stolen, it almost always disappears into the underground collector world and is never seen again."

"I still don't know why you called me. I know nothing about antique art or Dagons or how to buy and sell on the illegal market." I put the Mustang into gear and moved back into traffic. "I presume you had locked it in a vault. I'm sure the university's insurers will ask that question."

She was taken aback but said, "I'm on my way to Philadelphia for a conference; I'd left it on my desk with a note to Mary-Carol Kooi, telling her what steps I wanted her to take to identify it. Very few people knew that it was in my office, but the thief knew to go there. My lock is easy to circumvent, but they used violence, breaking the glass pane in the door. They also took my Inanna figure."

I was guessing that was the eight-breasted goddess, but I said politely, "I'm sorry for your trouble. That kind of invasion always feels like a personal violation. I hope you've also informed the FBI and Interpol."

I hung up but had barely turned onto Lake Shore Drive when she phoned again. I could understand why Felix answered my call with "Now what?" but I said hello with as much politeness as I could muster.

"It's Pete Sansen, Ms. Warshawski. I met you Monday in Candra's office."

Oh, yes, the balding, sunburned director of the Oriental Institute.

"We're all in shock down here. We have a collection of immense value in the museum, and we have the requisite security for it, but whoever came in was able to bypass our lobby security. They didn't try to get into the museum but went straight to Candra's office."

I kept my focus on the traffic, which was moving fast to beat the afternoon rush.

"I wasn't surprised that the Dagon made it into the news," Sansen said. "By the end of the day Monday, most of the Sumerian students and all the museum staff knew about it, including its dramatic arrival in the middle of the night. Of course they were all talking about it. But very few people knew Candra had it."

"The package was addressed to her," I objected.

He was silent. Only the ticking seconds on my car's computer screen told me we were still connected.

He came back on the line after a minute. "Yes, that's true. But she hadn't put it in the museum vault; she'd locked it in her own desk, hoping to study it more thoroughly today."

"I had no way of knowing that, Professor Sansen. But even if I'd known, I wouldn't have thought about it—she already had a number of other valuable-seeming objects in her office, including the figurine she says was also taken."

"We've talked to the police, we've spoken to the FBI's art crimes unit, and of course we've put it out on Interpol as well as advising the international artifacts project. But you have an eye for Chicago crimes. I'm hoping to persuade you to come down and look at our crime scene, to see if there's something we've overlooked."

I ran my afternoon schedule through my head. "I couldn't do it before seven-thirty this evening, and I would expect to be paid my usual fee, a hundred dollars an hour plus expenses."

"Even for a consultation?" he asked.

"In this case, yes. I've got an overfull caseload, and Professor Van Vliet began the conversation by accusing me of playing a role in your fish-man's theft."

"Ah, yes. That was awkward, wasn't it? Seven-thirty, then. I'll talk to our purchasing department about how to classify your work."

I didn't think I could do anything for them, but it was an odd problem: an unusual object shows up in the middle of the night and is stolen in the middle of the following night. It made me curious enough to want to see the crime scene.

I had reached my exit at Wilson Avenue when my phone rang again. This time it was Dick, furious that I'd been out to see Teri.

"She says you came with all kinds of accusations about my relationship with the company that Reno was working for."

It was hard to believe that his light baritone had ever made my heart flutter.

"What company was that?" I asked.

"Rest EZ, as you damned well know."

"When I saw you last week, you claimed not to know where Reno had been working," I objected. "Then you said Glynis gave her a list of prospective employers. Now you're hot and bothered about Rest EZ."

"I didn't want you butting your know-it-all nose into my business. It isn't perjury when you're trying to get your ex-wife to leave you alone."

Maybe that was supposed to be a joke, but it didn't come close to making me want to laugh. "Dick, I have been fed so many lies this last week that it's almost been like eating fois gras morning, noon, and night. After a while, the diet is so rich you start to choke on it."

"Before you say anything slanderous, you should know I'm recording this call," he said stiffly.

"Just like Teri. Tell me why you've called: I'm keeping a client waiting."

"Then *you* stay on the topic. You told Teri Reno was blackmailing me—"

"Jesus, Dick—*she* said Reno was blackmailing you. I suggested she urge you to dig deeper into Rest EZ and Trechette. They are highly secretive companies. If you are in on their secrets, I hope they are not illegal or disgusting. My words to Teri were to ask if Reno had come to you with evidence about illegal acts by either company."

"She didn't," he snapped.

"But she talked to you when she got back, right? Even though you and Glynis said she hadn't."

"That's because my actions with my nieces are my business, and I'm fucking tired of you making them *your* business."

"Right, Dick. You didn't suggest to your clients that she be one of their hostesses at their debauch in St. Matthieu last month. And so when she asked you for the directors' names, you felt you had to protect them, not Reno. Correct?"

"'Debauch'? What kind of word is that?"

"Sounds French to me, but I'm not a linguist."

"You know what I mean. My clients don't conduct themselves like that."

"So no one assaulted Reno, you don't know where she is, and you're not worried about her well-being."

"Those two girls know how to land on their feet, believe me."

"I think we know two different women. Or should that be four different women, the two you know and my two? Actually, I've only met one of them. Teri told you about Harmony being attacked on the lakefront?"

"That was unfortunate. Glynis tried to find out where she's staying so we could send flowers," Dick said even more stiffly. "I assume you know, since you've set yourself up as her protector."

"You might send lilies," I offered. "They're traditional for funerals, and I very much fear Reno is dead. Doesn't that worry you?"

He didn't say anything.

"Reno's fate isn't what Arnaud Minable wanted to talk to you about Monday night, was it?" I prodded.

"You have a hell of a nerve, Vic, thinking I'd collude in Reno's death, or stand by while she died. You go around saying that in public, and you'll face a slander suit so fast you won't be able to say 'subpoena' before you're reading it."

"Bravo, Dick. I can see the jury, all teary-eyed over the misunderstood, tenderly loving uncle. Until, of course, we start crossing you and Teri and your mom on your absolute refusal to help Becky or her daughters."

I paused for a beat, to let that sink in. He started to sputter, but I cut across him ruthlessly.

"Arnaud Minable seems to be representing Trechette in a suit filed against an insurance subsidiary by North American Ti-Balt. Trechette owns Rest EZ. Reno works—worked for Rest EZ. You connect those dots into a different drawing."

"How do you know about Trechette and Ti-Balt?" he demanded.

"Lawsuits are filed in court and court documents are open to the public." I put a maximum of patronage into my tone. "I've been trying to find out who owned Rest EZ so I could track down who Reno ran afoul of in St. Matthieu. The Trechette name popped up in dozens of places, but no human face was attached. So looking at legal action was the logical next step."

It had been the logical step, just not one that occurred to me until this minute. As soon as I got back from inspecting Rasima Kataba's apartment, I'd spend some time with LexisNexis, to see who else was suing Trechette.

"Runkel, Soraude and Minable are based in Havre-des-Anges," Dick said. "The firm needs a U.S. address, so they're renting space from us, but we don't handle any of their business. I may have offered some advice to Minable on key aspects of U.S. foreign tax compliance, but I'm not party to their actions."

"So you don't care if I do more research into *Ti-Balt v. Trechette?*" I asked.

"Would you stop if I did care?" he asked.

I laughed. "Nope. Just curious about how disinterested you actually are. After all, only two days ago, I saw you leaving for dinner with Minable and Gervase Kettie. You wouldn't bring Minable to that gathering if he wasn't important to Kettie. And if he's important to a power ranger, that means he's important to you."

"Be very careful what you say on an open line," Dick advised me. "Very careful indeed."

"Thank you, Dick," I said meekly. "I appreciate your caring enough about me to give me such valuable advice."

HOME WITHOUT A MINDER

I CHECKED MY e-mail. Martha Simone had come through with a formal document, describing her relationship with Felix and Rasima and listing me as an investigator helping uncover evidence that could be used in both Felix's and Rasima's defense.

I found an Internet café on Lawrence a few blocks from Rasima's building and printed out the document. I also checked online for a photo. Rasima didn't have a Facebook page, but she was in some student photos from the IIT engineering school, wearing jeans and sweatshirts, but covering her hair. Her distinctive face with its deep-set, thoughtful eyes looked much as it had in the photo of her at thirteen.

The caption described some of the water projects she'd worked on with her adviser. I could picture her and Felix, heads bent together over the machinery in the engineering school lab, creating their prototypes. Of course they'd fallen in love, or at least Felix had.

I cropped the group photos so that I had separate pictures of both Felix and Rasima. I left my car at the meter on Lawrence and walked to Rasima's building. In the middle of the afternoon, kids were starting to come home from school. I followed a group of teen girls up the walk to the entrance, but stopped to study the directory, looking for KATABA. 4P. I rang the bell. The girls stared at me, exuding a whiff of teen menace.

"No one is there," one of them said. "And the immigration, they already trashed the apartment."

"Don't talk to her, Raina—she's a cop, she already knows!"

"Yeah, you can tell—look at her fist—she punched someone too hard."

"Ooh, chill, Hania, white lady cop's getting mad, she's going to hit you with the other hand."

I'd been a tough teen myself, although with a cop for a father, I wouldn't have dared join in cop-baiting. To this group, I looked Anglo, which was mildly ironic: as a child I'd been the Jew's daughter or the Wop's kid.

I leaned against the inner door, blocking their way. "You girls are impressive, but I'm not with ICE or the city; I work for the lawyer who's trying to get Rasima Kataba out of detention. The lawyer is also trying to keep Felix from being arrested for murder."

I showed them my PI license and the letter from Martha Simone. They looked at each other, daring to be the one to read the letter or touch the license.

A couple of men came off the elevator and headed to the exit. I moved away from the door so they could leave. One of them spoke sharply to the girls in Arabic. They scowled, but the one called Hania pulled her scarf, which was wrapped around her neck, over her hair. The other two stared defiantly at the men, not covering their hair, but moving away from them into the building. When I followed the girls, the men eyed me narrowly but didn't try to question me.

"What was that about?" I asked as we waited for the elevator.

"Shaming Islam," Raina muttered.

"We don't really know Rasima," the girl with the scarf said. "She's like eight years older, but she's at college, she's going to be somebody, not just a mother staying at home behind the cooking pots."

"Her father is a poet," I said. "I suppose you know that? Does he live here with Rasima?"

A cautious exchange of glances. "You really not with ICE?" the boldest said.

"I really am not with ICE. You can call the lawyer, or you can look me up online and see the kind of work I do." I handed them cards with my website address. They studied them before tucking them into their jeans pockets.

Hania looked around. "He was here sometimes but he's illegal."

"When did you last see him?" I asked.

They hunched their shoulders; they didn't watch for him, they couldn't say.

"Maybe more than two weeks," Raina said, "because those men just now, they were trying to shame Rasima about being in the apartment without a—a *wasi*."

"*Wasi?*" I asked.

"A minder," Hania translated. "A man or an old woman who would be taking care of her."

"A man who would give her orders," Raina said. "But Rasima isn't wanting a man to give her orders."

"Yeah, but when those guys saw her with Felix, I thought they were going to kill both her and him," Hania said. "So maybe it would be better if she had a *wasi*."

The thought silenced all of us; no one spoke again until the elevator arrived. Once we were on board, the girls retreated into their own world, speaking in Arabic, not about me, I thought, since they were giggling and punching each other.

Apartment hallways smell like the cooking of the residents. No overboiled cabbage as I followed the letters on the fourth-floor doors, but sharp spices. I could pick out the cardamom and cloves, but the rest were too subtle for me.

Apartment P was locked, without crime scene tape. My picks are getting to be obsolete with all the new electronic door locks, but this building was old, and the lock still had the kind of tumblers I could handle.

It was a small place, one large main room with a desk, a pullout couch, prayer rugs, and a wall of books, mostly in Arabic. The one bedroom clearly belonged to Rasima—engineering textbooks had been tossed onto the narrow bed, as if dumped after being shaken for documents.

The law hadn't touched a shelf holding miniature gears and pulleys. These were like the careful work I'd seen at Felix's, but more domestic—an elaborate pulley turned the handle of a wringer on an open washing machine, foot pedals moved a carpet sweeper. I longed to pick them up and play with them, but I didn't want to add to the damage created by law enforcement.

The girls had exaggerated when they said ICE had trashed the place. Besides the disruption in Rasima's bedroom, they'd pulled papers out of drawers, books off shelves, and flung clothes onto the closet floor, but it wasn't nearly the mess the wreckers had created in Reno's apartment: the feds had reassembled the sofa bed in the living room, sort of, and hadn't emptied spices or flour in the kitchenette in the corner.

They'd knocked over the family photos on the desk in the main room. I picked them up and studied them: big family gatherings where Rasima was one small girl among many children, distinguishable even when young by her narrow face and deep-set eyes. Rasima in a school uniform, clutching the hand of a slightly older boy, and in another, both children with their parents. Pictures of a courtyard in the middle of a square of small houses, pictures of a man working on a bicycle chain. I took a picture of that one—Tarik Kataba in the days before Assad's prison and the Syrian civil war, grinning happily at the camera.

I set the photos back up on the desk, adjusting the edges where pictures had become dislodged, then picked up the papers from the floor and sat on the daybed to examine them. Some were in Arabic, which surprised me—I assumed the feds would have taken everything in Arabic to sift for proof of terrorism. The rest were the ordinary detritus of life, receipted bills, unpaid bills, a notice to Tarik from Force 5:

Dear Valued Employee,
Because you have missed your shift two nights in a row, we are taking
you off our work register. To return to work you must go to our offices
on Milwaukee Avenue and file your paperwork again.

By this point, I wasn't surprised to see that Kataba had worked for Force 5, although the confirmation was valuable. I looked at the postmark on the notice: almost a week before Fausson's body had turned up in the forest preserve.

Felix had blurted out *Where's he from?* to Lieutenant McGivney. It looked to me as though he was afraid that the dead man might have been Kataba. The poet had disappeared, and Rasima and Felix were scared about what had happened to him—I guessed.

Fausson and Kataba had known each other in Syria. They reconnected in Chicago, which made it likely that Rasima also knew Fausson. I was afraid that made it plausible that Felix also had known him, unless his relationship with Rasima was very new.

Rasima was in detention because ICE wanted to find her father. I thought again of the hundred-dollar bills under Fausson's floor. Maybe the cruds who'd shot at me really had been federal agents, but what was Fausson up to? Currency smuggling is an electronic business these days, but I suppose small-time hoods still did it the old-fashioned way, with actual bills. Or could Fausson traffic in refugees? I hadn't even thought of that, but given his attachment to his Syrian friends, he might be raising money to help bring people into this country. Tarik and Rasima, for instance.

I couldn't make sense of any of it, but I was getting hungry, which made it harder to do keen analytical work.

Before leaving the building, an impulse to help Rasima made me go into her bedroom to tidy up the engineering books. Among them was a small pamphlet, printed on shiny cheap paper in English and Arabic—*Treasures of the Saraqib Museum*. The museum building was on the cover, a whitewashed structure of brick or stone, about the size of a small house.

The treasures inside came from the Tell at Ebla, the text told me. The first few pages were in black and white—photos of figurines of cows and goddesses and bulls, some jewelry, a number of clay tablets, a few ivory pieces. The pamphlet fell open to a two-page spread with staples down the middle. There was a single photograph, in color, of the body of a man with the head of a fish.

TREASURES OF SARAQIB

AT A DINER near where I'd parked I ordered a bowl of tomato-chickpea soup, but it grew cold while I frowned over the centerfold in *Treasures of the Saraqib Museum*. In the photograph, you could see that the figure was of a giant fish embracing a man, rather than a man with a fish's head. The fish head covered the man's head like a headdress, leaving the man's eyes and nose visible. The fish's body was draped across his neck and back, with the tail hanging below his waist.

The man was naked except for a short skirt made of fish scales. He wore wrist guards and held something knobby in his left hand. I squinted—it looked like rows of teeth. In his right hand he carried what looked like a purse. When I met with Peter Sansen at the Oriental Institute this evening I'd ask him about it.

In the photo, the statue gleamed more golden than bronze, but as far as I could tell, it was identical to the piece I'd seen in Candra van Vliet's office Monday morning.

Dagon, Peter Sansen had called it. I looked it up online. Dagon apparently wasn't a god of fishing but of agriculture. He guaranteed fertile fields and had been worshipped in a part of ancient Sumer called Ebla. Until the recent mayhem in Syria, Ebla had been an archaeology mecca. It was near the modern town of Saraqib, where Lawrence Fausson had met the poet Tarik Kataba.

"You're not eating; soup is no good?" The waitress had appeared at my elbow.

I assured her it was delicious, but she was solicitous; it wasn't good cold, she'd bring a fresh bowl. When it came, I ate it quickly, to forestall her concern, and ordered a coffee.

Rasima or her father must have brought the treasure out of Saraqib to keep it safe from the ISIS looters. They had delivered it to Candra van Vliet in the middle of Sunday night. No, Rasima was already in custody. Her father, perhaps? The Syrian poet trying to safeguard his country's treasures? Or Felix, trying to help his lover.

I drummed my fingers on the diner counter. My impulse was to race back to the IIT to confront Felix, but I couldn't think what purpose that would serve. Did it matter if it had been Felix or Tarik Kataba who'd delivered the Dagon to the Oriental Institute? The more important question, after all, was: Who had wanted it badly enough to break in and steal it?

There was one other color photo in the pamphlet, the statuette of a horned woman holding snakes in her outstretched hands. The figure looked contemporary, the hair short with a circlet around it. In the photo, she looked greeny brown, with rouged lips. I looked at the black-and-white photos on the pamphlet's other pages. Clay tablets, rings, a necklace, some figurines. Also a small stone lion. I knew that lion, or one like it. I squinted at it. Part of the right forepaw was missing. It had been sitting on Lawrence Fausson's desk when I went into the apartment last week.

The lion, the fish-man—what treasure of Saraqib would show up next? And exactly what was Fausson's role in them? Thief, middleman, protector?

But if he'd spent the two years after he left Syria collecting artifacts to sell, where was his hoard? I'd been to his apartment an hour ahead of the shooters; other than the lion, he hadn't kept statues or clay tablets there, not unless he'd torn up floorboards throughout his apartment to create caches.

Apartments often had storage lockers in their basements. Fausson could have used one of those, but I was betting on an outside locker—he needed to control access to his treasures, and an apartment basement wouldn't be secure. Always assuming he had treasures to store.

I called Niko Cruickshank, to see if he'd found anything else on Fausson's hard drive—such as the address of a storage locker.

"I'm recovering part of his address book," Niko said, "but it's a jumble of names in English and Arabic and I can't match them to e-mail or phone. I have sentences here and there from documents; I'm compiling a file, which I'll send you, but it's pretty much gibberish. How much money do you want to spend, Vic? I've already put in eighteen hours."

At one-fifty an hour, that was $2,700. I was bleeding money on family matters. "See what you can retrieve in another six," I said finally. "Addresses and money are what I'm most interested in."

"I'll see what I can do," Niko said, "but there's not a lot here. You should have used something else as a shield, not the hard drive."

"That would have been my spine, Niko. In which case you'd be giving your information to my ghost."

"You're my favorite client, Warshawski. No one else has your sense of humor."

"It wasn't meant as a joke," I said, but he hung up.

I paid my bill, adding the price of the first bowl of soup to the tip. As I climbed back into my car, I tried to remember what else I'd seen in Lawrence Fausson's apartment last week.

The drama and trauma of escaping the shooting had dominated my memory. I leaned back in my car seat, picturing the apartment. I'd entered and had been overwhelmed by the aerial photo on the wall. I'd gone into the bedroom and found the book by Candra van Vliet. Receipts next to the bed for the Damascus Gate on Austin. I'd been in the closet, riffling through Fausson's clothes. No keys there or in his desk drawers.

If he'd carried all his keys with him, whoever killed him had the keys. Unless they'd fallen out of his pocket when he'd been dragged through the woods.

A trip to the squirrel home in Cap Sauers Holding would take whatever was left of daylight. Anyway, it was a job for a team of trackers, not one weary solo op.

Lieutenant McGivney with the sheriff's police had a team of trackers, if he felt like sending them into the woods. I thought about how to couch the conversation.

McGivney greeted my call with a rough grunt. I guess that was a step up from Felix's surly "Now what?"

"Did ICE tell you what they found in Lawrence Fausson's apartment?" I asked.

"ICE?" he echoed. "What the hell were they doing in there?"

"They don't confide in me," I said primly. "I thought they might share with a fellow law officer."

He snorted. "The day that anyone from Homeland shares as much as a football score with local LEOs is the day pigs fly. How do you even know they were there?"

"It came up in conversation with a local reporter," I said, figuring McGivney didn't need to know I was the one who mentioned it to Murray Ryerson. "Shots were fired in Fausson's building; the shooters claimed they were with ICE."

McGivney digested that. "'Claimed'? Anybody see ID?"

"If I knew I'd tell you. I don't know. Don't know if they were agents or home invaders, don't know if they were men or women, how many there were, how they got into the building, how many shots were fired, or even if anybody inside the building was hurt."

"So you got squat but you're calling me for a reason. Which is?"

"I hoped you'd heard from ICE. I hoped they'd found Lawrence Fausson's keys, and that they would have shared that knowledge with you. Unless you already had them, that is."

"Why do you want Fausson's keys? You want my sanction to go into the apartment? Why do you need that when Martha Simone can get you a court order to let you in?"

It was my turn to pause while I went back over my conversations with McGivney. Simone had told the state's attorney she had an investigator digging into Fausson's associates; McGivney had made the leap, but it was a reasonable guess.

"From what I hear, Fausson's apartment didn't have a lot of value in it. If he brought anything back from the Middle East with him besides his books of Arabic poetry, it would be in a storage locker. I suppose he could have rented—"

"What do you mean?" McGivney demanded. "What did he bring back from the Middle East?"

"I don't know, Lieutenant. That's why I'd like to find his keys, see if he rented a locker somewhere."

"But you have evidence of something. Was he a smuggler? What did he smuggle? Drugs?"

"It's true he spent a lot of time in the Middle East, including Afghanistan, but he flew home on commercial flights, and it's not that easy for a single person to bypass customs, immigration, and so on with a suitcase full of heroin."

"How do you know? About the flights, I mean."

Hell. I knew because I'd seen Fausson's passport in his apartment. In all my years at the public defender's, I had pounded on my clients to answer only the question asked, not to babble and volunteer information. I'd gotten out of practice.

"I talked to his old professors and colleagues. Any law officer could do the same. I guess I'll get a team together and go back to Cap Sauers Holding, see what we can find with a metal detector."

"It's still an active crime scene," McGivney said sharply.

I laughed. "You been out there lately, Lieutenant? I went looking at it a couple of days ago and the tape is down, helping litter the woods. If you want to preserve your scene, best take your deputies away from bird-dogging Felix Herschel and put them in the forest preserve."

"So that was you at the Herschel boy's apartment this morning."

"Young man," I corrected. "And I don't see that it's a big secret."

"What were you looking for at the crime scene, anyway, Warshawski?"

"Whatever I could see. Which was squirrels, rotting logs, and litter."

At the other end of the phone, McGivney was giving orders to someone; when he came back on the line it was to ask for the names of Fausson's old professors and colleagues.

"Lieutenant, I found these people through asking questions with an open mind. Yours is closed: you're sure Felix Herschel is guilty because his phone number was in Fausson's pocket, and because he's a Canadian who crossed the Boundary Waters into Canada. Let me know when you're looking seriously for credible suspects and I'll be glad to share what I've learned through unpaid hard work."

I hung up as McGivney peppered me with questions. Brava, V.I. You know as much as when you called him. Well, perhaps I had a tiny piece of negative knowledge—the county didn't have Fausson's keys.

BATWOMAN

I WAS ON my way to my office when Marilyn Lieberman called from Arcadia House. My heartbeat spiked.

"What's going on? Did someone find Harmony?"

"No. But she's making herself sick over this necklace. I know it's a long shot in a Chicago park, but you said you'd try to look for it. She says Clarisse gave one to her and one to Reno when they graduated from junior college; the locket has pictures of Clarisse and Henry?"

"Her foster parents," I said. "I'll ask at the Town Hall District, but it's a very long shot."

I was south of the district headquarters by then, and south of where we'd been attacked in the park. I got off the drive and turned back north. I was able to find parking near the underpass where I'd found Mitch, so I started there, walking slowly, shining my flash along the gutters. I even risked death by lying flat and peering into the drain at the edge of the underpass while cars honked at me; one driver stopped to swear at me.

The attack had happened quickly; people think trauma embeds a picture on the brain, but it's usually the opposite. You don't remember clearly. I went back to the hill where I'd been standing and then tried to retrace my steps to the exact spot where Harmony had been struggling.

Several joggers stopped to ask what I'd lost. After an hour I had to give up. I paid a courtesy call on the Town Hall station, but didn't have any luck there with lost and found. I put a message on the park district's Facebook page, offering a substantial reward if the pendant and chain were returned, although my expectation was of wasting time checking bogus claims.

Back in my car, I called Marilyn Lieberman to report my failure. "Do you need me to talk personally to Harmony?"

Marilyn said the counselor would take that on, but Harmony was doing better—Arcadia House had a walled garden in back that no one really attended to. The counselor had suggested to Harmony that she do something with the weed-choked beds. After an apathetic start, she'd become engaged in cleaning the beds.

I was close enough to home that I stopped to see Mr. Contreras and Mitch and take Peppy out. She seemed anxious not to be gone too long from her wounded son; we did a circuit of the block and she ran back to Mitch and my neighbor.

I told Mr. Contreras about Harmony's distress over her necklace.

"We should get her another one, doll."

"That would be a good idea, to show her you care about her," I said. "But this one was special, something from her foster parents that can't be replaced."

Mr. Contreras wanted to be doing something, anything, to stop feeling so helpless. I printed out a list of self-storage facilities, starting with ones in walking distance from Fausson's apartment, and asked if he could call them.

I explained why it seemed important. "Say you're Fausson's father or grandfather, that since his death you're trying to find the locker he rented so you can empty it out."

He wasn't enthusiastic at first, but the idea of finding hidden treasure sparked his interest. I told him he could use his own name, but he decided he had to be in character. "They named the boy for me, I'll tell 'em. Which is more than Ruthie ever did with my own grandkids."

His only child, Ruthie, rubbed him the wrong way, and vice versa, but he loved his two grandsons.

I went to my office to start a search for lawsuits against Trechette.

I was low in spirits, and time spent with litigants isn't exactly exhilarating.

Of course, any large enterprise is always involved in litigation, a lot of litigation, so it didn't surprise me to find over a hundred outstanding suits. The one I'd seen in Dick's office, *Ti-Balt v. Trechette,* dealt with a dispute over a completion bond. I did a quick sort of litigation by cause; seventy-one had concerned insurance in the secondary marketplace. Trechette had bought the upper layers of insurance but had not paid, or had paid only token amounts.

If you're a company, or even a person, who wants insurance in the value of hundreds of millions of dollars, your primary carrier will sell you the policy, but will resell chunks of it to third parties. It's a prudent form of gambling.

Perhaps you're a construction company with a big stake in a hydroelectric plant. If there's never a claim, or no claim for many years, your insurer happily invests the premiums and makes a lot of money. A flood destroys the plant, you present your insurance claim, and your insurer calls on all the third parties who bought a piece of the action to pay their share of the bill.

Trechette seemed to have reneged on their share of the claims, not once, but many times. Was that what Reno had discovered in St. Matthieu? She'd overheard conversations about the claims?

I went back to the Rest EZ website to see if they sold insurance. They offered some cheap policies—high-deductible auto and renters insurance with a twenty-thousand-dollar limit. The website didn't say which company provided the coverage—Rest EZ didn't have their own insurance company. Neither did Trechette.

I looked at the clock. Seven P.M. My appointment with Sansen down at the OI was at seven-thirty; there was time for a call to Donna Lutas, Reno's boss at Rest EZ.

"Have you found Reno?" she asked.

"Not yet. But I've found a whole bunch of lawsuits against Trechette."

"I'm not a lawyer," Donna said roughly. "I don't know anything about those."

Red-gold squares covered the floor where the setting sun shone through the skylights. I had a childish impulse to play hopscotch on them, but I turned on my desk light and drowned them out. "You know who Trechette is, though."

"All I know is they own Rest EZ."

"Their headquarters are in St. Matthieu."

"Yeah, well, I've never been there."

I ignored her studied rudeness. "What company provides the coverage Rest EZ sells?"

"What do you mean? You just said we sell it."

"I mean, when I buy the policy and look at the dec page—the first page that outlines the limits and so on—does it say 'The Rest EZ Insurance Company,' or is there some other name?"

"Buy a policy and see for yourself." She hung up.

We were definitely not BFFs these days. She must feel humiliated from revealing her secrets to me when I was at her home.

In the end I was almost fifteen minutes late to my meeting with Peter Sansen. I was on my way out when I discovered tomato sauce on my trousers. Red blotches on gray serge—a perfect Lady Macbeth moment, I realized after futilely trying to spot-clean them. By the time I reached the museum, the damp spots had dried to a dark rusty gray. I hoped my keen professional brain would keep Sansen from noticing.

On Wednesdays, the museum was open late, so I didn't need a guard to let me into the building, but I wasn't allowed to go up the stairs until Peter Sansen came down to vouch for me.

When we'd met on Monday, his sunburned face had glowed with a kind of energetic humor, as if he found life an engaging enterprise. Now, though, he was squinting from fatigue. The scar on the right side of his face seemed to glow redder.

"I've spent the day with more law-enforcement agencies than I knew existed. Our campus cops, the city, the FBI, Interpol, Homeland Security—which includes so many agencies I gave up trying to follow them. They wanted me to testify that this was the work of ISIS, or perhaps a lone wolf on campus recruited by ISIS."

"Could it be?" I asked.

He shrugged. "Anything's possible, but I don't see ISIS tracking down a lone artifact at an American museum when it's so much easier for them to do wholesale looting at the source. Unless the artifact has some special symbolism. The Dagon was unusual, perhaps unique—certainly the first example Candra or I had ever seen of a figurine instead of a bas-relief—but I don't see it as particularly meaningful to radicals."

"How did the thief get into the building at all?" I asked. "Those doors aren't easy to breach, and I presume you have good security, with all these treasures to protect." I waved an arm toward the gigantic Sumerian horsemen who guarded the entrance to the rest of the museum.

"Security cameras, motion sensors, trip wires in unexpected places. And our conservation area is also tightly safeguarded. We've been more cavalier about the faculty offices, although I'm sure that will change.

"As for how the thieves got in, the police or the FBI, I forget which, think someone hid in a classroom or unused office while the museum was being locked down at closing. Our guards do make a thorough search, or at least they're supposed to, but it's a rabbit warren when you get down to it."

"Do they ever find anyone?" I asked.

"People fall asleep, or ignore the closing announcements, but you'd be surprised at who tries to linger—scholars from other institutions, who could easily get a pass, or students trying to show up authority."

I followed him up the stone stairs to the second floor and down the hall to Candra van Vliet's office. Someone had already replaced the broken glass in her door. I tried the knob; the door was locked. Sansen was getting out his keys, but I stopped him and used a credit card to press the lock tongue back.

"They didn't have to break the glass," I said. "Whoever went in was making a statement. Did the police pick up prints?"

Sansen shook his head. "They say the intruder wore gloves."

I stepped aside to let Sansen enter the office first. When he'd turned on a light I took a quick look around, but so many LEOs had been through here that the main residue of the crime was fingerprint dust and empty DNA swab kits, some labeled FBI, others from ICE and Interpol.

"Professor Van Vliet said she was on her way to Philadelphia. Is she there now?" I asked.

"An antiquities conference. Ironic in a grim way. I suppose our brief ownership of the Dagon will be the main conference topic."

"Was anything else taken from the Institute besides her eight-breasted goddess and the Dagon figure?"

He smiled sardonically. "No one's reported anything, and no one else's office was broken into, but I can guess that for the next few months, every time someone has mislaid an inscription or a prized bead, it will be blamed on the thieves."

I made a slow circuit of the room, feeling like an actor playing Sherlock Holmes in an amateur drama. I stopped at the window to look out, expecting to see either the chapel bell tower or Fifty-Eighth Street, but I was looking down at an interior courtyard. Ground lights showed a greensward with a few trees and bushes surrounded by cobblestones.

I tried the window latch. It moved easily and the casement opened smoothly, without squeaking. Sansen watched while I shone my flashlight around outside the window.

"Hold my legs, will you? I want to look farther down the wall."

He cocked his head. "You're not joking."

"No, but I should have asked, can you hold my legs? I don't want both of us tumbling to our deaths."

"It's not the strangest thing archaeology has demanded of me. Roll up your pants: I'm going to hold your left leg, above the ankle; if my hands slip, they'll catch on your shoe. Ready?"

I unwrapped the dressing from my hand so that I could use my fingers more easily, rolled my trousers up, and knelt on the radiator under the window. The old cast-iron sections cut through my trousers into my knees, but in a moment, Sansen had seized me in a strong grip. I inched over the stone sill. When I was hanging upside down the blood rushed to my head and my hand sweated on the flashlight. I blinked back the spots dancing in front of my eyes and shone my flash at the wall.

"Pull me back up!" I shouted.

Sansen kept one hand on my leg and grabbed my waistband with the other. The serge ripped, but I had my left hand on the sill and boosted myself back into the office.

My arms and legs were trembling; I collapsed onto a chair and massaged my arms. I felt the back of my trousers, where the fabric had split—and not along a seam.

"Second pair of trousers I've damaged on this investigation. You have strong hands, for which, believe me, I'm very grateful."

Sansen grinned. "You often do Batwoman impersonations?"

"It's my second-favorite party trick. But I'm afraid this is how your perp got into the building. I can see the marks in the wall where he—or she—inserted holds, and there are scuffs about a yard below the sill that could have come from climbing shoes."

The scar along Sansen's jawline pulsed redder. After a long pause, he said, "Someone here in the Institute gave him precise directions."

"I'm afraid so. The smashed glass in the door was a misdirection. By the way, didn't that noise rouse your security?"

He shook his head. "This office is pretty remote from the lobby, where the guard waits for normal robbers to come in through the front door or ground-floor windows, which all have alarms on them, anyway."

"You don't think the guard—"

"Horace has worked here for seventeen years. I trust him absolutely. I'd believe Candra staged the whole thing before I'd accuse Horace."

"Could Professor Van Vliet have staged it? She could have delivered the package here, after all."

Sansen glared at me. "Absolutely not. Anyway, why go through a charade like that?"

"If not the guard, and not the professor . . ."

"Yeah. I know. Someone else who works here or studies here."

We sat in uncomfortable silence for some minutes. Could the young woman I'd met on Monday be hard up for money? It was difficult to believe such a dedicated archaeologist would do so criminal a favor for a thief. There were probably hundreds—well, maybe dozens—of university employees who were more likely suspects; that was a police job, to track them down, not mine.

Finally Sansen shook his head. "I can't believe we had all these FBI and Interpol idiots here today and none of them thought to hang upside down, when it was daylight and easy. Why the hell do I pay taxes, anyway? I'm sorry about your pants."

My arms had stopped trembling, although my legs were a bit wobbly when I stood. I rubbed my hip, the spot where I'd landed last week. It had been healing nicely, but was reminding me now that I wasn't thirty anymore.

"I could use a drink," Sansen said when we were back in the hall. "You a teetotaler?"

"I have been known to sip scotch in a Batwomanly way."

"What's that like?" He cocked his head, eyes amused.

"Mm, you know, as if you were daintily helping yourself to someone's blood."

38

THE THINGS THEY CARRIED

OVER DRINKS AT a bar in Bucktown, I showed Sansen the pamphlet I'd picked up at Rasima Kataba's apartment earlier in the day.

He turned the pages slowly. "I spent time at Ebla, years ago, but I never heard about the museum in Saraqib, although that isn't so surprising—every town of any size in Syria has—used to have—a small museum. You think Kataba brought the Dagon out with him when he fled?"

"That was my first thought." I turned the pages of the pamphlet back to the black-and-white photos. "This lion, with the right paw broken off, that was on Lawrence Fausson's desk in his apartment."

Sansen looked at me in surprise. "I thought you didn't know Fausson."

"I didn't. I learned his name from an anonymous phone call, and then I found where he lived. And I went inside, which I have not revealed to anyone in law enforcement."

"How did you get in?" Sansen asked.

"I didn't have to climb up the building side in the dark—a woman in the building let me in."

"Are you thinking Fausson smuggled them into the country himself?" Sansen asked. "But why then give the Dagon to Candra?"

"He couldn't have; he was already dead," I reminded Sansen. "That's why I was leaning toward Kataba bringing the artifacts to Chicago with him when he managed to get here. And then, when ICE started

turning up the heat on him, he or his daughter sent the most important piece to the museum."

"Specifically to Candra?"

"Kataba had met Fausson when Professor Van Vliet's team was in
Syria; the professor said she went to Kataba's bicycle repair shop. I'm
sure you know Fausson liked to leave the Tell and go exploring with
the locals. He loved the chance to build his 'Lawrence of Chicago'
image; he liked working on his colloquial Arabic."

"Kataba was in a Bashar prison for twenty-some months," Sansen
said. "Nobody knows how he arrived in the States or where he spent
the years after his release, but for a refugee on the move, carrying
around a bundle of priceless artifacts as he hid from one authority or
another would be pretty damned difficult."

"My mother was a refugee from Mussolini's Italy," I said. "She carried a set of eight Venetian wineglasses with her from her home in Pitigliano to a hiding place in the Umbrian hills, and then as she crawled
through the mountains at night to the Port of Livorno. She brought
them with her to Chicago without breaking one."

I was the one who had broken them. My headfirst dives into danger, imagining I was in the pursuit of justice—my mouth twisted in a
bitter grimace.

"You value artifacts," Sansen said, his voice gentle—he'd noted the
grimace.

He looked back at the catalog and paused at the statuette of the
horned woman. "This is a very nice figure. Might be almost as valuable as the Dagon—you don't often see a statue like this completely
intact, including the snakes." His lips moved as he read the Arabic text
underneath. "Yes, the snakes are gold, with carnelian tongues and lapis
eyes."

"Why does she have horns?" I asked.

"Oh, they show she was a goddess, although I don't know which
one. The snakes are fertility signs, so it might be Inanna, the goddess
of fertility—among her many other duties."

He put a hand over mine, stroking the bite marks. "It looks as though you could use a visit from the goddess Gula—she took care of healing. Did you get these at Fausson's building?"

"Different inquiry. Someone jumped my niece in the park; the creep bit me when I intervened." I nodded toward the scar along his jawline. "And this? Was this from a dig?"

"Collateral damage. I should have left Iraq sooner than I did— thought I could make arrangements to protect my dig at Tell al-Sabbah and got hit by an IED. I was lucky—it was early in the U.S. invasion, before the whole damned infrastructure collapsed. Someone found me fast and flew me to the medical ship, and I got away with these burns. It was the last straw for my wife, though."

"That's a pity," I said.

"It was more than a decade ago, long enough for me to get through my self-pity, along with my skin grafts, and return to the field, in Syria, where I was prudent enough to leave before the fighting turned horrific. I hope you don't have a partner who turns away in disgust from your wounds."

"I used to. He turned away so fast that he ended up in Switzerland. Where will you go next?" I asked.

He grinned. "My secretary says no government is going to let me in to dig when they see that civil war follows me. I'm still working on it. Turkey has quite a number of Sumerian sites, but I'm not sure. I'm fifty, I want a new venue, new adventure, maybe, before I get past surviving them."

He squeezed my hand and released it. "Include a bill for your pants when you send your invoice; I'll see the Institute reimburses you. And then, perhaps, we could have dinner. I promise I would not bite you."

I got to my feet and brushed my own fingers along the puckered skin on his face. "You have my number."

39

FIT AS A FIDDLE

I FELT THEM a second too late. One grabbed my keys as I pulled them from my pocket. Before I could react, the second pinned my arms under his own. Black leather-clad, massive as tree trunks, beyond my strength to break free. His partner had opened my apartment, and they were dragging me inside.

I made my arms and torso go limp. Hooked both feet around one massive calf and forced the leg back. The attacker flung out a hand to steady himself and I dropped, rolling toward the stairs, roaring for help.

The pair recovered fast, loomed over me. "Locked up. Need locked up, give."

Light glinted on steel, the knife that had cut Mitch. I didn't try to fight but plunged down the stairs, shouting to my neighbors to call 911.

The two jumped after me, landed in front of me.

"Locked up now, bitch. No more games."

"You are locking me nowhere," I spat. Grabbed the railing at the second-floor landing and swung my legs high, missed the knife but connected with chin.

Mr. Contreras's thin voice floated up. "Hold on, doll. Cops coming. I got you covered."

Behind him the dogs were baying, and then a loud protest from the woman across from him in 1B.

"Get those damned dogs under control. Do you think this is an animal shelter? You let those dogs race around, barking their heads off, while you scream up and down the stairwell. The condo board—"

I clung to the stair rail.

"Bitch! Bitch, you not attacking, you giving locked up." They each had a leg, yanking on me. I finally had to let go of the rail, fell heavily. The pair was rocked off balance just long enough for me to pull my legs free and slide down the stairs on my butt.

They followed me, but Mr. Contreras was at the bottom, swinging his pipe wrench. The man with the knife lunged at my neighbor. I chopped Knifer behind his ear. He grunted and staggered back. His partner growled, tried to grab me, but my neighbor's wrench connected with his kneecap.

Blue strobes lit the front walk. The hulks said something, harsh, Slavic, and lumbered down the hallway to the back of the building. I heard the areaway door slam.

The woman in 1B opened the building door for the cops. "High time you got here. These dogs are a menace to—"

"Easy. Easy does it. This an animal complaint?" The speaker was an older white guy, the lines in his heavy face showing he'd seen every strange or horrible thing humans could do to each other—including calling him in to complain about dogs.

"Home invasion," I gasped.

My legs had given way; I was sitting on the bottom stair. Peppy, who'd followed Mr. Contreras into the hall, was licking my face and hands.

"Two guys," my neighbor said. "They was upstairs and come after Cookie—after Vic—here. They was huge, I hit 'em with this"—he brandished the pipe wrench—"and it was like hittin' a big rock."

The senior cop and his partner, a younger black man, came over to me.

"This the dog that's menacing the building?" the older man said. "She going to bite if we ask you questions?"

I managed a smile. "No, officers. Not unless you have a steak concealed under your vest."

1B stormed over. "I have a report due tomorrow morning for an important client and these dogs—ten-thirty at night, you'd think—"

"You got no consideration," Mr. Contreras interrupted her roughly. "You got a neighbor attacked by dirtbags the size of Mount Rushmore and all you can think of is some stupid report for a company that probably don't care if you live or die."

His neighbor began an inflamed response, but the young black officer took her to one side, speaking to her in a soothing undervoice while his partner ushered Mr. Contreras and me into my neighbor's apartment.

We spent over an hour with the cops. They urged me to go to the emergency room to check me over, but the adrenaline boost that had carried me through the fight was gone. I didn't have the stamina to spend the night in the ER waiting for my turn in the triage queue.

I summoned the energy to say, "Same men attacked my niece. Lakefront. Yesterday."

That startled them. The officers took me through the attack on Harmony. I stressed the vicious way the man had yanked the necklace from her.

"It left a deep cut. A miracle it didn't sever her windpipe, but she's grieving for the necklace, not the injury."

The officers called over to the Town Hall station for a copy of the incident report.

"What makes you think they were the same men?" the black cop asked in his low, soothing voice.

"Their accents were Slavic. Said the same thing to her—locked up. I thought her sister, thought they'd locked up Reno, and wanted to lock up—"

I gave a spurt of laughter that bordered on hysteria. "Locket. Their accents, my mind on Reno's disappearance, I heard 'locked up,' but they wanted Harmony's locket. No, they took her locket. Special present from Henry and Clarisse. They're looking for Reno's locket. That's why they tore the apartment apart. Oh, my God. What time is it?"

The cops stared at me. "Who is Reno?"

"What about the locket?" Mr. Contreras asked.

I tried explaining—the identical lockets the sisters had received when they graduated, how Harmony, at least, never took hers off.

"Someone wants those lockets, but they could only know about them if one of the sisters said something. I need to talk to Harmony."

I didn't say it out loud, didn't want to jinx my tiny flame of hope, but if the thugs knew about the locket, there was the smallest chance that Reno was still alive. Locked up but without her locket. Because how would the creeps know about it if Reno hadn't told them?

"You got to go to bed, doll," Mr. Contreras said. "You been working way too hard lately. You need a good night's sleep, you need to go to Dr. Lotty in the morning. You officers, we appreciate you coming so fast and all, but you got to let Cookie here go to bed."

The cops had more questions, which I tried to answer coherently. They made a note of Lieutenant Finchley's and Sergeant Abreu's names as the cops with the most knowledge about Reno Seale's disappearance.

Before they left, I asked the pair to inspect the back of the building with me, to make sure the creeps weren't lurking in the basement or on the rear staircases.

They also climbed up to the third floor with me to check out the upper hallway. I was alone on the floor these days—Jake Thibaut, who owned one of the units, was in Switzerland. When he left Chicago—and me—he'd sublet the place to a drummer, who caused even more disruption than the dogs and me. All the tenants, not just 1B, had risen in fury, and the drummer had left. Jake hadn't bothered to find another renter.

The third unit on my floor had stood empty for some months now, too. I hadn't thought before how lonely it was with no one living behind the doors, but it struck me forcibly now.

My keys were still in the lock on my outer door—the creep who'd grabbed them from me hadn't had time to take them before he joined the battle. That was a bit of good news; I'd been worried that I'd have to spend part of the next day waiting on a locksmith.

"You going to be okay here?" the older cop asked. "You sure you don't need a doctor? You got that bruise on your hand and a welt on your face."

The bruise was where I'd been bitten, but I'd be answering questions for another hour if I mentioned that. "Ibuprofen and ice and I'll be fit as a fiddle and right as rain."

The words came from a deep place in my memory, a Golden Book from my childhood. My mother used to read it to me, laughing over the English idioms, which were funny to her Italian ear. When she became ill with the cancer that killed her, she used to reassure me, "Soon I will be fit as a fiddle," but when she was dying and English deserted her, she would say it in a strange Italian translation, *Sono sana come un violino*—I'm as healthy as a violin.

Sixteen years old and frantic as I watched her retreating from life, I used to argued over language with her, telling her it was just an expression; in Italian she'd say *"Sono in gamba,"* which would sound just as silly in English. *"Non sono, carissima,"* she murmured. What a painful mess that year had been.

Tonight, my sleep, when it came, seemed filled with dreams of absolution. I was standing at an ancient temple in Syria, looking at the Dagon in front of the altar—not the small figure I'd seen in Candra van Vliet's office, but a golden man with a live fish wrapped around his head and shoulders. My mother appeared next to him, radiant with health. When I ran to the altar to embrace her, the fish-man took the form of Peter Sansen. He said, *Your mother is as healthy as a beautiful violin. Soon you, too, will be as fit as a fiddle and right as rain.*

40

A PATCH OF BLUE

I MET WITH Harmony in a back room at Arcadia House. I'd slept in, but my second plunge down the stairs in a week had left me uncomfortably stiff; I did an extra half hour of stretches before taking the dogs on the short walk Mitch could handle.

I'd parked at my office and ridden the L to a stop beyond the shelter, walking a half mile around side streets to make sure I wasn't being followed. Of course if last night's invaders had been on my tail I would have seen them at once, but I couldn't believe they were working on their own. Someone wanted Reno's locket badly enough to hire foreign vermin and sic them on my niece and then on me; they could easily hire a harmless-looking op to follow me.

When I was sure I was clean, I went to the nondescript double graystone that housed the shelter. Once inside I heard the usual clamor—babies wailing, toddlers screaming or banging on noisy toys—but Marilyn Lieberman greeted me with her professional cheerful calm and sent me to talk to Harmony.

The room was small, used for private conversations. Like the rest of Arcadia House, it was furnished with thrift store finds along with castoffs from the affluent members of the board. A small round table with four chairs upholstered in faded maroon took up most of the space, but there was also an easy chair with a footstool, a scarred bookshelf holding children's books and toys, and two high-backed chairs that sternly faced each other in front of a disused fireplace.

Harmony came into the room a few minutes after me. At Lotty's clinic two days ago, her vacant eyes had frightened me. Today, although her expression was pinched and anxious, I could see she'd returned to the world around her.

I walked to the window, which overlooked the garden where she'd been working yesterday, and asked her what she'd found.

"Not much," she muttered. "A few bulbs may come up. They have some coreopsis that I may be able to rescue."

The ugly line across her throat where her assailant had torn the chain away stood out under the pale light from the windows.

I moved over to the round table and sat in one of the maroon chairs. After a moment, Harmony joined me, sitting as far from me as possible.

"I searched the paths where we were hit on Tuesday," I said. "I also checked in with the Park District and the cops, but I'm sorry to say that I think the men who jumped you did it specifically to steal your locket. They were waiting for me in the hall outside my door last night and attacked me—they were demanding the locket. I can only guess they wanted your sister's."

Harmony's face seemed to collapse. "Oh, no! Why can't they leave us alone! What is wrong with us that people want to hurt us?"

"Nothing wrong with you, sweetheart. It's something wrong with them. We can't fix them, but we can change the situation so they leave you alone."

When she was calmer, I asked her to tell me more about the lockets.

"When Reno and me graduated from junior college," Harmony whispered. She fingered the place where the chain used to hang, forgetting it wasn't there.

"They were so proud of us, they gave a party and we invited all our friends; there were like a hundred people in the backyard. Clarisse had made this incredible cake, shaped like a book, with me and Reno's diploma on it, done in frosting, you know. And before we cut it, they gave us our special presents. The lockets were from Clarisse, real gold, and the chains are real gold, too. We both had the same picture of Clarisse and Henry in them and mine had one of Reno; hers had one of me. We both wore them always."

Her eyes filled with tears. The only words that came to me were so banal I kept them to myself, just patted her hand.

"Would you ever keep something secret in them?"

"Honestly, Auntie Vic, they were lockets, not treasure chests."

"I'm trying to understand why someone would want them," I said meekly.

Harmony hunched a shoulder. "I don't know. The pictures were just us, just family. The lockets were real gold, but it's not like they had diamonds or emeralds in them to make them super valuable. Just to us, because they were from Clarisse. She had our names and the date engraved on them.

"Henry, he gave us these special scarves from China. His aunt who lives in Shanghai sent them, royal blue for Reno, rose silk for me. They were so beautiful we agreed we could only wear them for special times."

She took out her phone and opened her photo album. "This was at Henry's funeral. Clarisse was okay enough then to go."

The sisters stood solemn faced in front of Clarisse, whose face had already started to lose its definition as the early stages of her disease set in. All three women were dressed in white, but each wore a long scarf looped around her neck, Harmony's in rose, Reno's in blue, Clarisse's in gold. Under the sisters' scarves I could see the gold chains that held their lockets.

"In China, you wear white to the funeral. People shouldn't wear colors, especially not red, but we wanted to respect Henry with the gifts he had given us."

Blue silk: I stared at the photo and enlarged it with my fingers. I'd recently seen a strand of fabric that matched that color. In the squirrels' nest in Cap Sauers Holding. That couldn't possibly have been from Reno's scarf. If it was, she'd been in the same place where Lawrence Fausson had died. Which meant—a coincidence so gigantic I couldn't get my mind around it.

"Vic? Auntie Vic!" Harmony cried out. "What's wrong? Did I say something wrong?"

"Nothing's wrong; you didn't say anything wrong." My voice was hoarse. "I just need some water."

I found a drinking fountain up the hall, Harmony hovering close behind me. A staff member appeared, checking that we were okay— Harmony's outcry had been loud enough to alert someone.

"I'm okay," Harmony said, her voice back at a whisper. "Vic, my auntie Vic, looked like she was fainting and I got scared."

The staff member eyed me narrowly: I was on the Arcadia board, but that didn't make me sacrosanct. "I'm close by," she assured Harmony. "Holler if you need anything."

I didn't go back into the small meeting room but spoke to my niece near the drinking fountain. "Harmony, if I brought you a piece of fabric, would you be able to tell if it was from Reno's scarf?"

"Maybe. I guess, if I compared it to mine, but mine is in Portland." She wrinkled her nose in doubt.

"I may know where a piece of it is, but it's just a guess, not a certainty. I want to go back to the place where I saw it—if it's still there, I'll bring it to you."

Harmony tried to get me to take her with me, but I was firm on that. She was staying put until I was sure she wasn't in danger.

"The scum who jumped you in the park are sniffing around for you. You stay here where it's safe."

"How about you?" she demanded. "I have to follow 'women and children first,' but you don't? If you think you know where Reno is, I have a right—"

"You do." Her words had pulled me up short—the first sign of real fight I'd seen in her and she hit me in my feminist solar plexus. "You have a right to help find and save your sister. But not at the expense of your own life and safety, which have been severely compromised the last few days. Please stay here to build up your strength for another day or two, okay?"

"Oh, all right," she said. "I know you're trying to help. I just don't like being left on the outside of my own life."

I squeezed her shoulder. "I know that feeling. So go dig up the garden and get your muscles back in shape."

She gave me an awkward hug before disappearing into the kitchen. When I went back to the room where we'd been meeting to collect my things, I saw her appear in a jacket and Wellington boots with a handful of gardening tools.

Three preschoolers were also out there, bundled against the wind. The cusp of April, and it was still cold. Harmony began clipping branches from an evergreen, throwing them into a heap with almost savage energy. The biggest of the children went to the pile of evergreens and pulled one out. He began waving it around. In a moment, the other two joined him. Soon they were fighting one another with the branches.

I stopped in Marilyn Lieberman's office to tell her about my conversation with Harmony. My niece's riposte made Marilyn hoot with laughter.

"V.I. Warshawski as part of the patriarchy—I wish I'd been there to see your face."

"Hysterically funny," I agreed drily. "I didn't tell her where I'd seen this bit of silk, so I'm not worried she'll try to dog me to a forest preserve, but I don't want her to bolt. She doesn't have any place to run to that the creeps who are dogging her can't find. I hope the garden keeps her grounded here—so to speak."

Marilyn nodded, but said, "This isn't a locked ward, as you know damned well. We have no power to stop people from leaving, only to keep others from coming in. I'll ask a counselor to talk to her, but I'm afraid that's the only thing I can do."

I knew she was right, which only added to my worries. As I rode the L back to my office, I fretted over what Harmony might do, whether the volatile mix of hurt feelings, fear, and loneliness would send her away from Arcadia.

Everyone, from the Buddha to my own mother, reminds us not to worry about hypothetical outcomes. Breathe, Gabriella used to lecture me: deep breath in, feel it under your diaphragm. Do that ten times and you won't be able to worry about—what a girl had said to me on the playground, or my upcoming chemistry test, or . . . whether she was dying.

No one bothered me as I retrieved my car and headed to Cap Sauers Holding. I parked as close as possible to the trailhead and hiked back to the crime scene. My heart was thick in my chest, but I had come better prepared this time than before: I'd stopped in my office for crime scene gear and had pulled overalls on over my jeans, along with waterproof boots, a slicker, hard hat, heavy gloves, and a miner's headlamp.

When I reached the tree trunk where Fausson's body had lain, I blew a whistle into the narrow end of the log. I heard a rustling and a chattering inside, but the squirrels stayed put.

"Sorry, Madam Squirrel," I said. "You have something I want, but I hope this is the last time I disturb you."

I'd brought the tire iron from my trunk. When I lay flat to inch my way into the log, I extended my arm and used the iron to drag the nest toward me. Madam Squirrel attacked, gibbering: there were five naked bodies in the nest, squeaking in a heartrending way. I moved fast, as Madam bit my gloved hands. The blue strand was there; I pulled it free from the twigs and leaves and left behind a cotton hand towel I'd taken from the bathroom in my office building.

"That will keep them warmer than the silk will, ma'am." I pushed the nest back up into the log and scooted out.

"She walks with the animals, talks to the animals," I muttered. I sat on a neighboring log but heard an angry chatter overhead, and then a stream of urine hit my hard hat: Mr. Squirrel had taken my invasion as a sign of war.

I tucked the strand into my glove and moved down the path, away from the squirrel family. I took off my hard hat and turned it upside down on the forest bed, then removed the strand and looked at it under my miner's lamp. It was a kind of royal blue and very likely silk. Close enough in color to the photo Harmony had shown me.

41

THE BRAVEST GIRLS

IN CHICAGO

MR. WRIGHT, MY first-year physics professor, used to heap scorn on theorists who picked and chose data to support their ideas. "Collect the data, see where the data take you," he would say. "Don't start with a preconception and look for facts to support it."

The fact: a blue silk scarf. The meaning: Reno and Lawrence Fausson had been in the same place. Why and when could wait.

I returned to my car to shed my heavier gear and collect drinking water and specimen bags. I sealed up the blue strand, labeled it, and stuck it in my backpack. I had a handful of orange plastic pegs to mark spots where I found something.

The sun had come out, brightening the air. The branches were showing buds, but were still bare, which made it easier for an unskilled tracker to look for clues. The advantage of the bare branches was more than offset by the thickness of the leaves on the ground. I walked the perimeter of the log in a series of widening circles, but my own footsteps didn't leave a trace I could recognize.

I marked each circuit with an orange peg so I wouldn't repeat my steps. Even so, I couldn't be sure I wasn't missing something in the heavy ground cover.

I'd been walking for over an hour and was sitting on a stump, drinking water and massaging my shoulders, when I finally saw a second piece of blue. This was a mere wisp, caught on a sucker about a yard from the ground. I photographed it, then put an orange peg next to the tree before adding it to a specimen bag.

The find gave me new energy. I narrowed my search lane to a cone spreading from the tree and found another scrap about a hundred feet farther in. Two points mark a line; my line was heading northeast from the squirrels' nest into the densest part of the woods.

I'd found two additional bits of thread when I stopped cold: in front of me was a toe print made by something like a size twenty boot. It was pointing toward me; a big person had walked out the way I'd just come.

I knelt next to it. Close up, under my miner's headlamp, I could see that someone had been raking the leaves smooth behind them, but they'd missed this one print.

It was impossible to know if the print had been made today or yesterday. My neck turned hot under my slicker.

My slicker was yellow, to help me stand out on city streets in the rain. I took it off and bundled it into my backpack. Looked to see what I had besides water, orange pegs, specimen bags. Sunblock. A spare T-shirt. A few remaining wires from Fausson's computer. My picklocks. I put those in my front pocket where I could grab them quickly—they'd do to gouge someone.

I squatted and moved forward, duck-like, watching the dead leaves as if I were Jim Chee. Every few yards I found an indentation, showing where the size twenties had been.

I was so intent on the search that I hit my head on the shack. It was a ramshackle structure, jerry-built from weathered boards. They were gray brown with age and damp and blended almost seamlessly with the surrounding trees.

It was a small structure, about six feet by ten, put up for some unfathomable purpose—perhaps long-forgotten maintenance equipment. I tiptoed around it, ear close to the wood, but couldn't hear anything. There were no windows, just a door held shut by a very heavy chain with a very new padlock.

American Master locks are not easy, especially when nervous sweat is greasing your palms and fingers. When the metal loop finally came free, my neck was sore from tension. I buried the padlock deep in leaves and pulled the door open.

The smell inside was so rank it pushed me out the door again. The lion house at the zoo: blood, soiled clothes, shit, vomit. I swallowed a gag, turned my head for a deep breath, and switched on my headlamp.

The small space was crammed with junk: shovels and rakes, most missing their handles; rusted pipes; pieces of bathroom fixtures. A stool held cartons of moldy carryout food. Cigarette butts, a box of matches, a heap of empty vodka bottles, another three full ones.

The smell, the isolation, the massive feet, which could have smashed Fausson's skull with one kick. I could believe he'd been murdered here, but what about Reno? Had she been a spectator at his death?

I kept backing out, taking in air, looking again, but it wasn't until my third foray that I saw the body. It was against a wall under a filthy tarp, one grimy bare foot sticking out from the end.

When I pulled the tarp away, I saw she was manacled to a hasp in the wall, one cuff on her left ankle, the other on her left hand. She was naked from the waist down, with dried blood on her legs, burns on her abdomen. The blue scarf, in shreds and caked with dirt, was loosely looped around her neck. She wore a filthy knit top but it had lacy scallops around the buttonholes and wrists—she had dressed up for this abomination.

I knelt next to her, fingers on her neck. The faint thread of a pulse. Bent close to her ear.

"Reno. It's your aunt Vic. Stay with me, girl. I'm going to get you out of here." I massaged her arms, held the right one up, hoping for blood to get to her brain.

I tried calling 911, tried calling Lieutenant McGivney, but I couldn't get a signal. I tried sending a text to McGivney, tried Murray Ryerson at the *Herald-Star,* but I wasn't going to get help.

On your own, Vic. Deal.

I tried to wrench out the hasp, took one of the shovel heads to smash it out, but the rotting wood on the outside was a camouflage: they'd lined the interior with metal, and the hasp with its big steel hook was deeply embedded.

She was emaciated. I rubbed sunblock onto her cold hand and wrist and managed to slide her hand from the cuff. The manacle on her leg didn't move. I worked feverishly on the lock with my picks. Easy does it. Sweat ran down my neck. I had to keep fighting the bile rising in me.

When I finally freed her leg, I took the T-shirt from my backpack to cover her legs, creating a makeshift set of shorts. I was scooping her inert body into my arms when I heard the footsteps in the leaves and the rumble of voices on the perimeter.

I lay Reno back onto the soiled tarp, dumped the food containers from the stool and dragged it next to the door. The thugs were approaching from the back of the hut. I swung the door shut, grabbed a shovel, and clambered onto the stool.

One of them bellowed something that sounded like *"Shto za chort?"* followed then by a rapid exchange. The door was yanked open. I brought the shovel down on the head of the man who entered. It was like pounding steel. The man winced and staggered, an arm against a wall to steady himself, but the recoil knocked me off the stool.

The second man burst through the door, shouting at his partner. I had a one-second advantage before he saw me. I grabbed two of the vodka bottles and smashed them against the door.

The second man roared and charged me. I lunged forward with the bottles, striking upward, cutting him from chin to eye. His partner had recovered, was trying to get behind me. The space was too small for his bulk. I kicked a rake into his path.

Two against one; the one was exhausted. Dancing, kicking, hitting out with the broken bottles, but the man I'd cut rushed me, hit me on the chin, knocked me against the wall. And then blackness.

I never completely lost consciousness. I heard a pounding, like an ax on logs, and slowly sat up. I was dizzy and wanted to throw up, but not in the dark, not when I might befoul myself or Reno. I had landed on something hard and knobby. I fumbled with my miner's headlamp, but it had been smashed in the brawl.

My phone was in my hip pocket. I shifted enough to pry it out and turned on the flash. I was sitting on a pipe connected to a chunk of ceramic—part of an old sink dumped in here with the rest of the refuse.

I was close enough to Reno to put my fingers on her ankle. Slowed my own anxious breath, waited, finally felt a tiny flutter.

I'd have to get us out and the only way out was through the door, which the vermin had shut when they fled. I staggered over, pushed it. Put a shoulder into it. Couldn't budge it. The pounding I'd heard had been the attackers nailing the door shut.

I looked around wildly for an ax, anything to break down the door. I tried sticking the shovel into the hinged end but couldn't get a purchase.

My phone battery was down to 39 percent. The matchbook and cigarettes had disappeared when I tipped over the stool. I wasted precious battery time hunting on the floor, finally found the matches wedged between two of the decaying slats that made up the floor. Wrenched up the slats to stick in a vodka bottle for a makeshift torch. I took apart a couple of cigarette packs to use as fire starters and soon had enough light that I could put my phone away.

I hunted in the tiny junk room for anything that would let me break down the door or saw through the metal walls. I pulled up more slats to keep my torches burning. I couldn't keep going much longer, not at full strength. And Reno—that weak fluttering pulse could cease at any moment.

As I searched, I sang to her, sang the Italian folk songs of my childhood. Listened to Gabriella's voice in my head, sternly mindful of my breath, to keep the fingers of panic from strangling me.

The door's wooden frame had been covered with metal, but along the hinges and the top was a strip of exposed wood. I brought the stool over, stood on it, and emptied one of the bottles of vodka onto the top frame. I poured a second down along the hinges. Brought my torch over and held the burning end along the frame.

The wood caught more quickly than I'd expected. The entire side was in flames before I was ready. I scrambled for my backpack, put on my slicker, knelt to gather Reno.

When I picked her up, the fire glinted on gold. I blinked, looked at the door, looked back. A gold chain with a locket. Reno had dropped her locket through the floor slats that I'd pulled up for my torches.

I stared a moment, slack-jawed. A loud crack at the door, a piece of flaming wood falling into the room, jerked me into motion.

I couldn't carry Reno and kick the door. I laid her as close to the fire as I dared, took the shovel, and smashed it into the hinges. Once, twice, fifth try, and the wood and metal gave way.

I picked up my niece, tucked her under the slicker as best I could, lowered my head, and pushed through. Middle linebacker Warshawski, yes, she makes a hole, yes, the opposition is strong but she's stronger, and in another instant I was on the ground outside, gulping in air.

I didn't know where we were. I still couldn't get a signal on my phone, so I couldn't summon a map to see if there was a closer road than the one I'd driven in on: I had no choice but to go back the way I'd come. The thugs had crashed through the woods, not trying to hide their steps, I didn't want to follow them, but I had no choice.

I drank the last of my water and slung Reno over my shoulder, wrapping my slicker around her. She was a featherweight, but she was a weight. I staggered from tree to tree, following the steps I'd made coming in, occasionally seeing one of my orange pegs. I shifted Reno from one shoulder to the other but couldn't risk stopping to rest.

"You're doing great, you're doing great," I encouraged both of us out loud. "One step after the next, that's how we get to Kraków."

My father's patient voice, calming my frustrations over not being as fast, as smart, as rich as some neighbor or other. *Life doesn't have winners and losers. If you see it as a rat race, remember that the winner is never going to be more than a rat. Life is about savoring the good moments, learning from the bad ones.*

He'd taken Harmony and Reno into his loving heart that Christmas when they were five and six, seen how scared and hurting they were. We'd gone to his district station and he'd given them badges, the same kind he'd given me as a child. *Who are the two bravest girls in Chicago? Officer Harmony and Officer Reno.*

"Remember: Grandpa Tony says you're the bravest girl in Chicago. He'll be proud of you: you've stood up to the biggest monsters under the bed, now we're going to get you safe and warm. Yes, we are. You keep going, you're doing great."

42

ROUGH RIDER

IT TOOK THE better part of an hour to return to Fausson's log. As I staggered the final two hundred yards to my car, I heard sirens. I laid Reno carefully in the passenger seat, buckled her in, stretched the seat out as flat as it would lie. I took off my boots and put my socks on over Reno's icy feet. I'd just buckled myself into my seat when two fire engines turned into the clearing.

A voice on a loudspeaker told me to stop. I made a U-turn on a dime and floored the accelerator before they thought to block the road. Maybe they would have gotten an EMT unit faster than I could make it to Lotty, but maybe they would hold me up with pointless questions while Reno's body gave up the fight.

I called Lotty from the car. Lotty was in surgery, but Jewel Kim told me to get Reno to Beth Israel; she would have a team waiting at the ambulance entrance.

"She's alive, barely," I said. I hoped. "Probably dehydrated. Don't know about internal injuries. Shock, trauma, imagine the worst and you'll be close."

I had the heater on full blast and had pulled over long enough to cover Reno with the towels I kept in the back for the dogs. They were full of dirt and hair but would keep her warmer than the slicker. I couldn't see any motion in her chest, but I didn't want to feel for a pulse. Facts are good in their place, but sometimes you just can't handle them.

Once I turned onto I-55, I put my foot down, going over ninety, whipping around cars and semis, driving with a recklessness that took all my concentration. When the traffic gelled at Cicero Avenue my stomach clenched.

Think, don't react. One step after the next. I took advantage of my near crawl to call the Shakespeare station. I couldn't reach Terry Finchley, but Sergeant Abreu answered on the second ring. I gave her the details: finding Reno near death, en route to Beth Israel.

"We're stalled on the Stevenson just north of Cicero. I'm going to ride on the shoulder. If I give you my license plate, can you clear me with your patrol cars?"

"Give me your license plate; we'll get the nearest patrol to bring you in. The closest hospital is Stroger, you know."

"They're set up to take care of her at once at Beth Israel. Thanks, Sergeant. My plate is SP82VIW."

I hung up before she tried arguing or ordering me to the county hospital. They'd do a good job, probably. Possibly. But they weren't Lotty, they couldn't revive the dead.

A couple of squad cars picked me up on the shoulder at Pulaski and cleared a path across the expressways to the Wilson Avenue exit from the Edens. The cops stayed with me while a triage team lifted Reno from my car to a cart. They tried to start questioning me as I followed the gurney into the building, but I ignored them, watching a crew give her oxygen, insert catheters, start a saline drip, antibiotics, glucose. This must mean Reno was alive. They wouldn't do that to a corpse.

Relief undid me. Tension and fear were all that had kept me upright. There were no chairs in the hall. I collapsed onto the floor, head on my knees. The patrol team stood over me, not sure what to do.

An ebony hand appeared, grabbed my arm, hoisted me to my feet. "What is this? Hard-as-nails PI V.I. crying like a blonde in a six-hankie movie? I could post this on Instagram and ruin you for life."

Terry Finchley. Sergeant Abreu was standing next to him.

"He was in a meeting with the captain at Thirty-Fifth Street," Abreu said. "I figured he'd rather be here."

"Of course," I said hoarsely. "Wouldn't we all."

Reno had disappeared into the hospital bowels, but the ER charge nurse told Abreu that she'd been taken to the ICU in dangerous condition; they'd know more in an hour.

The patrol teams evaporated. Finchley looked me over critically. "If you step outside the hospital looking like this, people are going to toss quarters your way. You need a bed yourself and fluids and all those things. But PIs who spend their lives going head-to-head with the CPD don't need coddling, do they, Warshawski? Abreu, get her a Coke. Spike her blood sugar so she can answer some questions."

I didn't know if Finchley was trying to buck up my spirits or hoping to bring them down, but either way, my fatigue was a handicap. When people are at low ebb, they are easy marks for police questioning, too tired to monitor their words. Finchley and Abreu escorted me into a small room set aside for cops to interrogate suspects who come into the ER carrying the near-dead on their backs.

I told them pretty much everything I knew, but slowly, checking each sentence for weaknesses before I said it.

"You went back there on the chance that your niece's scarf was part of a squirrel's nest?" Finchley said. "If I hadn't known you all these years and learned that you don't think like most people, I'd throw the book at you for that alone."

"I take that as a compliment. Follow the data, not the theory."

Finchley said to Abreu, "Illustration of my point. That sentence means nothing to me, but it does to her. Go on, Warshawski."

I went on, through the woods, to the shack, to the horror story and back to the road. "I can't make sense of it, but that shack, it has to be where Lawrence Fausson was murdered. What Reno was doing there I have no idea. They were torturing her—" I broke off, pushing back the image of her legs with the dried blood on them.

"What did they think she knew?" Sergeant Abreu asked—dry questions to keep me from falling into the dark spaces. "Or what did she have that they wanted?"

The locket that I'd shoved deep into my jeans pocket. That was one thing I kept back from the cops. There were others—Rasima Kataba, the pamphlet from the Saraqib museum, the money under Fausson's floorboard.

"Did you ever search his place?" I asked. "Lawrence Fausson's, I mean?"

Finchley said, "Not my district, not my case. What should the Sixteenth have been looking for?"

I flung my hands up, clueless. "I don't know. I'd love one piece of data that explained what brought him and my niece to the same place in the woods thirty miles from where either of them lived. Fausson had been an archaeology student, but the University of Chicago cut him loose. He was working as a janitor for one of those big corporate companies. I can't see anything that puts the two of them together. However, she disappeared right around the time he was killed."

I drank the Coke and leaned back in the chair, head against the wall, drifting into sleep.

Finchley shook my shoulder. "Fausson's a county case, right? How come you're involved?"

I didn't open my eyes. "Dr. Herschel's great-nephew—the county keeps thinking he's involved in Fausson's death. Which he isn't. He's Canadian, so ICE is also harassing him."

Sergeant Abreu asked who Dr. Herschel was.

"Chief of obstetric and perinatal surgery here at Beth Israel," I said. "My friend, mentor, someone whose welfare is important to me."

"And your doctor." Lotty had swept into the small space. "I just finished a pelvic floor reconstruction and they told me you were here, that you'd found Reno. I went up to ICU before coming to see you. She's thready but stronger than she was forty minutes ago; you got to her in time. But you are not in any condition to be talking to the police, or anyone else."

She nodded at Finchley and Abreu, her force field making Finchley back up.

"I only have two more questions, Doctor," he said.

"Then you'll be able to remember them easily until tomorrow, Lieutenant," Lotty said curtly. "Victoria, we have a bed ready for you."

"Finch." I got to my feet, slowly, leaned against the wall to catch my breath. Finchley and Abreu stopped on their way out.

"Finch, Sergeant Abreu, however you write up your report on coming here today, can you keep Reno's name out of it? I don't know what she saw or did or knows that seems like a threat to whoever paid those monstrosities to torture her, but they're serious. I don't want them to track her here."

Lotty came back in to see what was keeping me. Finchley said, "I'll come up with something, as long as you remember that only my friends call me 'Finch.'"

Lotty snapped, "Enough!" and took me to a waiting wheelchair. I started to argue that I could walk, but every muscle in my body shrieked, *No, you can't*. I sat in the chair, let them strap me in, let them wheel me to an upper floor. Lotty oversaw the process of stripping me and bathing me, inspected my bruises, tutted, and ordered a nurse to start me on fluids, more antibiotics, and a round of steroids.

"Harmony," I said. "Harmony needs to know we found Reno. And Mr. Contreras—he'll worry terribly."

Lotty nodded; she'd take care of it. I was asleep before the nurse had finished calibrating the drip rate.

4 3

DISTURBING THE PEACE

IT WAS SEVEN the next morning when I woke again. I felt feather-light, newborn, free from all worries. I sat up and cautiously moved my arms and legs. They seemed pain-free, as if I'd never hoisted a dead-weight across my shoulders and marched across rough terrain for an hour.

A nurse poked her head in, saw I was awake, and marched over to take my vitals. "Dr. Herschel left orders not to disturb you, but we were beginning to wonder when you might wake up—you've slept for fourteen hours. You have a visitor, too."

She helped me into a hospital robe and let Mr. Contreras into the room.

He thrust a bunch of daffodils at me. "Dr. Lotty said you was okay, but I had to see with my own eyes. And you found Reno, saved her life."

"That was sheer luck. Luck and doggedness, anyway."

"Where was she?"

I gave him a complete history of how I'd discovered Reno, includ-ing creeping into the squirrels' nest, the fight with the mobsters, and how I'd torched the old shack to get us safely away. He pumped his fist in excitement.

"Vodka as a fire starter. You're unbelievable, Cookie, I never would've come up with that. They gonna let you out soon?"

"As soon as Lotty sees me," I said. I offered to drive him home if he waited for my discharge, but he wanted to get back to the dogs.

"I called that kid who does the walking when you're out of town, but Peppy, she don't like to be away from Mitch too long. Kid says she lay down in the middle of the sidewalk and wouldn't move until he turned around and brought her home."

Lotty arrived at nine, after making rounds. She rechecked my vitals, had me get out of bed and walk around for her, do neck stretches, knee bends, and stand on one leg with my eyes shut.

"You're doing well, Victoria. I'm going to let you go home, or back on the streets, although I wish you would rest for a few days."

I smiled. "Even though I've done almost nothing to help Felix?"

Lotty gave a reluctant smile. "Yes, I would like you to go back to work—but as your doctor, I counsel against it."

She told me that Reno's vital signs were stabilizing, although she still needed a ventilator. "Do you have any idea why the poor young woman was kidnapped and abused like that?"

"The terrorists who took her are working for someone, I'm sure of that—they're brutal and remorseless, but they were looking for something very specific that they wouldn't have thought of themselves. They were speaking a Slavic language. Not Polish—even though I don't speak it, I know what it sounds like." I repeated the one sentence I'd made out: *"Shto za chort?"*

Lotty shook her head. "I don't know any languages east of the Danube. What was it they wanted?"

"A locket. She had dropped it through the floorboards at the shack."

"What makes it so valuable?" Lotty asked.

I dug into my jeans pocket and extracted it. The locket was an oval, about an inch wide and an inch and a half long. When Lotty had cleaned away the dirt, we could see it was embossed with interlocking roses and lilies. The catch was stuck after its week in the ground, but Lotty worked it open—those surgeon's fingers were used to delicate tissues.

Inside the front face was a photo of Clarisse and Henry. Facing them was Harmony, grinning over a blue ribbon from a county 4-H plant competition. Lotty used a pair of surgical tweezers to pry up Clarisse and Henry's photo. Underneath was the engraved message: *To our beloved Reno. You always make us proud. Mama Clarisse and Papa Henry.*

When Lotty removed Harmony's photo, we found a key, just small enough that it fit into the long oval of the locket. It was wedged in tightly; Lotty eased it free with her tweezers and handed it to me.

I turned it over in my hand. It was lightweight, not meant for a door, but a box. Safety-deposit, maybe, or U.S. post office.

"This must be what the trolls were trying to find when they tore her apartment apart." I took it to the window, where I could see it more clearly. "372" was cut into the bow.

"What was she hiding that they wanted so badly?" I fretted out loud. "And where on earth is Box 372?"

Lotty said, "I can't answer those questions, and I'm not interested in them, for that matter. What I care about is her safety and the safety of the people who work in this hospital. If your horrible men were willing to attack Harmony and you and try to kill Reno to get their hands on this key, you can't let anyone know that you have it. And don't tell people that Reno is at Beth Israel. Please!"

I shook my head. "It may be too late for that. I talked to Jewel while I was driving here and mentioned Reno by name—if someone is monitoring my phone, they'll know. And Lieutenant Finchley and Sergeant Abreu—I asked them to keep it quiet, but police stations are the world's busiest gossip markets. Besides, there's always going to be someone who will provide tip-offs to the press, or interested outsiders, if the price is right. Added to that—Harmony. She has a right to know her sister is safe, but who knows who she'll talk to."

Lotty's shoulders sagged. "You're right: I couldn't reach Harmony, so I told Marilyn Lieberman at Arcadia, who promised to get the word to her."

Her phone pinged, a text message. Lotty stood. "I have to go—my resident is in over her head right now. Reno isn't in any condition to be moved. I don't want your life at greater risk than it already is, but can you help us with security here?"

"The Streeter brothers," I finally produced. "Maybe I can figure out a way to get Richard Yarborough to pay for their help."

Lotty kissed my forehead. "I'll explain it to the ICU charge nurse. Take good care, my dear one."

Round-the-clock surveillance isn't cheap, but at least here the target was stable. I texted Tim and Tom to see if any of the brothers were available. Tom could start today; as long as the ICU ward head let him sleep next to Reno, he could cover her until tomorrow morning, when Tim and Jim could pitch in.

The clothes I'd worn into the hospital were so soiled I could hardly bear to put them on. I didn't know how to hide the locket; I finally stuffed it and the key deep into my jeans pocket, where they could rest until I got them to a safer place.

On my way out of the building I passed the gift shop. They had a display of Chicago sports team sweatshirts in the window. Including, to my surprise, the Sky, Chicago's WNBA team—women's teams almost never get shelf space. At the checkout counter they had a row of blue plush pigs under a sign that read FOR BABIES BORN IN THE YEAR OF THE PIG. The pigs were holding miniature dragons between their front trotters.

I bought one along with the Sky shirt. After I'd changed into the shirt, stuffing my filthy top and bra into the bag, I went to the intensive care unit. I was going to leave the pig with the charge nurse, but when I told her I was Reno's aunt, the nurse told me I could visit her for a few minutes.

When I saw Reno in bed, I couldn't hold back a gasp: she was so thin it was hard to believe there was any room for blood or tissue around her bones. Someone had clipped her hair, which accentuated her gaunt face. She was moving restlessly in the bed, making strangled cries every now and then, but not waking up.

I knelt next to her and took one of her hands. "It's Vic, Reno. Auntie Vic. I've brought you a pig to look after you, but you are safe now. No one can hurt you. Your locket is safe."

When I said the word "locket," she scrabbled at the ventilator tube and tried to cry out. I took the locket from my pocket and fastened it around her neck.

"She can't have that on," the nurse said. "She's moving too wildly; she can choke on it."

When she moved past me to undo it, though, Reno began to scream, "No, no, no," turning even more frantically. The nurse made a face. "Better leave it on; she's calmer with it. I'll talk to the doctor, see what he says."

"You endured an enormous amount to protect that locket," I murmured in Reno's ear. "I have your key safe, but what does it unlock?"

If she could hear me, she didn't respond. I stayed on my knees near her head for several more minutes. Her breathing was stertorous, but she lay more calmly.

When I got home, and greeted the dogs and assured Mr. Contreras that Reno was still alive, I went upstairs to rest. What kind of private eye who's just spent fourteen hours asleep still needs more rest? Philip Marlowe, Amelia Butterworth, none of them ever lay in the bath for half an hour after burning down their prison doors and escaping with comatose women.

And nor could I. I had just climbed into the tub with a mask over my eyes when the street-door buzzer screeched through the intercom by the door. I ignored it, but two minutes later, multiple fists pounded on my door. I heard a shout that sounded like "Police!"

As soon as I paid all the bills I was accumulating working for other people's families, I would install security cameras in the hall. For now, I climbed from the tub, wrapped myself in towels, and went down the hall to look through the peephole.

Lieutenant McGivney was there in person, with a deputy, a muscular man who was doing all the pounding. Behind them Mr. Contreras appeared, puffing for air after climbing all three flights, beside himself with indignation.

"I'll be with you as soon as I'm dressed," I called.

My voice didn't penetrate their own racket; the deputy kept pounding, McGivney bellowed for admission, and Mr. Contreras continued to expostulate. I didn't feel like shouting, let alone opening the door covered with nothing but towels. I took my time in my bedroom, putting on clean jeans, a rose sweater I'm fond of, and the sheepskin slippers Jake had sent from Basel as a final Christmas present. I'd thought of throwing them out, but they were the most comfortable footwear I'd ever put on. I checked for my keys and went into the hall, shutting my door behind me.

McGivney said, "That took you long enough. I knew you were in there. Why didn't you come to the door?"

"It was that woman down in One-B," Mr. Contreras interrupted. "They was ringing all the bells, and when she saw it was cops, she let them in. Just to get at you. I was trying to tell them you just got out of the hospital, you're entitled to rest and privacy, but they're like all the cops I ever saw, they don't care nothing about anybody's rights. Just swagger around like they own planet Earth."

McGivney looked stunned as my neighbor paused for breath, but the deputy was openly resentful. He started haranguing Mr. Contreras for his attitude.

I cut him off before Mr. Contreras reached for his pipe wrench. "Deputy, this is an Anzio veteran who has limited patience with punks, so cool the attitude lecture. Lieutenant, you are getting exaggerated ideas about your right to barge in on people without calling and without a warrant."

"Why the hell didn't you tell me you were going through my crime scene before you set fire to it?" McGivney said.

I leaned against the door and whistled softly. "That's a mighty large soap bubble. Where was I, how was it identified as your crime scene, and did I set fire to it? Can you answer those three questions?"

"Were you, or were you not, in Cap Sauers Holding yesterday?"

"I was."

"And did I not tell you to keep away from my crime scene?"

I shook my head reprovingly. "Are you implying that all of Cap Sauers Holding is a crime scene?"

"Damn it, Warshawski!"

Below us the dogs started barking and the woman from 1B began hollering up the stairwell. Mr. Contreras leaned over the banister to yell back at her, but I pulled him away.

"Don't go tumbling down the stairwell because of her idiocy. Stay here and enjoy the show."

"You wanted me looking for the Fausson guy's keys and I told you it was an active crime scene," McGivney growled. "Did you go back there hunting his keys?"

"Nope. I went there to hike through the forest preserve. I saw no signs anywhere posting the land as off-limits to the public, not even at the log where Mr. Fausson's body was found. Have you been back there? Did you or your deputy find Mr. Fausson's keys?"

McGivney ignored that. "Someone reported a fire in the woods, less than half a mile from the scene. It was arson, the fire marshal tells me, and the Palos fire chief says you were leaving the woods just as the engines arrived."

I studied my hands in the dim hall light. I had burn blisters between my fingers that I hadn't noticed earlier.

"And?" McGivney prodded.

"And what?" I said.

"Did you set the fire?"

"Lieutenant, I think you're a good cop who's acting strangely for a good cop. I don't know the Palos fire chief. I don't know if he saw me leaving the woods as his engine arrived." It was one thing to be frank with Terry Finchley, whom I've known for years and trust. Quite another to be forthcoming with a county cop whose agenda seemed confrontational, if not downright hostile.

"One of the firemen photoed your car; we ID'd the plate," the deputy said.

"People are very creative these days with Photoshop," I said. "A suspicious person would think you were trying to pressure me into ending the work I'm doing for Felix Herschel. Is that your agenda here?"

McGivney made a visible effort to dial back his belligerence. "Did you set fire to a shed in the woods yesterday?"

I smiled. "Shall I call and ask my lawyer to meet us in Maywood? Or do you want to move on to something else?"

The woman from 1B started up the stairs, yelling so loudly that Mrs. Soong came out of her second-floor apartment to tell her to be quiet, she was waking the baby.

"Let's take this conversation inside, Warshawski," McGivney demanded.

"Do you have a warrant? No? Then we'll stay out here and take our lumps."

McGivney scowled but directed his deputy to go downstairs and talk to the broad—woman—who was making the racket. "Let her know we don't have jurisdiction for disturbing the peace here; she'll have to call the CPD. Get the old guy to go down with you and shut up the dogs."

The deputy didn't want to leave—he wanted me intimidated into confessing to arson, tampering with a crime scene, endangering animal life, and who knows what else—but McGivney ordered him summarily. I couldn't do that with Mr. Contreras, who wanted to see McGivney intimidated into apologizing, but the deputy seized my neighbor's shoulder and propelled him down the stairs in front of him.

44

PUREST WATER IN THE WELL

"WHAT'S GOING ON?" the lieutenant and I spoke almost in unison.

"You first," he said.

I leaned against the wall, one foot behind me. "As I said, I think you're a good cop, but you've galloped all the way in from Maywood to try to barge into my apartment. Almost as if you couldn't get a warrant but you were hoping to sidestep it. Are you looking for something specific?"

He turned a dull red. "Are you accusing me of wanting to plant evidence?"

"I want to know what questions were so urgent you couldn't ask them by phone."

He made an angry gesture. "You were in the woods yesterday, Photoshop or not. You're protecting the Herschel boy—kid—youth. You have a reputation—I wouldn't be surprised if you'd burned evidence that would have implicated Herschel in Fausson's death."

"I have a reputation?" Fury pulled me upright. "I have a reputation for integrity. If you think it's for anything else, we are done talking forever. My lawyer is Freeman Carter. From now on, he's the only one you speak to."

"Easy, Warshawski, easy." McGivney flung his hands up, placating. "You as good as accused me of trying to plant evidence and I didn't tell you to communicate through the SA."

I gave a feral grin. "I don't feel a need to communicate with you through any channel."

He made a heroic effort. "Okay. I want to know about the fire. I will not accuse you of tampering with evidence. And I want to sit down."

I gestured toward the hall floor.

"Don't push it, Warshawski."

I still had Jake's door key—I'd kept thinking I needed to turn it over to the building management, because I was no longer willing to do the little odd jobs Jake wanted as an absentee landlord (*Could you turn down the heat, Vic? Check the windows? See if the pipe under the kitchen sink is still leaking?*).

Jake had let the place furnished to the drummer, but it had been shut up unoccupied for so many weeks that it felt cold and empty. A stack of music stands was collapsed on the floor next to the couch. I was pretty sure the drummer had left those behind. McGivney stepped on the pile and the clatter annoyed him, as if I'd put them there myself to trip him up. I sat on a backless stool some other musician had forgotten.

"Who lives here?" McGivney asked. "You have a right to be here?"

"I used a key, remember? So no need to fear being caught on a B and E with a known investigator," I said. "The fire in the woods."

"Old equipment shed. I didn't know it existed until the Palos fire chief told me it burned. It's not listed in any county records."

"I didn't know it existed, either, until I bumped my head on it yesterday as I was hiking through the woods. You honestly never knew it existed?"

McGivney shook his head. "The county's a big place and some of those forest preserves cover a lot of ground. We patrol the roads, we leave maintenance to the forest crews."

He pulled a map out of his pocket and unfolded it onto the couch cushion next to him. I took it and laid it across the sheet music scattered on a table near the window. A desk lamp was plugged in there. The light came on. Either Jake or the drummer was still paying the electric bill.

The map showed the forest preserves near Palos. McGivney came over and stabbed the map in several places: the road closest to where we'd found Fausson's body; the spot where Fausson's body had been found; the location of the shed, which had been written on the map in a small, precise hand. An X showed the shed's location, but in the map's margins someone had written in the latitude and longitude.

The Fausson crime scene had another precise note on it. The direct route between Fausson's log and the shed was about a quarter mile, but of course I'd gone indirectly, sweeping the woods looking for traces of Reno's blue scarf.

"You can see that some buildings are noted officially—picnic buildings, garages, and so on," McGivney said. "This is a 1999 map, the oldest I had a print copy of, and it doesn't show the shed. What was in it?"

"Rusty tools, old toilet seats, that kind of thing, but someone had turned it into a prison-cum-torture-chamber. They'd lined the inside with metal sheeting. The door was padlocked shut. I managed to undo it and found a woman chained to the wall inside, close to death. Before I could carry her away, her torturers returned. We fought, they won, they locked me in with her and took off."

"They set the fire?"

"Is this a trap?" I said. "Your arson investigators can tell you the fire started on the inside, not the outside."

"Why didn't you call for help?"

"No signal."

"How did you set the fire?"

"The door was the only way out—there weren't any windows. They'd lined the door with metal, but the frame was all wood. Creeps had vodka in there. I doused the frame and was able to set it on fire and kick out the door when the wood burned away from the hinges."

"You think they were leaving you to die with her?"

"I think they were going off to get instructions from whoever pays them. Even if I hadn't had to get the victim out, I didn't want to wait around for the verdict."

McGivney's expression was sour. "I'm guessing that's where they murdered Fausson, but I'll never prove it now."

"Don't sit there moodily wishing I'd died in there. You didn't know the damned shed existed, so you'd never have proved it, ever, not even with my body as the cherry on the sundae."

He gave a reluctant smile. "Did you see anything?"

"Blood, but the woman had been bleeding. If she recovers, she might have witnessed something. Don't tell me the whole place burned."

"The floor, the exterior walls. If I can persuade the county to pay for it, we'll send the shovels and rakes and old toilet parts out for forensic evaluation, but for now they're stored in another shed. Which isn't inside the forest preserve, by the way. Give me a description of the men who shut you in there."

"They are musclemen in the most literal sense of the word. Arms like tree branches, legs like tree trunks. I couldn't make a dent in them, any of the three times they attacked me. Black hair. One has a three-day growth—I'm guessing he watched a lot of Clint Eastwood movies in his youth in Siberia or Sofia or wherever it was and thought grunge made him look tough. Black leather. My dog bit the Clint wannabe so he might have gone to an ER, but he knifed my other dog and very nearly killed him."

McGivney digested this before asking, "The woman you brought out with you, that was Reno Seale, wasn't it?"

"The woman I brought out was and is unconscious. She had no ID on her. I have no idea who she is."

"Come on, Warshawski, everyone knows you were looking for her."

I eyed him narrowly. "Even if everyone knows that, it doesn't stop my obligation as a human being, not to mention an officer of the court, to save the life of someone I find in extremis, even if I don't know her name. Even if I suspect her of being a right-wing nutcase or a mule for the Mendoza cartel."

"Or someone involved with a Canadian who's skating around a murder charge?"

I smacked the map hard enough to dislodge some of the scores underneath. "So that *was* the agenda that brought you into Chicago today after all! You can't find anything to link Fausson to Felix Herschel except a phone number, so you're going to accuse me of evidence tampering. But even in the era of Trump, a criminal court requires evidence, not imagination."

"Then give me some of the evidence you have," McGivney demanded. "You wouldn't tell me what professors or colleagues of Fausson's you spoke to, and I don't have the manpower to go around Chicago looking for them."

"Neither do I. No obliging taxpayers are paying my salary to avoid foreclosure on their homes. You've got a budget."

"And a board. You can do whatever you damned well please; I have a chain of command."

"Did you ever search Fausson's place?" I asked.

"No." He bit the word off, as angry as me. "Yes."

"One or the other, Lieutenant."

"The CPD executed the warrant. They let us tag along." He'd hated that: the Chicago cops don't give the sheriff's crew the respect they believe they merit.

"What did you see?"

"It had been tossed. Even the floorboards had been pried up. We found signs he'd stored cash in a hole by the kitchen, but whoever went through there was looking for more than that—there were holes everywhere. It was like walking through a field of gophers."

That jolted me. I wondered if I'd missed other caches. Instead of a storage locker, had Fausson buried everything at home? Could he have hidden a fortune in stolen artifacts between his floor and the ceiling of the apartment underneath?

McGivney was eyeing me suspiciously. "You look startled."

"I am startled. He didn't seem like the kind of person who cared about money. Syrian poetry, archaeology. Did he have an expensive wardrobe? An art collection?"

McGivney shrugged. "Anything valuable disappeared with the first intruders. We got the CPD to put motion detectors in place in case anyone comes back, but so far, not a whiff."

"And if there'd been trace elements of Felix Herschel you'd have arrested him. So you have nada but you keep trying to build a scaffolding around him." I didn't keep the contempt out of my voice as I walked to the door.

"It's nice to be a solo op without a boss. You can be the purest goddamn water in the well," he snapped at my back.

"There's always chemical runoff; any water can be poisoned." I spoke absently, as the subtext of his comment hit me. "Someone in the county wants Felix framed. They don't want you to put Fausson's murder in a cold case drawer, they want it finished so that no one, including me, asks any more questions. Who is pushing those buttons?"

McGivney looked back, uncomfortable, unspeaking, not quite meeting my gaze.

MY LUCKY DAY

I'D LEFT RENO'S key on my dresser when I was bathing. I zipped it now into a thin nylon money belt that I could wear inside my jeans. I was tying my shoelaces when Martha Simone called to see how I was doing on protecting Felix.

I felt like a pinball, bouncing between Felix and Reno. It was Friday afternoon; I wanted to get to banks in Reno's neighborhood before the end of the business week to see if the key belonged to their safety-deposit boxes, but I sat down so I could focus on my conversation with Simone.

I told her about McGivney's visit. "He as good as said someone is pressuring him to nail Felix and close the case. Do you have any sense of why? Are they protecting a power ranger, or trying to get leverage against Rasima Kataba?"

"It may be the second," Simone said slowly. "I'm not giving up on her, but so far I can't get the court to budge on a release. They want her father and they refuse to believe she doesn't know where he is. Apparently ICE has staked out her building. They've taken eleven other occupants into custody but haven't seen Tarik Kataba on the premises."

"My heroes," I said bitterly.

"Mine as well. What's this I hear about you burning down the forest preserve where Fausson's body was found?"

"That's how McGivney put it," I said. "Where did you get the language?"

She laughed. "I have access to some of those county reports. Seriously, what happened?"

I gave her a quick sketch, including finding my niece, but Simone wanted a description of the shed, what had led me to it, all the questions that a litigator thinks of when she's imagining a trial down the road. I told her everything. Almost everything—I omitted the locket and key. Simone was a lawyer, communications were privileged, but the fewer people who knew the better.

"If you're right that they killed Fausson in the shed and moved him to that log, why?" Simone asked. "That sounds as though they wanted him found, not that they wanted the body to decompose."

"The shed was a small space," I said. "They snatched Reno and Fausson right around the same date. If they were both in there, there was hardly space for two thugs. After all, the room was already crammed with junk. Once Fausson died, they had to move him."

If the goal had been to torture Reno and Fausson into revealing what they knew, the pair I'd been fighting didn't speak enough English to understand what their victims were saying. There must have been a fifth person present, the person who'd hired the torturers to make Reno and Fausson tell their secrets.

"Are you still there?" Simone demanded.

"I was thinking they hadn't meant to kill Fausson, at least not then. The guys I tangled with could kick a person to death with one swing of their steel-capped motorcycle boots. They swung too hard, and then they had a dead body. They might have pretended to their boss that Fausson escaped; they could have hidden the body in an effort to protect themselves from the boss's wrath."

That would explain why Reno was still alive—they hadn't yet been ordered to finish her off when I showed up.

"I hope your niece makes it," Simone said. "From my standpoint, the best news is that you can put faces on Fausson's killers. I'm going to ask for an emergency hearing with Judge Vivian; I will probably need you to testify to the probable identity of Fausson's killers."

"Only with a subpoena, Martha: I am drowning right now and don't have time to wait in a courtroom."

"You'll do what the law requires and what Felix Herschel needs," she said sharply. "Since Felix has never been formally charged, we don't need the extra hoop of asking the judge to drop charges, but we do want him to order an end to the surveillance by ICE."

I'd heard McGivney leave Jake's place while we were talking. As soon as Martha hung up, I ran from my building and drove to Reno's building at North and Fairfield. I'd mapped out the five banks within walking distance of her home and I trudged from one to the next, checking to see if any of them recognized her key.

I got to the last one, the Ft. Dearborn Trust, as they were closing, but the guard called a manager over who gave me the same negative I'd gotten from the other four. I'd passed a post office and confirmed that the key didn't work in their boxes.

This meant I needed to come back in the morning and begin a tour of all the UPS stores and their ilk. I tried to suppress a feeling of panic. The task was so large—not just tracking down the box, but also figuring out what had brought both Fausson and Reno to that shed in the woods. Dealing with Harmony, protecting Felix, figuring out what Dick's role in all this was.

I was climbing into the Mustang when I saw the storefront across the street: OLIVIA'S—YOUR HOME OFFICE WITHOUT THE RENT. I ran across the road, swerving around the traffic and nearly colliding with a bicycle. Olivia's door was locked but people were working inside. I rang a bell, holding up the key, and someone buzzed me in.

The woman behind the counter began telling me that I was supposed to bring my own front-door key with me after 5:00 P.M., but when I saw the wall filled with lock boxes I went straight to 372. The key turned smoothly. I opened the door, my hands trembling slightly, and pulled out a manila envelope containing a handful of documents.

I sifted through them. It was an eclectic collection: trading summaries for Climate Repair International; part of an e-mail that urged recipients to sell all shares of GGTHP as soon as the market opened. A loan agreement between the Trechette Trust and Legko Holdings of Saint Helier, Jersey, for two hundred million U.S. dollars.

The e-mail had been torn so that sender, date, and recipients were missing. Part of the loan agreement had been torn off as well. When the key turned in the lock, I was sure many of my questions about Reno would be answered, but these documents seemed to raise more than they answered.

I walked slowly back to my car, prudently waiting for the light at California before crossing.

Donna Lutas, Reno's boss at Rest EZ, had told me Reno had been trying to learn the identity of their CEO. These documents didn't seem to help with that, although at least the loan agreement involved Rest EZ's nominal owner, Trechette. If these were what Reno's torturers had wanted, they must mean something deeper than I could tell from the surface.

I drove to my office. I copied all the documents, but instead of locking them in my office safe, as I'd planned, I overnighted them to my lawyer, Freeman Carter, with a brief summary of their connection to Reno and Rest EZ: I didn't want to be the only person on the planet besides Reno who knew about them.

Niko Cruickshank, my computer consultant, phoned just as I got back from the FedEx drop box at the corner. Niko was excited: he had recovered most of a text exchange. However, it was in Arabic, so he had no idea what it said.

"Wonderful, Niko. Five gold stars for you today. I don't know Arabic, either, but e-mail it to me. I'll find someone who does."

I could take it to the woman at the Syrian-Lebanese center in Palos, but if it contained something negative about Fausson or any of the center members, she might improvise on the content. Peter Sansen from the Oriental Institute probably knew enough Arabic to read it.

When Niko's message arrived, I forwarded it to Sansen: *Do you read modern Arabic? Can you make sense of this?*

I turned again to Reno's documents and started to do some digging into them. Legko Insurance was headquartered in the Isle of Jersey, one of the tax haven dream spots of the modern world. An insurance company headquartered there would not be my first choice as a reliable payer of claims. When I dug into the files for Legko's board, it somehow didn't surprise me to find they had only two members: the Trechette Foundation and the Trechette Trust.

A. M. Best, the insurance industry bible, told me that Legko's capital adequacy ratio—whether they had enough money to pay claims if a lot came due at the same time—was not available. They had lent two hundred million to Rest EZ, so they must have some reserves, but where they were banked was a mystery.

Try as I might, I couldn't find any list of their insurance agents. None of the independent agent listings included Legko, which meant whoever sold for them was a direct employee of the company, but even so, an insurance company needs to sell policies to stay in business. Legko had a website, but every link on it sent me to a contact page, telling me to send inquiries to Inquiries@Legko.org.

I put Legko to one side to research the company whose stock report Reno had brought home. Climate Repair International, a company with a Delaware incorporation, had a website that proclaimed their commitment to products that would reverse the damage to fisheries and coastal waters caused by the rising temperatures in seawater. That seemed like an admirable corporate mission.

Climate Repair was interested in genetically engineering bivalves to make their shells resistant to increased acid in the water. Their financial statement said they had eight employees at their factory in Ningde, China. Their website showed all eight happily eating oysters. As was true of Legko Insurance, the links all led to a generic e-mail address.

GGTHP, the stock symbol in the e-mail Reno had hidden, turned out to be for Green Grow Therapeutics, a company that was jumping onto the reefer bandwagon.

Green Grow and Climate Repair were both pink stocks, trading through the over-the-counter bulletin board. In the days before electronic trading, OTC stock sheets were printed on cheap pink paper. Even after all these years, people in the business still call them pink stocks or penny stocks, but unsophisticated investors should think of them as colored bright red for danger. Pink stock can be issued by very small legitimate companies. However, the SEC doesn't inspect or regulate pink stocks as they do for companies listed on the NYSE; pink-stock financials range from sketchy to imaginary.

Green Grow, which the e-mail urged recipients to sell, had two million shares outstanding. It was trading today at two and a quarter cents a share, its low for the year, but its fifty-two-week high, last December 12, had been five dollars. The e-mail fragment was undated, which was frustrating—I would like to have known when all those investors had sold.

A banner ad on top of the stock sheet read, *"Nobody knows this company today, but soon the whole world will. Get in now, before it's too late."*

The ad sounded familiar. Perhaps it was the language of all flim-flam artists. I saved all the files I'd opened to my Pocket List. I was missing something crucial, but I couldn't put my finger on it.

"Reno, wake up," I cried. "Tell me why these companies mattered so much to you. Tell me where you found these documents."

SENSITIVITY TRAINING

MY PHONE RANG while I was trying to figure out what I could possibly do next to uncover the actual owners of Trechette.

It was Caroline Griswold, Darraugh Graham's right-hand woman at CALLIE Enterprises. "Vic, this isn't like you to be late, but we've been expecting a report from you since yesterday morning."

Damn and hell! My most important client, the man who kept me from drowning in debt and going out of business, and I'd forgotten him completely in the drama of Reno and Felix and the woods.

I apologized but didn't try to explain—a detective who gets herself locked in a shed in the woods when she should be tracking down a shipment of diamond wheel blades is not someone you trust in the future.

The blades weren't exactly missing: the shipment had arrived at JFK from Shanghai nine days ago. CALLIE's shipping agent had cleared them through customs and overseen their loading onto a semi, which drove them from New York to the factory in Elgin, forty miles northwest of Chicago. The shipping agent claimed to have examined the blades, but when the Elgin factory started using them, the teeth broke after a single use.

I didn't have to test the blades; my job was to examine the links in the delivery chain to see whether the shipping agent or the trucker could have substituted them. If not, then CALLIE would go after the Chinese manufacturer.

I had done some preliminary work on the case last week but hadn't uncovered anything. Today, though, the lapse in time worked for me. I had been monitoring a dozen tool auction sites, and today, on three of them, I found what looked like parts of the shipment.

I spent the rest of the evening digging into the life stories of everyone on the American end of the shipment. The shipping agent's brother-in-law had a machine shop near Toledo. The truck had stopped at a garage on the tollway to change a tire, had been there for ninety minutes. I pulled together all the information I could find on the work the brother-in-law did in his shop. He could definitely make blades that would look like the diamond-edged ones. I put the report together for Darraugh.

"It would be worth bidding on one of these blade lots. The serial numbers have been erased with acid, but a good infrared scope should bring them up again. I can fly to Toledo and examine the machine shop there for the blanks he probably uses for making fakes, or you can alert the local LEOs, but it looks as though the shipping agent and the driver are acting together."

The Toledo scam made me think of Felix and Rasima. They had access to sophisticated equipment at IIT, where it would be easy to make prototypes, or to create a fake. What if they'd made some kind of lethal weapon that looked like a mobile water purifier? Felix hadn't wanted me to touch his model. Maybe he thought I was knowledge- able enough to detect its real purpose.

What if for once ICE was on the right trail here? If they'd been tapping his and Rasima's phones, they'd know what the pair were working on. And if they were creating something ugly—I didn't want to think ill of Felix. I would not think ill of him.

Murray had called twice while I was working on my report for Dar- raugh, wanting to know about the fire in the woods and the woman I'd found there. Glynis Hadden, Dick's secretary, had phoned my cell, telling me we needed to speak about Reno. She'd also texted and left a voice message on my office line.

I ignored Glynis's message, but I phoned Murray while I started shutting my office down for the day.

"What have you been up to, Wonder Woman?"

"The usual, you know, saving the city and so on." I was cautious, wondering how much detail had made it on to the police reports.

"Did you set fire to a forest preserve?"

"I'll tell you the whole story, omitting no detail, if you'll tell me how to uncover the identity of the beneficial owner of an offshore company that's hiding behind trusts and foundations and whatnot."

"Who is it?" Murray asked.

He had never heard of Trechette, but after a moment while I heard him typing, he said, "Can't be done, not unless you have someone like the dude who leaked the Panama Papers. I still want chapter and verse on you committing arson in the forest preserve."

"Where'd you find that odd tidbit?"

"I follow all local crime. One of the Palos district fire stations had your license plate as the car fleeing the scene at the Cap Sauers Holding when they responded to a fire yesterday."

"Even private eyes sometimes go hiking in the woods to restore their sanity, Murray."

"Not when those woods are where a dead body was found two weeks ago. You haven't found the killer, right? It's not Lotty Herschel's nephew, that's still all we know?"

"More or less," I agreed.

"Who was the woman you took out of the woods with you? Your missing niece?"

"Don't know," I said. "The woman had no ID on her."

"But was she about the right age, race, coloring, things that would make a sensible person hazard a guess?"

"I'm not a guesser, Murray, I'm totally fact driven. Later."

I hung up, but the conversation left me jumpy. Murray wasn't the only person scanning police and fire reports. If he guessed I'd found Reno, everyone else would, too, even if I'd kept her name off the airwaves. I texted the Streeters, who were camping out in the ICU with her. So far, no one had tried to approach her except for the nursing staff.

"We're trying to get them to show us their credentials, but they aren't always willing to do that," Tom Streeter warned me.

I told him I'd talk to Max Loewenthal—besides being Lotty's lover, he was the hospital's executive director; the nursing staff presumably would listen to him.

Cynthia, Max's PA, promised to do her best with the ICU staff. "The nursing staff put patient welfare first, so if they see it's part of the protocol for keeping Reno alive, they will help out. But Reno isn't the only patient in that unit, Vic. If someone urgently needs help, the nurses absolutely have to put that patient ahead of inspecting IDs."

She was right, of course, which made me so depressed that I answered the next phone call without checking the caller ID.

"There you are," Glynis said. "It's important that Dick speak to you."

"Really? Why?"

She didn't answer, just switched her phone through to Dick's line.

"Vic! What's going on with Reno?"

"Oddly enough, I've been wanting to ask you the same question. Remind me of the last time you spoke with her?"

"We've been over this, and it's not relevant. I've been reading that you found her in a forest preserve yesterday."

"Gosh, Dick, where'd you read that? I'm googling 'Reno Seale' as we speak and I'm not seeing anything." I wasn't, actually, but if Murray hadn't seen her name, she wasn't in any report that the cops had issued.

Dick was silent for a beat, regrouping; I could hear Glynis breathing on the extension.

"My niece is at Beth Israel hospital," Dick said. "But they're denying that they have her there. Now you're denying that you found her. What kind of conspiracy are you running?"

"How do you know she's there?" I asked.

"Police reports," he said.

"Dick, corporate litigation must be slow if you're hanging around station houses reading reports. But if the hospital says Reno isn't there, why are you sure they're lying?"

"I know you were in the forest preserve yesterday. The same place where that guy's body was found. I know you discovered Reno in an old equipment shed. What's wrong with admitting that? If you rescued her, you're a heroine."

"Tell me the story, Richard," I said. "Tell me about the shed, and tell me how I rescued your niece and how you know she's at Beth Israel."

"From the police reports I've seen, she was in bad shape and you carried her through the woods and got her to Beth Israel."

"Anything else? Was there someone else at the shed who helped with the getaway?" I was drawing a large chain link on the legal pad on my desktop.

"I heard you were on your own, but that the shed caught fire."

I added a handcuff to it and drew an arm in navy suiting. Cuffing Dick to the truth.

"These are very interesting reports. I'll have to check with the cops myself and see what they have to say. What did Lawrence Fausson know about you that you wanted kept secret?"

"We had this conversation. I never met Lawrence Fausson and I refuse to let you take this discussion off the rails. I am entitled to know—"

"It's easy for a cleaning crew to go through the trash and learn things they shouldn't know. About Trechette holdings, for instance, and your involvement in the North American Ti-Balt lawsuit—"

"That's privileged information. Who told you about it?"

"Police reports," I said. "I read the police report on how senior partners snack on Snickers bars after lunch. It's funny, when I think of the lunches you eat at the Potawatomie Club—flounder with choron sauce or whatever—and then you're gobbling candy bars out of the vending machine."

"How dare you, Vic, how dare you go bribing the cleaning crew into going through my trash—"

"Dick, for a lawyer, you jump to conclusions faster than a rabbit looking for the briar patch. I haven't bribed the Force 5 workforce, with money or hockey tickets or promises of eternal salvation. I have talked to them, trying to find anyone who knows anything about Lawrence Fausson. It's easy for cleaners to look at garbage. People like you think cleaners are part of the furniture; you don't guard what you say or do or throw out. Which makes me wonder if Lawrence Fausson found something in your trash to use against you."

"I never met him!"

"You might have and not known it," I objected. "Let me phrase this differently. Has anyone tried to blackmail you within the last twelve months? Glynis, you can chime in. I know Dick has no secrets from you."

"Vic, when you're being as insulting as only you know how to be, it's usually to hide or avoid a topic," Glynis said. "Why don't you want to talk about Reno?"

"I'd love to," I said promptly. "What did Reno learn about Trechette when she was in St. Matthieu? She confided in Dick when she got back, right?"

"She had questions that Dick couldn't answer," Glynis said.

"Couldn't, or wouldn't?" I asked.

"Oh, Glynis, it's time to stop dancing around," Dick said. "Let me put it to Vic straight. I know this is the age of political correctness cubed, but Reno needed—needs to grow up. She took a simple pass as an attempted rape and thought I should step in and advise Rest EZ to offer sensitivity training to their male managers. I didn't, of course, and she took that in very bad part. I'm afraid we parted rather angrily."

"That sounds unfortunate," I said politely. "Glynis, is Dick looking at his fingernails?"

"Talk about rabbits jumping around briar patches," Dick said, "you are the champion at the long jump and the sideways topple."

"An unwanted pass is a violation that no one should have to tolerate. And being told to 'grow up,' 'suck it up,' or any other variation on that theme is a double violation. Especially for your nieces, who were violated plenty already as children."

Dick protested that my response was an outrage. "I knew it was useless trying to tell you this—you've always been on some feminist crusade or other. That's why I didn't tell you when you first came to me about Reno. I knew you'd start lecturing me on insensitivity and crap.

"You think I don't care about Reno and her sister, but they're my sister's children. Everyone knows how close you are to the Herschel woman who's a surgeon there; I'm sure she'd get me into the ICU if you sweet-talked her."

"You've got better sources than I do, Richard: they're telling you

Reno is at Beth Israel, which I don't know. Even if I were willing to abuse my friendship with Dr. Herschel—which I'm not—she couldn't possibly let you visit every woman in the hospital in the hopes that you would recognize one of them as your niece."

"I tried to do this the nice way," Dick snapped. "I can go to a judge and get a court order forcing you to reveal their whereabouts."

"Glynis, is he running a fever, or is he psychotic?" I said. "I know you're good pals with a lot of judges, Richard, but what grounds are you going to give? You're not your nieces' guardian, you never had a legal relationship with them."

"You really don't understand, do you, Vic?" Dick's voice was filled with contempt. "I can make a case because I know the players and I know what court to go to."

I added Dick's torso to my drawing, with flames shooting from his rear end. Pants on fire.

"You know members of the Cook County Board, too, don't you?" I said. "Are you the person who's pressuring the sheriff to close the investigation into Lawrence Fausson's murder?"

"I keep telling you, I never knew Fausson and his murder isn't interesting to me personally. However, I've been told that the sheriff's police have a suspect whom they're not ready to charge."

"If you're monitoring the situation closely enough to know they have a suspect, then you should know he's 'the Herschel woman's' nephew. If you or a friend is leaning on the sheriff's department, I can guarantee that arresting Felix Herschel will cut off all possibility of help from me or anyone else who's close to Dr. Herschel."

SIDE TRACKS

I HUNG UP on that fierce sentence. Afterward, though, I sat for a long time in my dark office, turning the conversation over in my mind. It was credible that someone had assaulted Reno in St. Matthieu: I'd wondered about that when Harmony told me her sister returned from the Caribbean in a troubled frame of mind. Reno wanted to identify Rest EZ's CEO to see if he had been her assailant.

But the idea that Reno had gone to Dick wanting help in setting up sensitivity training at Rest EZ beggared belief. I also didn't think he would have kept the story to himself the whole time I'd been looking for Reno. Dick was spinning a fancy web, trying to sidetrack me with a gratuitous attack on feminism and political correctness.

"Richard, Teri, and Glynis, the three of you are like a game of three-card monte, trying to get me to guess which one Reno spoke to when she got back from St. Matthieu. Did she come to your office? To the Oak Brook house? Phone you?"

If Reno recognized someone whom Dick knew or worked with, it could have happened in one of two ways: either she'd been in his office or home and saw someone whom she re-encountered in St. Matthieu. Or she'd had a bad interaction with someone in the Caribbean and then saw them in his office, or at Dick's house. Maybe even seen their photos on the Crawford, Mead website.

I turned my desk lamp back on and looked up the financials again for Green Grow and Climate Repair, trying to get their board members' names, or at least a registered agent. The firms were remarkably secretive, but they shared one detail: both had used the services of the firm of Runkel, Soraude and Minable in Havre-des-Anges, St. Matthieu, to handle their incorporation.

That wasn't just interesting: it brought Dick perilously close to something that was potentially illegal or even fraudulent. Pink sheet companies often existed only on paper as a way to seduce the greedy and credulous into parting with money. Had Reno discovered that on her Caribbean vacation? Is that why she came to see Dick?

Those documents were so threatening to someone that showing them to the wrong person put her life at risk. She'd talked to someone about what she'd learned. Surely not her uncle. I stirred uneasily in my chair. Dick would not, no, he could not have hired those brutal hit men to torture his own sister's child.

Reno had dressed for her meeting with her abductor: someone she wanted to impress was coming to see her but had snatched her instead. That was why her keys were home but her phone and computer were missing. When she saw she was in danger, she'd blurted that she'd put her evidence in writing and hidden it. The thugs had gone back to her apartment, where they'd torn it apart, looking for her secret document. Bit by bit as they tortured her, she'd revealed more, finally giving up the secret of the locket, but concealing her locket in the floor beneath her.

"*Poverina, poverina, che corragio,*" I muttered.

It was too late to try to see Donna Lutas at the Rest EZ branch in Austin. I could barge in on her at home, I supposed, but maybe I should start with Harmony. She was nearer, and she might be able to interpret her sister's notes.

I left my office as cautiously as I'd entered, but neither the two hulks nor any less obtrusive assailants seemed to be hovering. That was nerve-racking in its own way, wondering when the next boot would stomp.

I turned off my phone, along with all location permissions, in case someone cared enough about my movements to be tracking my GPS. I still parked a quarter mile from Arcadia House and took several side streets to make sure my back was clear.

The evening staff didn't know that I was coming. They could see me on their security monitors, though, and they buzzed me into the foyer, which was separated from the house itself by another door made of bullet-resistant glass. The person who came to the door recognized me, but still made me show ID. Since I was in charge of security recommendations for the premises, I was glad to see that they took the protocol seriously.

Harmony met me in the same little room where we'd spoken yesterday morning. Her eyes were bright, but it was a feverish brightness, not a sign of buoyancy.

"Did Dr. Lotty let you know I found Reno?" I asked.

She nodded. "She says Reno is really sick and isn't talking. Is she—did they hurt her brain?"

"She was out in the woods without a coat. She lost a lot of weight and is suffering from exposure, so they won't know for sure until she's feeling stronger, but Dr. Lotty tells me the brain scan looks good."

"Why couldn't you tell me yourself?" Harmony said, her eyes bright with tears. "You wouldn't even have known she was missing if it wasn't for me."

"I know, sweetie, but I was pretty wrecked myself. I only found Reno by chance. She'd been wearing her blue scarf and it snagged on bushes as she was carried through the woods to a decrepit shed. The same horror stories who attacked us in the park on Tuesday locked her inside. By the time I found her, she had lost consciousness. It was lucky that I got there when I did, but her assailants came back before I could move her.

"I fought them, they were too strong for me, they locked me in the shed with her. I had to set fire to the place to get us out, and then I carried her through the woods to my car. I got her to Dr. Lotty, but that took my last ounce of strength: I fainted and spent the rest of the day and all the night asleep. I came here as soon as I possibly could, even though it wasn't as soon as you needed or deserved."

I pulled out my phone and showed her pictures of the shed, and of her sister comatose next to the wall, but not of her sister in chains, or naked and bleeding from the waist down: she didn't need that image burned onto her visual cortex.

Harmony looked and looked away. "So now you're a hero. You saved Reno."

"I hope I saved Reno," I said soberly. "She hasn't yet regained consciousness. If you want to see her, I will take you to her. Hearing your voice might be the best therapy for her right now."

Harmony started scraping the dirt from under her fingernails with the nail of the other hand. The nails had broken off and there was blood on the ends of two of her fingers.

"Maybe tomorrow," she muttered.

"Whenever you want to go, all you have to do is let me know."

"Whenever I want to go, I'll go. I don't need your permission to see my own sister."

"Fair enough," I said. "I think I understand why she was kidnapped and why you were attacked. She had some papers that her attackers wanted. She'd put them in a lockbox and hidden the key in her locket. They thought your locket was the one they were looking for."

Harmony's hand again went reflexively to her throat.

"Reno had hidden hers under the floor in the shed where she was imprisoned; her captors never found it."

"Well?" Harmony demanded. "Where is it?"

"I put it around her neck," I said. "The nurses are afraid she may choke on it, but wearing it seems to bring her some comfort."

"You should have brought it to me. The nurses can steal it. You didn't have the right to decide what to do with it. I'm her sister. Don't you think I should decide what's best for her?"

"Hey, Harmony, what's going on here? You came to me for help—I didn't fly to Portland and demand that you come to Chicago so I could risk life and limb on your behalf. Now all of a sudden I'm the bad guy?"

"There's no 'all of a sudden' about it. For two weeks I've done everything the way you said it should be done and all that's happened is my own locket got stolen, I got beat up, and Reno almost died. And now I'm like some prisoner in this place. I want to leave, I want to see my sister, I want to go back to Oregon."

I felt a headache build behind my eyes. "You can do all those things. I just don't want you hurt again, which the two men who attacked you are well able to do. If you decide to leave, please be very careful. Don't go places alone, don't lead people to your sister, because she's at risk as well."

Harmony reddened. Fresh tears spurted from the corners of her eyes—fury, impotence.

She didn't say anything else, however, so I pulled a copy of the documents I'd found from my briefcase and showed them to Harmony. "Do any of these company names sound familiar? I'm hoping Reno might have discussed them with you."

Harmony took the papers from me, but only glanced at them briefly. "Reno always was interested in money, how to make money, I mean. She followed the stock market and tried to get Henry and Clarisse to invest, but they didn't trust it. So maybe these are two companies that she thought would be good investments. Look how cheap the stock is—you could buy a thousand shares for twenty-five dollars."

I nodded politely. "You could be right. What about the loan between Legko and Trechette?"

"How should I know? I never heard of either of them. Did you ask Uncle Dick? What did he say?"

"I didn't discuss the documents with him, but he does now say Reno called him when she got back from St. Matthieu. She complained about some of the men who were at the resort. He says Reno wanted him to put together sensitivity training for Rest EZ managers."

"She did?" Harmony's eyes widened. "Why did she do that?"

"Not saying she did. That's what Dick says happened."

Harmony's mouth returned to its mulish lines. "I forgot: you're the only person who knows the truth. Maybe she did call and ask him to do it and you're completely wrong about him."

I was feeling my own flash of fury and impotence, but it would be a mistake to give rein to it. I got to my feet. She looked small and fragile, hunched in her chair by the empty fireplace, but when I tried to hug her, she pushed me away.

48

A GOOD WINE WITH

STALE CHEESE

HARMONY TURNING ON me felt physical, a kick in the stomach, but I could understand it, even if it made me angry. Her world had spun out of control and now she was by herself—yes, living in a large house with many residents, but she didn't know any of them; the only person in Chicago she felt close to was close to death. She'd been assaulted; when her chain was stolen she'd lost her iconic connection to her foster parents. I could understand why she was acting out, but I still hated it.

I had deliberately not given Harmony Beth Israel's name. If she was enterprising enough to track that down, more power to her, but I didn't want to go out of my way to send her to her sister on her own. On top of my hurt and the anger was fear. The puppet master pulling the strings here was amoral and ruthless.

I drove toward my home, stopping to pick up enough food so that I could at least make sandwiches. I parked on one of the side streets near my building. My miner's headlamp had been destroyed in the shed yesterday, but I still had a high-power flash in the glove compartment, which I brought with me. I used the flash to study the cars on both sides of my block, walking down the west side and coming back up the east. I also inspected the shrubbery around my own building as well as several ones nearby.

Right now, I seemed to be in the clear, but I was still nervous: Was the thug-master planning a new attack that would come from an un-expected direction?

I stopped at Mr. Contreras's place to check on him and the dogs. Mitch was starting to put weight on his injured leg. I took him on a short walk with Peppy, still without finding anything untoward. When we got back, I filled my neighbor in on what I'd done after leaving the apartment. In exchange he gave me a word-for-word of the encounter between the sheriff's deputy and the woman in 1B.

"I think she's deranged, doll. You look out for her. She's the one who buzzed those goons into the building the other night, and she talked so crazy to the deputy, it was like she'd throw them a party if they killed you. She'd let them in again for nothing, just 'cause she hates the dogs, but she'll report on you for pay."

He offered to make me dinner, but I turned him down. As I headed upstairs, I shone my flash around the dark corners of the second-floor landing, the upper rails where someone could lurk and jump me, the corridor between my apartment and Jake's. I even went into Jake's place, which I hadn't locked after McGivney left. The hair on my neck was standing up, but this time no one was lurking.

The past few days had been so stressful that I deserved a treat. I took one of my mother's red Venetian wineglasses and opened a bottle of Brunello. Deep red, rich body. The perfect wine to go with a toasted cheese sandwich, which I ate lying on the living room floor, watching the Cubs play the Marlins.

I drifted off in the bottom of the sixth. The downstairs buzzer jolted me awake. I knocked over the wineglass as I scrambled to my feet, red wine spreading across the floor. My heart was hammering when I pushed the communications button on the intercom.

"I'm here to see Ms. Warshawski."

Mr. Contreras had beaten me to the bell. I went out to the hall and leaned over to listen: my neighbor demanded to know if the visitor had an appointment.

"Is she out? I was in the neighborhood and stopped by on a chance— if she's busy I'll send her a text."

I trotted down the stairs, calling, "It's okay, I know him."

Mr. Contreras was in the entryway, shouting through the outer door. The door to 1B was cracked open. I blew the woman a kiss as I hurried to the foyer. Peter Sansen was there, hands jammed into the pockets of a navy windbreaker.

I let him into the building and performed a flustered introduction, since Mr. Contreras was looking at Sansen as though he were a live grenade.

"We been having a lot of trouble in this building." Mr. Contreras was truculent. "People barging in, beating up on Cookie here, trying to kill the dogs, sheriff thinking he can ride roughshod over us 'cause he's got a badge. It's better if we know in advance you're planning on showing up."

"Is that your father?" Sansen asked as he followed me to the third floor.

"Old friend. We share the dogs. He's a good guy, but he hates knowing he can't rip an enemy battalion in half with his bare hands anymore."

"I should have called before I came," Sansen apologized, "but I was at a restaurant in the area and read your text over dinner. My modern Arabic isn't as good as, well, Fausson's, for instance, but it's good enough that I read the message chain. The texts were so startling that I wanted you to see them right away."

When we went into my apartment, I hurried over to where I'd been lying and picked up the wineglass. I held it to the light, twisted it slowly. It was intact. I'd been holding my breath over that—I'd already damaged three of Gabriella's glasses. It would break my heart if I lost another.

Sansen took in the wine I'd spilled. "You were fighting?"

My own cheeks flamed. "Wine. Let me mop this up and I'll pour you a glass."

I turned off the television and took Sansen into the dining room so we could spread papers and devices out on the table. I took out another of Gabriella's glasses and poured wine.

Sansen twisted his glass, watching the red of the wine against the diamond lines. "These are the wineglasses your mother carried through the Italian mountains on her way to Chicago? No wonder you treasure them."

He paused for a respectful moment before turning to the business at hand. "The document your computer wizard dug out is a text thread between Fausson and Tarik Kataba, the poet."

Sansen held the phone close to his face to read. "It starts with Fausson: he writes, '*Did you take it? They blame me.*' Kataba says, '*It is not for you. It is for history,*' something like that—perhaps he's saying, '*It's important historically.*' Then Fausson wants to know where he is."

Sansen looked over the top of his phone at me. "Arabic doesn't conjugate verbs the same way Indo-European languages do. Fausson might be asking, '*Where are you, Kataba?*' but he might also be asking about the object itself. Kataba doesn't answer. Fausson then asks if Kataba is with his daughter or if he is hiding with the daughter's Canadian friend."

"That would be Felix Herschel. He's an engineering student at IIT who has a relationship with Kataba's daughter. I got involved because he's the great-nephew of an old friend of mine—Lotty Herschel, who's a perinatologist at Beth Israel. . . ."

My voice trailed off; Sansen asked what was wrong.

"Not wrong, but I've been tense all day over when or where the uglies would strike again. Now I'm wondering if they're lying low because I can link them to the murders. Whoever is paying their bills may be rethinking strategy." I stirred uneasily in my chair.

"Frightened?" Sansen asked.

"Terrified. They're hired muscle, horrifyingly strong and totally without affect. I'm only walking around because of sheer damned luck."

I gave a half laugh, trying to cover up the fear I'd felt in the shed. "From their accents, I think they're Eastern European. The one set of words I could make out clearly was when I whacked one of them on the head with a shovel. It was like whacking a steel bollard—he blinked a few times, then fought back. Anyway, he shouted something that sounded like '*Shto za chort?*'"

Sansen nodded. "You have a good ear. Russian, for 'What the hell?' At least you made an impression on him." He put a hand over mine and pressed it gently. "You are an incredible woman, Ms. Warshawski, memorizing Russian while fighting for your life."

I ducked my head, pleased by the praise but embarrassed as well. I spoke quickly, to cover the moment.

"I hope whatever they think of next doesn't involve a grenade to the building or something like that—there are too many innocent bystanders here."

Sansen's lips twitched. "I thought I'd left IEDs behind when I evacuated Tell al-Sabbah. I should have known a lady who would hang upside down out the Institute windows could attract her own *quttae at-taruk*."

"Which are?"

"Brigands, bandits."

"They sound more dramatic in Arabic. . . . Is there anything else in the text thread?"

Sansen had been laughing with me about the brigands, but when he looked at his phone, he became sober at once. "Kataba never wrote back, after that one reply. There's one final message from Fausson, terrifying when you know what happened next. He says, '*Please, I beg of you; they are giving me only one more day to find it.*'"

One more day. Who had given the poor fool that day? Surely not Dick. Gervase Kettie? Had Fausson lifted something from Kettie's office? But then why was he trying to get it from Kataba?

My brain felt like a merry-go-round, thoughts rising up and down poles, horses' legs trampling me and Reno and Felix. Sansen caught my wineglass as it slipped from my fingers.

"You need to get to bed," Sansen said. "You don't have to prove you're the toughest camel in the train—I already believe it. Come on, detective. Up you get."

He helped me to my feet, his calloused hands unexpectedly gentle.

"Teeth," I muttered.

"I won't tell the dentist you went a night without brushing. Which way to your bedroom?"

49

INTERLUDE WITH

ARCHAEOLOGIST

WHEN I WOKE, the sky outside my window was turning a paler gray. Six-thirty in the morning and I was wearing only the knit top I'd had on yesterday, my bra dangling unhooked underneath. I didn't remember undressing; Sansen must have helped.

I took off my clothes and pulled on a long sweatshirt—it was chilly in the apartment. When I went to turn on the espresso machine, I saw Sansen's navy windbreaker slung over the back of the chair where he'd been sitting.

I found him stretched out on the pullout bed tucked into my living room couch. He'd foraged for a blanket and pillow in my hall closet but hadn't bothered with sheets. His shoes were lined up neatly next to the couch, his trousers folded across the piano bench.

I knelt next to him and stroked his face. "If you spend any more time lying on this lumpy thing, you'll have a crick in your neck."

He smiled at me sleepily. "It's more comfortable than a sheepskin laid across a sand dune."

"My bed is more comfortable than both choices. No IEDs, either."

"Does it come with or without detective?"

"With. Definitely with."

It was past nine when we finally got up again. Sansen had a meeting with a group of potential donors—Saturdays were when enough of them could leave work for a behind-the-scenes tour. I pulled a couple of shots of espresso while he showered.

When he came into the kitchen for his coffee, he said, "I confess: I almost brought my grown-up clothes with me last night, but I decided I'd feel like ten fools if I'd misread your response to me."

He put an arm around me and pulled me next to him. "Delicious coffee. Delectable detective. I need to get going." He didn't move.

"Yes. So do I." My head was tilted against his cheek, but half my mind was on my to-do list. I wanted to go back to Rest EZ, but that would have to wait until Monday. Today I could focus on Reno's papers.

Sansen squeezed my waist and let me go. "A shekel for your thoughts, Victoria."

"My New Year's resolution was to focus on the moment, and I love this moment—but I feel the hounds of hell gnawing on my feet. I need to work out how Fausson and my niece Reno ended up in the same forest preserve—presumably assaulted by the same hired muscle. And of course those papers that Reno had hidden must have some deep meaning. While you're raising money for the museum, showing them how to read ancient bits of clay, I'll be trying to read pink sheets."

Sansen looked at me seriously. "Treat your papers like an archaeology problem. When you excavate sherds, it's not at all clear whether you have pieces that belong together. You lay them on a table, you see which ones have the most likely connections—similar finish, similar soil content around the sherd, all those things. And then you try to fit them together. You don't try to jam them together without thinking about it first. Treat your documents like that."

I nodded. "There are also questions about the Dagon; I'm assuming that's the object Fausson was referring to in the messages you translated. If I get my sherds glued together I'll start working on that."

"I agree about the Dagon, although we don't know whether Leroy—Lawrence—was actually involved in bringing it to Chicago. Still, he formed a relationship with Kataba when he was working in Syria, and the Dagon came from Kataba's hometown. The fact that Fausson was here in Chicago could well be why Kataba came here when he was released from prison."

"Fausson probably brought it," I said. "I did wonder about Rasima Kataba, but I don't think she returned to Syria from Lebanon before coming to the States. I've spun a bunch of theories about where Fausson got the cash he was hiding under his floorboards, from drugs, through stolen artifacts, and even by smuggling refugees."

"What cash?" Sansen cried.

I made a face. "I'm losing my grip: I forgot who I told and who I kept this from, but I was in Fausson's apartment a few days after he died and stumbled on it."

By the time I'd gone through the whole story of my search, including my near-death, Sansen was eyeing me with a mixture of alarm and amusement.

"As for where he got the money, I have no idea, but there's so much theft these days all over the Middle East, from digs and from museums. There always has been, of course, but now, between the U.S. destabilization of Iraq, the wholesale collapse of Syria, and the way ISIS helps themselves to artifacts to fund their terror operations, important pieces are being destroyed or scattered around the globe. It's infuriating. Heartbreaking, too. Archaeologists steal, too, sad to say. We oldsters don't like to admit it, but the temptation is strong for students and postdocs.

"You're twenty-five years old, you've borrowed money for graduate school that you can't imagine ever being able to repay, you're digging up bits of pottery and old coins under a hot sun, and then you wander into an unguarded museum in a tiny town. You come face-to-face with a statue or necklace of unimaginable value—the temptation can be overwhelming. For Fausson, who wanted to be famous and wanted money to fund his own expeditions, the temptation might have proved irresistible. Especially with an object like the Dagon. He'd need a buyer, of course."

"I'm wondering if I might be able to name one or two possibilities."

I thought uneasily of the Mesopotamian statue in Dick and Teri's Oak Brook house.

Sansen grinned. "If you need someone to lower you upside down through a skylight into the heart of a nefarious antiquities thief's mansion, I'm your man."

I gave a perfunctory smile. "I'd like to talk to your postdoc at the OI again. See if she has any insight on how the Dagon spent a mere fifteen hours in your museum."

"I can't believe Mary-Carol—" Sansen cut himself short. "No one wants to believe anything unsavory of the people they work with. I'll tell them to talk to you when you call . . . I'm flying to Jordan Thursday night—big conference there and one of our hot topics is stolen artifacts. I know your time is as stretched as mine—but I hope we can have dinner before I leave."

"That would be very nice," I said formally, but I could feel myself grinning fatuously.

A last kiss and he was gone.

I showered and brushed my teeth, took the dogs for a quick walk. I couldn't see anyone watching me. Mitch was eager to run, but the vets had stressed no extraordinary strain on the joint for another week.

"Patience, big guy, patience. Everyone says it's a virtue even though you and I know differently."

When I brought the dogs back in, my neighbor looked at me critically. "You're up kind of late for a private eye with a lot of investigating to do. You check up on your niece yet?"

"Which one?" I asked. "The one who won't talk to me or the one who can't talk to me?"

"This ain't a joking matter," my neighbor said sternly. "Those two gals depend on you. You can't be lying around in bed with some gravedigger when there's lives in danger."

Gravedigger? Was that going to be his nickname for Sansen? He used to refer to Jake's double bass as a banjo. Mr. Contreras has never liked any man I've been involved with. I don't know if it was jealousy, or if he had an unacknowledged fear that I might marry and leave him in the lurch. I couldn't really imagine marrying again, but whether I did, I would never abandon him.

"Right you are," I said. "I'm racing upstairs this minute to get to work. Mitch is looking good, by the way, healing ahead of schedule. . . . You do know Mitch is the only man in my life, right? Besides you."

My neighbor turned crimson. "Oh, go on upstairs and let the dogs and me get some dishes washed."

When I got to my own place, I brought one of my big artist's sketch pads to the dining room table. I could have done this more easily in my office, but I was enjoying the lingering sense of Sansen in the room with me.

Before I started work, I called the hospital. My niece was still improving; rehydration and warmth had stabilized her heart and she had intervals where she seemed alert, although they weren't sure, because she wasn't talking to anyone. That provided some welcome reduction in my stress, but the faster I solved the problem in Reno's papers, the sooner her life would be out of danger.

I opened my computer case files for Reno and Felix and started copying the names of everyone I'd interacted with onto the artist's pad. I began with Rest EZ and the people I'd talked to there. I put in the locations of the various holdings in the Trechette name, from Latvia to Luxembourg, then moved on to the two law firms—Crawford, Mead and Runkel, Soraude and Minable—adding Dick, Teri, and Glynis. I threw in Kettie for good measure. Harmony, of course.

I added another column for the sheriff and the Cook County Board.

A column for Lotty, Felix, Rasima Kataba, and her father the poet, another for the people from the Oriental Institute. I included Peter Sansen. I was human, my judgment wasn't infallible—I'd married Richard Yarborough, after all.

The next step was to see which people or companies had the most in common. That was easy, once I laid all the names on the table. Trechette, the Trechette trusts, and the foundation connected with Reno and Dick, although not with Fausson. They connected to Kettie, too, in a roundabout way: Kettie had eaten with Dick and with Arnaud

Minable, who represented Trechette. Force 5, the cleaning company, cleaned Kettie's office as well as Dick's.

I had found the Trechette and Minable names in Dick's trash when I was cleaning his office. Fausson could easily have found other more incriminating documents if he had worked in there. I drew a dotted line from Trechette to Fausson. I still thought it was possible he'd found something that had made him try to blackmail Kettie. Or Dick. I drew another dotted line between the billionaire and Fausson.

I went into my corporate and legal databases and looked for links between Trechette and each of the other entities I'd written on the sketch pad. Even so, I almost missed the crucial connection, the lawsuit North American Titanium-Cobalt, aka Ti-Balt, had filed against Trechette.

Earlier, I'd read only a summary of the suit. Today I went through all the documents and attachments. And there it was: the Trechette insurance subsidiary that had actually sold the bond was Legko. Legko had sold a three-hundred-million-dollar completion bond to Ti-Balt's construction arm to cover the building of a new extraction plant in western Australia.

When new environmental regulations slowed construction and delayed completion by over a year, Legko refused to pay. The correspondence attached to the lawsuit showed that Legko referred Ti-Balt to Trechette Insurance, which sent them to the Trechette Trust in Havre-des-Anges. Trechette Trust sent them to the Trechette Foundation, which said they had no legal liability for Legko Insurance.

"Legko rented office space from Trechette Insurance Holdings' Jersey offices, but we had no legal relationship with them other than landlord and lessee," according to a lawyer for the Trechette Foundation.

The fee for a completion bond is typically 1 to 3 percent of the value of the project. As I grimly made my way through all the documents, I saw that Legko had underbid its competitors, offering a rate of .8 percent. Ti-Balt was having a cash flow crunch; this must have looked like pennies from heaven.

The insurer requires enormous amounts of data from the insured to show that they are doing business legitimately and aren't pretending to be contractors just to get a big insurance payout. I would have thought Ti-Balt's risk managers would have performed similar due diligence in looking at their insurer.

And then the other shoe dropped hard on my head: Gervase Kettie sat on the Ti-Balt board.

I sat down slowly, carefully, as if I were made of glass and might shatter on impact. What if Kettie had steered Ti-Balt to Legko? I put my papers aside and started a search through LexisNexis for lawsuits involving Legko. There were seven others, six by limited liability companies whose board members weren't named in the public documents. The seventh, though, was Keep Your Paint Dry, Inc., a well-known firm that built movie sets and architectural prototypes.

The bond was for sixty million, not a hundred, but again, Legko refused to make good on the completion bond and then led Keep Your Paint Dry through a dance that ended at the Trechette Foundation. To my disappointment, Kettie wasn't one of the firm's directors. By this time I was obsessed enough to look at the movie that Keep Your Paint Dry had been building sets for. Kettie was one of the producers.

Had Fausson found proof that Kettie was helping Legko defraud Legko's clients? Even if he was, why would a billionaire do something so sleazy? Because he liked proving that the law didn't apply to him. Because in the billionaire world, rules exist only for working stiffs.

Any good feelings left by my morning in bed with Peter Sansen had dried up completely.

UNGUARDED COMMENTS

JERRY, THE GUARD, was sitting near the door when I came into Rest EZ's Austin branch, the *Sun-Times* open to the baseball scores. He looked up, almost turned back to his paper, then did a double take.

"You're not welcome here. We made that clear a week ago."

The room was half full of people, some hunched over their lottery tickets, some working out compound interest problems at the loan machines. A woman with two small children scuttled for the exit, in case I was the next crazed person to open fire in a roomful of strangers.

"A lot changes in a week," I said, "especially in America's fast-paced society. People we couldn't stand a year ago are presidents and cabinet officers. Tell Donna Lutas I'm here with a couple of quick questions."

"You weren't listening, were you?" Jerry said heavily. "I had to escort you from the premises a week ago and I'm happy to do it again today."

It was Monday afternoon. I had spent most of Saturday immersed in lawsuits and tax reports, trying to find a direct link between Kettie and insurance or securities fraud. Failing that, I'd looked for the St. Matthieu lawyers, Runkel, Soraude and Minable. The lawyers had done a good job of sewing their trusts up tightly. The only name that appeared was "Trechette," and I couldn't find Trechette. I'd looked for Richard or Teri Yarborough and Glynis Hadden and hadn't found them, either.

By Saturday night, I had started to think I could smell burning rubber in my brain, I was working the gears so hard without anything to oil them. I needed a day off.

On Sunday I stopped at the hospital with Lotty to visit Reno, whose face had lost its gauntness. She opened her eyes when I spoke to her and seemed to be listening, but I couldn't be sure.

Afterward Lotty and I drove up to the botanical gardens north of the city and spent a peaceful afternoon among the plants. Lotty needed a break as well. Ten hours in the OR never wore her down the way her worries over Felix had.

We agreed to forgo any talk of Felix, Reno, and the troubles mushrooming around them for the day. Instead we admired orchids, walked through the Japanese garden, and finished with dinner with Max in the solarium behind his kitchen. Although I had worried about leaving Mr. Contreras and the apartment unguarded all day, everyone was fine when I returned.

Monday morning, I got Darraugh Graham to give me five minutes: he's the only person I know with the clout to move the Cook County Board. It's always a long shot, trying to reach a busy CEO who could be anywhere on the planet and in any number of high-power meetings, but Caroline Griswold got me in—my quick turnaround after her nudge the other day had bought me a reward.

I drove to the Loop and parked in a fifteen-minute zone—with Darraugh, five minutes means five minutes. Darraugh's wintry personality makes small talk impossible: I went immediately to the point. "If Gervase Kettie is a personal friend, I won't ask anything else."

"I see him at the Potawatomie Club sometimes. He sits on boards, we go to the same fund-raisers. He do something you're investigating?"

"Maybe," I said. "I'm trying to find proof, but he, or whoever is doing it, has all his tracks well covered. Would you know if he was in debt to the Russians?"

"Don't know it. Wouldn't surprise me—he wants people to think he's the biggest flame in the fire. Fake money. Just my opinion, of course."

"Fake? He counterfeits securities?"

"No, no." Darraugh was impatient—he was short on time and I wasn't keeping up. "CALLIE makes things. We build, we supply. Hedge funds, money chasing money, nothing behind it. So they collect money, art, whatever to make it seem like they have something to be proud of. Real estate, too—easy to get in over your head if you're not as smart as you think you are.

"You know the kind of boards people like me are on. Symphony, Art Institute. We give a few million around town. Kettie pledges but he never pays up. Could be he's a louse, or could be he's bankrupt."

"Two weeks ago, a man named Lawrence or Leroy Fausson was murdered and left in a forest preserve west of town." I gave Darraugh a thumbnail of Felix's connection to the murder and the various attacks against me and my nieces.

"I can't find the men who attacked me and who kept my niece locked inside a shed for over a week. I'm pretty sure they are Russian, in which case, they may have been sent back to Moscow until the heat dies down here. But someone is pushing on the sheriff to arrest Felix, despite my evidence that these two Russians are most likely Fausson's killers. I know it's asking a lot, maybe too much—but I was hoping you'd know someone on the county board who could tell you whether someone is pressuring the board to protect the Russians."

Darraugh thought it through, quickly but carefully. "See what I can do. You're hoping the name is Kettie, of course. May just be the sheriff wanting to close a case, you know."

"I know. One long shot after another these days. Thank you."

"You did a good job on that Toledo machine shop. Shell game, wasn't it, switching components on us."

He nodded—a courtesy, a truncated bow—Darraugh doesn't usually shake hands.

I drove from Darraugh's office out to Austin. I knew that if Jerry was on duty there would be a confrontation, perhaps even a physical one, but when he grabbed my left shoulder I ignored him: my attention had been caught by the big TV monitor on the west wall. I'd been vaguely aware of grinning people hawking Rest EZ financial products, but suddenly a man in a tie and starched white shirt was proclaiming the "Stock of the Day."

"Folks, the one percent got to be the one percent by paying attention to little companies that no one else cared about. Green Grow Therapeutics is a company that's going to create new billionaires. It's going to turn old billionaires

green with envy when they find out what they've been missing. Last week when it was selling for seven cents a share, nobody had heard of Green Grow, but believe me, this time next week, the whole world will know them. Buy today and wipe out that debt overnight."

"Yes!" I cried. "That's it, isn't it? The Stock of the Day will turn the one percent into the point one percent. Jerry, have you bought any of the stocks of the day? Have they performed well for you? You get a special rate on the debt?"

My outburst bewildered Jerry so much that he relaxed the grip on my shoulder. The audience, which had been keeping their distance from the crazy woman, moved closer. One man, with sagging blood-hound cheeks and a gray three-day growth, growled, "Yeah, Jerry. You buy these stocks?"

Jerry fingered his holster. "Company policy—employees aren't al-lowed to buy recommended stocks. Risk of insider trading."

"I bought me one of those stocks," a heavyset woman of about fifty said. "Three cents and something a share, how can you afford not to, the ad said. Lost every dime I put into it and then lost the rest of my dimes on the interest on the loan they gave me to buy the damn things. They's poison, those stocks."

"Stock market? Hell. Even the lottery is a better deal than the stock market," someone else said while the man with the bloodhound cheeks rumbled, "Better off playing the numbers if you can find a policy shop. Lottery put most of these out of business, of course."

While Jerry dealt with an increasingly belligerent group of cus-tomers I faded to the rear. When I was here the other week, I'd noted the number Jerry typed on the keypad to the back of the office. I shut my eyes, opened my left hand where I'd traced the numbers onto my palm. 611785. Poor security—they hadn't changed the code. I'd have to speak to Donna about that. When I finished speaking to her about other things.

The people who worked in the cubicles along the narrow hallway had all left their stations and were crowded into Donna's office, raising the alarm about what was going on in the front of the store.

"People are upset about the stocks, Donna, we have to do something." "They could riot." "It all started with that lady who says she's a detective—"

"Yes," I cut in. "The detective has a few questions about the stocks. Does every Rest EZ outlet in the country advertise the same ones on the same day?"

The loan counselors became quiet so fast that for a moment I could hear the hum of Donna's computer, and then Donna said, "Oh. It's you."

"Yep, it's me."

"How'd you get back here?" one of the counselors demanded.

"Jerry helped." I smiled blandly. "Back to the stock questions. Do you want to talk privately, Donna? Or shall I share my concerns with your whole staff?"

"Back to work, ladies." The words were authoritative, but Donna's tone was weary.

The women eyed one another, looked at me to see how dangerous I might be, but finally sidled past the chair full of documents that was keeping the door open. There were mutters of *We should stay. What's she know? She gonna hurt Donna? Someone should tell Jerry.*

I moved the chair, spilling some of the binders as I did. The woman who thought they should call Jerry ordered me to clean up the mess I was making: we all want some authority, even those of us who have none. I shut the door and leaned against it.

"Tell me about the stocks."

"Why do you want to know?" Donna's voice was still weary, but her eyes were watchful.

"I'm like the other Rest EZ marks—I want to get out of debt and join the point one percent. Does every Rest EZ store advertise the same stocks?"

She didn't say anything but started to fumble with her desk drawer.

"Panic button?" I said. "I'd rather you didn't, because if you call the cops, I'll file a lawsuit, which will mean you and your staff will get subpoenas to appear in court and answer these questions, which will probably end your career."

She gave an angry sigh but took her hand away from the drawer. "In Chicago, we all get the same e-mail telling us what will be advertised on a particular day. I don't know about the rest of the country."

"And do the stocks change every day?"

She shook her head. "They call it the Stock of the Day, but a lot of times there's no stock or sometimes the same one gets shown for a week or two at a time."

"So the message comes from corporate? From Eliza Trosse?"

"It's one of those corporate e-mails, you know, the kind that comes to a blind distribution list from a blind sender."

"And now the sixty-four-billion-dollar question. Answer this and you could be as rich as Gervase Kettie or the Koch brothers."

I walked over to the desk and leaned over her, my hands on two unstable stacks of documents. She clenched her hands together but didn't look at me.

"Did Reno Seale talk to you about the stocks when she got back from St. Matthieu? Or about an assault?"

Donna gave a tired smile. "Both. She wanted to call corporate, she wanted to know who was setting up the stocks, but she wanted to know who organized the gala, too. I tried to get her to leave it alone. I liked her, but she was getting people in corporate stirred up. In fact, after she left on Monday, Eliza called me to say Reno needed to calm down and cool off. So when she didn't come in on Tuesday, I thought maybe Eliza had called her at home to warn her. And when I couldn't reach Reno myself I thought maybe she was making up her mind about whether even to come back."

I stood up and one of the stacks teetered to the floor. I knelt to start gathering up the papers, but Lutas got out of her chair and pushed me away.

"Get up, get out. Don't come back."

MAKING GRANDPA

TONY PROUD

JERRY WAS WAITING at the door when I came back to the front of the store. Once again he grabbed me with more force than he needed; once again I let him shove me outside without fighting back.

"Hey, brother, there's no call for that." It was the man with the bloodhound cheeks. "She try to attack you? She threaten you?"

Jerry said, "Hey, brother, yourself. She comes around here threatening the managers."

The bloodhound followed me to the street. "That right about the stocks? You think they're a scam?"

"I *know* they're a scam. Just trying to get the proof."

He hesitated. "You with the government?"

"Nope. Private investigator." I handed him a card.

"V I—how do you say that last name?"

I pronounced it for him.

"My sister lost a lot on those stocks, Ms. V.I. People get addicted to trading 'em, like they do to playing the lottery. Worries me to see Rest EZ push them so hard. You need help out here, you call me, okay? Name's Andy Green. Don't have a card like yours, but here's my phone number." He pulled a scrap of paper from his pocket and wrote the number with a faulty ballpoint before heading up the street.

I stood next to my car, staring at the street but not seeing it, trying to figure out how the Rest EZ owners could make money from their Stock of the Day program. I wanted to look again at the companies whose tear sheets Reno had brought back with her. What made them so explosive that my niece had nearly died protecting the lockbox where she'd hidden them?

Trying to follow stock prices on a phone screen would be maddening. I'd have to crawl through the rush hour traffic to get back to my computer. I looked at the Rest EZ window and laughed to myself—I could rent time on one of their machines.

As I stood there, a call came in on my burner: Tim Streeter, calling from the hospital pay phone.

"Your niece Harmony was just here. She came with a guy she said was her and Reno's uncle. We had to let them in—Harmony's the next of kin, after all, but when the guy tried to talk to her, Reno began to scream. Security came and hustled them away, but I thought I'd better let you know."

"Harmony went to Dick?" I cried. "Oh, no! She's been angry with me, angry with the world and taking it out on me—but to go to Dick—" I stopped myself—this was beside the point.

"I'm in Austin, but I'm on my way—as fast as I can get to you."

This time of day, side streets were ten times faster than the expressways. I took Lake Street, cruising under the L tracks, turning north on Kedzie, and pulling into the visitors' lot at Beth Israel in just under thirty minutes.

I ran around to the rear entrance and up the stairs to the intensive care unit. The charge nurse came over to me at the entrance.

"Your niece has been very agitated. I don't want her more upset, so be careful how you speak to her."

"But she's conscious now?" I asked.

"In and out. She won't answer questions about the day or the president or anything, so we don't know how well she's understanding what's said to her."

I didn't waste time arguing with the nurse, but of course Reno wouldn't answer questions: she'd been interrogated under torture for more than a week.

Tim Streeter was waiting outside the door to Reno's room. I asked if he'd heard Dick talking to her.

"It all happened pretty fast. The sister ran to her and put her arms around her. She was crying and saying she was grateful that you'd found her—'Vic found you, Reno, she saved you, I'm so grateful, but now she's acting like a tyrant'—that's pretty much what the sis said. And then she said the uncle was there and he could help.

"Dude walks over to her and says he's her uncle and all she has to do is give him the papers and he can make sure she's safe, and Reno began to scream *no!* over and over. You'd better believe I had the asshole out of there faster than you could spit.

"Reno was thrashing around—the doctor came in to put something in her IV line to calm her down. He said it was good she was responsive, he wasn't going to knock her out, just get her to relax. And then he— the doc—tried asking her did she know who was president or mayor or those things and she lay there doggo."

When I went into the room, Reno's breath was coming in short stabs. Her eyes were closed, but she was holding herself rigid: she wasn't asleep, she wasn't unconscious; she was hyperalert.

I knelt next to her head. "This is Vic, Reno. Your auntie Vic. You're in Chicago, in a hospital. I found you in the woods and brought you here."

I didn't try to touch her: she'd had too many people pawing at her to enjoy the hands of someone she didn't really know. I saw that the nurses had left her locket around her neck.

"You were brave and smart, just like Grandpa Tony told you. You hid your locket, and the bad men didn't get it, they didn't see it. Now you have it back. I found your key and I got your papers. I have them safe; you don't need to worry about them. I'm trying to make sense out of them but I can't."

I sat cross-legged on the floor. I didn't want to use a chair, which would put my head a few feet above Reno's head, but the floor put me below her and I had to speak more loudly than I wanted. I waited several minutes in silence and then repeated what I'd said. I added a few details: I was a detective. I wished I'd known Reno was in Chicago all these months. I wished she'd come to me with her troubles.

Another patient silence and then I went through my litany again, voice always calm, pitched low. Her thin face, ravaged by hunger and pain, made me long to stroke her skin, give a physical comfort, but I restrained myself. At one point, Tim Streeter appeared with a stool for me—Goldilocks: it was just the right height.

"Papers," Reno muttered. "I was hiding. Warehouse. Free port. Statues, paintings."

She shuddered, eyes still closed. "Nightmare museum. Real, not real?"

"Real," I said. "Real and a nightmare. The papers were in there?"

She opened her eyes briefly. "Who are you?"

I repeated my name, that I was Grandpa Tony's daughter and I'd brought her out of the woods.

"Grandpa Tony. I want him, I want Henry." She said something in Chinese, and tears oozed from the edges of her eyes.

"I want them, too," I said. "They gave us the gift of courage and we will be brave because of that gift."

She might have drifted into sleep, but I sat still. Perhaps twenty minutes passed and then her eyes fluttered open.

"Auntie Vic? You are Auntie Vic?"

I pulled my wallet out of my briefcase and showed her my PI license.

"Uncle Dick is afraid of you."

"Good," I said. "He should be. Can you tell me about the papers? You brought them back from St. Matthieu, didn't you?"

"St. Matthieu," she whispered. "Men looking at us like fish in the market. I should have known. Mama Clarisse—don't tell her. She— she stopped me and Harmony, she saved me and Harmony, and if she knows—knows I went straight back to those men—"

"You knew the men from Oakland?" I ventured.

"No. New men, old look. Why Rest EZ sent me there. Uncle Dick said they want women who can get along with important clients. Should have known, should have known, should have known."

She was pounding the sheets with a feeble energy. This time I took her hands, easy clasp, easy to break away from.

"Hey, hey, baby. Clarisse loves you. She forgives you everything, she understands everything. And I love you, too. Your auntie Vic, sitting here, loving you. The company gave you a chance to take a fancy vacation—it sounded exciting. We all would go. We all would love a chance to be on a white sand beach when Chicago is freezing."

After a time, when nurses and doctors had come and checked on her and decided I could stay, Reno gave me the whole story, in little bits and pieces. I filled in the fragments as best I could and perhaps got some of the details wrong, but what it boiled down to was that Trechette was celebrating Carnival in a big way on St. Matthieu. Executives and clients had come from operations around the world, about three hundred men, and the company had brought in about a hundred young women who all looked good in bathing suits.

"Didn't understand until dinner the first night. They put me at a Chinese table."

Reno understood Cantonese from her years with Papa Henry. "One of the men said if they had a chance to bid on the women—whores, he called us—he would choose me. Pretended I didn't understand. He stroked my neck and I smiled. He laughed."

Another man at her table said he wouldn't give more money to the Russians. He had paid enough to attend the Carnival, and he knew all their money was going straight to pay off Russian loans. He said, "If the girls aren't free, I'm not interested in them. Plenty more in the town just as pretty."

The women had been divided into groups, and each group had a leader, who was essentially a minder, to keep the young women in the party rooms with the men, so Reno pretended she needed a bathroom. She found a back staircase, went to her room, and gathered a few essentials—passport, toothbrush, credit cards. Changed into jeans and sneakers and spent the night in a vacant cabana on the beach.

The next morning she tried to get on a flight out, but the airline said she could only use the ticket that her group leader was holding in her name. Reno left the airport while the ticket agent was calling the leader for Reno's group.

"Came to meals and parties long enough the leader saw me. Harmony and me, always learned secret ways in and out. Safety. The parties—" Reno shivered. "Bowls filled with Ecstasy tabs. Five-hundred-dollar bottles everywhere. Alcoves with couches and no one closing curtains. Men slapping my ass. 'Can't wait for the talent show, you got big . . . talents there.'"

She shuddered and fell silent. I let go of her hands, but she grabbed mine convulsively. "Don't leave, don't leave."

"I'm not going anywhere. I'm here with you. Right here, baby. I have you safe. No one will hurt you."

The last part of her story was the hardest. On the final afternoon of the trip, Mardi Gras, hotel security guards trapped her and took her to an enormous complex on the water's edge. She made out the sign over the entrance, FREE PORT OF ST. MATTHIEU, as they shoved her into a building with dozens of rooms, most filled with art as far as she could tell as they muscled her along a corridor.

They took her to a room lined with mirrors and a giant round bed in the middle. The Chinese man who wanted to bid on her was there.

"Screamed and ran. Down hallways, in and out of rooms, saw 'Rest EZ' over one door. Snatched papers from a shelf, kept running."

She somehow ended up at an emergency exit and ran down the beach into a bodega, where the woman behind the counter hid her in a supply closet. She gave Reno a mattress for the night. In the morning, she roused her son to take Reno to the airport on his pedicab.

"Group leader furious. 'We brought you here and you disappointed us. Your career is over.'"

Reno didn't answer back; she wanted to get her papers home safely and wouldn't risk fighting with the person who had power in the situation. She'd grabbed papers at random but recognized the names on the stock sheets as Stock of the Day promotions at Rest EZ. She wasn't sure what the documents meant, but was sure they showed something fishy, if not illegal—why else would they have been hidden in a free port building, where no government could get access to them? The loan agreement didn't mean anything to her, so she'd approached Dick.

"Thought he could help, get me Rest EZ CEO. Wanted CEO. Needed to show how wrong sex games were. Needed to learn why the stock pick. Uncle Dick said he didn't know Rest EZ bosses. He wanted the papers, but I didn't trust."

After that final burst of confidences, Reno fell heavily asleep.

I stayed another half hour, holding her hand. "You are the bravest girl in Chicago," I said when I finally got up to leave. "The bravest, the smartest. Grandpa Tony would be so proud of you. As I am myself."

52

A NOD IS AS GOOD

AS A WINK

BY THE TIME I left the hospital, the nursing staff had changed shifts and so had the Streeter brothers, with Jim taking Tim's spot outside Reno's door. The sun had gone down.

I expected bigger changes—I thought a century might have passed. I expected my hair to be white and my face deeply scored with wrinkles. It seemed strange to look at myself in the bathroom mirror and not to detect any difference. Reno's story made my whole body rise in revolt, not simple nausea, but as if everything inside me needed to come out, bones, blood, nerves, in a paroxysm of revolt.

Dick—we hadn't slept together for over twenty years, but the thought of his skin next to my naked body made me feel filthy. What were you thinking, Richard, when you came into this hospital to try to get those documents from your niece?

And Harmony—had you gone to Dick? Had Dick come to you? I called Arcadia House, but Harmony hadn't returned. The night director told me that she'd left without telling anyone where she was going.

Lotty and Max had both left for the day. The whole administrative wing had shut down except for an emergency night clerk. I'd hoped to find a place where I could rest, restore some semblance of balance to my tormented brain.

The cafeteria was almost deserted. I slumped on a chair against a wall, one of a handful of numb, dumb animals waiting for news on the direly ill. My whole body ached, as though the Russian enforcers had been pounding on me with their massive fists.

Even in the #MeToo era, it was hard for women to get their stories taken seriously. Whatever was going on at Rest EZ, they weren't as worried about their Caribbean debauch being revealed as they were about the papers Reno had taken. They hadn't tried to silence Reno's description of the orgies, with their bowls of Ecstasy tabs and high-priced alcohol, but they'd sent Dick to get the papers from her. The papers whose location she'd very nearly given her life to safeguard.

The hyperwealthy aren't like you and me. Not, as Hemingway supposedly told Fitzgerald, because they have more money, but because the money makes them think their needs, however debased, should be met on the instant. A billionaire's bacchanal in the Caribbean where members brought beautiful women as party favors for their friends seemed vile; the idea that the billionaires entertained themselves by bidding on the women was beyond vile.

My vocabulary was too limited for me to come up with a word for the disgust and rage I felt.

What Reno's story told me was that attacking Rest EZ and Trechette by exposing their debauchery wouldn't have any effect on them. The scumbags who'd gone to St. Matthieu cared only about money; they collected it along with their stolen paintings and statues.

My anger seemed to make my brain come to a point; I suddenly realized how the loan agreement Reno had brought home connected with the Stock of the Day.

The Trechette subsidiary Legko lent money to Trechette holdings. That meant that Trechette had a large debt, which it could use to off-set income, including capital gains. If they pumped up the price of penny stocks and sold at the top of the artificial market, they'd make a profit—offset by the debt to their other wholly owned subsidiary.

The high rollers had paid to go to the Caribbean. How much, I wondered, and how had they paid it? Direct deposit to a Trechette bank account? No, into a Russian offshore account: Reno's Chinese men had said that their money had gone to the Russians, because the person who organized the fête was in debt to them.

I'd been shot at, bitten, beaten, kicked—I was tired of being a punching bag for these monstrosities. Quadruple that for Reno. Time to dish it out. I called Niko Cruickshank, my computer wizard.

"Vic! I don't have anything else for you, I'm afraid."

I told him I didn't need anything else out of Fausson's computer, at least for the time being. "This is a new project, but there's risk attached."

"You know my hobby is skydiving, don't you?" he said.

"Joke?" I asked.

"I spend my days digging in the bowels of computers. I need to do something in the open air. And I get squirrelly in the winter—can't afford to get away to Arizona or Mexico more than twice before it gets warm enough in the Midwest to go up. You got something high-risk, it'll get the jitters out of my system."

I didn't want to discuss it over the phone, at least not over my phone, but Niko assured me he was encrypted and impenetrable. "As much as anyone can be, of course."

I looked around the cafeteria: no one was in earshot, but I still lowered my voice. "There's a computer system I need to break into. It's for a countywide system, maybe a nationwide system. Do you need to be in the IT department's machine to insert code?"

"I need access to a machine that connects with the IT department, but I don't need to be there physically. You're out-of-date, V.I. Go to a community college and take an intro to computer security."

I agreed, humbly. With every year that passes, I move further from understanding contemporary technology. I was at my peak when tracking meant a real person had to follow you. Listening in on someone's phone meant sweating bullets to get a bug into a handset, or shinnying up a phone pole to a junction box. Modern electronics make detectives lazy.

However, Niko was free tonight. He'd meet me in my office in an hour unless I aborted the mission.

I dug in my pockets for the scrap of paper with Andy Green's phone number on it. He was the man with the bloodhound cheeks who was angry about Rest EZ's stock program because it increased their customers' debt load.

I went out to my car so I could dig one of my burner phones from the trunk. Maybe I was only partly divorced from modern technology.

"Hey, detective. I wasn't expecting to hear from you again," Green said when I called.

I asked if he worked for Rest EZ.

"No, ma'am. I run a few errands for one of the gals there, that's all. You don't need a loan, do you?"

I thought of my accounts payable list. I could use a windfall. "Probably, but not from Rest EZ. I want to get in after the place closes and look over their computer system."

"You planning on stealing from them?"

"I'm hoping to shut down the stock trades. Don't know if I can."

He was silent for a beat, as if trying to assess my reliability. "There's a cleaning crew empties the garbage, runs a mop over the worst of the dirt, and so on, between ten and eleven. If they're shorthanded I sometimes help out. Come around the alley about eleven-fifteen in case the back door doesn't shut all the way."

I texted Niko that we were on. I had time to go home for an hour. And to check in with Dick, which I did from the hospital parking garage.

"Dick!" I cried heartily, although he'd answered his phone with a biting "Now what?"

"I'm just calling to say how pleased I am that you're reaching out to Becky's daughters. I heard from the hospital that you went with Harmony to visit Reno."

"I didn't do it to win your approval, Vic."

"That's what makes it so special," I said earnestly. "You were doing good for its own sake. Are you and Teri putting Harmony up now? I'm guessing she won't want to go to Portland until she sees Reno has really turned a corner."

"I don't know her plans, Vic. She's not staying with us; she didn't want to be that far out of Chicago without a car."

"Where did you drop her off, then?"

"I know you made these girls your business for the last two weeks, Vic, but Harmony doesn't want you breathing down her neck."

My mouth twisted bitterly. I couldn't tell if he was lying or not— my last conversation with Harmony had been unharmonious in the extreme, after all.

"Richard, this is going to be a very difficult thing for you, but start thinking of them as 'women,' not 'girls.' Where did you leave her?"

"That's privileged, Warshawski. She asked me not to tell you and I'm respecting her wishes."

The patronizing sneer in his voice was almost more than I could bear. "I hear you caused a major crisis in Reno's health by asking about some papers she brought back from St. Matthieu. The hospital isn't going to let you near her again."

He cut the connection a second before I could. How satisfying was that? Not at all.

When I got home Mr. Contreras was distressed by the news, but he had to agree that I couldn't take the time to scour Chicago for Harmony. "You got a plan to bring this whole shebang to a halt, you get on with it, doll. I'll leave a light on and stay up, in case our gal remembers she's got a bed here."

5 3

PAYDAY

REST EZ IS a payday loan company whose headquarters are in Chicago's West Loop.

I was sitting on Mr. Contreras's couch, watching Beth Blacksin present the noon news on Channel 13. The television showed Blacksin in front of the dreary building on Adams where Rest EZ leased their offices. Blacksin had a wool scarf wrapped around her neck: we were in the first week of April and the wind from the lake and river was still biting.

Blacksin gave a thirty-second précis of Rest EZ's business model and then told her viewers about the Stock of the Day, and the way in which consumers were enticed into buying the shares, driving up the price every time they made a trade.

"We made a quick search of a number of recent stock shares that were heavily promoted by Rest EZ. During the week Rest EZ was pushing customers to buy the stocks, prices rose dramatically. One company, Green Grow, saw its share price rise from pennies a share to five dollars. Climate Repair looked even more impressive, its share price rising to nine dollars. At the end of the week, a mysterious owner dumped five hundred thousand shares of both companies, and the customers who'd bought their shares on Rest EZ credit saw their holdings wiped out and their debt to the company notched up."

In the short time she'd had to prepare her story, Blacksin had come up with an elderly white woman who'd lost her home because of her debt to Rest EZ. The woman said they kept pushing her to buy the stocks as a way to get out of debt, *"and then I suddenly was owing them fifty thousand dollars. They took my house."* She was trembling and crying.

Next to me, Mr. Contreras reacted with exclamations of grief and outrage. "These the people your niece got involved with? Oh, Cookie, you got to get those girls safe."

He'd been up until one, hoping that Harmony might show up, and had gone to bed feeling wretched. There wasn't much I could do to comfort him, except to assure him I was working hard.

I myself had been up until four with Niko. We'd spent the first two hours at the Rest EZ store, so he could see how to get into the corporate system.

He had typed for a few minutes and clicked his tongue disapprovingly. "They deserve to be hacked: their security is so pathetic that *you* could probably break into it. Not really a challenge, V.I."

He next did something fancy with the security cameras, putting them on a loop that made them think they were looking at empty offices. Finally, he hunted out the programs that dealt with stock advertisements.

When he had the code he needed to put the stock information out on the video network for the company's three thousand North American loan stores, we left: no point tempting the fates.

We went back to my office—if Niko made a misstep and someone traced the hack, it was on me, not him. He made sure all my files were backed up on two separate 8-terabyte disks and dismounted those from my Mac Pro. He disconnected the machine from the cloud and went to work. When he finished, he cleaned the Mac Pro disk, zeroing it out, which took an extra hour. Finally, he reinstalled my files, so that the machine looked the way it had when we arrived that night.

"If it weren't so immoral, I'd be tempted to short some Green Grow myself before the markets open," he said when he finally finished. "It's a wicked scheme, and horrible that they got away with it for so long. I'm also tempted to forgive everyone's debts. I'll think about that one. See you in Leavenworth, V.I."

I'd slept for five hours on the daybed in my office: I didn't want the dogs to record my return home. If Kettie or Trechette or even Dick suspected me of jimmying Rest EZ's system and sicced the FBI on me, I could imagine the woman from 1B chirping, "Oh, yes, she came home at four that morning. Ask what she was doing out all night if she wasn't breaking into Rest EZ."

Niko and I couldn't come up with a real actor, of course, so he'd taken the authoritative-looking man already shilling stocks for the company and given him new dialogue. Niko had been sad that there wasn't enough time to change his jaw movements to fit the words more closely, but I read the script while Niko ran a program to turn my alto into a convincing baritone.

"Did you buy Green Grow or Climate Repair stocks? Did you lose your shirt? You're not alone. Those stocks made Rest EZ's rich owners even richer, but the owners rigged the system to make sure you lost money. Want to know how they worked the scam? Go to ShortStock .com for complete details."

ShortStock was a rudimentary website Niko had set up to step people through the details of the scam—including the loop of debt and profit cycled through the Trechette holdings.

"The simple version is—every time you buy a stock through Rest EZ, the owners are roaring with laughter over you for being a chump.

"Who are those owners? That's the pea under the walnut. We found a company called Trechette in the French West Indies but there's no one there we can talk to.

"By the way, don't ever buy insurance from a company called Legko. Legko has never yet paid a claim. They say they don't have any money, which makes it hard to understand how the Illinois and Minnesota and other state insurance commissioners let them get away with doing business."

Within twenty minutes of opening for business, Rest EZ had shut down their in-store TV program, Beth Blacksin told us. Every time they tried to override Niko's and my program, their whole computer network crashed. I was impressed—that was an extra step Niko hadn't told me he'd inserted.

"We've tried talking to Rest EZ's Chicago management team, but so far, no one is returning our calls. This is Beth Blacksin, live in front of Rest EZ's Chicago headquarters."

"That's where Harmony's sis worked, huh?" Mr. Contreras said. "And they was doing this to the people borrowing money from them? I thought I got taken to the cleaners, but the interest they charged me wasn't nothing compared to this stock mess. Hard to think a nice gal like your niece could be caught up in something like that."

He'd never met Reno, of course, but he couldn't imagine Harmony and her sister as anything other than "nice gals."

"She wasn't," I said soberly. I told him what I thought had happened, which left him horribly shaken.

Murray called while Mr. Contreras was digesting this. "Warshawski, they've got Blacksin out trying to corner someone from Rest EZ, but I'm looking for Trechette. What have you learned about them?"

"No more than what I saw on Channel Thirteen just now—they're the putative owners of Rest EZ, right? You on that part of the story?"

"Don't play naive with me," Murray snapped. "I can still count to ten without losing track of my fingers. Three days ago, you mentioned 'Trechette' to me. You were taunting me, as we both knew at the time. You tried to tap-dance over whether you'd found your niece in the Cap Sauers Holding last week. I looked up Yarborough's family, and his sister's married name was 'Seale.' Her daughter Reno has been on the Rest EZ payroll for about a year. Now talk to me about Trechette, and this bizarre hacking of the Rest EZ internal TV feed."

"You just summed up everything I know; I can't tell you anything else."

"Like, was it your niece who hacked the feed?"

"You apparently can't keep track of your fingers," I said, "or you'd know my niece is lying unconscious in a hospital bed."

"You? Was it you who hacked the feed?"

"If I had that kind of skill I'd be sitting on a fortune in Bitcoins, not racing around town trying to stay a half step away from some terrifying Russians. Did I tell you one of them bit me?"

"Don't try to sidetrack me," Murray snapped. "Unless it happened within the last twenty-four hours, it's not news."

"Share that definition with the president," I suggested, and cut the connection.

I was uneasy: Murray had put the pieces together very fast. He was a better investigator than Rest EZ might have on tap, but Dick or Glynis would think of my name pretty quickly. Niko and I hadn't left a trail that the FBI could follow, but the person behind the Russian mobsters wouldn't care about evidence. He'd care about things like tearing out fingernails to force an answer.

"Things are about to get even uglier than they've been the last few weeks," I said to Mr. Contreras. "I'd like to drive you and the dogs out to your daughter's place."

"First of all, I ain't going," my neighbor said. "Second, Ruthie don't want dogs in her precious ranch house. Third, I ain't being driven from my own bed by some foreign lunks."

"But—"

"Where will you spend the night? With that bald guy who was here the other night?"

I couldn't keep from blushing. I'd had a brief phone call with Peter while I was with Niko last night, enough to learn that his donor meeting had gone well Saturday; neither of us could fit in dinner before Thursday, when he was leaving for Jordan, but we set a date for the week he got home.

"I don't want to put anyone else in danger," I said to Mr. Contreras, "you, the dogs, Peter Sansen—not even that pest across the hall. If I could get you to move out, I'd sleep in my office. The place is fire resistant." That wasn't because of my work, but because my lease mate's sculptures involve high-powered blowtorches.

"Well, I ain't budging. What if little Harmony comes around and finds the place empty?"

IN THE CLEANUP SPOT

I WENT TO my office after taking care of the dogs, but I couldn't focus on work for my paying clients. I wished I had some way of finding out whether the two Russians were still in Chicago. Or who had hired them or what he or she might want them to do next.

I called Martha Simone to see what progress she'd made. The lawyer was happy: she'd found an immigration judge willing to order Rasima Kataba's release.

"She should be out tomorrow, maybe tonight if we're lucky. After that, it would be best if Dr. Herschel persuaded Felix to go to Montreal until you get the state's attorney to arrest Fausson's actual killer," Simone said.

"Right," I said brightly. "They're eagerly waiting for my opinion." The call reminded me that I wanted to talk to Mary-Carol Kooi from the Oriental Institute, to see what she knew about the Dagon's mysterious appearance and disappearance. Kooi's phone rolled over to voice mail.

I spun a coin around on my desktop. Should I drive down to Hyde Park and see if I could find Kooi? Or was it time to rejoin the Force 5 cleaning crew? If Kettie had been upset by the hijacking of Rest EZ's internal TV network, he would doubtless have been on the phone to his lawyers. Dick might have left notes lying around.

I'd rather be at the OI, with a chance to say hello to Sansen, but we learned in first-year English that duty is the stern daughter of something or other: Crawford, Mead took priority here. I sent a text to Peter Sansen, telling him I'd tried unsuccessfully to reach Mary-Carol Kooi. He said he'd try her himself and get back to me. That meager crumb would have to suffice.

As I drove home, I listened to news updates. Both local and national feeds gave a lot of airtime to Rest EZ's problems:

"The number two player in payday, or cash advance loans, in the nation, Rest EZ offices all over the country are reeling from efforts to discredit their stock-selling scheme. Someone hacked into the company's internal TV network to claim the company's stock-buying program was at best a sham and at worst a successful effort to defraud customers.

"Eliza Trosse from the Chicago headquarters said today that Rest EZ 'is trying to help ordinary people who can't afford a big portfolio take part in America's success story. We have no tolerance for anyone who would make our customers question the financial advice we provide and we are working with the FBI to find the perpetrators and prosecute them to the fullest extent of the law.'

"Meanwhile, business in some locations had dropped by fifty percent."

Prosecuted to the fullest extent of the law; that was a threat that should make the perpetrator shake in her running shoes. Instead, she ran her dog Peppy to the lake and back. Then changed into a white-collar outfit: tailored suit, silk shirt, light makeup. Put the purloined Force 5 smock into a briefcase, along with running shoes, jeans, and a T-shirt.

I walked over to the L stop on Sheffield and rode the train downtown. I hustled to the Grommet Building and got there just as the Force 5 van was pulling up. While Melanie Duarte—the crew chief I'd sparred with last week—conducted her roll call, I strode past them into the lobby. I was management: cleaning crews didn't exist on my radar.

I sat on a banquette, frowning over a document and texting. When the Force 5 crew came in, the security guard took a look at me, decided I belonged there, and went to chat with Melanie while he checked in the crew.

I sat until a pair of late-working women came in, heads together, laughing over some story. I held my phone down as if it were my ID and slipped through the security gates in their wake.

I took an elevator to 38. The changing room for the Force 5 women was there, and a security guard had just unlocked the door as I walked down the hall. I nodded to him—still regal, still management—but stopped to handle more texts until he'd taken off. Several other cleaners arrived while I waited. They stared at me when I came into the room, but I pretended not to notice, just hung my jacket and good blouse in an empty locker, put on my T-shirt, jeans, and the smock, then wrapped a paisley bandanna around my head.

Finally one of the women asked me in halting English if I was new to Force 5.

"I'm here as a temp," I said in English. "Usually I work at a hospital in Edgewater."

They shook their heads, not understanding, but two more women arrived; one of them translated my answer. "I'm supposed to go to fifty," I said. "Melanie didn't tell me who the team leader is for fifty."

At that moment, the woman who'd rescued me on my first visit arrived. When she noticed me, she snapped out a sharp query that even my feeble Spanish could follow: Who was I and what was my real business here?

The woman who'd translated for me started to explain, but my erstwhile rescuer cut her short, apparently recounting the story I'd told her last week about my nephew. A cluster of eight or nine women gathered around me.

The English speaker said, "We know you were here last week, hiding, telling Lidia a story about a nephew. Now you are here this week, telling a story about being assigned temporarily. In eight minutes we start work, so in seven minutes, you tell the truth or we call security."

I nodded: fair enough. "There are two stories, one about a nephew and one about a niece. The story about the nephew involves Lawrence Fausson, who worked for Force 5 until he was murdered two weeks ago."

I paused while the interpreter put it into Spanish. More women were arriving, but one of our group shushed their excited questions—time was short. Two women in hijab stood at the back, puzzled by what was going on but trying to follow what we were saying.

I cast about for a word to describe Lotty's relationship to me. "My godmother has a nephew named Felix who came to Chicago to go to college. The police think Felix murdered Fausson. When I came here last week, I hoped to talk to men who had worked with Fausson. Fausson spoke Arabic."

I was working hard, keeping verb tenses simple, sentences short.

"Oh! Elorenze Foessahn!" one of the women in hijab cried. "Elorenze speak Arabic very good."

I smiled at her but plowed on. "I was trying to find out how Fausson knew Felix. I didn't learn much. I came back today because of the second story. This story is about my own niece, a young woman named Reno. Reno was kidnapped and almost murdered. She is still very close to death."

I stopped again for the interpreter. A number of women made sharp comments. The interpreter said, "They say you could say anything; how can we believe any story you tell us?"

"I found my niece two days ago in a forest preserve west of town. The men who kidnapped her attacked me." I pulled my smock down my back and showed them the bruises, then showed them my hand, where the bite marks had faded to yellowing greens.

There were little murmurs of shock and sympathy in the group. I pulled out my phone and opened the photos I'd taken of Reno in the shed in the woods. The murmurs turned to horrified gasps.

"In this building many powerful people have their offices. One of these men is Gervase Kettie. I think Kettie hired—paid—the criminals who kidnapped my niece. The lawyers who work on the fiftieth floor are helping Kettie—"

"*Kettie!*" There was another outcry about Kettie and what he might have done.

"I have no time," I said to the interpreter.

She clapped her hands together and spoke to the others sharply in Spanish.

"I want to go into the lawyers' offices, to see if there is any proof about the kidnapping or how the criminals were paid."

I couldn't begin to try to explain the pink stocks, not in one or two minutes. I was hoping shock over my niece's damaged body would sway the group.

"*¿Policía?*" "*¿Inmigración?*" they demanded.

I said no, but the interpreter said, "Not good enough. Why do you have the authority to be here?"

"No authority," I said. "I have experience in this kind of inquiry. That is why my godmother asked me to help her nephew—her brother's grandson—and why I am trying to help my niece." I showed them my PI license.

This sparked a ferocious outpouring, but it was stopped when a bell dinged on everyone's phones: time to go to work. They began pushing supply carts into the hall. The interpreter nodded at me to follow her.

"Callista is in charge of the fiftieth floor; says she will take you to fifty. If you steal anything she will report you, but you may go with her."

She pointed me toward a woman with a dark, disapproving face, who nodded at me with a jailor's sternness. The wiry curls emerging from her kerchief were mostly gray and her fingers on the supply cart handles were starting to twist and thicken with arthritis. A hard job for someone no longer young. Two other women followed in her wake, whispering in Spanish.

On fifty, Callista used a special key card to open the locked doors. She stayed in the reception area, dusting the high counter and using cleaning fluid on the glass and metal surfaces, but the other two headed toward the offices on the west side of the reception area. Callista was limping—the arthritis might be in her knees as well as her hands—but she brushed off my attempt to help, pointing toward the corridor. I grabbed a garbage bag and plastic gloves from the cart—I could make myself semi-useful while I snooped.

I entered Dick's suite cautiously, head bent in case Glynis was working late, but the two rooms were empty. I turned on the desk lamps and went first for the trash, since that's where I'd struck pay dirt last time, but either my taunting had made Dick cautious or today's sensitive communications had been by phone or text. He had eaten another Snickers, but there were no meeting notes, nor any printed e-mails from Gervase Kettie demanding action against the felons who'd hacked Rest EZ's TV system. The only thing mildly interesting was a handwritten note from Glynis: *"Tonight's showing is canceled,"* but since it didn't say what was being shown or where, it wasn't very helpful.

In the outer office, I looked over Glynis's work area. She had brought in a salad from a place across the street and thrown the remains away less tidily than I would have expected. I emptied the remains into my garbage bag along with Dick's Snickers bar wrapper.

Her desk was a handsome piece of oak with two shallow drawers. The surface was severely tidy: a landline, her computer monitor, and empty in-and-out trays in a leather just darker than the desk. One regulation green plant and family photo.

The computer keyboard was tucked on a sliding tray under her desk, but as I'd learned on my previous visit, her machine was password protected. I tried opening the drawers to see if she helpfully kept her password where she—or I—could see it, but they were locked. It wouldn't be prudent to jimmy them.

Dick's desk wasn't quite as tidy as hers; he'd left a brief open to a page marked with yellow highlighter. The brief dealt with an agriculture conglomerate's response to a lawsuit about improperly sealed waste tanks. After our summer together dealing with hog waste, Dick had developed a specialty in litigating for agribusiness, but unless Kettie was a stakeholder in Sea-2-Sea's Animal and Animal By-products Division, this suit had nothing to do with Rest EZ.

I sat down and tried Dick's computer. Also shut down for the day, also password protected. However, he hadn't locked his desk. I was going to rummage for his password, but when I opened the top right drawer, the first thing I saw was a figurine of a naked woman.

She was about four inches high, but the detail was intricate. Her short hair had a gold band restraining it; her eyes were wide, rimmed in white, all-knowing. A pair of stubby horns sprouted from her head.

The figure was copper, with a green sheen across the hips and face where the metal had tarnished. She looked modern. I would have thought she had come from current-day Africa, if I hadn't seen her photo among the pictures of the treasures of Saraqib.

In the photo, though, she was holding snakes in her outstretched arms. This figure's arms had been broken off. Could there be two goddess figurines, identical but for the arms, one in Saraqib, one in Dick's desk drawer?

I picked her up with the hem of my smock and looked at her closely. The left arm had been torn or cut above the elbow; the right had been yanked out of the armpit. The dismemberment had been recent: the metal shone bright copper there, not the dull brownish-green patina of the rest of the figure.

"Who did this to you, goddess?" I asked her. "Was it Gervase Kettie? Did he want those snakes so bad—"

I stopped midsentence. When I was mock-groveling to Gervase Kettie outside the elevator ten days ago, my hair had caught in his ring and dislodged an inlay of a serpent set in lapis.

"You take?"

Bad detective. I hadn't noticed Callista coming into the office. If it had been Dick or Glynis, I'd be in serious trouble.

"Nope. I'm studying it." I was laying it back in the drawer when I saw there was a card underneath it, a thick cream stock with an ornate *K* done in gold with lapis flourishes. *"Thanks, Yarborough."*

For—what? The card didn't say, but I could come up with a pretty good short list.

I photographed the card and took a dozen shots of the goddess, with Callista watching me, tight-lipped. My brain was frozen. Kettie had given Dick the statue, which had come from Saraqib. The Dagon from Saraqib had arrived at the Oriental Institute and just as quickly vanished. Kettie must have played a role there.

"You finish!" Callista demanded.

"He does two things," I said. "He works the accounts with his right hand and steals artifacts with his left. Or he acquires artifacts other people have stolen."

"You finish!" It was a command, not a question. *"Porque* Melanie—" She fumbled for English but, frustrated, finished in Spanish. *"Melanie vendra a inspeccionar el trabajo."*

Melanie was coming to inspect the work. I thanked Callista and hastily laid the figurine back in the drawer. I longed to take it with me, to cherish the poor armless goddess, or at least give her to Peter Sansen, but best not.

I fled down the hall toward the reception area, but saw Melanie getting off the elevator. I turned and ran back up the hall to an interior staircase that connected Crawford, Mead's six floors and left their offices through the forty-ninth floor.

5 5

TRANSGRESSIONS

AFTER CHANGING BACK to my corporate clothes I stood at the far windows on the thirty-eighth floor, watching the city below. Inky water to the east, but mile on mile of sodium-lit grids in front of me and to the west.

My phone dinged; incoming text. It was from Sansen.

I'M AT TRANSGRESSIONS IN LOGAN SQUARE WITH MARY-CAROL KOOI. CAN YOU JOIN US? IMPORTANT.

I went to the elevators, looking up Transgressions's address while I rode. I flagged a cab. Logan Square was becoming one of Chicago's happening neighborhoods; the cabbie knew Transgressions and didn't need the address.

It was a converted storefront, with old-fashioned streetlamps outside the entrance. Inside, it was so dark that the waitstaff had LEDs on their trays. The only real lighting was at the end of the bar, where I saw a small stage for live music—fortunately not happening tonight. However, the canned music was well amped, a trying backdrop for conversation.

I squinted, trying to make out Sansen, and finally spotted him waving the flashlight on his iPhone. I stumbled my way to him, trying to avoid the waitstaff, but knocking into knots of happy drinkers. He and Mary-Carol Kooi were sitting at one of a row of spindly wrought-iron tables and chairs perched on a wooden ledge next to the glass storefront.

Sansen got to his feet and kissed my cheek, murmuring in my ear, "Mary-Carol lives nearby; this is where she likes to drink, and I wanted her to feel at ease." He squeezed my hand briefly.

Mary-Carol remained seated but looked up at me anxiously. The ledge was just wide enough for the table and two chairs.

"I'll stand," Sansen said. "I've already heard Mary-Carol's story."

I sat gingerly in the chair; the iron poked the bruise in my back where the computer had taken a bullet for me almost two weeks ago. It was mostly healed but the iron reminded me it had happened. "What's up?"

Mary-Carol flashed another anxious look at Sansen, who smiled reassuringly. She spoke, but so softly I couldn't hear her over the noise in the room. I leaned over the spindly table so that my head almost touched hers.

"The Dagon," she repeated. "When it came, I was surprised, I didn't know anything about it. But—how it got stolen. From the OI, I mean, that's what—that's why—I had to talk to Peter. And he said we need to talk to you."

I nodded—a "with you so far" gesture.

"Rasima Kataba, you know, Tarik Kataba's daughter."

My neck was starting to ache from leaning over the table, but I tried to be patient. "Yes."

"I met her a few times at the Syrian-Lebanese center. She's being held by ICE right now."

Another pause and then the story finally tumbled out. "She's dating this guy named Felix; they're in engineering school together. And Felix called me Monday afternoon and asked me if I knew where the Dagon was being stored."

A waitperson was holding a menu under my nose. Mixed drinks with fanciful names and dozens of micro-beers. They didn't have anything as pedestrian as Johnnie Walker Black. I ordered house-made tonic water with a twist of lime. As pricey as a whiskey at my usual bar.

"You're sure it was Felix?" I asked.

"When Rasima was born, her father wrote a poem for her. In English, it goes something like, *Nothing in life is planned, Not my fate, To fall in love with a tiny scrap / With solemn black eyes / And so we call this scrap*

Rasima, the plan, the design. Felix doesn't speak Arabic very well, but he stumbled through it in Arabic, and so I believed it was him, because who else would know that about her?"

That seemed like a credible if unusual proof of identity. "Did you tell him about the Dagon?"

She nodded, not looking at me.

"So when the Dagon went missing, you figured Felix had stolen it?"

"I didn't know what to think," she said. "When he called, he asked how hard it was to break into the Institute. I thought he wanted to make sure the Dagon was safe, but after the break-in—anyway, I called him and asked if he'd taken the Dagon. He said, 'No, of course not,' but I didn't know if I could believe him."

"You didn't tell Professor Van Vliet or Peter about the call?"

She shook her head, not looking at Sansen or me. "I didn't want to get him in trouble. I mean, if Rasima and Tarik were being detained by ICE and Felix was connected to them, then telling on Felix could send him to prison."

I wanted to sit on the floor and howl. Her motives were noble, but they'd made an investigation into the theft impossible.

"Why are we having this conversation now? And why are we having it in a place where the music is so loud my brain is getting scrambled?"

"Because what happened next scared the bejesus out of her," Sansen said. "She told me that someone had called her tonight, demanding the location of the Dagon."

"I told them I didn't know, that it had been stolen. And the man, it was horrible, he said, 'We know that, bitch.' He said the one in Candra's office was a fake and they wanted the real one." She started shivering, wrapping her arms around herself.

"Why did they call you?" I asked.

"They had a note addressed to me, telling me what to do with the statue."

Sansen nodded grimly. "Before she left for Philadelphia, Candra had written down instructions for Mary-Carol, telling her how to test it and what authorities to question about it."

"Why didn't they go after Candra, then, instead of Mary-Carol?"

"She's out of town," Mary-Carol said. "But anyway the man said I must have switched the pieces. I kept telling them I didn't know anything about it, and then he said, 'No games, bitch. You ever see pictures of girls in Pakistan after someone threw acid in their faces? Tell us where the real statue is.'

"They told me they were coming to my apartment to get it. I tried to reach Felix, but he isn't answering his phone. I couldn't call Rasima because she's in that detention center, so I called Peter. He was going to come over to my place, but I heard someone outside my apartment door. I screamed my head off and ran out through the kitchen down the back stairs. I came here, because it's close to where I live and I didn't know where else to go."

I squeezed my eyes shut, hoping the situation would go away, would be a mirage compounded of the loud music, the shrieking customers, the late hour. The noise seemed worse when my eyes were closed.

"Did you and Professor Van Vliet know it was a fake, or suspect it, when you saw it?" I asked Sansen.

"We didn't have time to inspect it. It looked authentic, in the sense that it had the detail you'd expect from a Mesopotamian artifact of the early Akkadian period. And the work was beautiful."

I turned back to Mary-Carol. "How did Felix know the Institute even had the artifact?"

"It was on the news," Sansen reminded me. "The whole city knew about it—actually, the whole archaeological world. We were already fielding calls from institutes in Jordan and Israel as well as Europe and North America—it's the kind of piece scholars covet, even though we didn't have its provenance."

One of the waitstaff bumped into me trying to deliver drinks to a nearby table. I was blocking traffic; I needed to move. I especially needed to get out of the noisy bar, but if Kettie's Russians were monitoring Mary-Carol, she wasn't safe. Assuming it was his muscle who'd threatened her.

Felix had played some role in this and I needed to talk to him. At once. I couldn't imagine a reason he would have staged a theft of the piece from Professor Van Vliet's office, but he was involved.

"I need to get some air," I said. "If I have to listen to five more min-utes of this music I am going to lose all capacity for thought."

"I can't go home," Kooi said.

I had a fleeting thought of parking her in the ICU next to Reno, where the Streeter brothers could keep an eye on her. Maybe Mr. Con-treras and the dogs and I could curl up in there, too, and sleep for a week. I couldn't help smiling at the image, even while I worried about where Mary-Carol Kooi could spend the night. If I ever had an extra hundred thousand lying around, I'd invest in a safe house where fright-ened clients and their detectives could huddle.

"She could stay at my place and I could stay at yours, if that works for you," Sansen suggested.

I pressed his hand, but said, "That would be great, but I need to find Felix and see what he was up to when he put Ms. Kooi on the spot. If he's not answering his phone, I'm going to the IIT campus to find him. You'd be welcome to go to my place by yourself—"

"And face your downstairs neighbor alone? I've dealt with Taliban who didn't frighten me as much. I'll come with you."

I tried to protest, but Sansen said, "If it's a question of authenticating a Syrian artifact, you need me, Ms. Warshawski, no matter how many pink stocks you buy and sell."

5 6

MISSING PERSONS

SANSEN TOOK MARY-CAROL out through the kitchen exit to the alley. He'd parked across the street. I watched through the long picture window, waiting for them to appear around the corner. When he pulled away from the curb, I went to the front entrance, scanning the street, but no one was following.

Sansen lived in Bucktown, a mile or two from the bar. It took him half an hour to get her settled into his place and return. While I waited, I went into one of the unisex toilets, where the sound system was muted, and tried reaching Felix. He answered neither his phone nor my texts.

When Sansen returned, we agreed to go in his car, which he'd left in the alley behind the bar. He drove a few loops around the area to make sure we weren't being followed and then headed for the expressway.

Neither of us spoke until we were sure we were clean and then Sansen said, "This is hard news from Mary-Carol Kooi. How could she have jeopardized the Institute in such a way? She's one of our most promising young fellows, but when all this is cleared up, we'll have to let her go."

"What I don't understand is Felix. It must have been he who told the thieves where to find the Dagon. Until I've had it out with him, I don't think you should make any decisions about Mary-Carol."

Felix wouldn't have—couldn't have—wanted to harm anyone at the OI. He'd cared about the Dagon because it came from Rasima's hometown, but why would he have engineered its theft from the In-stitute? And the fact that it was a fake—I suddenly thought of Felix's work, and the ghost of an idea stirred in the back of my mind.

Dean Pazdur had said Felix had a sculptor's understanding of how to shape metal, something like that. I had a vision of him in the IIT metal engineering shop, working with Rasima—not on their water purification model, let alone on weapons. What if they'd been creating a fake Dagon? I began wondering about the armless goddess in Dick's drawer—was that a replica as well?

In the drama around Mary-Carol, I'd forgotten I wanted to tell San-sen about the figurine in Dick's desk, but before I could say anything, my cell phone rang: it was Dick himself.

"Richard!" I pretended a liveliness I didn't feel. "How lovely to hear from you. It's been a long time since you've missed me so much that you phoned at midnight."

Sansen gave me a quizzical look.

"This isn't a romantic call, Vic, as you damned well know. My nieces are both in considerable distress because of some papers that Reno has. Harmony said you showed her copies but that Reno has the originals. I need to see them."

"Why?" I asked.

"It's clear Reno is in over her head. She made a lot of hysterical ac-cusations at Rest EZ before she disappeared. These papers can help me sort out what went wrong and maybe get them to let her have her job back."

"You are glib," I said, my tone admiring. "If I didn't know you and the facts I'd believe you. But the only way you could know about the so-called hysterical accusations is if someone in Rest EZ's management chain told you."

"Only to protect my niece."

"Is that why you badgered her at the hospital? Where is Harmony in all of this? Is she in Oak Brook, nestled safe in one of your three spare bedrooms?"

"You don't have a need to know. What you need to do is give me those papers."

"Or you'll huff and puff and blow my house in? Is that what Gervase Kettie wants you to do in exchange for that cute little statue he gave you?"

"How do you know—" He cut himself off midsentence. "If you have been in my office I will have you arrested for trespass."

"Richard, don't make empty threats."

"Don't talk to me about empty threats," Dick said. "That's the emptiest one yet. There's nothing wrong with Kettie—you just can't stand for anyone to make a success out of capitalism."

I laughed. "You could be right. But next time you talk, ask him about Legko."

When he didn't say anything, I added helpfully, "They're an insurance company that's involved in litigation with Trechette, which is the name on the ownership documents for Rest EZ. Since they don't seem to have any capital reserves, I wondered how Legko got Ti-Balt's surety bond business, but then I saw Kettie was on their board. And I dug some more and there he was on the boards of lots of companies that bought insurance through Legko and were suing for failing to meet their policy agreements."

"You always thought you knew more about the law than me," Dick said, overlooking the fact that my exam results had usually been higher than his. "But you haven't been near a courtroom or a lawbook in years. You be very careful what you say about Gervase Kettie—it could get you back into a courtroom in a way you'd hate."

"It's only libel if it isn't true," I said. "But things are going to get uglier for Kettie before they get more beautiful. If you really are in bed with him, get out before someone sets fire to the mattress."

When I hung up, Sansen said, "I don't know what that was about, but if you pronounce 'Legko' slightly differently, it's Russian for 'easy.'" He said the word, softening the *g*.

I groaned. "If you're right, someone with a perverse sense of humor set up all these holding companies. It's hard to believe Gervase Kettie, or even Richard Yarborough, performed those linguistic tricks. Kettie is the kind of man who rips arms off statues to get the gold serpents."

"What?" Sansen bellowed. "Please tell me you're joking."

"Sadly, no. Do you remember that goddess in the *Treasures of Saraqib* who was holding two serpents?"

"Kettie has it?" Sansen cried. "How—oh, hell, I just missed our exit."

We were on the Ryan, going through the spaghetti that connected the expressway to Chinatown, Bronzeville, and Lake Shore Drive. We got off at the next exit and backtracked.

When we were heading east on Thirty-First, I said, "I saw it in Richard Yarborough's desk drawer tonight."

"How did you do that? After listening to you talk to Yarborough, I wouldn't think he'd let you within a mile of his office."

"He didn't exactly invite me to inspect his desk," I said primly. "When I opened a drawer, the figurine was there, but she was missing her arms. The metal was raw, as if they'd been torn off, or cut roughly with a metal shear. The statue was in Dick's desk along with a thank-you note on Kettie's personal note card."

"You think it's the Saraqib statue but Dick tore off the arms?" Sansen was furious.

"I think Kettie took off the arms and then the statue had lost its value for him, so he gave it to Dick—a discard, in a way. The first time I saw Kettie, he was wearing a big gold ring with a gold serpent embedded in a lapis square."

"Damn him to hell. Damn him, damn your ex-husband, and damn every other asshole who thinks their money gives them the right to fuck with our history. A figure like that—she's irreplaceable." He smacked the steering wheel hard enough that the horn sounded.

I didn't try to respond to his rage. "I took photographs in situ, but I don't know how much you can tell from a picture. Would you know if it's the same figure as the one in the Saraqib catalog?"

"At least show me the pictures. . . ." Sansen's voice died away. We'd reached Indiana Avenue where Felix had his apartment, but the road was blocked by a pair of blue-and-whites, their strobes sweeping the night. Behind them was an array of cars, some city, some county.

Sansen straightened the wheel and continued west. He turned the corner on Indiana, the next street over, and pulled to the curb. He'd had a lot of experience with ducking danger.

My arms and legs didn't seem to have any muscles in them. Felix. Arrested? Shot?

"I have to go back there." My throat was so tight my voice barely came out.

"I'll go with you," Sansen said.

"Trouble," I whispered.

"I can see that, Vic. Oh. You mean trouble for me? Don't worry about that."

I cleared my throat and straightened my neck. "If Felix is being arrested or he's been—been hurt, they may take me for questioning. I need you free to call his lawyer. And Lotty." I texted the two numbers to him.

He looked at his screen. "Right. Put me on speed dial—if you need me to act, call but don't talk. I'll send for the marines."

He got out of the car with me and stood watching me. I didn't try to get past the squad cars blocking Prairie but ran down Indiana, cutting across a vacant lot and coming to Felix's building from the south.

A crowd had gathered in the street. The mood was tense: students who thought they were going to witness midnight deportations were shouting anti-ICE slogans; African-Americans who thought the cops had cornered someone they planned to shoot were yelling, "We can't breathe."

My stomach knotted at the sight of the crime scene unit's name on one of the vans, but I walked to the door with an authoritative stride.

"You live here, miss?" said the officer guarding the entrance.

"I'm looking for Lieutenant Finchley or Sergeant Abreu from the Shakespeare station. Are they inside?"

While the guard was trying to decide what to do, a pair of techs got out of the crime scene van and brushed by me. I followed them in. They went for the elevator, but I took the stairs and ran down the hall to Felix's place.

It took a minute for the confusion of floodlights, bodies, broken bits of metal scattered across the worktable and floor to resolve into images. The bodies were all upright and moving—law officers. No dead people on the floor or the bed in the corner. I looked at the tabletop: the little models of machinery that Felix had built had been smashed. An angry arm had swept all the little models to the floor. Only the copper flask from the water distiller was still on the table.

The room had seemed crowded with lawmen and women, but there were actually only seven people, nine when the crime scene techs followed me into the room. The one person I recognized was Lieutenant McGivney. He saw me at the same time.

"Warshawski." I had never heard my name spoken with such loathing. "I might have known."

"Lieutenant." I gave the slightest nod of the head. "I hope you're not responsible for the destruction of the scale models that were on this table. They were valuable."

"When you're looking for fugitives you care more about evidence than artwork," he said, but his voice had thickened—embarrassment or anger, I couldn't tell which.

"Fugitives? You searched the tabletop for someone fleeing justice and were so enraged you had to break the evidence?"

The room had become completely quiet. We could hear the L rumbling in the background; the tap in the kitchen sink was dripping.

"You tell me, Warshawski," McGivney said. "Where are Felix Herschel and Rasima Kataba?"

5 7

NATIONAL SECURITY

V. MURDER

I WAS GIDDY with relief. Felix wasn't dead. He hadn't been arrested. I took a breath, counted to ten, steady, steady, don't give way to emotions that would put me off balance.

"I didn't know they were missing," I said, voice level. "When did you last see them?"

"That's our question to you." A woman in a navy trouser suit stepped out of a knot of people near Felix's bed. "I take it you're V.I. Warshawski? We've been briefed on you, that you're working on behalf of the fugitives."

"Your briefing is remarkably inaccurate, or at least lacking in detail," I said.

Her lip curled. "Suppose you fill in the details."

"Suppose you show me some ID."

She flashed a wallet at me, fast, the way they do in cop shows.

"Let me actually *see* it," I said, tone level, nonconfrontational. I couldn't afford to enrage her. If I had any friends in the room, they hadn't spoken up.

She sucked her lips inside her mouth, but held the ID out again: Deenah Montefiore, with Homeland Security, Immigration and Customs Enforcement.

"I've been hearing a lot about you, how you think you're the answer to law-enforcement questions in Cook County," she said.

"I look for evidence; I don't manufacture it. Is that the answer to the county's law-enforcement issues?"

Someone in the corner near the bed turned a bark of laughter into a coughing fit. Montefiore stiffened. "Tell me when you last heard from, or saw, Herschel and Kataba."

"I've never met Ms. Kataba," I said. "I've never spoken to her, texted her, Skyped her, e-mailed her, nor heard back from her through any medium."

"But she's connected to Felix Herschel."

"That could be. But in my lexicon, that's hearsay."

"You know Herschel. Is that correct?"

"We've met, yes."

"What has he said to you about Kataba?"

"Do you know that I'm a member of the Illinois bar? My interactions with Mr. Herschel have all been as his lawyer. Everything he has said to me is privileged."

The room was in disarray. I began walking the perimeter, looking at the books and papers that had been tossed on the floor. The azure volume of Tarik Kataba's poems seemed to be missing. That was a relief—anything written in Arabic and Montefiore would have put out word to shoot Felix on sight.

I looked around, too, for the book that Felix had grabbed from me. I shut my eyes, visualizing the book as he'd grabbed it. *Art in Copper: A Technical History*. I didn't see that, either.

Montefiore said, "We heard that Martha Simone was Herschel's lawyer. All the pleadings and so on for his girlfriend and for him have been made by Simone."

"Many people have more than one lawyer working for them," I said. "Look at the U.S. president—he's got dozens. Why can't Mr. Herschel have two?"

McGivney cleared his throat. "Listen, Warshawski: I assume you know that Martha Simone got the Kataba girl—woman—released earlier this evening."

"No," I said. "I hadn't heard that. But well done."

"Maybe, maybe not," Montefiore snapped. "ICE and the rest of Homeland are trying to keep America safe, but you and your friends think by protecting terrorists, you're doing something noble. Instead, all you're doing is endangering the country."

"Ms. Montefiore, it's after midnight. I'm weary, so I'm not going to dissect all the flaws in your logic, starting with your conflation of college engineering students to terrorists. Tell me what happened, without any more propaganda, if you please."

Before Montefiore could order my arrest or shoot me, a man in jeans and a sports coat spoke up. "I'm Braden Levine, lieutenant from Area One—CPD. I'm late to the party, but as I understand it, some fifteen women, all with long braids and blue head scarves, were waiting for the Kataba woman outside the detention center. ICE tried to follow her, but the women kept getting on and off the train in different groups and they couldn't be sure they were following the right person."

"Yes," Montefiore put in bitterly. "Two or three would leave, but more were waiting along the route. Three rode out to O'Hare, where it turned out one of them works. Others switched from the Blue Line to the Red and Red to Green and back."

"It was well planned, the kind of plan someone like you would make," McGivney added to me.

"That's a nice compliment; thank you."

I saw the tiny Mason jar from the water purification model on the floor. I put it on the table next to the copper flask, but I couldn't see the tubing that connected them.

"Were you involved in Kataba's escape?" Montefiore said.

"It doesn't sound as though she escaped," I objected. "The immigration court ordered her release."

"Don't make us take you in as an accessory to aiding and abetting a fugitive from Homeland Security," she snapped.

"I can't make you do anything, Ms. Montefiore, but just because Ms. Kataba evaded Homeland surveillance doesn't make her a fugitive. Anyway, why are so many officers from so many jurisdictions in Mr. Herschel's apartment?" I asked.

"The whole situation is confusing," said Levine. "The CPD patrol team"—he nodded toward a uniformed pair who were keeping as far to the back as they could without falling into the tiny bathroom—"responded to a report of shots in the building. When they got here, they found the locks had been shot off the door and all these little models thrown around. Whoever was here tore the place apart, looking for valuables. Hard to know what they took, if anything."

"Shots?" I cried. "Was anyone—what did you find—"

Levine shook his head. "No bodies, and no blood. We found a couple of shell casings for a nine-millimeter Sauer. We searched the hall and the stairwells but didn't see any signs of a struggle or a wound. We're pretty sure the only shots fired were those that broke the locks into the apartment."

"What do you think happened?" I spoke directly to Levine, since he seemed to be the one person in the room acting like an investigator. "Does it look as though they seized Herschel?"

"Can't tell. My guys called in the situation and then all hell broke loose, with Homeland and the sheriff's police showing up and trying to force them to leave. Possible murder versus national security. My guys called into the station for advice and I got the short straw. No one had thought to call a tech unit, so we did that."

"I hope the representatives of the nation and the county haven't touched everything in sight," I said, "because this looks like the work of some imported creeps who trashed an apartment in the Shakespeare District. I'm thinking they also killed Lawrence Fausson, but the sheriff hasn't wanted to look into that."

McGivney and Montefiore started shouting at me in unison, but Levine wanted to know more about the break-in at Reno's apartment. He said he knew Finchley. Despite the late hour, he called Finchley to get his version of the break-in at Reno's and alert him to the fact that his perps might be active again on the South Side.

While he talked to Finch, I kept looking through the room for anything that might tell me if Felix had been here during the break-in. Montefiore asked me whom Felix and Rasima would turn to if they were in trouble.

"The U.S. government," I said earnestly. "Isn't that the refuge for people yearning to breathe free?"

Levine finished his call to Finchley before Montefiore could react. "He confirmed your report and he wants to send someone over to look at this place. I told him he was welcome," Levine said, adding to the tech unit, "Prints from Reno Seale's apartment have been processed, so see if anything here matches."

"Felix Herschel's phone," I said to Levine. "He's not answering, but I'm not seeing it here. He thought ICE was listening to his calls: Any way of finding where he is now?"

"Montefiore." Levine touched her shoulder. "You're monitoring Herschel's phone, right? When did he last use it?"

After a moment, when Montefiore seemed to struggle about whether to cooperate or go all National Security Act on him, she typed something into her phone.

I moved to the doorway but waited for her answer. "The Kataba woman texted him at nine-seventeen, after she was released. He wrote PLAN A and that was the last communication from him to Kataba." Montefiore scrolled through the screen.

"Warshawski texted him and left a voice mail for him to call her, someone named Kooi texted him multiple times, but he wasn't answering. The last few hours, the phone has been moving around the city and briefly to DuPage County."

Everyone in the room stopped what they were doing. Felix was clearly laying a false scent, but what did it mean? Where was Rasima?

"He's been making a lot of calls," Montefiore said. "The last one was from Ninety-Seventh and Wentworth. He said, 'Dog, you in business or what? Where you at?'"

She typed a query, waited for a response, then turned to me. "We don't have a record of a 'dog' in Herschel's list of contacts. Who would that be, Warshawski?"

Levine and his tech unit exchanged glances and looked away, smothering laughs.

"Someone has his phone, Ms. Montefiore," I said gently. "Either he was robbed or he gave it away, but your trackers are following a drug dealer around the metro area. We don't know where Felix is."

That was my exit line, but I saw the laughter wiped from Levine's face as he listened to a call on his vest phone. He beckoned his two patrol officers and the crime scene techs.

"That was a relay from 911. There've been break-ins at three South Side museums; a security guard was shot at the Oriental Institute."

A HARD RAIN IS GONNA FALL

SANSEN WAS STANDING outside his car at the top of Prairie Avenue, engine running. An unmarked car whizzed past, light flashing—Levine, heading to the OI.

"Did you hear—" I started to say at the same time he said, "Vic, a guard has been shot at the Institute. I must go down there, at once."

"Two other South Side museums were attacked just now, DuSable and the Smart. They're trying to find the Dagon where they think Felix and Rasima parked it. You go on south; I can take the L or get a Lyft."

I gave him a quick kiss, remembered to take my briefcase from his backseat, and jumped onto the sidewalk as the rest of the Chicago Police squads roared the wrong way up Prairie. Sansen followed them to Lake Shore Drive. The county and federal cars didn't move: McGivney and Montefiore seemed to be staying put, probably hoping Felix would return and drop into their arms.

A thin rain was falling. I pulled my coat collar up over my ears, wishing I'd worn a hat. The rain had driven away most of the protestors, but a few hardy souls remained, still chanting.

I jogged along Thirty-First Street as fast as I dared in my dress shoes. There wasn't any protected place where I could stop to change into my running shoes.

Rasima's friends had been switching L lines, and some had ridden the Green Line, which was the line that served IIT. I couldn't believe she had been heading for Felix's apartment—she and Felix were very aware of the surveillance against them. But what if they were going to the engineering lab. If they had made the Dagon replica, they could have stored the original there.

The original treasure of Saraqib was made from gold, and Kettie somehow had known that. Felix and Rasima couldn't afford to make a replica in gold, but they did it in copper or some alloy, and that was how Kettie knew it wasn't the real Dagon. Kettie wouldn't want anything but gold. He ripped the arms off the goddess because she was worthless to him. He wanted the gold snakes.

I hoped someone was working late at the lab; I hoped they'd buzz me in. At State Street, all that went out of my head: more cop cars, the red of a fire engine's strobes mixing with the cops' blue. Two blocks down. Close to the engineering school.

I ran flat out, heels on my pumps squelching in the mud on the sidewalk. A man in a campus security uniform was gesticulating with a city cop while a firefighter was pulling a blanket over a figure in the road near the curb.

I pushed past them, ignoring their protests, and knelt next to the figure. Felix Herschel, looking horribly small, his face waxen as the lights streaked it.

"He's not dead, is he?" I cried to the firefighter.

"Do you know him?" Cops converged on me.

"That's one of our students." A man in a windbreaker appeared next to me. He was wearing Nikes but no socks—he'd pulled clothes on in his hurry to get here.

I pushed myself to my feet. "Dean Pazdur! It's V.I. Warshawski—I met you—"

"I remember you," he said heavily. "How did this happen?"

"I just got here."

I knelt down next to Felix again and put my fingers on his throat pulses. As if aware of me, he opened his eyes, blinked, and cried out in pain.

"It's Vic, Felix. We're getting you to Lotty. You will be fine."

The firefighter and one of the cops joined me on the wet tarmac. "You awake, son?" the cop asked. "That's good. Can you tell me your name?"

"Felix," he muttered, his eyes shut.

An ambulance arrived, bells clanging. I left Pazdur providing details to the cops and hoisted myself into the ambulance along with the EMT crew.

"I'm an aunt," I said. "His parents are in Canada."

I woke Lotty to give her a thumbnail. She demanded to speak to the EMTs, so I handed my phone to one of them and knelt on the floor next to Felix's head.

I found one of his hands under the blankets they'd wrapped him in and pressed it lightly. "It's Vic, Felix. Do you know where Rasima is?"

"Light hurts my eyes," he fretted.

"Yes, I expect you have some concussion." I kept my voice calm. "You'll be fine. What happened?"

"Thought we were clear. Went to engine lab—" His eyes fluttered open but he winced at the light and closed them again.

"Yes, for the Dagon," I said. "Did Kettie jump you?"

"Big men. Grabbed Rasima and me, shoved us . . . into SUV. . . . Kicked door open. We got out but they . . . backed up . . . door hit me. Rasima—didn't see. Where is she?"

The tech on the phone with Lotty was giving her Felix's vitals, but the other tech told me to stop talking to Felix—his blood pressure was spiking.

I sat back on my heels, but Felix clung to my hand. "Rasima."

"I'll find Rasima," I promised him.

"Sorry, Vic, sorry . . . for . . . didn't . . . trust. Trust." His voice slurred on the repeat and he lapsed into silence.

I stayed next to him, holding his hand, although his own fingers had gone slack, until we pulled into the ER bay. I went inside with him and gave what information I had to the ER charge nurse. The cops wanted to talk to me, too, but I couldn't focus on their questions. I needed to find Rasima but I couldn't leave Felix until Lotty arrived—

which she did about ten minutes after the ambulance pulled in. She's a reckless driver even at her most relaxed. Tonight, she must have beaten Indy speed records.

Lotty swept up to the desk, demanded the attending on call, and overrode the admission clerk's efforts to put her at the back of the queue.

"Of course you may see my credentials, but it will save time if you also page Dr. Deverel and tell him I'm here." She caught sight of me. "Victoria! Thank you. How did you come on Felix?"

Someone in scrubs came through the doors to the hospital interior and asked for Dr. Herschel. I walked—trotted—next to her.

"I have to go. I need to see if I can track down Rasima Kataba. She and Felix were nabbed together at the engineering lab; he managed to get the door of the car open and the two of them fell out. But she's disappeared."

Lotty nodded. "Go, go, I'll let you know what happens here."

THE PURLOINED DAGON

I CHANGED FROM my mud-clogged pumps into the running shoes I'd worn to my Force 5 cleaning shift. My tailored trousers were so stained with mud and oil from kneeling in the road that there didn't seem a point to changing into my jeans.

I was running on fumes, but I was afraid if I came to a halt I wouldn't be able to get back in motion. I summoned a Lyft car and rode back to Thirty-Third and State.

It was past two in the morning now, and the area was completely deserted. No squad cars, no fire engines, not even a drunk to share the street with me. Only a few lights in the IIT buildings, showing students pulling all-nighters, kept me from feeling completely alone. At least the drizzle had stopped, since I still didn't have a hat or an umbrella.

My phone battery was low, but I needed its flashlight. Felix had fallen into the road only a few steps north of Thirty-Third; the churned-up mud along the curb showed where all the emergency crews had gathered. The Force 5 smock I'd wrapped around my head was there in the muck as well.

Rasima must have lingered, at least for a moment, hoping to save Felix. I shone my phone around and then saw the tire tracks in the ground. I could just make out an occasional footprint—small foot, moving fast.

Rasima had fled away from the street. The SUV had followed her. I lost the tracks for a bit but then found a big gouge in the wet soil where the SUV had made a U. Rasima had doubled back; she'd crossed the road. The tire tracks followed her over the median and then halted near the student center.

Rasima had been heading for the L. The SUV had turned around again in the mud and returned to State Street, but whether with Rasima I couldn't tell.

I climbed to the L platform, checking the stairs for signs of a struggle—a dropped scarf, torn button. I didn't see anything. I couldn't think of any way to track Rasima further. In the morning I would go to the Lebanese-Syrian center and beg for help, but for now I could scarcely keep myself upright. A train was approaching, rattling the corrugated tunnel. I lurched on board and collapsed into a seat, blending with the homeless people slumped across the seats in their stained clothes. I kept myself half awake until we reached the Loop stops, staggered over to the Red Line, and slept until we reached Belmont.

As I walked the half mile home, I tried to stay alert to danger, but I kept thinking about my bathtub. I had just enough remaining mental presence to walk the perimeter of the building. No one seemed to be lurking, but I still went in through the alley: I'd check the front stairwell from the inside. At the top of the third flight, as I was fitting my key into the back door, I heard a movement behind me. I turned, clumsy in fatigue, trying to brace myself against the door so I'd have leverage for kicking.

"Victoria?"

I gaped at the small figure emerging from the neighboring landing. In the streetlight I could see a long braid hanging below her head scarf. "Rasima?"

I hurried her into the kitchen. She was shivering, feverish—she'd been running ever since the immigration court decided to release her.

"Felix? Is he— Do you know—" she asked disjointedly.

"He's okay," I said. "Okay enough. He was knocked out when the car door hit him, but he can talk; his worry was for you. Dr. Lotty, his great-aunt, is with him at the hospital."

The worry lines in her narrow face eased; she murmured something in Arabic and squeezed my hand convulsively. I showed her the bathroom, so she could get herself clean and warm before we tried to talk further. While she soaked in the tub, I sponged myself off in the kitchen sink, changed into clean jeans, made hot tea with honey. I was going to pour whiskey into mine but regretfully decided I'd best not add anything that would knock me out.

I tried to find some clothes that would fit Rasima, but she was six inches shorter than me and probably fifty pounds lighter. While she sat on a kitchen chair, lost inside my bathrobe, I sponged the worst of the mud from her jeans.

Her story came out in nervous bursts: the release from prison, the text to Felix. "Plan A" meant he'd texted sixteen of her friends, who were standing by to help cover her escape from surveillance, all in blue paisley hijab. Her face lit briefly with laughter—that part had been scary but fun.

"Felix and I, we finally connected at the end of the Blue Line, on Ninety-Fifth Street." Her voice was soft, with a slight accent that was more French than Arabic. "We were very careful. He was wearing a kaffiyeh; I put on niqab." She rummaged in her backpack and pulled out a black face cover to show me. "We acted like a very traditional Arab couple, which was not fun for either of us but meant people stepped away from us. We were too foreign, too unpleasing—we got more insults than I usually hear in hijab."

I could imagine, but I just nodded and put her jeans in front of a space heater to dry.

"We were going to go to Felix's apartment—my release was so sudden he hadn't had time to collect his bag, with everything he needed for a journey. But when we reached his street, we saw a big SUV arrive. A man who looked like, I don't know, every criminal who ever worked for Bashar, only three times as big, got out.

"We knew they were coming for Felix, whether they were with ICE or the police, or the man who stole the Dagon from my baba. We decided to get the Dagon; we had put it with our models in the engineering lab—I told Felix it would be like the 'Purloined Letter'—you know that story? Yes.

"We waited at the lab, pretending to work, until everyone else left.

That wait was agony. Every time the door opened, we were afraid it would be an immigration agent. But finally we were the last engineers in the building. And so we took the Dagon. We had made a shell for it. It sat among our materials like an uninteresting cube of tin. When we got outside, the criminal from the SUV was there; he grabbed us. He had a comrade, also enormous. They carried us into the SUV—we were like sacks of oranges, we were so—so weightless in their hands!"

Her eyes flashed with remembered fury and fear. "And then, they thought we were too weak to fight, so they didn't bother to restrain us. As they started to drive off, we kicked open the doors and jumped out. Felix fell. The car hit him. I wanted to stay for him, please believe that, but we couldn't both be victims."

She started to weep then, her slight body shaking so hard that I feared she might injure herself. I put my arms around her, petted her, and said, "You did absolutely the right thing. You would not have survived a night in the hands of these monstrosities."

She drank her tea and calmed herself. "This kind of weeping, it wastes time. It wastes energy. I learned this when Bashar seized my baba and it is not good to forget this lesson now, when we are again in danger. Now I must bring the Dagon to my baba."

"You have it?" I gasped.

"A special pocket inside my jacket." She went to the chair where I'd draped her beige wool jacket and unzipped an inner pocket, then unfolded a figure wrapped in soft black cloth.

When she set the Dagon on the kitchen table, the ancient gold gleamed like the noonday sun. The dishes and used tea bags looked sordid and dreary; I picked them up and put them in the sink and knelt to look at the fish-man. Despite the smallness of the figure— only about five inches—the scales on the carp covering the man's head were individually incised. Its eyes were round, with the pupils clearly marked.

The man was naked from the waist up, wearing a short skirt and laced sandals. He carried a bucket in one hand and a pinecone in the other.

"He is sprinkling water on the seeds; he is guaranteeing a good crop to the king or noblewoman whose palace he guarded," Rasima explained.

She let me admire the figure for another few seconds, then restored it to her pocket, repeating that she had to take the Dagon to Tarik.

THE FROZEN NORTH

THE LAND HAD looked green from the plane, but close up it was brown. Brown trees waiting for leaves; brown ground, where mud mixed with ice. Broken branches on the trails. The spruce and cedar canopy we'd seen from the air was above our heads.

It was still winter in northern Minnesota, some fifteen degrees colder than in Chicago. If I got home—when I got home—I vowed never to complain about the cold again. Rasima and I had been walking for almost an hour, but it felt as though we hadn't moved, except to pull our mud-caked boots out of one bog after another.

I hadn't wanted her to come with me, but she refused to give me the Dagon unless I took her. "You mean well, Victoria, but you don't understand. My baba sent me to Beirut to school to keep me safe, and it did keep me safe, but I didn't see him for seven years. And ever since this American president has begun chasing immigrants, rounding us up like so many frightened sheep, my baba has had to be so careful who he talks to, where he sleeps, that I almost never see him anymore. I have to know he is safe. He needs to see me so that he knows I, too, am safe."

Tarik was in northern Minnesota, near the Canadian border.

"Felix thought he could find a way through the wilderness so that my baba could come and go between Canada and the United States. He wanted my baba to be safe in Canada, but until I could be with him, my baba would not want to stay in Canada."

She made a sad face. "It could not be done. Everything was still half frozen and it was too—too overwhelming for him. For Tarik, I mean. Even Felix found it hard to hike through this arctic wilderness, and for Tarik to stay there by himself—he survived Bashar's prisons, but to be cold and alone in a wilderness—Felix said he saw my baba would not be able to endure it."

With the help of the Anishinaabe Nation, Felix rented an unused house for Tarik in the Grand Portage Indian lands.

"We hope my baba is still there, but communication is impossible. Everything that comes to me or to Felix, whether it is a text or an e-mail or perhaps even a paper letter, is monitored now by ICE. I can see when friends from Lebanon write me that someone has opened my mail. They left greasy fingerprints on the paper—I could barely bring myself to read the letter."

I stopped trying to argue Rasima out of going north and turned instead to figuring out how we'd get there. We couldn't take a commercial flight: Rasima was on a BOLO for every law-enforcement department in the country, and I wasn't far behind. My car might also be on a watch list, but if I rented one, I had an uneasy feeling Kettie would know—through Rest EZ he had access to credit monitoring software.

A private jet would be nice. Dick could probably get one from his high-end clients. His firm probably owned a fleet, now that I thought of it. I sat up straighter: I had a client with a jet. He already knew part of the story.

Darraugh Graham's terse response was the same in the middle of the night as it was at a midafternoon meeting. He listened for two minutes, grunted that he was putting me on hold, and came back to tell me that a car would pick me up and get me to the DuPage county airport where the plane was docked.

"Pilot will arrange a car to meet you in Grand Marais, take you where you want to go. I need the plane back here in two days, so if you're not ready to come home, you'll have to find your way on your own. Don't let Kettie shoot it, not sure insurance covers WMD damage." He hooted with laughter—that was apparently a joke.

He hung up before I could thank him.

It was almost five when we left my apartment. I pushed a note to Mr. Contreras under his door—I didn't have the time or energy to explain my trip in person. Peppy barked sharply when she heard me, but didn't rouse him—or more important, the woman across the hall.

Darraugh's driver was happy to take us to an all-night Buy-Smart on our way to the airport. I outfitted Rasima in hiking boots, clean jeans and underwear, a parka, almost all from the youth department. From a sale bin I grabbed some micro-spikes for our boots. I had my own winter gear stowed in a duffel bag along with a flashlight, extra batteries, two burner phones, water bottles, granola bars.

During the flight, Rasima and I lay on couches, dozing, but at one point I asked her about Fausson.

She smiled sadly. "Lawrence was my father's friend in Saraqib. He admired Tarik's poetry greatly and loved sitting with the men at night, smoking and talking about the history of the region, when Syria was a great power. After Bashar arrested my baba, Lawrence promised to look after the treasures of Saraqib. When the civil war began and the country started to crumble, Lawrence took the two most valuable treasures—the Dagon and the goddess—for safekeeping. They are small; they are easy to transport.

"Of course, I wasn't there—I was at the lycée in Beirut—but my baba told me when he reached Chicago, finally, two years after his release—I was here on a student visa and he found a way to me."

It seemed prudent not to ask what way he found.

"Lawrence lost his scholarship—perhaps you know that?—and he found a job with Force 5 because so many of the men he met at the Syrian center worked with them. He liked a chance to speak Arabic. When Tarik arrived in Chicago, Lawrence got him a job with Force 5 as well—the pay isn't terrible and they don't ask for papers. Then they were sent to clean Kettie's office and Lawrence saw all those artifacts he had—many of them stolen.

"Lawrence wanted money. He had his fantasy of creating a big expedition to go to Syria or Iraq when the fighting ended. He started doing business with ISIS, imagining they would be his patrons. Kettie paid him to buy stolen objects he found on the dark web. Tarik thought it was terrible, but how could he report Lawrence and not be deported himself?

"And then Lawrence did a wicked thing: he sold Kettie the Dagon and the goddess. He was keeping them safe, because often ICE would come to my building, even to my apartment, looking for illegals. They might find my baba or they might steal gold artifacts and claim we were smugglers.

"My baba was cleaning in Kettie's office the night Kettie gave a big party, showing off the Dagon. Tarik couldn't believe it! He went to Lawrence, who said the money would help them go back to Syria and save more treasures. So Tarik waited until the party was over, pretending he had extra cleaning to do. He broke the case and took the Dagon with him—the goddess he didn't see, although he looked for her. He made it to the Force 5 van just as they were pulling away and rode to the Syrian-Lebanese center.

"The night watchman let him in—men often spend the night there if they are late getting off work—but the next day, Sanjiiya—the center's director—made him leave. She was terrified that ICE would track him to the center and that everyone's documents would be checked.

"He didn't dare carry the Dagon with him, so he put it into a hole in one of the pillars outside the front door."

I remembered the cracked stone and concrete at the Syrian center.

"Those were two terrifying days, for him and for me, because I did not know where he was. He lingered among the homeless men near the L stop on Thirty-Fifth Street until a day when he saw me. And then Felix took him in, but suddenly Fausson was killed and Felix came under suspicion."

She brought the end of her hijab over her eyes, as if trying to hide herself from the memory.

"Kettie thought Lawrence had stolen the Dagon back from him. He called Lawrence and demanded he give the Dagon back. He made Lawrence afraid, and so he told that Tarik had taken it. Then Kettie demanded that Lawrence tell him where Tarik was hiding. Lawrence knew that Felix and I were friends, down at IIT. He was desperate, looking for people who might give Tarik a roof for the night. He came

to see me, pretending he was worried about Tarik. While I was making tea, he invaded my address book, the one I write by hand, and tore
the page with Felix's name from it.

"The rest you know: we thought we could fool Kettie with a copy
of the Dagon. I knew Mary-Carol Kooi because she used to come to
the Syrian-Lebanese center in Palos, so we chose the Oriental Institute because we thought she would help. If our copy was in a museum
and Kettie had to steal it out of the museum, he would believe it was
real."

I didn't know whether to laugh or cry. Youth, impetuosity, imagination, all mixed together but made lethal by Kettie.

"The fun part was making the Dagon. We learned so much! The alloys they came up with five thousand years ago were so sophisticated."
She had sat up, eyes sparkling, but the light went out just as quickly.

"I thought when I reached America and Tarik found his way to me
that we would be safe. I know it isn't as dangerous as Bashar's Syria,
but this man, Kettie, he is like an ISIS warlord himself. He has his own
private army, he has so much money he can buy the government and
get it to do what he wants. For me and Tarik, America is not the land
of the free, but has the watchful eyes of a dictator. I can't travel, can't
come and go as I wish, even though I have the right papers. And my
baba, after being tortured for writing his poems, now he has to be in
hiding."

When she finished speaking I lay back on the leather couch and
slept. The pilot shook me awake when we'd landed and escorted us
from the plane to a waiting Jeep Wrangler. He reminded us to text
him when we were ready to return to Chicago, "or anywhere else.
Mr. Graham said to take you where you need to go, but to make sure
his plane is back at the DuPage airport in two days. And your driver
will get you where you need to be while you're on the ground here."

ASSAULT FROM ABOVE

OUR DRIVER WAS a short, stout woman named Lenore Pizzola. She said she'd lived in the area for over twenty years; she could hook us up with any supplies or destinations we wanted in the north woods.

While Rasima settled into the Jeep's backseat, I stood outside to make phone calls from one of my burners. I called Lotty first.

Felix had fractured a bone in his skull but it was a mild break with no apparent brain damage; he did have concussion and couldn't remember the previous night's events, including how he'd ended in the road, but he'd broken his shoulder in his escape.

"Tell him his friend is well. We're going to the same poetry reading he attended last month."

My next call, to Mr. Contreras, wasn't nearly as pleasant.

"Doll, if you never want to talk to me again I wouldn't blame you. This strange lady arrived about eight in the morning, but she had Harmony with her, so I thought she was okay, thought maybe she was your ex's new wife. She said they was worried about you, and Harmony said I could tell them where you was.

"Well, I hadn't been up but maybe five minutes, had just put the coffee on, and only had that bathrobe you gave me over my altogethers, so my wits wasn't what they should be.

"I said I expected you were still in bed, because if you was out running you would've taken Peppy, and she said you'd disappeared off the map. And then she saw the note you left me—doll, I swear on Clara's grave I didn't even know it was there." Clara had been his beloved wife, dead now for almost thirty years.

"It's okay," I said. "You would never betray us, I know that."

"But she grabbed it, and off she went, taking Miss Harmony with her. So I don't know where you are or what you're up to."

I told him where we were. I didn't try to explain about the Dagon but told him Felix had been injured and that we were looking for someone who could clear him once and for all of Lawrence Fausson's murder.

I reassured Mr. Contreras as best I could, but I was rattled. I tried not to show it when I got into the front seat next to Lenore, but twisted around to talk to Rasima.

"I spoke to the doctor; your brother will be fine. He has a broken shoulder and mild concussion—maybe he'll learn that skateboarding in the street requires a helmet and shoulder pads."

"That is good news." She smiled radiantly.

"I also spoke to your grandfather. He's unhappy that we left without saying good-bye." I paused to make sure she knew whom I meant.

"Oh, I am glad the dogs didn't wake him," Rasima said quickly.

"One of your aunts apparently stopped by and read the note we left for him. You know what a busybody she is—she may get your uncle to bring her up here, so if we want to get in any serious hiking, we'd better do it before they arrive."

"You're here to hike?" Lenore Pizzola asked. "I can drop you at any of the trails and come back for you later."

"It would be better if we rented our own car or SUV so we could move to different trails without having to wait for you," I said.

"No real car rental places around here," Lenore said. "There's me, with this Jeep, and Mike Norgaard, he has a Land Rover, but he does like me, hires himself out with the car. I guess I could drive you down to Duluth if you want to rent something of your own there, but if you're worried about needing to wait around for me, don't: your company hired me for two days and I'm at your disposal."

Rasima nodded at me: best do it. She pulled a piece of paper out of the pocket that housed the Dagon and handed it to Lenore.

"Cowboys Road, half a mile past the Portage Trailhead?" Lenore stared at us. "You gals sure? That's wilderness, and not to judge a book by its cover, but you neither of you looked equipped for wilderness hiking. Ice only broke on the Pigeon five days ago, and the trails are slick mud with ice and rocks mixed in."

Rasima bit her lip and took the paper back, studied it for a long minute, then nodded. "Yes. That's what we want. We'll see when we get there how strong we are."

Lenore looked us over again, shook her head, but put the Wrangler into gear. The first part of the route ran next to Lake Superior. It was beautiful, with the surface shimmering silver pink in the morning sun, but it felt alive and threatening. Michigan is not a tame lake, but Superior looked as though it could rise from its shore and swallow us.

It was a relief when Lenore turned inland, into the forested hills. Although the road was paved and better maintained than the streets of Chicago, winter's freeze-thaw cycle had created cracks and holes. The Jeep had a bone-jolting suspension; I began to suspect that Lenore was heading straight for the holes to show us we were too delicate for the route we'd chosen.

Once we left the county road for Cowboys Road, we left pavement as well. The Jeep grabbed the gravel surface, but the jolting became more intense. I thought I heard a louder engine above the noise of the Jeep, but I didn't see anything else on the road.

Lenore heard it, too. She slowed down long enough to stick her head out the window.

"Steve Thuxton's up there in his helicopter. Wonder if someone's lost. It is goddamn easy to disappear in these woods; you two understand that? Bogs that aren't on any maps, lynx, bears coming out of hibernation—you got to know what you're doing."

Rasima paled. I probably did as well. Even sheltered in a house, how had Tarik managed on his own?

We were passing a sign pointing to the PORTAGE TRAILHEAD when a thunderclap shook the Jeep. A boulder splintered and a fist-size piece struck the windshield. A series of loud whines and pops and the ice and dirt along the road churned and spat.

"What the hey—" Lenore shouted.

"They're shooting from the chopper!" I cried. "Get off the road, get under the trees!"

She wrestled with the steering and the gears and drove into the ditch by the road and up the other side into the woods. The gunfire stopped; the helicopter noise receded.

Lenore was furious. She hit a speed-dial button on her phone. "Steve Thuxton, what in hell was that about? You taking wolf hunters up? You damn near—what? Who?"

She was silent as someone spoke at length on the other end. When she hung up, her face was white with anger.

"Okay. You two, out of the car, now. When I saw this gal with an Arab scarf, I wondered, but it's a free country, more or less. I have a gun with me and I'm prepared to use it: we're on the lookout for terrorists this side of the border, whatever they want to do in Canada."

"Who is Steve Thuxton?" I asked. "And what was that shooting about?"

"As if you didn't know." She pulled her gun from under her seat. It was a Glock, but had dirt on it from the car floor.

"Pretend I don't know. We're up here to hike near the Pigeon River. Who was shooting at you?"

Lenore shook her head, eyes blazing. "Thuxton told me he has a couple of ICE agents looking for Arab terrorists, father and daughter, hiding in these woods."

"If you think I'm anyone's father, let me explain the difference between the x and y chromosome," I said. "But please ask Mr. Thuxton to describe his ICE agents. If they are the size of redwood trees, with bearskins on their heads passing for hair, they are not with ICE: they are members of the Russian mob. They will kill him and you, and me, and my niece for no reason other than they get a great deal of pleasure out of hurting people."

"Maybe, maybe not." Lenore's mouth was uncompromising. "You get out. You hike if you really are hikers and I'll go back and see who's who."

She waved the gun at Rasima, whose own face was pinched with fear. Rasima unbuckled herself and got out of the Jeep on shaking legs.

"You'd best keep that gun in a box or a holster," I said as I climbed out with our backpacks. "The Glock Nineteen doesn't like a lot of dirt in its muzzle; it could backfire on you."

Lenore only ordered me to shut the door; she needed both hands to handle the Jeep but she was afraid to put the Glock down in case I or my terrorist companion dove for it. She backed up the side of the ditch with an energy that almost tilted the Jeep onto its left side.

"I'm sorry, Victoria," Rasima whispered. "Now I have put you in danger of your life."

I shook my head. "This is like the weeping that you said wastes time and energy. Recriminations also waste time and energy. We're near the Portage Trailhead; we'll put on our boots and micro-spikes, get water and snacks, and map our route."

FIRE AND ICE

THE HELICOPTER STAYED close to the Border Trail. As much as possible, Rasima and I kept to the trees, although pushing through bracken and sidestepping bogs made our going rough. I wasn't sure how visible we were through the spruce canopy above us, but at least no one shot at us. No bears came after us, either.

We should have bought walking sticks when we were at the Buy-Smart. Large chocolate bars, a utility knife, air mattresses, a camp stove, all these things would have been a help. No wonder Lenore Pizzola thought "we gals" weren't really hikers: we weren't. When we found some fallen branches, we used them as improvised walking sticks, which made the going easier.

We were working with a compass and Felix's handwritten instructions—he had worried too much about someone hacking into his computer to type them up.

As we walked, Rasima filled me in on Felix's part in the story. When he drove up here with Tarik, he had rented a cheap cabin near Grand Marais, one where the owners didn't provide any housekeeping. Tarik hid there during the day while Felix scouted the border.

"They couldn't call me, of course, and I sat in Chicago for four days completely terrified, but they were frightened, too. Several of the native people had noticed Felix on repeated days: very few people live here, and a stranger stands out.

"The native people told Felix he needed to be very careful, as the immigration border patrol was—there is a word, I can't remember it— anyway, they are active. Finally, Felix felt he had to confide in someone and he took the risk with these people."

They offered Tarik the use of an abandoned house, deeper in the woods, not on a marked trail, but not hard to walk to if you knew where you were going. They promised to look after Tarik until Felix and Rasima came back with the Dagon; then they could try to cross the border farther inland, when the weather made walking easier.

It was that house Rasima and I were trying to reach. We followed Felix's instructions painstakingly, left the Border Trail after hiking alongside it for 1.23 miles, struck northwest-north through the woods. Over the singing of birds and the rustling of ground animals, we kept hearing the helicopter circling, moving away to the west, looping out toward the big lake, returning.

Rasima tripped over a log and fell headfirst into a thornbush. She didn't let out as much as a whimper as I pulled thorns from her face and hands. I slipped on an ice patch and landed in mud. Good camou- flage, I muttered, using my jacket sleeve to wipe enough mud from my eyes to carry on. We took turns with the compass and directions. Our spirits sagged as cold and fatigue sapped our reserves: neither of us had slept last night, but I worried especially about Rasima, weakened by her time in prison. It was past three o'clock and the dark woods were darkening further as the sun began to sink behind the hills.

We had veered off course when Rasima spotted the house to our left. Its moss-covered gray stone walls blended in with the surround- ing woods.

The house wasn't much bigger than the shed where Reno had been held in the forest preserve. As we approached, we saw a stovepipe emerg- ing from the single window on the north side. Additional pipe had been added and laid on the ground so that smoke emerged some thirty feet from the house, where it dissipated into the underbrush.

Rasima ran to the door, fatigue forgotten, crying, *"Baba, Baba, enema Rasima!"*

The narrow door opened and a man emerged, almost as small as Rasima. He flapped his arms, shooing her away, shouting something in Arabic. Rasima stopped, her face suffused with hurt. I caught up with her and grabbed her arm. A big white man appeared behind Tarik. He was wearing a new orange hunting jacket, but his graying hair was still pomaded away from his face in a sculptured side sweep.

"Gervase Kettie!" I stepped forward, smiling. "I think of you more as the Havre-des-Anges beach kind of guy, not a woodsman. I hope you left your Sumerian serpent at home—if it got caught on the trees you'd have a hard time finding it."

"Whoever you are, get out of the way. I want the girl and I'll shoot you to get her."

"I'm V.I. Warshawski, Gervase. We met outside the elevators in the Grommet Building a few weeks ago. You were with your lawyers, who don't seem able to protect you from people hacking into your Rest EZ system, do they? What is it money can't buy? Not just happiness, but savvy. You have so much money and so much power you forget you need a little old-fashioned common sense."

"Vic!" Rasima gasped next to me. "Don't stir him up."

"He's like Bashar," I said. "Placate him or stir him up, he'll still move forward like a puffing bull." I lowered my voice. "Tell your baba in Arabic that when I start to run he must drop to the ground and get out of the way. You, too."

I kept walking toward the house, keeping a tree more or less between me and Kettie. A movement on my right side caught the corner of my eye. Mitty, the bodyguard, automatic weapon under his arm.

"Yarborough's first wife. The ballbuster," Kettie said. "I remember you now. Dickie will be glad to know I've shot you for him, cleared one mess out of his life. I want the gold statue, I want it now. And I will shoot to kill."

I stuck my hand in my backpack and pulled out a dark sock. "It's in this bag. You want it, come and get it."

I ducked low and began to run a zigzag course past the house. Rasima shouted in Arabic. Gunfire. Shouts, screams, feet crashing after me. I couldn't risk turning. My skin prickled, expecting a bullet.

I stepped in a bog, pulled my foot free, swerved right. A stich in my side, but the crashing and flailing behind me propelled me forward.

The river appeared so unexpectedly that I didn't have time to stop. I fell forward, face landing on ice, feet in water so cold they were numb almost before I pulled them out.

Brown water, churning uneasily under blocks of ice. I didn't try to stand but began sliding on my butt across the ice toward the far bank. The block I was on cracked, started to break. I stretched out an arm for another piece and managed to slide across just as the first block splintered.

I saw Kettie's orange jacket. He was running full tilt, but Mitty grabbed him a second before he fell into the river. Mitty fired at me. My second ice block began to crack, and I slithered, feet down in the water, arms grasping the edges. I twisted, flopped forward. The ice bounced but righted itself. A small branch floated by. My hands were almost useless, lumps of ice themselves, but I managed to grasp the branch and use it as a makeshift paddle.

I was in the middle of the river. The current was strong and spun me around, pulling me toward the big water. I braced myself with my branch and heaved myself to my feet.

"Come for your Dagon, Kettie: it's going to be in Canada in five minutes."

I swung the sock over my head in a loop. Mitty started to fire again, but Kettie shoved him away—if a bullet got me midriver the Dagon was gone forever.

I turned my back on him and began a clumsy steering of my ice sheet. It was shrinking, water was sloshing over my feet. I banged into a tree that the river was carrying. The impact knocked me off my feet. I grabbed at the tree as I fell and managed to straddle it. The tree slammed against an ice mass that heaved with the swollen water. An unstable dam of ice connecting the United States to Canada sixty feet away. I can go sixty feet to Canada. One inch after another, it's how we get there, get to safety, to freedom.

River fog rose in front of me. Cold owned me. I turned and saw

Kettie's orange jacket, coming toward me fast. He'd made his way to the American end of the ice dam and was almost running toward me.

"It's yours, Gervase, you win," I screamed, and hurled the wet sock toward him.

Kettie lunged and grabbed the sock as it hit the water. He pried it open and stuck his hand inside. When he realized all he had was wet wool, he roared with fury and flung it into the river. Mitty fired again, a rifle spraying bullets across the ice. There came a sudden roar; the ice dam broke and the river hurled billionaire and bodyguard out toward the big water.

6 3

BORDER CROSSING

SOMEONE GRABBED ME from behind but there was nothing left
in me. They rolled me in a blanket; I had no strength to resist. I was a
lifeless rug locked into the back of a van. I woke to bright lights, a hand
on my neck. I beat at it feebly.

"Stop, miss, stop. You're safe. You're at a hospital."

Members of the Anishinaabe Nation had lifted me from the icy
rocks along the riverbank on the Canadian side, but I learned that only
later. Later, at the hospital in Thunder Bay. Later, when I was recovering from hypothermia and frostbite, while Canadian immigration authorities confronted me over my illegal crossing.

My passport was in my backpack, which I'd dropped as I ran through
the woods on Wednesday. I took refuge in my injuries and feigned sleep
under the weight of their interrogation. I didn't want to explain what I
was doing at the border until I knew where Rasima was and whether I
needed to protect her from authorities on either side of the river. The
Anishinaabe provided more help: they found my passport and delivered
it to the Canadians.

Lying in my Thunder Bay hospital bed, I saw Kettie's dead body
on the evening news. He and Mitty had been swept down the river
toward Superior, but the current had thrown them onto a rock at the
river's mouth. A Thunder Bay camera crew showed the heroic efforts
of the local paramedics to revive the pair.

"The Pigeon River claims more than one life a year from inexperienced tourists who think they can beat the ice or the rapids. Chicago detective V.I. Warshawski was exceptionally lucky to emerge with mild frostbite; the American mogul Gervase Kettie and his bodyguard, Dmitri Rakitin, were not so fortunate."

In the close-up of the rescue efforts, the camera lingered on the serpent ring on Kettie's right hand. "We've learned that this unusual charm is a museum-quality piece from the ancient Middle East. Mr. Kettie was well known as a collector of artifacts from Iraq and Syria; his daughter told our reporter that this was a recent acquisition, one that he thought would bring him good fortune in the many-layered enterprises he oversaw. Sadly, it could not protect him from the Pigeon River's treacherous crosscurrents."

I liked to think that the goddess had exacted revenge against Kettie for his savage dismemberment of her arms. My salvation had been a side effect, for which I was grateful. I would have to ask Sansen what kind of sacrifices a Sumerian goddess would expect for bestowing such an outsize favor.

I hoped that her favors extended to protecting Rasima and her father, but I fretted all night in my hospital room, unable to ask about them for fear of alerting border patrols.

The next day, the hospital allowed one of the Anishinaabe elders to visit; she told me what had happened. The elder said that the Anishinaabe had been alerted by the gunshots at Tarik's hideout. They do not allow weapons on their land, except with a permit to hunt, issued by the tribal leadership. A group of men had raced to Tarik's hideout, but by then Kettie and Mitty were chasing me through the woods. Mitty had tried to shoot Rasima and Tarik, but Kettie yelled that they would keep for later; they needed to get moving before I disappeared.

The Anishinaabe wanted to take the Katabas to the tribal building for warmth and safety, but Rasima insisted on following Kettie: "We aren't going to sit in safety while Victoria risks her life for us," she said.

It didn't take much skill for the Anishinaabe to follow the trail of broken branches and muddy footsteps Kettie and I left. They reached the river as Kettie and Mitty headed onto the ice.

"My cousins saw you in the river and were terrified for your safety but had no way to reach you. They texted our cousins on the Canadian side. Our cousins drove up with a raft but you were already falling off your log onto the riverbank."

She gave a dry laugh. "You were trying to fight them and they were trying to save you. As for the two dead men—when the ice broke last week, dead tree branches formed a natural dam that blocked some of the ice. That's where they were crossing, but when they started firing those weapons, the sound waves broke up the dam. I don't know why they thought they could come onto our land to murder people, so I feel no grief at their passing."

I felt no grief myself. Someone with Kettie's money and power could wrap himself in so many protective legal layers that I hadn't been able to imagine a way to bring him to justice.

Lenore Pizzola helped deal with authorities on both sides of the river. On my second day in the hospital, she showed up full of contrition. After she dumped Rasima and me out to meet our fates, she'd driven down to the U.S. border station at the mouth of the Pigeon River.

"I said I knew they were after a pair of terrorists, but that their agents damn near destroyed my Jeep in the process. That got the border guards all lathered up because of course they didn't have any agents up in a chopper. They radioed Steve, wanting to know what the hey was going on. By then, these two giants were pointing guns at him to make him stay up. I don't know what they thought they'd do when he came down. Shoot him, too, maybe."

"They're used to getting away with everything they do—assault, rape, murder," I said. "They worked for a billionaire, their home is in Russia—no one ever arrested them, let alone made them face a judge."

Lenore made a face. "I guess that's right. Steve told me they was looking for the house where your young gal's father was living in the woods. They were guiding that Kettie fellow and another Russian from up above. Every now and then Steve would get a glimpse of you and your friend, and those two Russkies would laugh, but Steve couldn't make out the lingo so he didn't know what they were saying."

She took a deep breath. "I had a long day with the border patrol. Of course, I know some of them, one of them lives in Lutsen and we train our sled dogs together, but they needed to know who hired me, who sent you up here, why I thought you was a terrorist."

She fidgeted with her watchband but looked me resolutely in the eye. "I shouldn't have acted like I did, judging that young girl just because she wore a scarf on her head. Being so close to the border we get ten alerts a week, so we shrug them off, and then I come face-to-face with an actual Muslim girl and I act like she was fresh from Iraq with grenades strapped to her body. I'm truly ashamed."

I wondered if it would have made any difference to the outcome. Even Lenore's Wrangler couldn't have navigated the woods we hiked through once we left the Border Trail, but if she'd driven us closer we might have beaten Kettie to Tarik's hideout. And then faced Kettie and Mitty somewhere else, I suppose.

"We all live too fearfully these days," I finally said, as close as I could bring myself to offer absolution. "It's not easy to prove you're not a terrorist. I will probably always show up on watch lists when I fly, and that does not make me happy."

"I understand," Lenore muttered.

She finished her tale in a subdued voice. The head of the border station ended up speaking to Darraugh, since the plane we'd flown up on was registered to CALLIE Enterprises. He sent Caroline Griswold, his PA, up to vouch for me. She came with videoed testimonials from Lieutenant Finchley and various Chicago power brokers. The most important was Darraugh's, of course: as CEO of a multinational with substantial Canadian interests, he carried more weight than a Chicago cop. Darraugh recorded a short comment for me—"thanks for keeping your Russian mob from shooting my plane"—followed by a hoot of his dry laugh.

Caroline also assured me there would be a plane to take me back to Chicago as soon as I wanted to go. Darraugh had needed his Gulfstream to fly to Nairobi, but the firm had a smaller plane, which had brought her north. She would send it back to Grand Marais after she returned to Chicago.

When I checked out of the hospital, I was astonished to find that Darraugh had taken care of the charges. My fight in the backwoods had nothing to do with any work I was performing for him.

I was less astonished by the cameras that surged toward me as I left the hospital grounds—a dead billionaire is always news. One who's drowned in a river in the company of a Russian mobster is big news.

"Kettie collected artifacts looted from Syrian and Iraqi museums," I told the reporters. "He thought I had one and chased me across the river trying to get it back."

"What was it?" they all wanted to know.

I spread my hands. "He was wrong: I don't have any artifacts, stolen or otherwise. He got confused. He was dealing with a scandal in one of his core businesses, his payday loan company, and he wasn't thinking clearly."

I tried to step them through the stock price manipulation, but that wasn't interesting; pilfered Syrian gold was news.

"You should talk to his Chicago lawyer, Richard Yarborough. Kettie gave Dick several ancient figurines, including one whose arms Kettie pulled off so he could get at that gold serpent he wore on his right hand. Dick can tell you all about it." I kindly gave them Dick's private number as well as Glynis's direct office line.

Lenore drove me back to Grand Marais, where I spent a night with Tarik and Rasima before going home. Lenore proved more than a match for the gang of TV reporters who followed us. I decided I could start absolving her. After all, it wasn't her fault that Kettie had known where I was headed. Dick had done that or, at least, Glynis Hadden, who had taken Harmony to wheedle the information out of Mr. Contreras.

Lenore had arranged a vacation-house rental for Rasima and Tarik, with a room for me. She'd persuaded the owner to let us have it free of charge for a week. Okay, I absolved her.

Rasima flung her arms around me when I came through the door.

"Victoria, you are my hero for life. What you did for two strangers—it is unbelievable to me."

Her father stood behind her, smiling fondly at his daughter's enthusiasm. When she released me, he took my right hand in both of his and spoke to Rasima in Arabic.

"He says to tell you how grateful he is. It is true that many worries remain, but they are easier to bear when a stranger steps forward out of nowhere and becomes a friend."

The worries that remained, of course, had to do with Tarik's undocumented status. The border agents here in Minnesota had focused on Kettie, the Russians who'd been in his entourage, and my own activities, but they wouldn't leave Tarik alone forever. Even if they wanted to, the pressure from Washington would force them to act, and acting would mean deporting.

"The Canadians are inviting Baba," Rasima explained to me. "He can be a poet at a college in Toronto, where there are many Syrians and many Arab speakers. But then, how can we see each other? He won't be able to return here, and on my student visa I can't be coming and going to Canada. But if he stays in the United States, then they will come for him and deport him."

"You could apply to a school in Canada," I suggested. "Montreal has a fine engineering school."

She blushed. "Yes. Felix and I have, we have talked about that. . . . But now that you have taken the weight of arrest for murder from Felix, and the fear for the Dagon's safekeeping from us both, I want to see whether I like Chicago when I'm not fearing for my or Baba's safety. Or Felix's."

Felix was home from the hospital; he and Rasima had spoken several times and seemed to be texting constantly. Martha Simone told me with a great deal of satisfaction that the sheriff had agreed that Felix had nothing to do with Lawrence Fausson's death. The border guards had arrested the two Russians who'd been tracking Rasima and me in the helicopter. When they learned that Kettie and Mitty—Dmitri Rakitin—were dead, the Russians instantly blamed all the crimes that they knew about on Rakitin, including Fausson's murder and the kidnapping and torture of Reno.

Tarik said, through his daughter's translation, that he did not want to make one more decision under a twenty-four-hour gun. "Ever since Bashar's men came for me, it has been like that. Twenty-four hours to get Rasima to Beirut, to get my wife and son to Jordan. When I was released, twenty-four hours to choose to board a ship bound for Havana. And then a chance to get in a boat to America to see my daughter: again, twenty-four hours. This time, no. This time I need to think before I cross another border."

The best I could do was to put him in touch with Martha Simone, to see whether she could help work something out.

Over dinner, I asked Tarik about the translation of Mandelstam's poem that had sent him to prison.

Tarik knew Russian. He explained: during the cold war, when Syria was closely allied to the Soviet Union, he'd spent a year in Moscow as an engineering student, but his first love was always poetry. He'd made friends among people who circulated samizdat; through them he learned the work of the great dissident poets of the 1930s.

"Akhmatova, Pasternak, Tsvetaeva. For me the best was always Mandelstam. I tried to translate. The language is hard, but also the—" He beat his hand on his thigh while Rasima fumbled for a word.

"Rhythm," I suggested, "or meter."

"Yes. It was hard, but wonderful. When I returned to Saraqib, I married, I had a son and my beautiful, clever daughter. I repaired bicycles, led tours, but I was always writing poetry. Kind French friends collected my poems and that turned out to be my—" Again Rasima fumbled for a word; we settled on "undoing."

"My own poems, and some of my favorite translations from Russian, they were gathered together and published in Beirut. One of Bashar's 'thin-necked half men' saw the Mandelstam poem and showed it to Bashar."

Tarik recited "Stalin's Epigram" for me in Russian and then in Arabic. It sounded beautiful in both languages, although I understood neither. When I pulled out my phone and looked it up, I saw why it would rile a dictator. Mandelstam wrote that Stalin had a mustache like "cockroach whiskers," his followers were "a rabble of fawning half men" who "whinny or purr or whine" at his command, his laws were "horseshoes" that hit people in the head or the eye or the groin.

"In 1933, after the 'Epigram' reached his ears, Stalin had Mandelstam arrested and, ultimately, killed," Tarik said. "Of course no poet should be surprised when the police arrive in the middle of the night."

I thought of the fawning half men in my own government, braying about "fake news," and shivered.

"The problem was the mustache," Tarik added. "Stalin's was big, like a cockroach resting on his lip. Bashar's mustache is tiny, like a pencil—" Tarik rubbed his fingers on the table, imitating an eraser.

"Smudge," I guessed.

"At my three-minute trial I did try to say that Bashar couldn't be confused with Stalin because his mustache was too small."

"I'm sure that didn't help." I couldn't hold back a laugh and instantly apologized, but Tarik laughed softly as well.

"Yes. Not help," he said in English. "Bashar *want* big cockroach mustache."

Tariq had spent twenty-two months in Assad's prisons, twenty-two months where he was whipped with electric wires, among other tortures. When he was released, he left Syria immediately. His wife was dead, his son remained in Jordan, but Rasima, his beloved "tiny scrap," was in Chicago. He made his way there.

SELF-JUSTIFICATION

I FLEW BACK to Chicago in Darraugh's second-best jet with Rasima, who was eager to see Felix. Tarik remained in Grand Portage, as a guest of the Anishinaabe Nation. It wasn't a good long-term solution; the United States might well send agents into the tribal township at a second's notice, but this would give him some breathing room so that he didn't need to make a twenty-four-hour decision.

Sansen was returning from Amman the following week. Rasima and Tarik agreed that she should turn the Dagon over to him to house at the Oriental Institute until such time that the treasures of Saraqib could return home.

"It may not happen in my lifetime," Tarik said. "But it will happen. I cannot live a life without the hope that the wheel will turn and good will follow evil."

The morning after I reached home, I enjoyed a long sleep-in, followed by French toast with Mr. Contreras and Harmony, who was once again staying with him.

"I hope you can forgive me, Vic," she whispered. "I stayed until you got back so I could apologize."

"That's all water over the dam," Mr. Contreras said heartily, but Harmony shook her head.

"I was confused and angry and made big mistakes. I wanted Uncle Dick to want me in his family and so I believed him when he said he needed to get those papers Reno had so he could protect her. I guess I only half believed him, but Glynis treated me so differently from when I first got here. Then she acted like I had some bad disease, but she suddenly started treating me like—I don't know—a niece, I guess. She and her husband put me up in their guest room. But after that morning, when we came here and she took the letter you'd left for Uncle Sal, then I saw she and Uncle Dick were just using me."

"That's right," Mr. Contreras said. "She saw who her real friends were. She ran away from that Glynis person and came straight back here."

Mitch and Peppy were ecstatic to see me home. I took them and Harmony to the lake. Daffodils and crocuses were blowing near the paths where Harmony and I had been assaulted two weeks earlier. Spring was coming to Chicago.

Harmony returned to Portland later that day: she'd remained in Chicago long enough to make sure Reno was mending and, after that, to apologize to me. When Mr. Contreras and I drove her to the airport, he handed her a flat jeweler's box.

"It ain't what your ma gave you, but maybe it'll help you remember you got another family here that cares about you."

I slept again and then went to see Lotty. We'd spoken while I was in the Thunder Bay hospital, of course, but it was important to be with her in person. She held my hands, inspecting my fingertips for any lingering frostbite.

"Thank God you got the right care in time," she said. "Thank you for risking so much for Felix."

"I didn't do it for Felix," I said, "but for you."

In the end, though, I did it out of my rage over Kettie. For years he'd gotten away with theft—theft of artifacts, theft of money, theft of dignity from the people at the bottom of the pyramid who turned to Rest EZ to keep food on the table. It wasn't enough that he could charge them 400 percent interest, but he swindled them with his stock scams, all to add something to his own billions.

"It was a fluke that he drowned. In some ways I wish he'd survived so that everything he'd been doing would come out in the open, but then I think of how easy it is for today's hyperwealthy to evade the law: it's possible he would have skated away from everything."

"He needed the Russians to shore up his companies." Max had been sitting so quietly in the corner while Lotty and I reconnected that we were both startled when he spoke.

"I had our own portfolio manager at Beth Israel do some digging to make sure we weren't holding any Kettie Enterprises assets. He'd over-extended his development projects over the last decade and had gotten himself in debt to some of Putin's friends. Not a good place to be."

"Why did he care so much about that gold statue?" Lotty asked. "Why did he try to kill you and the Katabas himself?"

I shrugged. "My guess is that he was furious at being crossed. That's why he had Lawrence Fausson murdered, after all. And then, when his mobsters couldn't take care of Rasima and Felix, he was going to show them how a real man handled interference in his affairs."

Max agreed. "You know that billionaires are investing in technologies to end the aging process? They think that since they can buy and sell everything, it's only fair that they should be immortal, too."

Lotty flung up her hands. "The story never changes. I can't stand it. One after another, people want to strut around in jackboots controlling everyone around them. Enough of this."

"They're not the only story," I said. "You heal the sick."

"And you drive the swine over the ice into the raging waters." Max grinned, pouring me another glass of wine.

"Did Kettie have a family?" I asked. I'd never thought to look up his private life.

"Two ex-wives," Max said. "Two adult daughters. One likes to spend money in Switzerland and the Mediterranean, but the other is apparently her father's sharklike daughter. You'd better hope she doesn't sue you for her father's wrongful death."

He chuckled, but I flinched—that was all I needed, more Ketties trying to destroy me.

IN THE MORNING I went to Beth Israel to visit Reno. The Streeter brothers had left the hospital. With Kettie's and Mitty's deaths, and the arrest of the two Russian enforcers, it seemed safe to leave her on her own. She was walking unaided now and eating, so she'd been moved to a regular ward.

She didn't recognize me until I spoke: she'd been so depleted when we talked earlier that only my voice had registered with her. As soon as I said her name, though, her face lit up.

"Auntie Vic. Thank you for keeping me safe."

We spent most of the morning going through the events of the last several months. "You are a woman of incredible strength," I said. "You brought crucial information out of St. Matthieu with you, and you kept Kettie's mobsters from finding your locket, even at the risk of your life. I don't know anyone, man or woman, who could have done what you did. Because of you, Gervase Kettie is dead, his mobsters are gone, his companies are in tatters."

She blushed. "I think it's because of you that Gervase Kettie is dead."

I talked to her about the Greta Berman Institute for Victims of Torture. "You can't stay here any longer, but that's a place that is immensely helpful to people who have been through the kinds of traumas you suffered. I spent a month there after I had been imprisoned and assaulted."

It wasn't a part of my history that I liked to remember, but when she asked for details, I told her: perhaps my example would help sustain her through the next hard part of her recovery.

I went to see her every day for a while, helped her settle in at the Greta Berman Institute on Chicago's outskirts, made sure she knew I was there for her. In one of our conversations, she told me briefly about her interactions with Dick.

"They helped me find a job, Uncle Dick and his secretary, but they wouldn't talk to me when I got back from St. Matthieu. I tried to tell him how awful it was, but Uncle Dick said there was no room for crybabies in his world."

A tide of fury rose in me but I tried to speak in a neutral voice; if I let my rage loose, it might knock her over in her frail state. "Was it Dick or Glynis who persuaded you to talk to the men who kidnapped you?"

"Not them. I didn't recognize the voice, but a man phoned. He said he heard I wanted to talk to the head of Rest EZ and that was him. He said he hadn't known the shocking things that went on in St. Matthieu and he'd like to come to my apartment and apologize in person. I was such an idiot. I put on a good outfit and my lucky silk scarf that Henry had given me, and then it wasn't the head of Rest EZ, it was these monsters who rushed in and grabbed me." She started to choke.

"It was a lucky scarf," I said when her retching subsided. "The pieces that caught on branches brought me to you."

As soon as I left Reno I headed downtown to the Grommet Building. Neither Dick nor Glynis wanted to let me past the security desk. I had the guard put me on the phone with Glynis.

"My next conversation is going to be with Murray Ryerson at the *Herald-Star*. He's been begging for an interview ever since the Anishinaabe pulled me out of the Pigeon River, and you are going to feature prominently in my remarks. I plan to tell him how you brought Harmony to my home, stole the letter I left for my neighbor, and alerted Gervase Kettie to—"

"We will give you five minutes," Glynis said.

She was waiting for me when I got off the elevator on the fiftieth floor. She started to push me toward the offices, but I stopped to look at the wall. Soraude, Runkel and Minable's name had been taken down.

"Good idea," I said to Glynis, pointing at the empty space. "All the attention they're getting from different international law-enforcement and securities monitors can't be good for Crawford, Mead."

"You don't understand, Vic."

"That's why I'm here. I want to understand. I want to know what drove you to use Harmony to get my location to give to Kettie. I want to know why Dick was so deep in bed with him that they couldn't unknot the bedsheets binding them together."

A young associate passed as I was speaking. He looked so startled that Glynis almost tackled me to get me into Dick's office, with the door shut.

I walked over to his desk and opened the drawer where I'd seen the goddess. She was gone now, but the cream stock note of thanks from Kettie was still there.

"What the fuck—" Dick began.

"Is she out at your house with that stone goddess, or did you prudently throw her out?" I leaned against the desk drawer, almost touching his legs in his ergonomic desk chair.

"I don't know what you're talking about."

"That is so lame, Richard. I can't believe a litigator with your experience wouldn't have a better line than the lamest ones used by perps since the dawn of time." I unfolded a copy of the *Treasures of Saraqib* to the photograph of the goddess statue.

"Your pal Kettie bought her from Lawrence Fausson, knowing she was stolen. He liked bright shiny things, so he ripped her arms off to get at the golden serpents. He destroyed forty-five hundred years of history to get that gold snake he had in his ring. And then the statue didn't appeal to him; its value had gone down. He gave it to you, a discard. That was your value to him. You did his dirty laundry, but he didn't think you deserved more than his broken toys."

Dick's skin seemed to thicken and his breath came faster. "You can't prove this."

"I don't think that matters," I said. "Your work depends on trust. Maybe clients like Kettie trust you to cover up their crimes, but you must have other clients who trust you to follow the law and look after their interests with probity."

"Oh, fuck. Fuck, fuck, fuck." He dropped his face in his hands.

"What happened?" I asked. "Was being close to all those billions so exciting you overlooked what he was doing to get them?"

"It wasn't like that," he muttered.

"It never is," I said. "Tell me what it was like."

"We do some work for Kettie Enterprises around their leases and taxes here in Chicago." He spoke to his lap. "He gave me a chance to invest in a property he was building in Jakarta, but the deal went south. I had mortgaged the house, but we—Teri and I—it was millions of debt. He showed me how to make some of it up with his penny stocks, but I was still in a hole. He said if I could get office space for his St. Matthieu lawyers, he'd forgive half of it. We did that—Glynis and I, I mean.

"When Reno came around looking for work, he'd made remarks

more than once on the value of a good-looking piece—woman in a loan office."

"And you thought, what better-looking piece of womanly ass had you ever seen than your beautiful niece," I said, smiling savagely.

"That's unnecessarily crude," Glynis said.

"Necessarily crude when the boys say it, but bad when I do? Do you fill in for Miss Manners when she's on vacation? Did either of you uncrude people know that the women who get to go to the Caribbean are picked because of their womanly pieces? Did it occur to you that your niece could use a little help and protection?" I kept my hands jammed in my trouser pockets so that I wouldn't strangle him with his silk Talbott tie.

"She could look after herself," Dick said. "She went out to Oak Brook when she first got here—she had a hell of a nerve, walking in on Teri, trying to give her a sob story."

"Okay." I stood up straight, suddenly tired of it all. "I know what happened, more or less, the information on the stock swindle Reno brought back with her, you in debt to the Russian mob. But what did you do to Harmony?"

"Nothing." Dick looked up in surprise.

"Don't 'nothing' me, Richard. Glynis took her to my home the Wednesday I flew to Grand Marais."

"Oh, that." He was back in his sullen, boy-hero-caught-shoplifting voice. "She'd been staying with Glynis. Kettie came to me, needing to know where you were. I figured he wanted it badly enough to forgive the rest of the debt. We haggled—twenty-five million down to seven! He loved every second of it, loved being a billionaire watching a man with a family sweat and beg over what was chump change to him."

"Yes, you were hard put upon," I agreed. "So hard put upon that you were willing to send Kettie after me, knowing he wanted to kill me."

"I didn't know that!" Dick cried. "He wanted to reason with you."

"Right. Because he was such a reasonable guy. Tell me about Harmony."

"She was pretty unstable, all over the place," Dick said. "One minute she hated your guts, the next you were her and Reno's savior. Anyway, she told Glynis the old guy would know where you were. We knew Dr. Herschel wouldn't give us the time of day, but Harmony said Contreras had a soft spot for Harmony. So Glynis took her there. But then Harmony turned on me."

"Richard, I have zero interest in your financial woes, but your nieces need years of expensive therapy. You will come up with the money, you and Glynis and Teri. All those bills will come here, and you will pay them promptly."

"I can't—you can't—"

"I can, and I will. Your other choice is a public airing of this entire business, which will lead to your disbarment."

I waited until he looked me in the eye and understood that I was implacable.

I didn't think I would ever calm down again, but when I got to my office, Rasima and Felix were watching for me from the coffee bar across the street.

They were full of gratitude, of apologies for not trusting me with their story, of thanks for saving their lives and Tarik's.

"My favorite poem of my father's is 'The Haunted House,'" Rasima said. "He wrote it in his head while he was in Bashar's prison, and it's a long allegory about what it means to be in prison and to be free. It's full, too, of the demons and angels of Islamic legends. My favorite angel is Artiya'il; she removes depression and grief when they are more than we can bear."

She handed me a framed parchment sheet, which she or Felix had illustrated with gold leaf.

I woke in the reaches of the night and wept at my weightlessness; a fever had broken. Artiya'il, you found me, lifting from me the weight of grief.

6 5

TRUE GOLD

MY DOORBELL RANG that night at midnight, just as I had fallen asleep. The dogs began to bark. The woman in 1B came into the hallway screaming at them. I pulled on my jeans and ran down the stairs, where Mr. Contreras and his neighbor were yelling at each other.

Peter Sansen was standing at the door. "I know it's late, I know I should have phoned. I was going straight to my place, planning on calling in the morning—but somehow the taxi ended up here."

"They do that." I was grinning stupidly. "Maybe you should come upstairs."

Mr. Contreras and the woman looked at us and abruptly shut up, returning to their respective apartments.

"You're a hero in Amman," Sansen said. "The recovery of the Dagon, your dispatching an artifact looter—they may want you to come to a state dinner sometime soon."

He followed me into my bedroom and started to take off his clothes, but I went to the safe built into my closet and returned with the Dagon. He took it from me, his square hands gentle on the gold figure, his face alight with awe.

The tail on the golden carp seemed ready to move, to sweep away all that was ill and evil in the world, while the arm raised with the pinecone offered a kind of benediction. *Lifting from me the weight of grief.*